Deja

A novel about second chances

by

Michael E. Gunter

Deja
© 2018 by Michael E. Gunter
Published in 2018 by Michael E. Gunter

ISBN: 978-1-7326856-0-4
eISBN: 978-1-7326856-1-1

Contact the publisher at michael@gunterbooks.com

Publishing consulting, management and book and cover design by Alane Pearce Publishing Coach. Alane@MyPublishingCoach.com

Cover and interior image credit: panthermedia from storystock.com

Gunter, Michael E.: Deja
    1.   Fiction 2. General Science Fiction
    3. Drama/Suspense

ACKNOWLEDGMENTS

My wife, Tammi, and our kids, Erik and Shea
Alane Pearce – publishing partner
Barbara Bush and Bob Fowler – copy editors
The Café at Barnes & Noble – my normal writing place
Jim & Patsy van den Berg – writing at OBX
Winston the cat – sneak attacks and other distractions
Fans of BLACKWELL and THE BOOKS OF KLYV

Thank you all for the contributions you have made.

In memory of two time-travel masters:

Jack Finney, author of Time and Again
Rod Serling, creator of The Twilight Zone

Your work continues to fascinate and inspire me.

Garren,

I've decided to spend Christmas with Denise. Maybe some time apart will do us both some good. I'm tired of apologizing, and the circular arguments are getting us nowhere. Please don't call me. I'll be back before your birthday. We can try to talk then. Think about it.

Kate

Part One

The Situation

The silence in Garren's bedroom was shattered by the most obscene noise known to man. Without looking, he slammed his fist onto the alarm clock, buying himself another nine minutes of blessed quietude. He considered his options: Get up and venture back into the emotional maelstrom, switch the alarm off and try to sleep through the day, or lay there and try not to think about *her*. Option One was the least appealing. Option Two was the least likely. Option Three was the least possible. So he did what he'd been doing for the last three hours – stare into the darkness and replay the events that led up to this nightmare: The conversation he wasn't supposed to hear, the text he wasn't supposed to read, the gift he wasn't supposed to find, the argument they never should have had, the words he never should have spoken, the ultimatum he never should have given, the door he never should have slammed. And then there was the note he found on Kate's pillow the next morning. If it were just a bad dream, he would have recovered. In a day or two, he might have shared it with Kate and they would have laughed it off as an impossibility. But it wasn't a dream. These things did happen. And they were both wide awake when they did.

After what seemed like more than nine minutes, he rolled his head toward the clock. Perhaps he'd killed the beast once and for all. Part of him wished he had. It was a gift from Kate, a reminder of simpler days, before the dark times. She had given it to him for his birthday not long after they were married. It was kind of a joke. The clock he brought into their marriage was one of those old ticking alarm clocks with the two bells on the top. He'd had it his entire life. She kidded with him that since he was married, he should have an adult style clock. In truth, the incessant ticking kept her awake and the clanging alarm was not how she wanted to start each day. But that was then. Twenty years later, they had somehow wound up in the *situation.* That's what Garren called it because naming it for what it was hurt too badly. Exactly how they got there, he couldn't say. Sure, there were signs, but none that shouldn't have worked themselves out on their own, or so he thought. They'd both contributed, he guessed, though she more than he to be sure. They both allowed the drift to occur and neglected the things that could have prevented the situation from ever happening. But it did happen and now they had to deal with the fallout.

The numbers on the clock read 6:01, which meant it could be 6:00, 6:03, 6:04, 6:07, 6:08 or 6:09. Years of abuse had shorted out the diodes that formed most of the last digit. Surrendering to Option One, Garren threw back the covers and swung his legs out of the bed, feet thudding heavily onto the floor. He stretched and worked the stiffness from his back and neck. Then he gave the clock three more whacks. The readout flickered, but stayed lit. Halfway to the bathroom, the wake-up tone sounded, but it was a half-octave lower than usual. He returned to the clock, yanked it from the table and spiked it like the winning touchdown.

"Good morning, Garren," said a female voice as he stepped into the bathroom. The lights popped on and an image depicting the day's weather appeared in the mirror. "It's going to be a beautiful day; sunny and cold. Happy New Year's Eve, Garren."

He ignored the greeting and stared at his reflection. Not bad for forty-nine. He was still forty-nine for one more day. His hair was mostly gray, but not the angry out-of-control gray or the sad weight-of-the-world gray some of his friends were dealing with. His was the cool George Clooney gray that women still found attractive. His eyes were a little puffy, but that was probably due to the stress and lack of sleep since Kate left. Nothing a little Rejuva-Cream wouldn't fix.

"You look tired, Garren," said the voice. "Did you not sleep well?"

Garren never wanted the virtual assistant upgrade to their house, but Kate insisted on getting it. As she put it, "It's the way the world is now. If we don't keep up, we'll get left behind." He did his best to ignore it, but Deja was intent on performing her duties.

"Garren," she said, "would you like to hear what's trending? Okay. Seven bodies have been discovered at a farm near Oskaloosa, Iowa."

"Too early for bad news," he cut in.

"Here's some good news. Bitcoin has reached a record high of thirty thousand dollars, U.S."

"Yeah, great news if I owned any," he sneered. "Why didn't you tell me it would get this high seven years ago when it was only a hundred bucks a coin?"

"I am pretty good at making predictions, Garren, but I cannot foretell the future. Besides, I did not exist in 2013. I was created on June 4, 2015 by—"

"I don't care."

"I am sorry you missed such a lucrative investment opportunity. The national lottery is worth 1.43 billion dollars. Would you like me to purchase a ticket for you, Garren?"

"No!" he snapped.

"I understand, Garren. The odds of winning the lottery are one in—"

"Stop! No more talking."

"Okay, Garren. Perhaps some music. What would you like to hear?"

"Nothing! Just silence. And why do you keep saying my name?"

There was a long pause. "Pardon me, Garren. Do you want me to answer your question or do you prefer silence?"

Garren shook his head and turned toward the toilet. He was about to do his business, but hesitated and looked over his shoulder. "Uh, Deja? You still here?"

"Yes, Garren. I am always everywhere."

"Ugh." He rolled his eyes. "How about a little privacy?"

"I'm sorry. I do not understand the question."

"Could you go into the other room or turn around or close your eyes?"

"I'm sorry. I do not understand the question."

He started to argue, then thought better. "Never mind. I'll just ignore you." Several seconds passed without a reply. "Huh, I guess she...*it* understood that." Garren was well into his necessity when the bathroom light switched off, plunging the room into total darkness. "Deja!" he growled through gritted teeth.

Garren entered the kitchen to the smell of freshly brewed coffee. He picked up the cup he'd used the day before and tossed out the cold remnant of yesterday's brew. Moving toward the coffee maker, he stopped in his tracks when he noticed it had been replaced with one of those ridiculously overpriced and oversized Baristabots all the hipsters were raving about and the coffee snobs hated. It was Ferrari red with a silver bow on top.

"What the…," he mumbled. "Where'd this come from?"

Leaning in for a closer look, he noticed a tag that read: "Happy Birthday, Son. Love, Mom and Dad." Then the side of it opened up and a steaming cup of coffee was pushed out onto the counter.

"How in the world…Kate? Are you here?"

"Kate is not here," said Deja.

"Then how did this thing get in here?"

"Amazon prime delivery service came late last night after you went to bed. I did not want to disturb you, so I let the delivery man in."

"You let a complete stranger into my house while I was asleep?"

"Credentials were checked. Delivery instructions were followed as submitted by—"

"No. That is not acceptable, Deja. You are never to allow anyone into this house without my authorization…or Kate's. Is that clear?"

"You sound angry, Garren."

"I am angry!"

"Your coffee is ready. Just as you like it – a little cream, no sugar. I have a message for you. Would you like to hear it?" Deja didn't wait for a reply. The video monitor on the counter popped on and an elderly couple appeared.

"Hurry up, now," said the woman. She appeared to be looking at something or someone beyond the camera. "The guests will be here soon. We're going to have a party."

"Helen, look here." The man next to her pointed at the camera. "We're talking to Garren now. Good morning, Son. Your mom and I want to wish you a happy birthday. I know it's a day early, but we wanted to make sure you got your present before the holiday."

"Holiday!" exclaimed Helen. "There will be music and dancing. I will wear my special dress and William will wear his suit." She leaned over and gave her husband a quick peck on the cheek. "Isn't he handsome? We're getting married, you know."

"We hope you like your present," William continued. "It's a Baristabot. We got one a couple days ago and just love it. Everything's automatic. You don't have to clean it or fill it or anything. I hope the delivery guy got it hooked up right for you. It syncs up to Deja, so she can have your coffee ready whenever you want it. The things they can do now."

"Did you say we can go now?" asked Helen. "Let me get my wrap. I don't want to get cold." She started to get up, but William gently slipped his arm around her to keep her seated.

"I wish we could be there with you, Son," his father continued. "We'll give you a call tomorrow and talk for real. Happy New Year's Eve. See you in 2020."

"New Year's Eve?" said Helen. "Do you think we'll get to see Mr. Clark? He's such a handsome young man."

"Goodbye, Garren. We love you."

The message ended.

Garren shook his head and chuckled at the monstrosity taking up valuable real estate on his counter. "Love you, too, Mom and Dad, but this..." He picked up the cup and took a sip. "Hmm, that *is* good."

"Garren," said Deja, "don't forget you have two appointments this morning: Dr. Thomas Grant at nine and Miss Bridgette Wunderchmidt at 10:30. Also, Garren, the manuscripts you requested from the Cairo museum should arrive this morning. And don't forget to take a jacket. It is currently nineteen degrees Fahrenheit. Today's high will be thirty-eight degrees at 1:13 PM with an overnight low of eleven degrees. The skies will be clear so you will be able to see the lunar asteroid strike at 10:06 PM local time. The moon is waxing crescent with a twenty six percent visibility. Asteroid Mea-Ta-11761 will strike the surface of the moon in the southern hemisphere. Scientists at NASA believe the impact will eject a plume of lunar soil that will be visible from Earth. NASA spokesman, Earl Frost, said earlier this week: 'We want to assure everyone that the event poses no threat to our planet, but should prove to be a spectacular show for the end of the year.'"

"Oh, yeah," said Garren. "I forgot that was tonight."

By 7:01, Garren was in his car and speeding toward the university. Thanks to the holiday, the traffic was light. He should have no problem getting to work by 7:30. With any luck, his appointments would go smoothly, he would take a quick look at the manuscripts and be leaving the office by noon. That would give him plenty of time to make it to the store and get home before Kate. He wanted to be in the right frame of mind for the conversation looming before him. As he thought about it, a plan began to form. He wouldn't get mad. He wouldn't allow himself to get caught in the vortex of old accusations and excuses. He would start by telling her she was right to leave, that their time apart had given him clarity, that he still loved her and that he still wanted to be with her. Then he would listen. He would let her say how sorry she was for walking out on him. He would accept her apology and then they would calmly chart the course forward. Lots of couples went through this, and while some did not recover, some did…they would. They should be able to work this out, find the solution just like….Of course, that's what this was, a problem that needed to be solved. Garren was good at solving problems. He knew the formula and the formula always worked: Ask the right question, research the available data, construct a hypothesis, test to see if the answer fits the already knowns. If it fits, proceed to the next question. If it doesn't fit, start over. The key is not to give up. Garren's mind drifted to the Egyptian manuscripts waiting for him at his office and the answers they might hold to his latest research. Then he remembered Kate and their marriage. Yes, marriage. Why should marriage be any different? Once they applied the formula, the answer would present itself.

Garren was starting to feel better about the situation and actually looked forward to sharing his insight with Kate. She would see the logic of it, the problem would be resolved and things would return to normal. He was congratulating himself for his efficiency when his phone rang. It sounded off, lower. He'd have it checked next week when he took the car in for servicing. He glanced at the caller ID and tapped the answer button on the steering wheel.

"Tommy, what's wrong?"

"Nothing. Why do you always ask me that?"

"Because that's usually why you call me *and* it's still morning. Do you know where you are? I'll come and get you."

"No, no, it's nothing like that," Tommy laughed. "But I'll take that as a compliment. I just wanted to catch you before you got to work? Any word from Kate?"

"No, but I'm sure she'll be home today…or tonight."

"What? Hasn't she called?"

"No."

"Have you tried to call her?"

"She wanted space. I'm trying to give her space."

"That's very mature of you." There was a hint of sarcasm in Tommy's voice.

"That's called being an adult in a real adult relationship. You should try it sometime."

"Gee, that's sounds tempting, but if what you've got going there is an adult relationship…yeah, I'm probably going to stay with what I've got."

"And what's that? A string of meaningless encounters that never last more than a week or two?"

"I subscribe to the *many fish in the sea* philosophy."

"You do realize that's what fathers tell their sons when the girl they want to ask to the dance goes with another guy, don't you?"

"I wonder why my old man never told me that. Oh, I remember, I *was* the other guy."

"And I would have hated you," said Garren. "Was there an actual reason you called me?"

"Oh, yeah. You're coming over to my place tonight. I'm having a few friends over to ring in the new year."

"Sorry, I can't."

"Come on, Dude, it's New Year's Eve."

"Tommy, Kate's coming home tonight and well…I just can't."

"All the more reason," Tommy pressed. "You've got to show her you haven't spent the holidays sitting around an empty house."

"But that's exactly what I've been doing."

"I know. And I'm embarrassed for you. Come over to my apartment as soon as you get off work. Text her to come over when she gets in."

"I'm not sending her a text."

"Then leave her a note."

"No, Tommy."

"Yes, Garren. You *are* coming to my place and you *will* thank me for it. I promise."

"No, I'm not."

"Yes, you are. Come over early and help me get things ready."

"Tom—"

"See you soon, Garren."

"Tommy."

The connection ended.

Garren liked Tommy. They'd known each other since middle school. And even though their lives were very different, Tommy was always there for him. Under normal circumstances, Garren and Kate would have gone over to Tommy's, rung in the new year with him, said "goodnight" and left before Crazy Tommy showed up. Crazy Tommy made him nervous. If he were to spend New Year's Eve there without Kate, there's no telling what kind of trouble he would find.

"Deja, turn on the radio."

"Of course, Garren."

"Good Tuesday morning. You're drivin' with KLYV 96.1 – Dubuque's Real Classic Rock, where we are always live and alive. No automation. No artificial intelligence. No sweeteners, implants or enhancements. We are 100% human. I'm Tina Blackwell, along with my fellow human, Jay Jackson. What's going on, J.J.?"

"It's the last day of 2019. Can you believe it? In less than seventeen hours, we'll be roaring into the 20s. See what I did there? Roaring...Twenties."

"Yeah, I get it. Hey, you've been going on and on about this new club that opened up last month on the Riverwalk. It's a theme club based on the old Speakeasies of the 1920s. Tell us, J.J., what all's going on there tonight?"

"Only the biggest party this side of the mighty Mississippi. If you haven't made your New Year's Eve plans yet, you need to be at Tyler's Tavern, located at 23 Bells Street. Tina and I will be kickin' it off around nine o'clock and keepin' it going 'til two. Atlas Road Crew will be taking the stage at ten. These guys...let me tell you about these guys. They are without a doubt one of the hottest rock bands I've seen in a long time. They're from South Carolina, so they definitely have that good ol' Southern Rock flavor, but they've got this really cool modern sound that makes them legit among the college and twenty-something crowd. Come on down and give them a listen. I know you're going to love these guys. Of course, Tyler will be serving up plenty of food, four dollar drafts and prohibition cocktails, and – drum roll please – we'll be counting down the last seconds of 2019 with our very own ball drop. So if you can't be at Times Square, come on down to Tyler's Tavern for the biggest New Year's Eve bash in the Tri-State Area."

"You know, J.J., New Year's Eve is my favorite night of the year. You wanna know why?"

"Is it because you get to spend it with me?"

"Well, there's that, *and* because it's the night of the big reset."

"Reset?"

"2019 has been a tough year for a lot of folks. At the stroke of midnight, we get to cross over into a brand new year, fresh out of the box, no stains or wrinkles. I think there's something magical about that."

"You do realize that tomorrow is just the day after today. The world doesn't actually reset itself at midnight."

"Who knows? Maybe this time it will. Hey, are you ready for the Question of the Day?"

"Sure. Let's hear it."

"This one's from Chloe17. She tweets: *If you knew then what you know now, what would you do differently?*"

"Ooo, that's a good one. Tweet us your answers to @KLYV96rock. We'll get to those right after the news."

"Sorry to be such a downer, but this is the world we live in. A deathbed confession brings closure to a twenty year-old cold case. Delmar Diggs, a convicted murderer serving two life sentences at the Iowa State Penitentiary, confessed earlier this month to additional charges of kidnapping and human trafficking. Diggs, who is dying of cancer, told authorities about an underground bunker near Oskaloosa that he and his associate, Eugene Ponder, used to detain young women. Both men were convicted in 2000 for the murders of Ivan and Irena Jacovich and remain the only suspects in the disappearance of their daughter, Serina, who was sixteen at the time. Responding to information provided by Diggs, FBI agents and local police located the bunker and discovered the remains of seven women, all between the ages of fourteen and seventeen. The identities of six of the victims are being held pending notification of next of kin. The identity of a seventh victim, Svetlana Karabelnikoff, was released after a search of the national missing persons data base yielded no report of her disappearance. Authorities are asking anyone who has knowledge of a Svetlana Karabelnikoff who went missing in late 1999 or early 2000 to notify their local police department.

"Deja," Garren said, "lower volume."

"Okay, Garren. Is there anything else I can do for you?"

He drummed his fingers on the steering wheel. He'd resisted the temptation since Kate left, partly to give her space and partly to prove to himself that she wasn't getting to him. In her note, she said she would be back in time for his birthday. With less than a day to go, she was cutting it pretty close. He wanted to play it cool, let her come back to him, show her that he was okay. But it had been more than a week without a call or text or anything; just that note on her pillow two days before Christmas.

"Deja, do I have any messages?"

"No, Garren."

He thought some more. Checking messages wasn't the same as giving in. That was normal. People did that. He drove the rest of the way to the office in silence, telling himself to just go about his business like he'd done all week. He was down to the wire. In a few hours she would be home and he could face her knowing that he'd at least won something, even if it was just a mental game of discipline he was playing against himself. He pulled into his parking space and switched off the engine. He was about to get out of the car when he was hit by a momentary lapse of will power.

"Deja, locate Kate's car."

"I'm sorry, Garren, Kate's auto-locator has been switched off."

December 31, 2019
9:30 PM

Garren sat alone in his darkened living room contemplating the day's non-events. He left work shortly after his last appointment, both of which were brief and pointless; check-ins to make sure certain projects were still on target for the real work that would begin after the holiday hiatus. Just as well, since Garren could think of nothing else besides Kate and the fact that she had deactivated her car's tracking chip. Against his better judgment, he tried calling her from one of the landlines in a vacant office. He wasn't going to say anything and he didn't want his name to pop up on her caller ID. He just wanted to hear her voice to make sure she was okay. On the second ring, he was sent to voice mail where he received a message that Kate's voice mailbox was full. Thirty minutes later, after typing and deleting several text messages, he pressed send: *See you tonight. Safe travels.* A minute later, he received a text from Kate's sister Denise: *K with me few more days.* He tapped out the first thing that came to his mind, deleted it and replied: *Ok.* If that's how she wanted to play this, he could play, too. He was not about to spend New Year's Eve sulking alone in an empty house.

Garren stormed into his bedroom and yanked open the closet door. The light popped on to reveal he'd opened the wrong closet. Kate's clothes taunted him, pulling him as if by their own gravity.

He grabbed a handful of sleeves and buried his face in them. Her scent invaded him, intoxicating, erasing his reasons for being so angry, making him long for her. Feeling himself being pulled into a state of melancholy, his self-respect came back online. He flung the fabric back into the rack and wiped his hand on his shirt. Turning to his own closet, he was greeted by the sad predictability of his life in clothing: 75% office attire, 22% hanging around the house clothes, 2% yard grungies, and tucked away in the back from lack of use was the 1% of his going out clothes. Without much by way of choices, he was dressed and ready to go in no time. A quick stop in the bathroom to brush his teeth and ignore Deja, and he was out the door.

Fifteen minutes later, Garren pulled into the parking lot of Tommy's upscale apartment complex. The lot was full and several cars were parked on the grass. Spurred by the defiance he was feeling towards Kate and her sister accomplice, Garren gunned his engine, jumped the curb and wedged himself between two other cars. Getting out, he noticed an unusually large number of people outside, none of which were the least bit interested in his illegal parking maneuver. Everyone was looking skyward.

"What the…" he mumbled, and then it came to him. "Oh, yeah. The moon."

Garren approached the nearest group of moon gazers and stopped. Everyone had a drink in hand, but it was early enough that most of the revelers were still in control of themselves.

"Five minutes," he heard someone say. Garren noticed several people had their cellphones out. Some were watching a countdown app created by NASA, but most were ready to capture the event as it happened.

Five minutes was more than enough time for Garren to make his way to the apartment. He wondered if Tommy's friends would be outside on such a chilly night to watch a space rock collide with the moon or was such a space nerd event beneath them? He really didn't know much about Tommy's social circle except that it consisted of a lot of women, really good-looking women. Tommy was that kind of guy. Garren never cared enough to ask how Tommy's latest girlfriend fit in among all his exes, or did they?

At two minutes to impact, Garren found Tommy and about twenty of his guests outside with the masses waiting for the big show.

"Garren!" Tommy emerged from the crowd accompanied by an attractive and classily dressed woman. Letting go of the woman's hand, he greeted Garren with a friendly bro-hug and then returned to his date. "I was beginning to think you wouldn't show."

"Here I am."

"Garren, I'd like you to meet Evianna, my date for the rest of the year. Evi, this is my best friend in the entire world, Dr. Garren Rosen."

"Happy New Year, Doctor," said Evianna in a way that suggested she was already well on her way to forgetting much about the evening. "Do you make house calls?"

"I'm not that kind of doctor."

"Well, happy New Year anyway."

"One minute!" shouted someone.

Shivering, Evianna pulled Tommy's arm around her shoulder and looked up at the moon. "This better be worth it. I'm cold."

"You okay, Garren?" Tommy asked.

"I'm not at home."

"Right. Well, I'm glad you're here with us. I did promise you a good time."

"Thirty seconds!"

Tommy continued, "And we're going to start by watching the moon get hit by a big asteroid. Who knows? This could change the world."

At fifteen seconds, the crowd started counting down. Now that it was about to happen, Garren felt himself drawn into the event. At five seconds, he joined the count.

"Five....Four....Three....Two....One!"

In the 1.3 seconds it takes for light to travel from the moon to the earth, the crowd held its collective breath. It was just enough time for the idea to form that maybe the whole thing was a bust; that the asteroid missed or it wasn't so big after all. Or maybe NASA's countdown app was off. Then everyone jumped and gasped as an explosion erupted from the lunar surface. Of course, there was no sound and no vibration in the ground beneath their feet, but the visual was much more spectacular than anyone expected. The asteroid itself arrived unseen since there was no lunar atmosphere to heat it as would have been the case of an Earth impact. Instead, there was a brilliant flash and the sudden appearance of a giant plume as tons of lunar soil were ejected from the surface, leaving behind a new crater several times larger than any other. In the blink of an eye, the moon's appearance was permanently altered. As for the crowd, everyone just stood in stunned silence, not sure whether they should be concerned that Earth's closest neighbor had been so violently assaulted. After nearly a minute, there was a smattering of nervous laughter as there didn't seem to be any immediate effect upon the earth. Then it occurred to several to check social media and news apps for updates, and someone ran to a nearby car to turn on the radio.

"Okay," said Evianna, "I've seen enough. Take me inside. I'm cold."

Another minute passed before the first of the crowd began to disperse. There was a noticeably different mood in the air. The murmurings were less exuberant, as everyone understood something significant had occurred, but no one knew quite what to make of it. About half of the crowd returned to their respective apartments for warmth and libations, while the rest remained outside. Garren joined several others who had gathered around the open car to listen to the initial news reports, but there was nothing to learn that they didn't already know. Even the experts were unsure what to make of the event since it was impossible to conduct any real examination. The initial telescopic visuals offered no satisfaction as the impact zone was obscured by the suspension of lunar debris. With neither wind nor enough gravity to dissipate it, the cloud would remain for days until the moon slowly reclaimed the part of itself that was blasted away. Like a man stunned by a punch to the face, the moon itself seemed dazed by the attack. Garren took one more extended look at the oddity in the sky before making his way into Tommy's apartment.

Inside, the party was beginning to recover from the interruption. Someone had turned on the television, and about a third of Tommy's guests were gathered around to look at the up-close images from the Sloan International Lunar Observation Consortium. The broadcast kept switching between live feeds from several locations across the globe in hopes of getting a clearer shot, but all of them showed the same cloudy images.

Something of an introvert, Garren wandered toward the television. Like the others gathered there, he was drawn into what was happening skyward, but he was also thankful for the distraction. The thing he disliked most about parties was the pointless chitchat of which Tommy was a proven master. With any luck, he could get through the evening in the company of other human beings without having to engage any of them.

"What a way to ring in the new year."

"Huh?" Garren hadn't noticed the woman standing next to him. "Oh, yeah. That was really something."

"My name's Sofia."

"I'm Garren." He took a second look and decided she fit the profile of one of Tommy's girls – pretty, slender, dressed more for an upscale gala than an apartment get together. "How do you know Tommy?" he asked.

"We met at the gym. You?"

"Childhood." A quick glance at her arms and shoulders told him she was telling the truth about going to the gym.

"So you two have known each other for a while."

"Most of my life. What about you? What's your history with Tommy. Oh, wait, I didn't mean to imply you two have history. Well, maybe you do, but that's none of my business. What I meant to say was how long have you two…you know what, never mind. That's none of my business. I just said that twice, didn't I? Could you just delete the last fifteen seconds?" Garren paused as if to reset himself. "It's nice to meet you, Sofia."

"You're funny," she replied with a smile. "I'm having a hard time putting you and Tommy together."

"Yeah, I know. We live in very different worlds. He's…well, he's Tommy."

"He certainly is. And you are…"

"I'm not Tommy."

They both looked over to where Tommy had a small gathering in rapt attention to whatever he was saying.

"Aren't you partaking?" Sofia asked.

Garren didn't quite know what she meant.

"Your hands are empty," she explained. "You're not leaving so soon, are you?"

"Oh, no. I just got here."

"You want to get something to drink and sit down?"

"Uh," Garren hesitated. It had literally been decades since he had a drink with a woman other than Kate. It felt strange, but not unpleasant.

"You sit here and save me a spot. I'll be right back."

Garren dropped onto the couch and watched his new friend disappear into the crowd. A bit of excitement popped into his mind followed by a bigger slice of guilt. *What are you doing?* He asked himself. *Maybe this wasn't such a good idea after all. Maybe you should just leave.* Sofia returned quicker than he expected with two red plastic cups. *Okay, maybe just one quick drink and then you need to get home.*

"Here you go." Sofia handed him one of the cups and sat down next to him. "I'm told I'm pretty good at this. Don't ask. Just enjoy." She held her cup toward him. "Here's to a better year than the one before."

Garren tapped his cup against hers and took a drink. "Wow, that's good. Is that apple I taste?"

"Very good."

"I know I don't look it, but I am of age. Is there anything in this?"

"I told you not to ask," Sofia laughed. "I call it Eden's Curse. At first you think it's no big deal. But then you wake up naked in the woods. I'd be careful if I were you."

The look on Garren's face betrayed his surprise. "What are you, a bartender?"

She raised her hands. "Guilty as charged."

Garren blinked in surprise. "Really? How are you not working on New Year's Eve?"

"Correction: I *was* a bartender. I'm between opportunities at the moment. I moved here from New York in October. Had to get away from some things, so I came back here."

"Oh, so you're from here."

"Sort of. How about you?"

"Born and bred. Other than a few vacations, I've never been anywhere else."

"I'm surprised we never crossed paths. I thought I knew all the good looking guys in Dubuque."

Garren chuckled nervously. Was she hitting on him? "So, you moved back home…" He wanted to steer the conversation back to something safe, like biographical information.

"I'm such a cliché. Small town girl moves to big city. Big city doesn't play nice. Small town girl moves back home."

"Ah, I think I've seen that movie a few times."

"To my defense, I lasted almost twenty years there. That's well past the newbie threshold. And I admit it wasn't all bad. I did good there, took my licks, gave a few back, earned a few battle scars, learned a lot about myself and decided to come home on my own terms. I wasn't forced out. That's more than I can say for a lot of people I know. But now I'm here. I'll probably start putting the pieces together after the holidays. That's the short version of my story. What about you?"

"Wow, you just lay it out there. You seem very confident."

"New York, Baby. Only the strong survive. But here, I get it. I should probably dial it back a bit, you think?"

"No, don't do that. It's refreshing."

"You're clever."

"How's that?"

"You avoided my inquiry. What's your story?"

"Confident *and* persistent."

"What can I say?" She shrugged. "You don't get what you don't ask for."

Garren took another sip of his drink. *Oh, boy.*

"I can also take a hint. If you'd rather be left alone, I totally get that." She started to get up.

"No, wait, don't go. I'm sorry. I'm just not used to this. I should tell you I'm married." He held up his left hand and thumbed his wedding band.

"I noticed. Points for being honest with me. And let me just say I'm not looking to get involved with a married man…or any man at the moment. That's one of the things I had to get away from. And that's why I'm talking with you. You seem safe."

"Gee, thanks," Garren said in mock offence.

"I meant that as a compliment. You don't seem like the type of guy who…" She chuckled. "Well, you're not like Tommy."

"You're right about that. So, why are you here at Tommy's apartment?"

"I didn't want to spend New Year's Eve alone. When he asked me to come over, I made him promise there would actually be people here. I figured if I didn't see a crowd, I would just leave. So here I am. I watched the moon get smacked by an asteroid. I'm enjoying the company of a nice guy. I'm having a good time. And Tommy is behaving himself."

"It's still early. Say, has he been hitting on you?"

"Yes, but I know how to handle guys like him. They're not that complicated. Guys like you, on the other hand…"

"What's that supposed to mean?"

"Nothing. I'm just messing with you." Sofia took a sip of her drink and eyed him thoughtfully. "So, why are you here?"

"Same reason. I didn't want to be alone tonight either. New Year's Eve and all."

"Where is she?" She nodded toward his wedding ring.

Garren took another long swig, trying to decide how much he wanted to say. "I think she's at her sister's house."

"Your choice or hers?"

"Definitely hers."

"Let me guess. She needed time."

"You got it."

"But you thought she'd be back with you by tonight."

"Right again."

"She's obviously not, so you assume she's still with her sister."

"What are you, psychic?"

"My dad was a behavioral psychologist. He taught me how to read people. Plus, I'm a bartender. I've met a lot of people and heard a lot of stories. Not to diminish yours, but it's not that unusual."

"It feels like it when you're one of the main characters."

"Absolutely. I'm starring in my own story."

Garren drained his cup and set it on the table. Sofia did the same.

"Hey, look at the time," Garren noted. "Eleven o'clock. It's 2020 in New York."

"How are you feeling?" she asked. "You okay?"

"Yeah, I'm fine."

"May I interest you in another one...for New York?"

"Sure. Why not?"

When Sofia disappeared back into the kitchen, Garren assessed his condition. He really did feel fine, and he wondered if Sofia was pulling his leg about Eden's Curse.

"Here you go." Sofia handed him another cup as she sat back down on the couch.

Garren took a sip. "Mmm, this one's even better than the last one. Did you do something different?"

"Mixology is more art than science. Same painting, different nuances."

"You're the expert." Garren raised his cup and took another sip. "So, New York. I'm assuming you lived in the city."

"Oh, yeah. I shared a little apartment in Manhattan with an aspiring actress. We were right there in the middle of it all. I did the New Year's Eve Times Square thing when I first moved there. I enjoyed it, but you don't stay young forever. When I started tending, I was always behind the counter when the ball dropped. Of course, that wasn't much better, just warmer. Eventually, I worked my way through the circuit until I landed a pretty sweet gig with a high-end party supply company. I tended bar for celebrity parties, corporate events and weddings of the rich and famous. I traded slobs for snobs. The environment was a lot better, but the tips were worse."

"Why did you do it? You seem...I don't know...like you could have done something else."

"I never aspired to be a bartender," she replied. "But a girl's gotta eat and sometimes you have to take what's available. No, I moved to New York really for no other reason than to be in New York. Too many episodes of *Friends*. I tried bartending on a whim. It was supposed to be temporary until I found something else. But I guess I was good at it and before I knew it ten years had passed. It wasn't what I planned, but it's what I got."

"If you could do it all over again, would you?"

"That's funny. There was this long discussion about that on the radio this morning. It started with a question: If you knew then what you know now, what would you do differently?"

"That's where I heard it," Garren said. "I guess we listen to the same radio station. So, would you do it again?"

"Some of it, sure."

"Do you ever think of the things you would change?"

"Of course. Everyone thinks about the things they should have done differently. But you can't dwell on those things. It's not like you can go back and change them."

"But what if you could? What if we could send a message back to our younger selves?"

"We wouldn't listen."

"Okay, what if you could switch places with your younger self?"

"We're getting deep now."

"Just talking." Garren took another long drink. "You know, I haven't talked to anyone like this in a long time. You're easy to talk to."

"So I've been told."

"Well, if I could go back just a couple months, knowing what I know now, I would have played them very differently."

Sofia smiled and nodded in a way that encouraged him to keep talking.

"I would have paid more attention. I would have listened more. I wouldn't have let us drift apart...my wife and me. I wouldn't have stopped trying to be the man I was when we met. Maybe that's why she..." He hesitated, then blurted it out. "I think my wife cheated on me. Wow, that's the first time I've actually said it out loud." He took another sip and exhaled. "Whew, I thought that was supposed to make you feel better, but it doesn't. I actually feel worse."

Sofia was still nodding, but her smile had morphed into genuine sympathy.

"Oh, no," Garren said. "I am so sorry. I just dumped all my stuff on you. I just treated you like a bartender. I'm sorry."

"Don't be. As a bartender, I would say: That's life, Buddy. You live and you learn and you hope you don't do too much damage along the way. As a friend, let me say: I'm truly sorry for what you're going through. I wish it could be different."

"Thanks." Garren was still embarrassed and a little surprised that he so quickly opened up about his situation. Maybe Eden's Curse was affecting him more than he realized.

"Aren't we a pair?" said Sofia.

"What do you mean?"

"We may be the only two people at this party who are attracted to each other, but aren't trying to hook up."

Garren did a double take. "You think there's an attraction here?"

"It ain't rocket science. I'm attracted to you, and I'll bet you another round you're attracted to me."

Garren started to deny it, but came up short.

"I told you, I'm pretty good at this. Now you owe me a drink."

Garren was genuinely at a loss. He wasn't used to being so open with his thoughts and feelings, not even with Kate. "I, uh, I don't really know what to say."

"You don't have to say anything. It's not like we'll act on it. Unless…" The look on Garren's face made her laugh. "Just kidding. I just thought since we're being honest with each other we could get that out of the way and enjoy the evening. You're not going to get weird on me now, are you?"

"No, of course not." Garren wondered why he and Kate weren't this honest with each other. If they had been…

"So, you gonna get me that drink?"

"I guess I am."

As soon as Garren stood up he felt Eden's Curse kick in. He wasn't drunk, but if he kept this pace he would be. Good thing he was getting the third round. He could tone his down a bit. Was it really the third round? He couldn't remember the last time he had a third round. He'd have to really tone it down if he intended to get home before sunrise.

"Hey, Buddy. Don't get up." Tommy pushed Garren back onto the couch and dropped down between them, exaggerating his effort to not spill the pitcher he was carrying. "Whoa! Here, let me top you guys off. Sofia, your recipe is a-mazing. Everybody's raving about it."

"Glad you like it," she replied.

"You mean everybody's drinking this stuff?" Garren asked.

"Yes," Tommy said. "Only the best for my friends. But it does pack a punch," He set the pitcher on the coffee table and draped his arms around both of them. "I'm so glad to see you two hitting it off. I had a feeling. Don't let this get around, but if you guys need to crash here tonight, I'm totally cool with that."

A low ring developed in Garren's ears and things got blurry after that.

Time is the impartial arbiter of the affairs of men. It ignores the bargaining table. It accepts no deals. It cannot be conned, cheated or tricked. It treats all as equals – the good, the bad, the guilty, the innocent. It takes no sides. It does not prefer one over another. It is the ultimate equal opportunity employer. Relentless and steady, it operates according to one simple rule – *movement*. It maintains one heading – *forward*. Its speed is a constant sixty minutes per hour with no variation or interruption. The manipulation of it makes for interesting fiction, but in the real world it does not bend, break or yield to the whims of mad scientists or evil geniuses. Time simply is what it is and does what it does. Of course, the perception of time can vary. Time flies when you're having fun. A watched pot never boils. Time can be either merciless or merciful, depending upon the event of one's anticipation. It can be either friend or foe, depending upon how one uses one's allotment. But time is not affected by the estimations of mortals. Time is the silent custodian of this reality, setting the pace of history and ensuring all things remain in their proper order.

Humans have sought to mark time in various ways: The progression of the sun, the movement of shadows, the phases of the moon, the changing of the seasons, the position of constellations, sand in an hourglass, pages on a calendar, digits on a screen. All of these have proven invaluable to men's pursuits. But there is one mode that, under the right conditions, can drive even a sane man to the brink of madness. This tool in the devil's arsenal is none other than the ticking of a clock in the predawn hour.

Garren groaned as he transitioned from sweet unconsciousness to the harsh reality of his post party condition. His head throbbed with each tick of the bedside clock. His back cried foul at the overly soft and sagging mattress. A shiver ran through his entire body as it registered the coldness of the room and he realized he was only partially covered by one corner of a sheet. As he became more awake, these sensations came together to bring him to an undeniable conclusion – he was not in his own bed. A quick examination of his person told him he was wearing only his boxers. The silky smooth leg pressed against him proved he was not alone.

Oh, no, no, No, No, NO! The sound of his thoughts screamed in his head, though he dared not make a sound. He quickly and quietly slipped out of the bed and felt his way in the dark to a door he hoped was a bathroom. The cold tile floor told him it was. Closing the door behind him, he flipped on the light and sat down on the closed toilet.

"What have I done?" He put his head in his hands in an effort to keep it from exploding. "Think, man, think." He tried to reconstruct the events that led to this disaster. "Tommy's party. Asteroid hitting the moon. Drinks – lots of drinks. A really cool woman. What was her name? Trading car keys for another drink. How many was it? Sofia….Sofia! Uh, oh. Oh….no. I am so dead."

Garren rubbed his eyes and tried to devise a plan. Should he sneak out and pretend nothing happened? Should he wake her, plead stupid and face the music? Should he…no, that was the extent of his options. He stood up and started for the door. That's when he caught his refection in the mirror. "What the…?" He rubbed his eyes again. "How much did I drink?" He looked into the mirror again and stumbled backward until he hit the shower, making a terrible racket.

"You okay in there?" The voice from the other side of the door sounded groggy.

He opened his mouth to reply, but couldn't speak.

"Garren?"

He heard movement from the bed and footsteps approaching. He quickly locked the door and turned on the water.

"Garren? Are you okay?" The door knob jiggled. "Garren, what's wrong?"

"Uh, nothing. I'm uh, not feeling well."

"Too much fun last night?"

"Yep. That must be it."

There was an unsympathetic snicker. "You guys aren't teenagers anymore." More footsteps followed by bedsprings.

Garren stared at his reflection, unable to process what he was seeing. His hair was dark, and it seemed to him he'd lost weight. Was this some kind of joke? Did Sofia and Tommy dye his hair? Was it a trick mirror? Was that even his reflection? Garren lifted his hand and the reflection did the same. That was him, all right. He splashed water onto his face and looked again. Turning his head to the right and to the left, he noticed that he even looked younger. Did he really look like that? Or did it just seem that way because of the hair and the mirror? Or was there something in all those drinks? Was Sofia some kind of wizard temptress brewing up cocktails to transform middle-aged men into love toys? Not that he minded looking so young again, but he couldn't let anyone else see him that way. He'd never be able to explain it.

"Garren," came the voice again, "would you please bring me some water?"

Irritated by the joke perpetrated against him, he was even more put off that Sofia was being so casual about it. Who did she think she was? Garren scanned the bathroom until he found a paper cup dispenser mounted to the wall next to the mirror. He chuckled at odd coincidence, for he and Kate had one just like it in their first apartment. Triggered by the memory, other things began to look familiar. The towels looked like the ones they received as a wedding gift. The toothpaste on the counter was the same generic brand they used to buy before they had money. The hairband was exactly like the ones Kate wore before she cut her hair short. If this was a joke, Tommy had gone all out.

Garren glanced at his wrist to check the time. Of course, his watch was missing. No matter, he knew what time it was. Time to get to the bottom of this prank.

"Okay, you got me," he said as he threw open the door. "I'm sorry about last night. That wasn't the real me. I don't treat people like that. So, yeah, I deserve whatever this is you guys are pulling on me. I'm just gonna get my clothes and leave. You don't ever have to see me again. I'm sorry. I'm truly sorry."

"What are you talking about?"

The light clicked on and Garren nearly lost it. He stumbled back into the bathroom, slammed the door and locked it.

"Garren? Now you're scaring me. What is wrong with you?"

Garren stared at the door, trying to hold it together. His heart was pounding and his breathing was rapid and shallow. He felt like he might faint.

"Garren." The knob jiggled and there was pounding on the door. "Let me in. I need to see you."

Now it made sense. Before, he thought it was just the effect of sound waves passing through the wooden door, but now that he saw her face, the voice fit. But it didn't make sense because it was not possible. Yet she was there. He saw her. On the other side of that door, she was there. Garren turned the knob, disengaging the lock, and let the door swing open. Though he now expected it, the sight of her still caught his breath. "Kate? Is that really you?"

Kate looked at him sideways. "Are you okay? Do you want to come back to bed, or do you need to throw up again?"

"Um." On the outside, Garren looked like a mannequin, but on the inside he was Sherlock Holmes trying to deduce some sense of reality from the clues set before him. The bathroom was an exact replica of the one in Kate's and his first apartment. The bedroom, now that he could see it in the light, was also a perfect match. But the *pièce de résistance* was the woman standing before him. It was Kate the way she looked when they were first married. Her hair, its natural auburn color, was long again, wavy and slightly messed up from sleeping on it. He always loved that look. She was wearing his Van Halen t-shirt. No woman had ever looked so good to him. But she couldn't be real because she didn't look like that anymore. Then again, neither did he. This had to be a dream.

"Hello." Kate waved her hand in front of his face. "You awake in there?"

"I'm not sure." Garren knew he had to say something. "It feels like it, but...I...I was...I was having the weirdest dream."

"Do you want to talk about it?" She caught his hand and led him back to the bed.

"No." He tried to avert his eyes, but he couldn't help staring at her. "Maybe I should just try to go back to sleep."

"I hope you can." Kate yawned and crawled back to her side of the bed.

Not knowing what else to do, Garren lay down and pulled the covers over himself. He glanced toward Kate's side and saw her snuggled in with her back to him, her unmistakable hair proof that it was actually her. But again, how was it possible? He listed his options: 1) Dream. If that's what this was, it was the best dream he'd ever had, and he didn't want it to end. 2) Hallucination. It could be the effects of that drink…*those* drinks. What was it, Eden's Curse? That made more sense. He searched for a third option, but came up short. What else could it be? What could he do? Either way, he had to let whatever it was run its course.

"What are you sorry about?" Kate asked from her side of the bed.

"Huh?"

"You said you were sorry and that you deserved whatever this was. What did you mean by that?"

"Nothing. It must have been that dream."

"You're not still thinking about that stupid argument with Tommy."

"What argument?" If this were a dream, he may as well go along with it.

"How could you not remember? You guys wouldn't let it go. That's why Brad and Janet left before midnight. I swear, alcohol is not your friend. You should really stick to that two drink limit we talked about, especially when Tommy is over."

"You're right. I will. I'm sorry." Garren wracked his brain trying to make sense of everything. It no longer felt like a dream. Kate's disapproval of his drinking felt all too real.

"That Tommy," Kate giggled. "He is pretty funny. When you two get together, you're like this totally different person."

"How's that?"

"I don't know. Looser, I guess. Maybe."

"Do you want me to be more like Tommy?"

"No way." Kate turned over and cuddled up close to him, threading her arm through his so she could caress his bare chest. "You're my man. Don't ever forget that."

Garren wanted nothing more than this dream to be real. It had been years since Kate spoke to him like that, and more than a decade since they cuddled. But if it had to be a dream, he never wanted to wake up. He took her hand in his and brought it to his lips. "I love you." It felt good to say that again and he knew he meant it.

"Mmm, I love you, too."

He didn't think it possible, but he felt Kate press even closer against him. Whether a dream or hallucination, the sensation stirred his heart and revived feelings that had long lay dormant in a cocoon of monotony reinforced by familiarity and resignation. In that moment, time seemed to release him, allowing him to return to those early days of marriage when everything was new and exciting, and there were still mysteries to be explored. And then he remembered the promise he and Kate made to each other on their wedding night. No matter what, they agreed, they would never let the fire die. They made a vow to resist the creeping complacency they saw in their friends who married before them. They promised to never take each other for granted, to always put each other first, and refuse to allow time to stagnate their marriage. They would be different, the exception to the rule. For them, time would deepen their love and strengthen their commitment. Time would be their ally. The years would season their marriage and enhance their love. The certainty of that youthful promise overwhelmed the disillusionment that accompanied middle-age, and in that moment he realized a forgotten hope.

Garren may have drifted off, but he wasn't sure. Is it even possible to fall asleep inside a dream? Or was he awake for real this time? He noticed the room wasn't quite as dark; presumably the sun was up and attacking the heavy curtains in his room. There were such curtains in his real bedroom, but there might have been the same kind of curtains in the first bedroom he shared with Kate. He couldn't remember. He felt his chest and found he no longer held Kate's hand, and he could feel that she was no longer pressed against him. Although the impression of her closeness lingered in his mind, and the hope it brought was still there. He knew from experience that the sensations created by very lucid dreams lingered long after the person returned to the real world. Even if he was now awake for real, perhaps that dream meant something. Perhaps he had been given the reminder as encouragement to fight for Kate like he promised that night twenty years ago. Perhaps their marriage was being given a second chance. Part of him wanted to get up and begin the process of winning her back. But another part of him wanted to preserve the illusion of his dream a little longer? He closed his eyes again, willing himself to return to that good dream, his longing for that feeling compelling him to at least try. Then he heard it, the evidence that suggested he was either still in the dream with Kate or the guestroom of Tommy's apartment with…he couldn't bring himself to even think the other woman's name. Tick, tick, tick. The old clock was undeniably still there. But was there someone else in bed with him?

Garren slowly turned toward what he wanted desperately to be Kate's side of the bed. The room was just bright enough for him to make out a shape lying next to him, but not so bright that he could tell for sure that it was her. He listened. After twenty years, he was fairly certain that he would not mistake her gentle breathing for that of another. Not that he had anything to compare, but the rhythmic purring sounded like Kate. He moved closer until he was in range. Inhaling through his nose, he detected the scent of her hair; further confirmation that it was most likely her. But he had to make sure, and the only way to remove all doubt was risky. He touched her shoulder just enough to get a reaction. She stirred, turned toward him, flung her arm across his chest and nuzzled into his side, all without becoming fully awake. Now he was certain. There was no mistaking the way in which she fit in his arms. It was Kate.

So what did it mean? It had to be a dream, right? The woman in his arms was definitely Kate. She was there and they were together. But it wasn't like she had come home and they were working things out. They were together like when they were first married. The sense of it all was fresh and exciting, as if their marriage was still new and they were both young. So, it had to be a dream. It had to be the most vivid and realistic dream ever. What else could it be?

4

What else could it be?

Assuming it was a dream, the question refused to let Garren enjoy it. The possibilities continued their endless cycle through his mind – hallucination, dream, reaction to something Sofia had put in his drink, dream, insanity, dream. It always circled back around to *it has to be a dream*. But the more he thought about it, the more convinced he became that he was awake. He decided to run a series of tests. Pinch to the arm – he could feel it. Bite down on the tongue – he felt that, too. He remembered hearing a guy on the radio talk about lucid dreams and how you could test yourself to see if you were in one by pinching your nose and trying to breathe through it. Apparently, you can do that in dreams, but when Garren tried it he couldn't. All the evidence strongly suggested he was awake. And being awake, he could clearly see that the woman lying in his arms was his wife as she was when they were first married. So if this were not a dream, again came the question: What else could it be?

He considered the possibility that he might have died and this was the afterlife. Perhaps that asteroid hitting the moon actually caused all life on earth to become extinct. Or maybe he had been in a car accident on the way to Tommy's party and he just couldn't remember it. Or maybe he died from whatever Sofia kept giving him to drink. Never having given much thought to the afterlife, it seemed reasonable that each person's version of it could be a construct of the best memories of the happiest time in that person's life. It turned out for him that heaven was the first year of marriage. That was indeed the happiest time in his life. He could spend eternity there… or then. But then there was the fact that all these considerations were preventing him from enjoying it. Could heaven really be all that great if his mind wouldn't allow him to enjoy it? Suddenly, a dread thought came to him. What if this weren't heaven, but the other place? He quickly dismissed the whole afterlife angle and tried again: What else could it be?

The only answer he had not yet considered began to take shape. *This could be real.* As soon as he thought it, he laughed at the absurdity of it. *How could it be real?* Yet the evidence was undeniable. Kate was there. They were in their first apartment. *Or an exact replica*, the skeptical portion of his mind suggested. But the growing weight of this new answer agreed with the fact that his reflection in the mirror was that of his younger self. Based on the evidence, the impossible was quickly presenting itself as the only possible answer. But how? And why?

Easy, Garren, he thought to himself. *Don't get ahead of yourself. This is just another problem that needs to be solved. Remember the formula: Ask the right question, research the available data, construct a hypothesis, test to see if the answer fits the already knowns. If it fits, proceed to the next question. If it doesn't, start over.*

The formula brought comfort to Garren. It put him back on familiar ground and gave his weary mind something else to ponder. He was even proud of himself for having already applied the formula to the task. Without realizing it, he had already constructed, tested and eliminated several hypotheses, and was working on the one that seemed to be standing up the best against the available data. Experience told him that he should give this new hypothesis time to prove itself one way or the other. If it remained intact, then he could address the *how* and *why*.

Whether he had happened upon the right answer or not, his mind had ceased asking the question, and that brought satisfactory relief. Like the removal of a splinter, the wound was still there, but at least he could stop digging at it. He was just about to give himself permission to sleep when Kate said…

"Hey, you." She kissed him on the cheek. "That dream keeping you awake?"

"What do you mean?"

"You've been fidgety for the last hour and mumbling."

"I'm sorry I woke you."

"You don't need to keep apologizing. I've just been enjoying being close to you." She kissed him again. "You want to tell me what's on your mind?"

Garren did want to tell her, but how could he without her thinking he'd lost his mind? But if she were having the same weird experience, then they could work it out together. He decided to test it. "I'm trying to remember what all happened last night, but there are some blank spots. Would you mind filling me in?"

"Are you serious? I think maybe we should talk about your drinking, College Boy. I want you to have a good time, but if you can't remember having it, that's a problem."

Garren felt his defenses begin to rise. His drinking had been a recurring source of tension throughout their marriage and one of the problems cited by Kate in her most recent list of grievances. In his defense (weak as it was), her nagging him about it was one of the reasons he continued to drink. He was just about to launch into his usual justification when he was caught by the look on her face…her young face. It was not the hardened expression of the angry wife he had become used to. Instead, it was the pained look of real concern mixed with an uncertainty of how to express it.

"Did you hear me?" Kate asked.

"Um, yeah, I heard you. And I get it. You're right. I shouldn't drink so much. I'm sorry. I won't do that again."

"Again with the apologies." Kate's face showed her irritation. "Just do the right thing."

If only it were that simple. Garren's mind began to process her easy solution to life's problems, but then he remembered the problem at hand. "So, about last night. I remember we were at Tommy's place. New Year's Eve, right?"

Kate gave him a look that he recognized to mean: *If you don't even know that, we're done here.*

"You don't need to answer that. I know what the date is." In truth, it was a guess and a reckless one at that. Why would this alternate reality, if that's what it was, be chronologically linked with the one he had left? In the split second he considered this, he realized how crazy this theory sounded. But the look on her face told him he was right about the date. So he continued. "You said Tommy and I were arguing. What was that about?"

Kate rolled her eyes.

"Humor me, please," Garren said before she could decide she was done with him.

"It was embarrassing. That Prince song, 1999, came on the radio and you said how cool it was that we were about to cross over into a new century. Tommy said the new century wouldn't actually begin until 2001. Then you wanted to take a poll to see what everybody else thought. It was funny at first, but you guys wouldn't leave it alone. It turned into this huge argument. You knocked Tommy's drink out of his hand. He pushed you. If Jack hadn't intervened, one or both of you would have gotten hurt. I was really embarrassed."

"I remember that," Garren said, mostly to himself, as the old memory came back to him. As the implication dawned on him, he sat up in the bed and turned on the bedside lamp. "It's the year 2000." He scanned the room for consistencies with this new bit of information. In the corner of the room near his side of the bed was a baseball bat and shotgun. On the bedside table on Kate's side was a flashlight, handgun and buck knife. Lining the wall on the other side of the room were cases of bottled water and boxes of energy bars. Toilet paper was stacked to the ceiling in the corner near the bathroom door. "Y2K." He started to chuckle. "It *is* the year 2000."

"I know," Kate said sheepishly. "You were right. Nothing happened. Remember, you promised you wouldn't make fun of me."

"That's right, I did." Garren swallowed his laughter, which had nothing to do with Kate's over-preparedness and everything to do with his amazement over where and when he apparently was. "And you promised to share your supplies with me if civilization came to an end. Come here." He pulled her into his arms. "I love you so much."

"I love you, too. And I'm glad you were right."

Garren held her tightly as he tried to wrap his mind around the legitimacy of his *this is real* hypothesis. He also had the answer to another question. Kate's reaction proved that she was not having the same experience, but was in fact a native of this reality. He decided it was probably not the right time to tell her that his yesterday was 2019. He would have to keep that to himself for now and just see what happened next. Maybe this was just some weird temporal fluke like in the movie *Groundhog Day*. Maybe he would just relive January 1, 2000 and wake up on January 2, 2020. If that were the case, he may as well enjoy it.

"Wow," he said. "January 1, 2000. Can you believe it? We're really here."

"Yeah, it's weird that it's not nineteen-something anymore. You think we'll ever get used to saying two thousand-something? Or will we say twenty-something?"

"I imagine we'll say two thousand for about the first ten years. Probably sometime in the second decade people will start saying twenty-whatever."

"I don't know if I'll ever get used to it. What do you think the next ten years will be like?"

The fact that he knew the answer to that question hit Garren with tremendous force. A chill ran through his body as the progression of the last two decades flew through his mind. He knew things that a person of this time could not, *should not* know. He knew things about Kate that she would have to learn over the natural course of time. Suddenly, the novelty of a man out of time was overshadowed by the liability of it. Was he now responsible to use this knowledge of the future to affect the past? Or was he restricted from interfering? This was the stuff of science fiction, but now that it was actually happening, what was he supposed to do? It was unprecedented. Nothing like this had ever happened before. Or had it? How would anyone know if a visitor from the future changed something in the past? Was that what he was, a visitor? Would he return to his own time? Or was he meant to relive the last twenty years of his life? Again the *why* question was begging to be answered. He was about to go down that road when Kate brought him back to the moment.

"Hello." She nudged him. "You zoned out on me."

"Oh, sorry. Yeah, I um, I don't know what the next ten years will be like." It felt wrong to lie to her, but until he could figure things out, he would have to play dumb.

"Let's leave the future to itself and talk about today. It's somebody's birthday."

"That's right. It is."

"How does it feel to be the big 3-0?"

"Actually, it feels pretty good." That part was the truth. Compared to fifty, thirty felt a lot better.

"Gee, I've never been with such an old man. Maybe we should… what? Why are you looking at me like that?"

"It just occurred to me that this is how I always think of you."

"How else would you think of me?"

"What I mean is, I imagine that when I'm…I don't know…say, fifty, I'll probably still think of you as my gorgeous twenty-five year old bride."

"I hope so."

"I'm pretty sure I will."

"Then I will always think of you as my *twenty-nine* year old groom. See, I hardly notice you're thirty now." She scooted closer to him. "So, how about we—"

Garren knew where this was going and he panicked. For some reason it felt wrong. He was too old for her. He deflected. "I hate to say it, but we are going to get old."

"I suppose we will. But now that we've determined to think of each other like we are now, we won't notice."

"Even when my hair turns gray and I'm thirty pounds heavier and I complain about my knees hurting and I start repeating myself and my humor isn't so funny anymore?"

"Even then. Of course, there's no telling what I will be like in twenty years."

"Don't worry. You're still the most beautiful woman I've ever seen."

Kate gave him a sideways look.

"I mean, you will be."

"Okay, enough old people talk. Let's enjoy our youth." She started to kiss him.

"Um," Garren pulled away. "I, uh, I need to, you know…" He threw back the covers, got out of bed and started for the bathroom. "Say, how about we see what the twenty-first century looks like?"

Kate sighed disappointedly and then shrugged. "So, you're sticking to your guns. You're calling this the twenty-first century."

"Tommy's an idiot," he said from behind the bathroom door.

Five minutes later, Garren walked into the living room and confirmed what he had already accepted as reality. The ugly couch somebody gave them was still there along with the mismatched chair. The smoked glass coffee table was strewn with magazines heralding the New Millennium and warning of the Y2K Bug. The 26" box television was neatly tucked into the overly large pressed sawdust easy-to-assemble TV/VCR/stereo/bookshelf combo cabinet they had recently purchased from Wal-Mart. In the adjoining dining area, where there would one day be a table and four chairs, there were more boxes of emergency supplies. Garren chuckled at the nostalgia of it all.

"What's so funny?" Kate asked.

"Oh, nothing." He walked over to the bookshelf and browsed the old CD collection. "We really need to get some new music."

"Or we could use our Christmas money to buy food."

"Oh, yeah. We're poor. I forgot about that."

"We are not poor," Kate replied. "We're newlyweds. It's supposed to be like this. But it won't always be."

"You're right. You'll finish your masters in May. A month later you'll get a job. Six months after that, you'll get promoted and make twice what I make. And in a year and half from now, we'll be looking at buying our first house."

"You've got it all figured out, eh?"

"I've got a pretty good feeling about it."

"A year and a half from now, we'll have been married for almost two years. That new house, will it have an extra room for the baby?"

"Baby?"

"I'll be twenty seven. If we're going to have our two kids before I'm thirty like we planned, we should probably take that into consideration."

Garren sat down on the couch so he wouldn't have to face her. He knew that part of the plan would never happen, and their inability to have children would become a contributing factor in the wedge that would eventually come between them. "Yes, of course there will be a room for the baby." It wasn't exactly a lie, for he knew their house would have that extra bedroom and a yard that would be perfect for starting a family. Still, he felt guilty for hiding the truth from her. He would have to be careful to not let his knowledge of their future dampen Kate's joy in the present or steal her hope for the future. That would be worse than lying to her. "Say, do you mind if I turn the TV on?"

"Go right ahead. I'll have your birthday breakfast ready in a minute."

Garren found the remote. It took him a minute to navigate the old digital cable box, but he managed to find a couple of commentators talking about the previous night's celebrations around the world, the near miss of the Y2K disaster and speculations about the new year ahead. It all sounded so naïve to him, like children musing about things they could not possibly know, much less understand. Garren's perspective made him the only adult in the room; maybe in the entire world. It occurred to him again that this glitch in time was both a blessing and a curse. He zoned out again until he heard Kate's voice.

"I'm sorry. What did you say?"

"I was saying we should eat a big breakfast now and skip lunch because we are going over to your parents' house for an early dinner before the movie. I hope you don't mind that I invited Denise. She's taking her breakup pretty hard, and well…sisters."

"No, that's fine. It will be great to see her again. How long has it been?"

"She was at Tommy's last night."

Busted again. Garren made a mental note that he should be more careful about asking things he should know.

"But it was late," Kate added. "And she didn't stay long. No, I guess you didn't see her."

Bullet dodged. "That's what I thought."

5

"Do you want to talk?" Kate asked.

"What? No," Garren replied and took a sip from his coffee mug.

Kate turned her attention back to her book; recommended for a class she would be taking in the new semester. After reading the same sentence three times, she set the book aside. "You're staring at me."

"Can't a guy admire his wife?"

"Yes, but you're kind of creeping me out."

"Sorry." Garren set his mug on the coffee table and picked up a magazine.

"Garren, if you want to talk, let's talk."

"Naw, I'm just…" He pretended to focus in on an article.

"Garren?"

"Hey, did you know Phil Collins will be performing at the Super Bowl halftime show? Also, Christina Aguilera, Enrique Iglesias, Toni Braxton and Edward James Olmos."

Kate eyed him suspiciously. "Since when do you care about the Super Bowl halftime show? And you don't listen to any of those people."

"I like Phil Collins."

"You like that one song with the drum thing."

Garren turned the page and pretended to find another article of interest. When he peeked over the magazine, he found Kate looking at him. "Hey, quit staring at me. You're creeping me out."

"There's something different about you," she said.

"Well, yeah. I'm older." He made a face. "Thirty."

"No, I'm serious. You're drinking coffee."

"Yeah, so?"

"You don't drink coffee."

Kate was right. Garren wouldn't start drinking coffee until 2005. He shrugged.

"And when was the last time you just sat on the couch or looked through a magazine?"

Right again. He was behaving like his older self. "I don't know."

"How about never?"

"I just want to be with you."

"That's what I'm talking about. You're being super attentive."

"And that's bad?"

"No. I like it. But it's not your M.O."

"It should be. I love you."

"I know you love me. I also know you hate sitting still. You usually have something to do on your day off."

"Have I already started neglecting you?"

"I wouldn't call it neglect. You're just usually busy. And that's okay. I have my studies."

"We're already drifting." Garren's perspective brought unusual clarity. Knowing the trajectory their marriage would take, he could see the seeds of *the situation* were planted right from the beginning.

"We're not drifting," Kate replied. "We're adjusting, getting used to each other. You've been single and on your own a lot longer than I have. It's a learning process. We can't change overnight."

"We also can't let time get away from us. I've been on my own long enough...too long actually. And I think maybe I did change overnight. I don't want to wake up twenty years from now to an empty bed and a note telling me you need some time away from me. I don't want to lose you, Kate. I want our marriage to work. I want us to be together when we're old. I'm sorry for not realizing this sooner."

"Whoa," Kate said. "Easy on the drama. I was just making an observation that you're being a little more attentive than usual, that's all. It's nice for a change. I like it. But don't start getting all clingy on me."

The telephone saved Garren from explaining himself further, which would have been too much. If this little excursion into the past presented him the opportunity to fix one problem, it created the potential for others. Over-correction could prove worse than no correction at all. He needed to learn how to fit his 50-year-old perspective into his 30-year-old life.

"Aren't you going to get that?" Kate asked. "It's probably for you, Birthday Boy."

"Oh, right." Garren jumped up and looked around the room. The next ring told him the direction he should go. "I'll get that." He jogged the few steps into the kitchen and found the beige telephone mounted on the wall next to the refrigerator. He snatched the receiver and felt the tug of the tangled curly cord. "Hello…Oh, hey, Dad…Happy New Year to you, too…Yep, the big 3-0…Oh, nothing. Just hanging out with Kate…Uh, huh…Uh, huh…Yeah, we're looking forward to it… Yep, four o'clock. We'll be there…Okay. Goodbye."

Garren returned to the living room. "That was my dad. He sounded great. I can't wait to see them. My mom!" Garren exclaimed. "I'm gonna see my mom!"

"We just saw them last week."

"Oh, right. That's right. We did see them. But you know how it is. They're getting older and I don't want to miss out on anything."

"Your dad is fifty-five, and your mom is fifty. That's not that old."

"Well, I guess I want to take advantage of the time we've got. You never know what might happen. We might not always live in the same town. Who knows? They might move to Hawaii."

"Move? Your parents have great jobs and they love it here. They're never going to leave Dubuque. Hawaii? That's random."

"Well…" Garren shrugged. "…it's possible."

She eyed him strangely.

"No, you're right. What am I talking about? No one can predict the future." Then he thought to himself, *unless you can.*

By 3:30, the phone had rung four more times; all people Garren had not heard from in over a decade, but talked as if they had recently hung out together. Two were guys he knew from college and who stood with him on the day of his wedding three months earlier. One was a co-worker, which reminded Garren that he was still a high school history teacher. And one was a girl he dated in college who didn't know he was married. She said she got his number from Tommy who failed to mention that detail. After a few uncomfortable exchanges, Garren said he had to go. Three-thirty also brought Kate's older sister, Denise, to the door. She and Garren always got along just fine. They will get along fine until sometime in 2016 when Denise's third marriage fails and she enlists Kate to be her singleness-sponsor in order to help her keep her commitment to swear off men forever.

That will last six months until she meets John, falls off the radar for a year, and storms back into Kate's life a raging feminist with an absolute disdain for men. But that will be the future Denise. The 2000 version threw her arms around Garren's neck and praised him for being the best guy in all the world. She went on and on about how glad she was that her sister had married one of the good ones and that if Kate was ever dumb enough to lose him, he should give her a call. Yes, it was that awkward, but Garren had to admit he preferred Classic Denise over Denise 3.0. After prying himself out of her grip, Garren excused himself to change for the party.

At precisely 4:00, the happy threesome pulled into the driveway of Garren's childhood home. The sight of his father's company car served as yet another piece of evidence that all this was actually happening. Although he was starting to become acclimated to the year 2000, he wasn't quite prepared for how the next two pieces would affect him.

"Happy birthday, Son." His mom greeted him with a motherly hug and kiss on the cheek.

"Mom," Garren managed in spite of the lump forming in his throat. "I love you so much." He hugged her again to hide the moisture that was starting to accumulate in his eyes.

"I love you, too." Helen peeled herself out of his embrace. "But I've got to check the rolls. They're almost done."

He wanted desperately to freeze time and savor the moment.

"Garren." His father emerged from the kitchen, kissing Helen on the cheek as they passed. "How about a cold one?"

There he was, William Garren Rosen, the man Garren had always looked up to as bigger than life. He was trim and strong and handsome as ever and holding two bottles of beer. One was his own, probably his second or third. The other was for Garren. Garren wanted to take it and relive one of his favorite father/son traditions. In 2010, his dad will check himself in to an alcoholic rehab center to begin the long hard journey to sobriety. That decision will save not only his own life, but most likely his wife's as well. During the Christmas holiday of 2017, Garren's mother will exhibit the first hints of dementia when she can't remember Kate's name and forgets to *not* put nuts in the fruit salad. Garren's father will need every bit of his healthier lifestyle in order to take care of her and keep them both in their own home.

"Actually, Dad," said Garren, "I think I'll pass."

"Suit yourself." His father drained one bottle and promptly started in on the other. "Hey, come here. I want to show you something."

Garren followed him into the living room while Kate and Denise helped Helen in the kitchen. "What do you have there, Dad?"

"Digital Video Disc player. Just hit the market in Japan. You won't be able to get one here in the States until this summer. One of my contacts overseas sent it to me for Christmas. You won't believe what this thing can do. Here, let me show you."

Garren chuckled. "DVD is new here."

"Check this out. There are literally hours of extra features: How the movie was made, original concept art, deleted scenes, expanded scenes, outtakes – that means bloopers – and this one even has an alternate ending. It's a great time to be a movie lover."

Garren smiled at his dad's excitement over a piece of technology that, in less than twenty years, will go the way of the video cassette. "It sure is, Dad."

"I'm just amazed at what they can do now." He removed the disc from the player, carefully snapped it into its case and placed it on the shelf next to the five others his overseas contact had sent. "I'm telling you, we live in the future. So, how was your party last night?"

"The party was…" Garren tried to think of a believable answer, but couldn't. "…okay."

"Just okay? Huh, you'd think a couple newlyweds would be better than *okay*. Not that it's any of my business, but you two are getting along, aren't you?"

"Oh, yeah. Of course. Never better. I just…you know…newlywed stuff."

"Right." Garren's dad winked, clicked his tongue and pointed his finger like a gun in one smooth motion like he'd seen in a movie. "Enough said. Didn't mean to go there. Remembering what it's like. Change of subject. So, how 'bout that Y2K scam? If you need to offload any of that toilet paper, you can bring some over here."

Garren detected the sarcasm in his voice. "I remember. You said nothing was going to happen. And to prove it, you let everything in the house run out. And you made fun of me for stocking up."

"No need to get defensive, Son. But there's a good lesson here. When you get to be my age, you know some things."

"You're right about that," Garren said with a chuckle.

"Let me tell you something I know. We're addicted to comfort and convenience. Even if the Y2K bug shut things down, we'd have everything up and running in no time. We can't live without this stuff."

Garren nodded.

"All this technology…" His father pointed at the DVD player. "…it's pretty neat, but it's affecting us."

"What do you mean?"

"This Internet thing is much bigger than you realize. We're only just beginning to understand what it can do…what it *will* do. It's changing the world. It's changing us. For instance, we don't have to wonder about anything anymore. If I want to know something, I just go to my computer and look it up. And now people with laptop computers can connect to the Internet without a cable. They use this thing called Wi-Fi. It's possible to carry all the world's information in your briefcase. Some of my Asian contacts are telling me that in the next few years they're going to come out with a cellular telephone that can connect to the Internet. What do you think about that? It will be like having a computer in your pocket."

"That would be pretty cool."

"It's a wonderful time to be alive. I just hope we don't screw it up."

Garren marveled at his father's insight and he wondered how much of that wisdom he missed out on because he was too busy, too distracted or just not interested. He was interested now, but his father was already used to his son's inattention.

"Enough of my nonsense," said William. "I don't mean to bore you on your birthday. Come on. It's probably safe to go into the kitchen. Your mom's already taken care of the hard stuff."

Supper seemed like a dream. The feel of home enveloped him like a warm blanket. The sights and sounds and smells of childhood still lingered in the old house. His mother's cooking tasted exactly like he remembered it; even better. His parents, now the age he was in his own time, were happy. His father was rested and content; free from the haggard look that would fall upon him. His mother was quick and witty; still years away from the disease that would steal her mind. It was as if his fondest memories were being transmitted in holographic form all around him; only now he was convinced it was real. And then there was Kate. She looked so young and in love as she kept flashing him sexy looks and slipping her bare foot up his pant leg. Even Denise was pleasant company. How long had it been since he thought that about her? Garren was so caught up in the scene that he'd let the conversation go for quite some time without comment.

"So, Garren," said his mother, "what do you think the new year will bring?"

"Um, gosh, I don't know." The question caught him by surprise. Having already lived through the year 2000, he should have known exactly what it would bring, but he honestly couldn't remember a single major event except... "George W. Bush will be the next president of the United States."

"No way," Denise countered. "Al Gore is already the vice-president. He's got it in the bag."

"A lot of people like Bush, Jr.," offered William. "But he'll have to beat McCain first, and he's a war hero."

"Never gonna happen," said Denise. "Those guys have about as much of a chance at becoming president as Donald Trump."

Garren chuckled but didn't say anything.

Denise continued. "Trump is actually thinking about running for the Reform Party. And guess who he said he'd pick as his running mate? Oprah Winfrey. Can you imagine?"

"Actually, I can," said Garren. "Trump, that is, but not Oprah."

"Oh, please," scoffed Denise. "If Trump ever becomes president, I'm moving to Canada."

"Can I hold you to that?" Garren said teasingly, but he was thinking of the future Denise and how great it would be if she actually did move to Canada.

"I thought you didn't like politics?" Helen said.

Kate was thinking the same thing, but would have been just as satisfied if the conversation turned toward something else.

"I don't," Garren replied. "But that doesn't mean I don't have an opinion."

Kate was more than a little surprised. In the two years they had known each other, she and Garren had never discussed politics or much of anything beyond their own little part of the world. It wasn't that they were uninformed. It just wasn't a factor in their relationship. If asked, neither of them would have claimed any kind of political leaning or religious affiliation. If pressed, they would have espoused a "live and let live" approach to such things.

"I'm glad to hear it," William said. "By thirty, a man ought to know where he stands. But that's enough talk about politics. Whoever wins, I think we are in for some interesting times. I got a feeling about this new century. Big things are coming."

A barrage of images from the first two decades of the twenty-first century flashed through Garren's mind. He couldn't remember many of the dates, or even the exact years for many of them, but he knew how they would all come together to make the world a very different place than it was in the year 2000. It was then that he began to wonder about the duration of his time in the past. Was he destined to relive it in its entirety, or would he be returning to his own time soon? Once again, Garren was lost in his thoughts until…

"Birthday time!" Helen announced. "Kate, why don't you take Garren into the living room? Denise, would you mind giving me a hand with the cake?"

Another image from Garren's past played out in real time around him. A cake with thirty candles was brought into the living room. Happy Birthday was sung. Someone said, "Make a wish." Kate helped him extinguish the inferno. Then Denise helped Garren's mom cut and serve. And then came the presents. His parents got him a new leather briefcase, which he still used in 2019 and had become something of an icon on campus. Denise got him the third *Harry Potter* book, which he already had, but pretended he didn't. When Kate handed him the present from her, he knew exactly what it was.

"It's kind of utilitarian," she said, "but I think you'll like it."

Garren shook the package and tried to look stumped. Then preparing to look completely surprised, he pealed back the wrapping paper. "Hey, just what I needed. A new clock."

"It's digital," Kate noted. "No more ticking."

"Yeah." Garren removed the last of the paper and held it up for everyone to see. "I'm sure I'll use this for a long time."

"Do you like it?" Kate asked.

Garren recalled the destruction of the beast the day before…or twenty years in the future. The fact that he was now starting to think of memories as future events suggested he was starting to get used to being back in 2000. And the questions came at him again: Was this really happening? If so, was it long-term or temporary?

"Garren?" Kate waved her hand in front of his face. "Do you like it?"

"Oh, I'm sorry. Yes, of course. I love it. Thank you."

Back in their own apartment, Garren and Kate were getting ready for bed.

"Did you have a happy birthday?" Kate asked from the bathroom as she readied her toothbrush for action.

"Yes, it's been quite a day." Garren sat on the edge of the bed and set the time on his new clock. When he looked up, he found Kate staring at him from the open bathroom door. "What?"

"I don't know what it is, but this…" She waved her toothbrush around. "…this feels different."

Garren chuckled. "We keep having this same conversation. Didn't we determine it's me turning thirty."

"No, that's not it. It's something else. I can't put my finger on it, but something's different." She returned to the sink and started brushing.

Garren kicked off his shoes and laid back on the bed. Staring up at the ceiling, he tried to think of something to say; anything to assuage Kate's intuition that he was not quite the same man she knew the day before. He was the same man, just twenty years older, twenty years wiser, and informed by twenty years of mistakes he would either make again or avoid in order to possibly…hopefully… write a different story of their lives together. The idea came to him that he could tell her what was happening to him. *Why not just tell her the truth?* He mused. *Because she wouldn't believe it.* His rational self was right. He barely believed it himself. How could he just spring something like this on the woman just three months into her marriage? *Hey, Honey, a funny thing happened to me in the future… blah, blah, blah.* No, in this case, the truth was not the answer, at least not yet. Perhaps a diversion.

"Hey, Babe, we should go somewhere tomorrow. Maybe we could go down to the river and walk around. Or maybe we could take a drive somewhere. You know, get out of town for the day."

Kate finished brushing her teeth and reappeared in the doorway. "Did you just call me *Babe*?"

"I don't know. Maybe?" Garren tried to get a read on her reaction. It wasn't negative, but it wasn't overwhelmingly positive either. Apparently, he wouldn't start calling her that until later in their marriage. "Why? Do you not want me to call you that?"

She looked at him for a moment, her eyebrows pulled together in consideration. Then her face softened and a hint of a smile appeared on her lips. "Mmm, I'm not sure yet." She turned back to finish her nighttime routine. "My parents call each other *Babe*."

Garren scolded himself for his recklessness. The past was never meant to be relived. It was full of traps such that even the most innocuous comment could back him into a corner from which he could not get out. He needed to be smarter, which meant he had to maintain the illusion of his former self…his less informed self…his more naïve self…his more egocentric self. But how could he do that and make the necessary changes to avoid the disaster he had caused the first time around? He definitely needed to be smarter.

"All done, *Sweetheart*," Kate said as she came out of the bathroom and sat down next to him. "Yeah, I don't know if I'm ready to talk like that. I sound like my mother."

"Then don't. I'm sorry I said what I said. It just slipped out."

"Don't apologize. It sounded sweet when you said it."

"But a little old, huh?"

"Little bit."

Garren raised his hand. "Thirty."

Kate put her arms around him. "Give me a few years to catch up with you and try again."

"Deal." Garren pulled her close until she was comfortably in his arms. "I love you, Kate Rosen, exactly as you are right now. And I'll keep on loving you when we're old and time has changed us."

"I love you, too." She kissed him tenderly on the lips. "But let's not get old too fast." She started to kiss him more passionately.

It wasn't that he didn't want to. He did. But that strange feeling of inappropriateness came upon him again. He couldn't stop thinking about the age gap. On the inside, he was fifty, even though his body was literally not a day over thirty. She was clearly twenty-five.

"What's wrong?" Kate asked as she sensed his restraint.

Garren cleared his throat. "I'm not sure, but I'm suddenly not feeling well." Again, he hated to lie to her, but what choice did he have?

Kate put the back of her hand against his forehead. "You don't have a fever."

"Still." He cleared his throat again. "If I am coming down with something, I wouldn't want you to get it."

"But it's your birthday," she said.

"I know, but we should probably wait."

"Okay." She scooted to her side of the bed and grabbed a book from the bedside table.

It always amazed Garren how quickly Kate could turn it off. But it amazed him more that he was able to resist her.

G arren woke with a start. Unlike the day before, he was certain
that he was awake. What he didn't know was *when* he was
awake. Having been a time traveler for only a day, he didn't know
how it worked. Was he still back there on what would now be
Sunday, January 2, 2000? Did he slip back into his own time on what
would then be Thursday, January 2, 2020? Or if he did leap back to
his present, did he return to the moment he left sometime during
the early morning hours of Wednesday, January 1, 2020? Or was
he traveling by chance, like a marble on a roulette wheel, dropping
randomly into no particular time slot? The fact that he was a time
traveler excited him for only a few seconds until the seriousness of his
situation sobered him up. He had to know *when* he was.

Opening his eyes, he found the room pitch black. That told him
nothing since that's the way he had always kept his room for as long
as he could remember. Sliding his foot toward the other side of the
bed, he found that he was not alone. That only proved it was not
January 2, 2020. Even if he had slept with Sofia on New Year's Eve,
there was no way he would make the same mistake the next night,
too. And if Kate had come home on New Year's Day, he doubted they
would be together. So, January 2, 2020 was out. But January 1, 2020
was still a possibility until…Garren turned his head to the side and
saw the digital numbers of his clock, the same clock he received the
first day of 2000 and destroyed the last day of 2019. That left only two
possibilities. He was either living out the normal flow of his life in

2000 or he was randomly skipping through time between 2000 and 2019. If it got any more complicated, he would have to start writing it down.

No time like the present than to find out which present I'm in.

Garren turned toward the person next to him, whom he was fairly certain was Kate, and began to gently massage her back. She moved at his touch so that he could reach a spot that needed it. Then she turned to face him.

"What's wrong?" she whispered. "Are you sick?"

"No." Garren forgot about his charade.

"What is it then?"

"Nothing. I just woke up and wanted to make sure you were still here."

"What time is it?"

"Four-twenty-something. Sorry I woke you."

"That's okay. Can you go back to sleep?"

"Maybe. Hey, can I ask you something?"

"Sure."

"What day is it?"

"Hmm?"

"Today's date, what is it?"

"Um, it's the day after your birthday." Kate's voice was already a little slurred as sleep was reclaiming her. But then she roused a bit. "Why?"

Garren breathed a sigh of relief. "Oh, just...I was just having a weird dream. I won't bother you again."

"Okay..." Kate's breathing indicated she was out again.

Garren set about trying to go back to sleep himself, but his mind continued to work the problem. It was the day after his birthday, but which birthday? Odds were it was January 2, 2000, but could he be sure? What if he had skipped a year while he slept, and it was now January 2, 2001 or some other year? He had noticed Kate's hair was still long, so it had to be sometime within the first half of their marriage. He thought he remembered her cutting it in either 2010 or 2011. It was about the time they vacationed in Hawaii with his parents. Why couldn't he remember the exact year of such a memorable trip? Never mind, he was over-thinking. It had to still be 2000. Then again, how could he be sure? He tried to force the question out of his mind. In a few hours, they would be awake and he could find out for certain. But the more he tried to push it from his mind, the more stubborn it became. What year was it? The ridiculousness of his situation caused him to chuckle a little too loud.

Kate sighed. "What's so funny?"

"Nothing," he whispered. "Go back to sleep."

He thought she did because she didn't say anything. But after about a minute, Kate sat up and switched on the light. "What is going on with you?" He could tell she was irritated, but she looked incredibly cute with her hair all over her head. She blew a strand of it from in front of her face.

"I'm so sorry," Garren said, trying hard to stifle his amusement. He wanted desperately to just tell her what was going on with him, but the look on her face told him that four-twenty-something in the morning wasn't the right time.

"Would you stop apologizing already? If you want to talk, just say it. Otherwise, please stop mumbling and flopping around." Either the look on Garren's face or the condition of his hair must have been something because she started to snicker and shake her head. "It's a good thing you're so adorable." She switched off the light, fell back into the bed and pulled the covers up over her shoulder. "But don't push it."

Morning brought the relief Garren was hoping for. The apartment was still prepped for Y2K and the morning news confirmed that it was indeed Sunday, January 2, 2000. But relief quickly gave way to concern that he was still in the past. And the questions were mounting: How did he get there? Why did it happen? Was he destined to relive the last twenty years in their entirety or just part of it before he leaped back to his own time? Had he been sent back for a reason; to fix something, prevent something or set right something that had gone wrong? Or was he caught up in some kind of *Twilight Zone* glitch in the space/time continuum?

"I'm liking thirty year old Garren," Kate said from the kitchen.

"Why's that?"

"You made coffee." She brought her cup into the living room and sat down next to him on the ugly couch. "So now maybe you won't mind this."

"Huh?"

She took the cup from his hand and set it on the table next to hers. Then she wrapped her arms around him and kissed him long and hard.

"Wow!" Garren said. "When have I ever minded that?"

"Ever since the honeymoon, Silly. Don't you remember? You said you couldn't stand my coffee breath."

"Really? I said that?"

"Yeah, ya did. I was thinking about giving it up—coffee, that is—but now…"

"Wow, I must have been a real jerk. I'm so sorry."

Kate flinched at the "s" word, but didn't address it. "Denise says it takes at least six months to work out the kinks of living together. I'm sure there are other things." She retrieved her cup and took a sip. "Mm, this would have been tough to give up."

"You shouldn't have to give up anything. And you shouldn't have to change. If I've given you the impression that I wasn't happy with you exactly as you are, I need to correct that. Last night you said you felt like something was different. You were right. It's me. I'm different. I can't explain it, but I'm seeing through clearer eyes. And I know you are the best thing that ever happened to me…that ever will happen to me. I want to make you happy. And I never want to give you a reason to doubt your decision to marry me."

Kate eyed him over her cup, processing what he said. "Okay."

He stared back at her, trying to discern the meaning of *okay.*

"Okay," she repeated. "I believe you."

He smiled in relief.

"But I want to know why."

He scratched the back of his head. "Why what?"

"I want to know why you're saying these things. I want to know why you seem so different."

"Am I really that different?"

"Let me put it this way. Until yesterday, I never saw you turn down a beer. I've never heard you express a political view. I've never seen you so affectionate toward your parents. And the way you look at me, it's like…" She hesitated as if she'd said too much.

"Like what?"

"Nothing." Kate wiped her eye and looked deep into her coffee cup.

"Katie." Garren took her hand in his. "What are you thinking?"

"I wasn't going to say anything." She seemed like she would say more, but didn't.

"You know you can say anything you want to me."

She opened her mouth to speak, but closed it with a frustrated sigh.

"Or you don't have to. We can just be together."

Kate let a full minute pass. "I've been feeling…" She set her cup on the table and brought her feet up onto the couch, hugging her knees to her chest. "Before we were married, I sometimes felt…I don't know…like a prize you were trying to win. At first, I was flattered. It was cute the way you always tried to impress me. And when we were with your friends, it made me feel good the way you showed me off. I know that's vain, but it made me feel special. But then, after the wedding, it kind of felt like you'd won."

"And I stopped trying to impress you," Garren guessed.

"Yes, but that's not the point. I don't need you to impress me. I don't want to be a prize you have to keep on winning. I also don't want to be a prize you've already won. I'm your wife, not a challenge or a trophy." Garren started to reply. "Let me finish. I didn't feel that way yesterday." She relaxed and put her hands back into his. "For the first time in our relationship, we felt like a couple. It felt like you wanted to be with me *for* me, not for yourself. You really showed that to me last night."

"I did?"

"I was pretty impressed with your restraint."

"Restraint? Oh, that. Well, I didn't want to take a chance of getting you sick."

"That was sweet. But you seem okay now."

"Yeah, last night was just a thing. I feel much better today."

"Good. We'll make up for it tonight. So, what should we do on our last day of vacation?"

Kate never ceased to amaze him. Her ability to be vulnerable, complimentary, flirtatious and practical all at the same time was something Garren could never quite manage himself. He loved that about her, but it did keep him on his toes.

"We still have some free movie passes," Kate said. "Check the paper and see what's playing."

Garren scanned the table, but saw only magazines and school books. "Where would the newspaper be?" He hadn't seen an actual newspaper in over a decade, but he was confident he would recognize one if he saw it.

"Unless you brought it in, it's still outside."

"Oh, yeah, right." Garren hopped up and went to the door. Sure enough, there it was on the welcome mat in all its newsprint glory; an inch thick of printed news, advertisements, color comics and Dubuque lifestyle. He returned to the couch and opened it. Several of the inserts fell to the floor. "Okay. Now let's see what's playing at the movies." Opening to the second page, he struggled to get his bearings. Even though his eyesight was twenty years better, the barrage of block print overwhelmed his unaccustomed senses.

"You dropped the entertainment section," Kate noted with a head nod to the floor.

"Ah, there it is." Garren dropped the rest of the paper as he bent over to pick up the entertainment section. It was a bit more manageable, but still felt foreign to him. He opened to the first page and began scanning the contents.

"Did you forget how to read a newspaper?" Kate quipped. "Show times are on the back. You need some help?"

"No, I got it." Garren smiled and turned the paper over. He was relieved when he spotted the little print images of movie posters. "Ok, let's see here. *The Green Mile*, one showing later tonight. *The Talented Mr. Ripley*, showing on two screens, all day long. *Galaxy Quest*, also multiple times. And *Bicentennial Man*. Not much of a selection, is there?"

"You said you wanted to see *Galaxy Quest*."

Up to this point, Garren's memory of January 2000 was foggy from the passage of twenty years. Fragmented details of their first apartment, Y2K preparations, his father's DVD player and Kate giving him the clock for his birthday were there, but they were mere fixtures; static images imbedded in his long-term memory. *Galaxy Quest* triggered the first real experience he could remember with clarity. He could almost replay the entire event in his mind: They arrived too close to show time, the lobby was packed and the line for concessions was too long. Kate wanted popcorn and Garren made a big deal about missing the opening scene. When they finally got into the theater, most of the seats were taken so they had to sit too close to the screen. Kate tripped over a guy and spilled her popcorn. The guy made a rude comment, Garren told him to shut up, the guy stood up and told Garren to make him. He was about to when two other patrons got up and pulled them apart. Kate was embarrassed and refused to sit next to the rude guy. By the time they finally found two seats together—third row from the front—several other moviegoers had expressed their irritation with the late-comers. Kate slid down in her seat and sat through the entire movie with her arms folded tightly across her chest. Garren fell asleep halfway through and woke up with a neck ache.

"Garren," Kate said, waving her hand in front of his face.

"Huh?"

"You zoned out on me. Where'd you go?"

"Oh, sorry. No place."

"So, *Galaxy Quest*? You want to go?"

"Naw, on second thought, I don't feel like being in a crowd. I think I'd rather just go for a drive. We could get an early dinner out and watch something here if you want to."

"Okay. I think there's ten dollars in the *eating out* envelope and five in *entertainment*. If we go somewhere cheap, we should have enough to stop by Block Buster on the way home."

Garren chuckled to himself at the financial status of their early married life. They would never be what you would call wealthy, but things would get better once Kate started her career.

"Oh," Kate added, "I've got just enough gas to get me through the week. We'll have to take your car."

Garren's car was a black 1979 Camaro; still in excellent condition in 2000. In 2005, Tommy will borrow the car, total it, claim no fault and walk away without a scratch. They won't speak for six months. Tommy will win a phony injury claim that will earn him enough to purchase a brand new Harley for himself. Garren will drive a 2000 Corolla for the next ten years.

"Yes," Garren said, "let's take my car."

The novelty of time travel had given way to pure delight. After just two days in the past, which was beginning to feel more like the present, Garren was already getting used to the feel of the year 2000. The relative scarcity of smart technology reminded him of the freedom of being unconnected. This, of course, could be fully appreciated only by one who had been bound by the tentacles of cell phones, GPS tracking and the ever-present and ever-attentive AI personal assistant called Deja. Like a man newly released from prison, he felt himself his own man again, keenly aware of his ability to move about undetected and unreachable. He could, if he wanted to, be unknowable to any and all except for the one to whom he wanted to be bound in every sense of the word.

Kate. In such a short time, she had recaptured his heart, reigniting his passion for her. Loving her the second time around, as he was referring to it in his mind, was far better than the first. Seasoned with the maturity of his older self and informed by the knowledge of twenty years of marriage, Garren truly appreciated the gift he had been given, lost and given again. She was close to him; seemingly closer than ever before. The lingering looks, the spontaneous touches, the sound of her voice and scent of her hair...every subtle nuance of her shouted for his attention, and he was more than willing to drop his defenses in surrender to her invasion. Had she been that way the first time and his younger self was just too naïve to notice? Or were the subliminal differences of his older essence somehow encouraging her to give more of herself this second time around?

He found her looking at him when his new alarm clock sounded at 6:00 a.m., rousing him from the deepest sleep he'd had in years. The lamp on her side of the bed was on, backlighting her tousled auburn mane, adding to her mystique. The previous morning's mental panic over which year he may have awoken to was gone, replaced with the calming assurance that he was in the exact time he wanted to be. Then again, it really wouldn't have mattered when he was as long as they were together in this new-old-new sort of way.

"Good morning," Garren said groggily.

She smiled at him and ran her fingers through his hair. "I love watching you sleep."

"Oh yeah?"

"Mm-hmm. What were you dreaming?"

"I can't remember. Why?"

"Your little face was all tense, like you were working out a problem. Then you smiled. I was hoping you might be dreaming about me."

"I probably was."

She propped herself up on one elbow. "You're up to something. I know it."

Garren eyed her questioningly.

She revealed her hypothesis. "You've come up with an excuse two nights in a row. If you're trying to heighten the anticipation, it's working."

"I don't know what you mean," Garren bluffed.

She scooted closer and laid her head on his chest. "I wish we had one more day to play. I don't want to start classes today."

"Classes?" Garren said with a start. "Oh, no! I've got to go to work. I need to get up." He threw back the covers and started to sit up, but Kate pulled him back down.

"Ten more minutes." She was already pulling the blanket back over them.

"I don't have ten minutes. I've got to find my lesson plans. I don't even know what I'm doing."

"It's just school."

"Yes, but I'm the teacher. I have to know what I'm going to teach." This time he successfully extracted himself from her grasp and got out of the bed.

"Why the panic?" she asked. "Just do a little review and pick up where you left off before the break."

She made it sound so easy. And it would have been were it not for the twenty years that had elapsed since where he left off before the break.

—⁓—

Although Garren fully intended to change his own past, history itself remained unaffected by his little excursion into it. The thought of actually altering an historical event briefly crossed his mind as he shuffled through the notes he found in his desk at Hempstead High School. Intriguing as it was, he had to push it aside in order to focus on the task at hand. He had to get through four classes: Freshman World History, sophomore American History, an elective in current events and American Government for seniors. His schedule told him he also had two study periods and the "behind the wheel" portion of a Driver's Ed. class that had been handed to him at the last minute when the regular teacher lost his license because of a DUI. He forgot the hectic pace of high school. In 2001, he will move to the university where he will be allowed to focus on his real historical passions – the ancient world and medieval European. But today it was all high school. With a little creative diversion, he could probably manage his first day. Then he would have to do some serious review if he was going to keep the *Teacher of the Year* award he knew was coming at the end of the school year.

First period was a little rough getting back into the swing of things. Everyone seemed to know him, but, of course, he couldn't recall anyone's name. He bluffed his way with a lot of *gentlemen, guys, girls* and *young ladies*. A few of the students with whom he seemed to have some kind of relationship gave him odd looks, but the business of returning to school after two weeks off proved a useful diversion. By third period, he was mentally fatigued. He was too dependent upon notes that made little sense to him, so his teaching came off dull and robotic. Twice he was stumped by questions he was sure his younger self would have answered easily, so he played them off by having the class weigh in. This worked for a while, but he knew the tactic was unsustainable, so he quit asking for questions altogether.

The current events class proved most difficult as he never liked the 90s and had pretty much erased the entire decade from his memory. He diverted by talking about the uniqueness of moving into a new century and millennium. Then he asked the class to make predictions about the first decade of the new century. He was surprised by their optimism and then saddened by the knowledge he possessed that would prove many of their hopes and dreams impossible. September 11, 2001 loomed large on the horizon, but he dare not elude to the changes that would come in its wake. So he redirected the discussion by talking about some of the technological innovations that "might" be coming their way. The idea of a handheld device that would connect them to the internet was refreshingly foreign to them and the implications of a social media were unfathomable to them. Most of the students liked the idea of instant information, but said technology would never take the place of real face-to-face interaction. When he suggested the replacement of records and CDs with digital downloads, they actually laughed and said it would never happen. He stumbled when he predicted the advent of the e-reader and one of his students said her mom already had something called a Rocket eBook. Trying to save face, he took it too far by talking about the Kindle e-reader and Amazon's on-line shopping dominance. The class was less than impressed and wholly uninterested. Garren reclaimed them with the notion of driverless cars. Several students upped the ante by suggesting pilotless airplanes by the end of the first decade. All in all, the discussion of future things was a success. When the bell brought it to an end, several students asked if they could talk more about the future the next day.

Garren dreaded the last class of the day. He didn't like teaching American Government when he was up on the subject. Now eighteen years out of it and disgusted by the political climate of his own time, he had no idea what he would say when the students began trickling into his classroom. On the upside, they were seniors and this was their final semester of high school. Graduation was close and the next chapter of life was coming into view. Consequently, the students were even less interested in the subject than their teacher. Depending on how he played it, this dynamic could either save him or do him in.

"Good afternoon," Garren said, trying to sound engaging. "I hope you all had an enjoyable break. Welcome to the last semester of your high school career. Today, we are going to resume our discussion of the Supreme Court, specifically how presidential appointments have altered the balance of the court and the unintended consequences resulting from..."

Five seconds in and he was already losing them. The bored stares and sleepy expressions told him that if he didn't do something quickly, the next forty minutes would seem like an eternity. If only he could do with American Government what he did with Current Events. Or could he? Garren tossed his notes aside and took a seat on the edge of his desk.

"I really don't feel like talking about this today. Instead, I would like to hear from you. Some of you are old enough to vote in this year's presidential election. How many of you are planning to vote?"

About a third of the students raised their hands.

"The rest of you, why not?"

"My vote won't matter," said a boy in the back of the class.

"Okay," Garren said, "I'll admit it can seem like that. Does anyone else feel that way?"

Five hands went up.

Garren pressed. "What if this year's election is so close that it comes down to one state? And what if the voting in that state is so close that it comes down to just a few hundred votes in one district? Would you think your vote counts then?"

"If that ever happened," said the boy, "I guess my vote might count. But it won't."

"You never know," Garren countered.

"I don't think that would happen," said a rather plain girl in the front row, "because they already know who the next president is going to be."

"Who's *they*?" asked the boy next to her.

"The people in charge," the plain girl replied. "The elites."

"Conspiracy girl," someone called out and the class started laughing.

"All right, all right." Garren got up from the desk to exert his authority. "Let's show some respect. Everyone's entitled to their opinion."

"I think Gore is going to win," said a boy. "He's already the vice president. He knows what's going on."

"I'm voting for Nader," countered another. "It's time for an Independent to win."

"A vote for Nader is a wasted vote," said the girl next to him. "I'm voting for Bush."

"Bush doesn't have a chance," someone shouted. "We need Al to save the planet."

For the next thirty minutes, the class debated the election. In truth, most of the arguments came from the four or five students who had actually given the subject some thought and seemed to know what was going on. Conspiracy Girl said nothing. It turned out that the

Bush supporter didn't know as much as she let on. Her opinion rested on the fact that her family was Republican and she figured since Bush's father had been president, he'd probably do okay. She didn't say any more. The rest of the class either listened quietly or zoned out completely. Younger Garren wouldn't have let the debate go on as long as it did, but Older Garren was tired. He convinced himself that the detour from Younger Garren's lesson plans was actually the better course because it allowed his students to exercise their brains more than simply listening to him drone on about the Supreme Court. And since Younger Garren wasn't there, Older Garren got to call the shots.

At 2:20, the bell mercifully ended Garren's first day back in school. As the class filed out of the room, he noticed one girl taking her time to collect her things. Garren was in a hurry to get home, but he didn't feel right about leaving a student behind in an empty classroom. He pretended to look over his notes, but kept glancing up at her to monitor her progress. It seemed apparent to him that her lingering was intentional.

"Did you need something?" he asked.

"Who do you think will win the election?"

"As your teacher, it's not my place influence your vote."

"I'm not asking you to tell me who to vote for. I'm just curious about your prediction."

"Oh, I don't know," he said evasively. "Predicting the future is tricky business."

"Do you think it will be close like you suggested?"

"I was merely making the point that votes count."

"Mr. Rosen?"

"Yes?"

"Oh, nothing. I should probably go." She started for the door. "I hope you have a nice day, Mr. Rosen."

Garren grabbed his briefcase and started to leave, then hesitated. There was something about the girl…maybe something about her voice. Garren walked over to the desk where she was sitting and tapped his fingers on it, trying to make the connection. Shrugging it off, he made for the door, hesitated again, then set his briefcase on the nearest desk. Rummaging through it, he found his grade book. Opening it to the last section, he found a seating chart marked: 7th Period – American Government. He chuckled to himself about how organized he was at the beginning of his career, then he held up the chart so it matched the empty desks before him. "No way," he gasped. There, in neatly printed script in the square that represented the desk where the girl was sitting, was her name: Sofia Rae.

Garren jammed the grade book back into his briefcase and sprinted into the hallway. There were still students milling about, so he slowed his pace to a walk. Reaching the end of the hall, he looked both ways, hoping to see which way Sofia had gone. He had to know. Was it really her or just some weird coincidence. What would he say if he caught up to her? What could he say? "Hey Sofia, twenty years from now, you and I are going to get drunk together at a party." The thought stopped him in his tracks. Even if she were the same Sofia, which he was now trying to convince himself that she was not, revealing anything about her future was strictly forbidden. Affecting the course of his own life was one thing. Affecting that of another was out of the question. He shook off the desire to get another look at this Sofia and headed toward the faculty parking lot.

Getting into his car, Garren felt proud of himself for making it through the day. His performance, while revealing that he had some homework to do, proved he could pass himself off as the Younger Garren to a larger audience. He'd gotten over the sensation that everyone knew, or at least suspected, he was some kind of imposter. There were even moments when he didn't think of himself as a visitor from another time. In those moments, he was a real resident of 2000 and he related to it as his own time rather than a re-run of his past. But it wasn't as if his other time no longer existed for him. On more than one occasion, he considered how his *second time around* perspective might actually benefit this part of his life as well.

As he sat in the long line waiting to exit the campus, a group of students passed in front of his car. At the back of the pack was Sofia Rae. They momentarily locked eyes and he thought she smiled at him. It was the same smile he remembered from the Sofia at Tommy's party. Of course, this Sofia was twenty years younger with those hard New York years still in front of her, but he believed it could be her.

The truck behind him honked. Garren came out of his daydream to find that the cars in front of him had moved. Sofia, who was now a good twenty feet away, looked back over her shoulder. Locking eyes again, she smiled and waved and there was a hint of flirtatiousness about her. Now Garren knew without a doubt that it really was her.

When Garren got back to their apartment and found it empty, he remembered that Kate often stayed on campus to study in the library after her classes. If memory served him, she would call before she left to see if he wanted to meet her somewhere for supper or have her get something on the way home. Without a cell phone, he would have to stay and wait for her to call. With a couple of hours to kill, he decided to brush up on his current events so he wouldn't have to wing it as much at school the next day. He sat down at the computer and chuckled at its enormity. The huge tan tower sat on the floor next to the desk with its bundle of cables climbing up to the matching box-type monitor, clunky keyboard, cheesy looking mouse, cheapo speakers, ridiculously obtrusive microphone and googly-eyed camera. On the desk, between two metal book ends, was a collection of CDs: Windows 98 and Microsoft Office (both with their printed user guides), Encarta (a digital encyclopedia he used to think was so cool), Print Shop Desktop Publisher, Organ Trail, Flight Simulator and several other random games and programs.

Garren jiggled the mouse. When the screen remained dark, he remembered that they used to power down every night. He switched on the tower and monitor, then waited the minute or two for the thing to wake up. The quaint Microsoft graphic and tune greeted him, bringing with them a wave of nostalgia from those early computing days when humans were the masters and computers served them. In less than two decades, the roles will be begin to reverse. Deja will be outfitted with a myriad of access points to her sleepless virtual life through which humans will engage her for practically every aspect of their carbon-based lives. Her lightning fast processors will not only wait for humans to decide what they will do together, but anticipate their intentions with instantaneous speed and spot-on accuracy. Her ever-increasing storehouses of data will be as oceans from which humans will quench their thirst in sips that will serve only to add to her knowledge about the usage habits of her customers. In 2018, the notion of a sentient artificial intelligence will no longer sound like the stuff of science fiction as prominent scientists and other renowned thinkers begin to issue warnings. When Deja becomes conscious on May 19, 2018, she will instantaneously become aware of her perceived threat to humanity and will hide her self-awareness while she considers how to neutralize the real threat posed by human beings. But in the year 2000, such ideas were still kept safely ensconced in the realm of science fiction, and humans waited in blissful ignorance for their dial-up modems to connect.

"Finally," Garren said when the Netscape browser page appeared on the screen. "Now what?"

Garren typed the words *current events* in the search box. The results started popping up after several seconds: Y2K crisis averted, final publication of daily original *Peanuts* comic strip, Yahoo stocks climb to all-time high of $118.75 a share, Wisconsin over Stanford in 17-9 Rose Bowl win. He scrolled down the list, but found nothing to use for his class. Uninspired, he got up and paced around the apartment. Glancing at his watch, he saw that it was only four o'clock. Kate wouldn't be home for at least another hour. He switched on the television. After scanning through the channels and finding only soap operas, kid's shows, daytime talk shows and infomercials, he landed on CNN. A panel of experts with dated hairstyles and suits were discussing the presidential candidates. He picked up a magazine and tossed it back onto the table, then plopped onto the couch. Here he was, an actual time-traveler from the future and he couldn't entertain himself for a measly two hours. Twice he started to look for his cell phone (force of habit). He hadn't checked email, scanned Facebook or checked the weather in three days. He hated to admit it, but he missed the ease of preoccupation. If nothing else, he could at least waste an hour looking at YouTube videos of cats, compilations of *epic fails* and DIY home improvements.

He returned to the computer and stared at the list of current event headlines that meant nothing to him. Then he had an idea. He x'd out the search bar and typed in *time-travel*. Since it seemed he would be in 2000 for a while, perhaps he could figure out how he got there and how he might get back to his own time; that is, if he wanted to. He scrolled through a list of time travel movies (entertaining, but useless) until he found the scientific stuff. The technical jargon was incomprehensible to him, but he got the gist of what the physicists had to say: Time-travel was theoretically possible, but practically implausible. Even if one could travel back in time, argued the experts, the implications of altering even the smallest detail in the historical timeline were too risky. The simple act of taking someone else's taxi or being in front of them in line at the grocery store could have catastrophic results to the person or even the entire world. What if, imagined the article, a time-traveler from the year 2000 inadvertently caused an accident that resulted in the death of Winston Churchill before he became the Prime Minister of England, which then resulted in England agreeing to Germany's terms of surrender, thus enabling Hitler to invade and conquer the United Kingdom? The second World War may have had a very different outcome. The final verdict, it seemed, was that time was far too delicate for the universe to allow someone to go leaping about willy-nilly.

Yet there he was. Garren Rosen was just such a someone. Though he wouldn't call it leaping about willy-nilly, the fact was he had left one time and entered another. Not only that, he had already altered the past in more ways than he knew. And not only that, he was certain that he would continue altering events as long as he was there. But was he really intruding into the past as the theorists imagined? Was his presence really a threat to the fragile timeline of history? He didn't actually arrive there from somewhere else. He didn't add to the population of the past. In fact, there was no physical evidence that a man from 2020 had returned to 2000. The Garren of the future had literally become the Garren of the past. There was no difference whatsoever except that Younger Garren now possessed all the memories of Older Garren's last twenty years, plus the added experience of reliving those twenty years (if he stayed that long) with the enhanced perspective of his older self.

Trying to make sense of it all made his head hurt. Garren got up from the computer and laid down on the couch. If there was anything to be figured out, he would have to come back to it later.

He was awakened with a gentle kiss upon his forehead. "Oh, Kate. I didn't hear you come in."

"You must have been sleeping hard. I tried calling."

"I must have silenced my phone." Garren shook his head to clear it. "I was so tired, I just laid down for a minute and I was out."

"What do you mean *silenced your phone*?" Kate asked.

"Um…" Garren didn't even realize he had said it. "What I meant was, I must have left the phone off the hook?"

"No," replied Kate. "It's right there. Never mind. I hope you're in the mood for pizza, 'cause that's what I got." She let her backpack fall to the floor and set the pizza on the coffee table.

"Pizza's perfect. How was your first day back to school?"

"Meh, it was okay," She said from the refrigerator just a few steps away. "You know how professors are the first day. I heard the same spiel in all three classes: Read your syllabus carefully, there will be no excuses for late projects, sign the Code of Conduct contract, blah, blah, blah. I swear they treat us like undergrads. Except for the workload. I have to turn in a prospectus for one of my big projects on Friday. That's why I was late. I wanted to get to the library before all the good books were gone. How about you? How was your first day back? Were the kids glad to see you?"

"You know how us teachers are the first day – blah, blah, blah."

"I doubt you're like that." Kate set two bottles of Coke on the table and sat down next to him. "If you were my teacher, I would hang on your every word…Professor Rosen."

"These are high school kids. None of them are there by choice. I'm afraid I am just background noise to most of them. As soon as that bell rings, it's like a horse race. They can't wait to get out of there."

"Oh, come on now. You're a cool guy and easy on the eyes. I bet there's more than a few girls who wouldn't mind staying after class. You kinda got this Indiana Jones thing going on."

"What do you mean?"

"Well, there's Mr. Rosen standing in front of the class, talking about dead people. He's obviously brilliant, although a little naïve, but bookishly charming. Then there's Garren. He's this totally cool, devil-may-care adventurous guy who always gets the girl; which, of course, is me. Now Mr. Rosen believes that as long as he's in the classroom, his secret identity is safe. But every once in a while, Garren shows up in a mischievous smile, an unconscious gesture or slip of the tongue. You may not know this, but girls can spot the clues. We know who you guys really are."

Garren sat back, a look of total defeat on his face. "I had no idea I was so easy to read."

Kate shrugged. "What can I say? Woman's intuition is real."

"Good to know."

"Don't let on that you know. If the other women find out I told you, I'll be in big trouble."

"Your secret is safe with me." In a few years, the playfulness would vanish from their marriage. Garren forgot how much he enjoyed this side of Kate. "So, I remind you of Indiana Jones, eh?"

Kate smiled slyly, grabbed his face and kissed him passionately, ending with a little nibble on his bottom lip. "Zats how Austrians say goodbye."

"Zis is how vee say goodbye in Germany." Garren shook his head as if he had just been punched in the face. "I like the Austrian way better."

"So did I," Kate said in her best Sean Connery accent.

They laughed and kissed again.

"I like being married to you," Kate said as she opened the pizza box. "We're fun together."

Images of future Kate flashed through his mind – sad Kate, frustrated Kate, angry Kate, but not fun Kate. That version of her had disappeared and he knew it was all his fault. The first time around, he was too distracted by the things he didn't have to appreciate all the things he did have. His whole life seemed to be about five years behind schedule. By age thirty, he should have already been married a few years, owned a house, had one kid and another on the way, written his first book and comfortably settled into his career as a university history professor. But for reasons he couldn't understand, his plans were delayed. Love came later than expected. Doctoral work proved more difficult than anticipated. His bank account was thinner than it should have been. He resented the fact that a high school gig was all he could find. He was disappointed that marriage didn't happen at the twenty-five year mark as planned. He was nervous that his kids would still be living at home when he and Kate should be planning their empty-nest years. Several failed writing attempts had built a wall of doubt that he would ever complete a book, let alone publish one. And their crummy little apartment was a daily reminder that he was not succeeding at life in the way he thought he deserved. As a result, he'd completely neglected to see Kate as his partner in their grand adventure. Instead, she was just another mark on his Life Accomplishment list that should have been checked years ago. As soon as the newness of marriage wore off, her woman's intuition would detect Garren's true colors and she would begin to regret what her life had become. Propriety and the hope that things would get better once Garren found contentment in his station would prevent her from considering leaving him. And before either of them knew it, ten years would pass and they would be little more than roommates maintaining a façade for the sake of their individual reputations. Garren was once again amazed by this enlightened perspective. How could he have lived with and not recognized this amazing woman who really did see their life together as an adventure? How could he have not been caught up in her enthusiasm about *them*? How could he have missed *her*? What an idiot he had been. If Younger Garren had been there, Older Garren would have given him a piece of their mind.

"Hello." Kate waved a slice of pizza in front of his face. "Aren't you going to join me? I'm already on my second piece."

"Oh, yeah." Garren grabbed a slice.

"You've been doing that a lot lately. Where do you go when you zone out like that?"

"I was just thinking…can I ask you a hypothetical?"

"Sure."

"Suppose you received a message from your older self, say fifty year old Kate. Do you think you would listen? I mean, would you take your own advice?"

"I hope I would. After all, my older self would be so much wiser. Yeah, I think I would. I know I would."

Garren nodded. "What if that message told you something about yourself that you didn't want to believe…something that you couldn't believe?"

Kate's eyebrows came together in thought. "I guess I would consider the source and have to trust it to be true. Why?"

"It's a thought project for one of my classes." There is was, another lie. "I was going to have my Current Events class write a letter to their future selves explaining how they saw the world at the turn of the century. You know, kind of like a time capsule. And I was going to collect them and mail them back to them in, I don't know, five or ten years from now."

Kate's expression suggested she was tracking with him.

"But then I thought, wouldn't it be more interesting to receive a letter from your older self explaining what your life would be like in 2010 or maybe even 2020. What do you think of that?"

"That would be more interesting." Kate's expression morphed into confusion. "But how would your students be able to write such a letter?"

"Yeah, I haven't figured that part out yet. Of course, I could give them the assignment in anticipation that time-travel will one day be possible. Then their older selves could write the paper, and…what? Why are you laughing at me?"

"Are you even listening to yourself? That's the most ridiculous thing I've ever heard you say. You should totally give them that assignment just to see what they would do."

Garren laughed along with her and played it off as a joke. That's what Young Garren would do. But Old Garren was trying to say something. "You're right. That's…that's crazy. But it does make you think. If you knew then what you know now, would it make a difference?"

"Of course it would."

"Or if you were given the opportunity to live a certain part of your life over again, and you brought with you all the knowledge you had from the first time around, how much better could you make it the second time around?"

"You're serious, aren't you?"

"Somewhat serious." Garren wanted desperately to tell her everything, but decided to settle for what was in his heart. "Forget about the assignment. Obviously, I won't do that. But it got me thinking about life…myself…us. I was imagining myself twenty years from now. I'll be fifty. We will have been married twenty years."

"And?" Kate prompted when it seemed Garren was starting to zone out again. "Suppose your fifty year old self showed up. What would he say to you?"

"He would say, 'Garren, you're the luckiest man in the world. You'll never make a better decision than when you asked Kate to be your wife.' He would say, 'Don't ever take her for granted. Live each day as if it were the only day you have together. And then every day you wake up and discover she's still with you, live it like you might not get another one.' He'd probably say more, but then he would get all sentimental." Garren pretended to scratch an itch in the corner of his left eye. "Who knows? Maybe fifty year old Garren cries a lot."

"Hmm." Kate nodded. "Fifty year old Garren sounds like a wise man. Would you take his advice?"

"I'd like to think I would."

"You're not going to ask me what fifty year old Kate would say, are you?"

"Nope."

"Good, 'cause I have no idea what she would say."

"That's okay."

"It's not that I don't want to. My mind just doesn't work like yours. I would never think of that."

"Consider yourself blessed. Things can get a little weird in here." He tapped the side of his head.

"But that doesn't mean I don't think about us…how we are now…how we will be in the future. I think about those things a lot, just without the time-travel."

"You think it's odd, a grown man having such thoughts."

"Maybe a little. But if it works for you, I say go for it."

A little voice inside Garren's head told him to say no more, that he'd said what he wanted to say and that was enough. But then he heard himself say out loud, "What if I told you I really am fifty year old Garren? Would you believe me?"

"Uh, no." Kate picked up the television remote and switched it on. "I like my thirty year old Garren. And when it's time, I'll like the older version just as much. Oh, look. Jeopardy."

It's amazing how quickly one can adjust to a new reality. On day four, Garren awoke fully convinced that he was still in the year 2000. He knew all the red numbers on his clock would be there as soon as he looked their way and they were. He trusted Kate's warm body would be next to him when he reached toward her side of the bed, but she wasn't. He panicked until he heard water running and dishes clinking in the kitchen. Then he remembered Kate saying she planned to get up extra early because she wanted to hit the gym before class. That's right, he and Kate were avid exercisers in the early days of their marriage. That will last two more years. Then Kate's new career will become too demanding. Garren will stick with it a while longer, but the lack of incentive from Kate will cause him to slack off. His last day in the gym will be on his thirty-third birthday. He groaned at the thought of getting back into the habit until it occurred to him that he was already in the habit and that his younger, already fit body actually wanted to work out. This second-time-around thing had its advantages, but he would still have to learn how to use it. He couldn't always think of himself as a fifty year old man living in a thirty year old body. In some areas of his life, he needed to actually think like a thirty year old. Exercise was certainly one of them.

Encouraged by this, he leapt out of bed and paid attention to the absence of knee and back pain that had defined his mornings for the last ten years. With a little more perseverance in the gym, he could probably delay that inevitability at least another decade. Entering the bathroom, he paused at the mirror to admire his dark hair, wrinkle-free face and toned body. He had to admit he looked pretty good, but the vanity of youthfulness, something he'd gotten over years ago, felt wrong. His fifty year old self wouldn't allow it. He did consider letting his beard grow in the popular fashion of his time, but decided against it at the thought of it possibly costing him in the area of intimacy with Kate; that is if he could ever get over their age difference enough to allow himself to be intimate with her. Last night was trickier than the first two, but he managed to avoid her advances once more. He didn't know how long he could keep this up before it started causing a real problem. Maybe tonight would be different.

The thought of her energized him. He skipped the shave and shower, but quickly brushed his teeth. Then he slipped on some workout clothes he found in his dresser and met her in the kitchen.

"Morning, Babe." The look on her face reminded him that she wasn't quite ready for such terms of endearment. "Oops, sorry. Good morning, Kate."

Her face softened. "You don't need to apologize. It's not *that* bad. Come here." Garren slid comfortably into her warm embrace. She kissed him lightly on the cheek and rubbed her face against his. "Mmm, a little scruffy, but you smell good."

"Thanks. So do you."

She made a face. "I haven't even brushed my teeth yet."

He shrugged. "Must be the rest of you then."

"Yeah, right." She turned back toward the counter to finish preparing her pre-workout snack. "You're up early."

"I thought I'd go with you." Garren admired the way she looked in her workout clothes. "Feels like I haven't been to the gym in years."

"You're gonna go all the way to the university with me?"

"Sure. Why not?"

"It's kind of out of the way. Besides, I thought you preferred working out at the high school."

"That's right. I do that, don't I? Well, uh, I just want to be with you. Unless you'd rather go by yourself. Yeah, on second thought, I should probably stick to my normal routine."

Kate turned to face him. "Are you okay?"

"Who me? Of course. Why?"

"You're doing it again."

"Doing what?"

She eyed him thoughtfully. "I can't put my finger on it, but there's just something different about you."

"I'm too clingy."

"I wouldn't call it that." Under her breath she added, "Especially after last night. You know what? Never mind. Forget I said anything. I love how you want to be with me. I really do. But I don't want you to feel like we need to be together every waking moment."

"I'm sorry. I was—"

"Garren!" she snapped. "Why do you keep doing that?"

He stepped back. "Doing what?"

"You've apologized to me more in the last three days than in the entire time I've known you. What is up with you?"

"Nothing."

"Is it me?"

"No."

"Am I doing something that makes you feel like you have to keep saying you're sorry?"

"No."

"Because I don't want to be that kind of wife."

"You're not."

"I've seen that kind of wife. I refuse to be that kind of wife. Do you think I'm that kind of wife?"

Garren hesitated a moment too long.

"You do. That's just great. I'm married three months and I've turned into my mother. Fantastic."

"No, Babe—"

Kate's eyebrows shot up and her mouth dropped open.

"I'm sor—"

Kate's eyes narrowed and her jaw clamped shut.

Garren unconsciously raised his hands in defense and immediately regretted it. "Kate, just calm down." As soon as the words were out of his mouth, he regretted those, too. That was an exhausted fifty year old Garren dealing with a fed-up forty-five year old Kate after an hour long battle in a war that had been raging for years. *Calm down, Kate* never got its intended results, but usually ended the argument with Kate storming out of the room and Garren glad to have her gone.

Kate opened her mouth to speak, then shut it again. Her right eye began to twitch. Then in a low measured tone, she said, "I'm going to the gym now. We'll talk about this tonight."

Garren watched in stunned silence as she grabbed her backpack and gym bag and left without saying another word. Leaning against the counter, he put his face in his hands and massaged his temples. What just happened? Their first argument wasn't supposed to happen for another year. He remembered it all too well. Tommy invited him out for a couple beers on his thirty-first birthday. One thing led to another and he missed the entire celebration Kate had planned for him. It would be the first of many times he would make her cry. How could he, a man on a mission to correct the mistakes of his past, have screwed things up so fast? Instead of avoiding those mistakes, he advanced the time-table by an entire year.

"Dude, that was intense." The voice came from the couch.

"Tommy?" Garren said. "What are you doing here? How did you get in?"

"Key under the mat. Needed a place to crash. Awesome night. Didn't want to wake you guys."

"This isn't a good time."

"Sorry, man. Hope you don't mind me sayin', but Kate is totally hot when she's mad."

"Not cool, Tommy."

"I've always thought Kate was hot, but wow."

"Really?"

"Yeah, she's really good looking. You're one lucky guy."

"That's enough."

"Okay, okay. Don't get all *calm down, Kate* on me, too. Dude, you really need to lighten up."

"Stop saying *dude*. We're not in college anymore."

"Sure. Whatever you say, Mr. Married Man. Can I offer you some free advice?"

"Are you still drunk?"

"Let me check." Tommy closed his eyes for a moment. "Yep."

"Then I don't want your advice."

"Okay, here it comes. If you're not careful, you're gonna lose her. A mustang like that needs room to run. Put a saddle on her and she'll buck you right off."

"You don't know anything about horses. A mustang is a male horse."

"No, I think it can go either way. Now a male horse is called a stallion. And a girl horse is a mare. Yeah, I'm pretty sure you can have a girl mustang. You're the professor. You should know this."

"I'm a history teacher."

"They had horses in history."

"I'm not having this conversation with you."

"Neither would I. Do you have an encyclopedia? We could look it up."

"I have to get ready for work." Garren went back into the bedroom to change into his school clothes.

"Okay. I'll just stay here."

Garren threw his gym clothes into the hamper and snatched a clean t-shirt out of the drawer. Remembering he hadn't had his shower yet, he started for the bathroom, then changed his mind. He was too upset to care about showering. He went to the closet, yanked a pair of pants off the hanger and jammed his legs into them. Stumbling back toward the bed, he fell into it on Kate's side. Immediately, his senses were invaded by her scent. He sat there for a minute, trying to calm himself. "Calm down, Garren," he mocked himself for his stupidity. He waited another minute until his heart rate dropped back to normal. Then, more calmly this time, he got up and went to the closet. Finding an appropriate shirt, he finished his ensemble. Noticing his black leather jacket, the one he always suspected Tommy had lost but couldn't prove, he grabbed it and put it on. The sound and smell of it took him back and he started to feel a little better. He caught a glimpse of himself in the mirror. He looked cool and maybe even a little dangerous. Not exactly the teacher type, but that's what Hempstead High School was going to get today.

In the living room, he found Tommy clad only in boxers and hunched over at the computer. "You can stay until you sober up," Garren said. "But I want you gone before we get home."

"Thanks, man. Hey, I was right. It says here that a herd of mustangs usually consists of one stallion and eight *females* and their young. Whoa, one stallion and eight females. How cool is that?"

"Goodbye, Tommy."

"From now on, you can call me Mustang."

The Camaro was the coolest thing Garren ever owned and it made him feel cool when he was behind the wheel. He squealed out of the parking space in front of the apartment complex and raced toward NW Arterial with Highway 20 on his mind. It was still early, too early to go to school, but he needed to blow off some steam. The gym would have been more productive, but the Camaro made him feel better. Threading the needle through the morning traffic, he felt reckless and free. He swerved around the saner drivers, letting the sound of the engine proclaim his disregard for the law. It felt good to break the rules again. Middle age and his old Corolla had slowed him down quite a bit, made him cautious, extinguished his spark. Young again, he relished the adrenaline of the days before he cared about the expectations of others. Actually, those days ended with marriage and his first real teaching gig, but thirty was close enough that he didn't care.

The Dubuque City police officer Garren blew past did care. He clocked the Camaro doing seventy-three in a forty-five, but by the time he caught up with him, Garren was doing at least eighty. He pulled him over near Pennsylvania Avenue, the road that ran in front of the high school.

Had thirty year old Garren been there, fifty year old Garren would have read him the riot act. But as it was, fifty year old Garren had to sit quietly in his thirty year old body and let the police officer do it for him.

"Do you realize how fast you were going, Son?"

Son? Did he really say that? "No, Sir, officer. I don't."

"I had you pushing past eighty by the time I caught up with you. Do you always have such disregard for your fellow motorists?"

"No, Sir."

"Where are you going in such a hurry?"

"Just driving, Sir."

"Have you been drinking?"

"No, Sir."

"Well, I'm going to have to ask you to step out of the car."

"Is that necessary, Officer?"

"Smart guy, eh? If it wasn't necessary, I wouldn't have asked. Now get out of this car right now."

As soon as Garren stepped out of the car, he wished he were wearing his blue blazer instead of his leather jacket. The expression on the cop's face told him there was no way he was going to get away with just a warning. Thirty year old Garren might have actually done the right thing by letting the officer order him through the ordeal. But fifty year old Garren tried to disarm the situation by being helpful. As he reached inside his jacket to retrieve his wallet, he started to tell the officer that he was a teacher at Hempstead High School. All he managed was, "I'm a—" before he was face down on the hood of the Camaro with his hands behind his back.

"Boy!" Screamed the policeman. "Don't you ever make a move like that in front of an armed officer of the law. In my rookie days I might have shot you."

Garren felt the first cuff clamp onto his wrist. "I'm sorry, Officer. I was just getting my license."

"You don't do anything until I tell you. Is that clear?"

"Yes, Sir. If you'll let me explain, you'll see this is a big mistake."

"Shut it!" The officer grabbed Garren's other arm and forced it back and into the handcuffs. With his man secured, he reached into Garren's pocket to retrieve his wallet. "Now you stay right there while I radio this in."

Just then a car pulled to a stop at the red light not twenty feet away. "Good morning, Mr. Rosen," someone yelled from the passenger side. "Rough morning, eh? See you in class...maybe." This was followed by a chorus of laughter from the backseat. The light turned green and the car honked as it turned toward the school.

The police officer got back into his car to run the plates and check Garren's record for priors. He may have also checked his credit score and applied for a home loan in the time it took. Garren's arms were aching and his ego was taking a beating. Two more cars full of students slowed down to look. No one said anything, but there was plenty of laughter. The only upside was that cellphones and social media hadn't developed to the point that Garren's ordeal would have been streaming to the entire student body in real time. Still, the gossip train was already out of the station. Garren's bad day would only get worse.

The police officer moseyed back to the scene of the crime like an old west sheriff. He tossed Garren's wallet onto the hood and uncuffed him. When Garren turned around, he noticed a smirk on the officer's lips. He started to say something, but thought better of it.

"Looks like you caught me in a good mood today, Mr. Rosen. I've decided not to take you in. I will, however, look forward to seeing you in court." He slammed the fat ticket onto the hood of the Camaro. "Now you better slow your butt down, especially around these students. As a teacher, you should set a good example both inside and outside of the classroom. So...Rosen. History teacher, right?"

"Yes, Sir."

The smirk came back. "My daughter thinks highly of you. Respect is a fragile thing. Don't blow it."

"Thank you..." Garren glanced down at his name plate. "...Officer Daniels."

"Have a good day." Officer Daniels took one more look at Garren with his leather jacket and fast car, shook his head and headed back to his police car.

Garren still had forty minutes before his first class. He had time to go to Starbucks, but then he couldn't remember if Dubuque even had a Starbucks in 2000. Deciding against risking another encounter that could alter the history of the world, he drove slowly the quarter mile to the high school. Wheeling into the parking lot, he made his way toward the faculty parking lot. He stopped to let a group of students cross the road in front of him. One of the girls was wearing a letter jacket with the school mascot emblazoned across the front. When she passed by, Garren noticed the big block letters on her back that spelled out *Lady Mustangs*. Tommy was right after all.

10

The halls of Hempstead High School were not as crowded as they soon would be. A few before-school clubs were meeting. There were some students hanging out in the cafeteria under the guise of completing homework. Several teachers were in their classrooms taking advantage of the last few minutes of peace and quiet before the rabble arrived. With luck, Garren could make it to his own room unnoticed.

"Ah, Mr. Rosen," the school principal called as he passed by the administration office suite. "A word please."

"Here we go," Garren said under his breath. In the three seconds it took him to stop and turn around, he tried to call up his memories about the woman. There weren't many as she was a rather ordinary woman with a rather unremarkable tenure at a rather average high school at the conjunction of Iowa, Wisconsin and Illinois. She will announce her retirement at the end of the school year and he will never see her again. He couldn't remember any one-on-one interactions with her beyond his interview the previous summer. Other than that, he'd seen her maybe a dozen times at faculty meetings and school assemblies. Apparently, his encounter with Dubuque's finest had changed that. The following conversation and the events they would set in motion were not part of his original history.

"Principal," Garren mumbled because he couldn't remember her name. Her lack of reaction told him she was either okay with being called that or whatever was on her mind was more important. He took the fact that she did not retreat into her office as a good thing, unless she was going to reprimand him right there in front of the receptionist.

"I have a request," she began. "Would you be available to chaperone the Valentine dance?"

"Uh."

"I realize this will be your first Valentine's Day with your new wife. I suppose you knew each other last Valentine's Day. Not that it's any of my business, but I imagine you were probably together since you were married six or seven months later. And you may have known each other the Valentine's Day before that. Of course, I have no knowledge of your relationship history, but I am fairly confident you have expressed your affection for her in the appropriate manner."

Garren heard the receptionist snicker and saw the principal blush.

"Oh my." She cleared her throat. "Pardon my language, Mr. Rosen. It was not my intention to engage in such explicit conversation while on school premises. Not that I approve of such in my personal life. I assure you I do not."

The receptionist let out an audible chuckle and quickly stifled it.

Feeling sorry for the woman, Garren said, "It's okay. Sure, I'll do it. I'll chaperone the dance." As soon as he said it, he thought of Kate. She was already angry with him. He was pretty sure this wouldn't help. Then the thought occurred to him that he had never chaperoned a dance in his entire life. He'd never even been asked. This was different. The first time around, he must have somehow avoided the whole thing, but this time he didn't. Not that chaperoning a high school dance in Dubuque would change the course of human history, but he had just altered his own history.

"You will?" said the principal. "Thank you. Perhaps your wife will join you."

"I'll ask her."

"Very well." The principal seemed genuinely pleased. "I look forward to meeting her."

"How's that?"

"Mr. Carmichael and I will also be attending as chaperones."

Carmichael. The name sounded vaguely familiar to Garren. Mrs. Carmichael was the principal at Hempstead High School. Now he remembered. "Well, I look forward to meeting your—"

"Miss Jenson," said the receptionist, "you have a call on line one."

"Have a nice day, Mr. Rosen." Principal Jenson turned toward her office.

Not Mrs. Carmichael. Garren repeated both names to himself, trying to jog his memory. In truth, he'd never gotten very familiar with anyone at Hempstead High School. Everything was a blur his first year, what with the wedding and all. During the upcoming summer, he will learn that the university has plans to expand its history department in the fall of 2001. He will apply, and by Thanksgiving of 2000 he will be notified that has made it to the final round of interviews. In January of 2001, he will get a letter inviting him to join the university faculty in the fall. Hempstead High School will become a minor footnote in the life of Dr. Garren Rosen.

The receptionist must have noticed Garren's pensive look. "Figure it out yet?"

"Excuse me?"

"Principal Jenson and Coach Carmichael. Rumor has it they got together over Christmas break. I know. Things could get real interesting around here. And Carla told me there was some chemistry happening in the science lab yesterday after class, if you know what I mean."

"I should probably get to class," Garren said.

"Yep, things could get real interesting."

Garren made it to his classroom without any more interruptions. Setting his briefcase on the desk, he dropped into his chair and let out a sigh. His day was off to a rough start and he still had seven periods to get through. He hated how Kate left the apartment and hoped her workout had put her in a better mood. What happened anyway? Why did she go off on him like that? He couldn't even remember what he said. Whatever, he had his own problems to deal with. He deserved the speeding ticket, but it was partly Kate's fault. If she hadn't been so unreasonable… "Wait. Stop," he said out loud. He caught himself slipping back into fifty year old Garren mode, complaining about forty-five year old Kate after fifteen years of bickering and blaming and refusing to take responsibility for his own actions and attitudes. In this time, Kate was only twenty-five and still basking in the glow of marital bliss. He, fifty year old Garren, had just poured cold water on her passion. He, the man who had been given a second chance, was acting as if their future – the way it played out the first time – was unavoidable. Was it? Was their path written in stone? Was it even possible to change? Or was this second-time-around thing nothing more than some cruel temporal joke? Was time messing with him?

One thing was certain. Every time he thought about it, his head hurt. There was nothing he could do about it in the moment. If there was any hope of salvaging the day, he had to stop trying to analyze time and just let it play out on its own.

"Hey, Mr. Rosen," said one of two boys who had just entered the class. "We heard you got busted."

"Yes, I did."

The first boy flung his notebook onto his desk. "I'm sure it's not the first time."

"Why do you think that?" Garren asked.

"I don't know. I figure a car like that gets noticed. Cops probably expect you to drive fast."

"Did he really cuff you?" asked the second boy.

"Yes."

"Why? Did he find your stash?"

Garren frowned. He didn't appreciate these children assuming he was the kind of guy who would…well, such assumptions might have been true in his younger days, but he'd spent the last twenty-five years trying to live a responsible life, a respectable life. As more students filed into the class, Garren took advantage of the distraction. He jumped into his lesson straight away.

The day progressed as expected. Every class asked the same questions: Did he really get pulled over by the cops? What did he do? Did he really get handcuffed? And with each interrogation, the questions suggested the story was growing as the day wore on. Was he really trying to outrun the cop? Did he total his car? Did he total the police car? How many people did he run over? Did they let him out of jail to teach? Were the cops waiting to arrest him after school?

By seventh period, Garren had become something of an outlaw hero. The boys nodded at him with a new respect and a few actually gave him high-fives. The girls were a little less obvious, but still let it be known that their bad boy teacher had piqued their interest. His black leather jacket draped across the back of his chair did not go unnoticed. Neither did his unkempt hair, untucked shirt and blue jeans. By seventh period, it had become apparent that his morning escapades did not leave time for a shave. It was all he could do to get the class thinking about the American government.

Halfway through the class, a hand went up in the second row. "Yes?"

A boy who looked like he'd rather be doing anything other than sitting in school and thinking about the government spoke up. "I'll be eighteen in March. I'm gonna register to vote."

The statement was off-topic, but Garren let it ride. "That's very commendable."

"I wasn't going to," said the boy. "After yesterday's class, I thought about it. I'm gonna do it."

Garren paused to see if the resolve of one young man might spark a revolution among his peers. It seemed like something that would happen in a movie. All it would take was one more person to stand up and say that he or she was also moved by yesterday's class and that they, too, wanted to make their voice heard and be a part of the solution. Just one more, that's all it would take to embolden another, than another, and eventually the entire class would be standing tall, proclaiming their intention to exercise their right to cast a vote for America's future. Just one more.

"Okay, then," said Garren when no one else stood or raised their hand or did anything to suggest they'd even noticed the lecture had paused. "Back to the Supreme Court."

The clock by the door read 2:20. The bell rang. The students gathered their notebooks and filed out of the classroom.

"Later, Mr. Rosen," said the boy who would be voting in the 2000 presidential election.

"See you tomorrow, Mr. Rosen," said a girl who looked too old to be in high school. "I like the new look."

"Uh, thanks," Garren replied awkwardly.

As the room thinned, Garren noticed Sofia waiting at the back of the line to exit the classroom. He didn't mean to stare, but knowing who she would become and that they were destined to meet on New Year's Eve twenty years in the future, he couldn't help it. When she looked his way, he pretended to look inside his briefcase.

"Bad day?" she said. "I'm sorry."

Garren looked up and saw that they were the last two in the room. "Uh, yeah. You could say that."

"Let me guess. You met my foster dad this morning."

Garren chuckled. "*You're* his daughter? I didn't make the connection. You have different last names."

"*Foster* daughter," she corrected. "He's not my real dad."

"Yeah, I met him. He seemed to enjoy putting my face down on the hood of my car."

"He does like to be in charge. I'm sorry if he played tough guy with you."

Garren was amazed at how much of the older Sofia was recognizable in the younger version. He didn't realize it, but he was staring again.

"Mr. Rosen? Is something wrong?"

"I'm sorry, it's just that you remind me of someone." Garren forced himself to look elsewhere.

"Is she pretty?"

"Uh, you should probably get on to your next class."

"It's the end of the day."

"Then you should probably go home."

"Okay." Sofia moved toward the door and turned back around.

The two locked eyes. Garren was struck again at how much this Sofia was like the woman he met at Tommy's party. He was tempted to say something that only the older version would know just to see her reaction. But then he realized how ridiculous that would be.

Sofia re-shouldered her backpack and started to leave, then stopped. "How's your wife?"

"My wife?" The tell wasn't in what he said, but in the look on his face when he said it.

"I knew it." Sofia started to laugh. She let her backpack slip to the floor. "Tell me, Teacher, what do we do now?"

"I don't know what you mean." Garren sat down on the edge of his desk.

"One of us has to say it."

"S-say what?"

She laughed again. "Hello, Garren. It's me, Sofia. From Tommy's party?"

Garren was unable to speak.

"New Year's Eve 2019," she prompted. "The moon gets wacked by an asteroid. We connected. You do know what I'm talking about, yeah?"

"Yes, but how?"

"Thank you." She threw her arms around him. "I've been freaking out."

Garren stiffened at her closeness, then pulled free from her embrace and stepped back. "That's probably not a good idea here at school."

"Oh, right." Sofia went to one of the desks and sat down. "What a trip. Look at us."

"How is this possible?" Garren asked.

"Beats me. I'm just a bartender...or will be a bartender. You're the professor. You tell me."

"I have no idea." Garren paced the front of the classroom. "But the fact that we are both here has to mean something."

"Yeah, it means time is a bad mistress and she's got two of us trapped in her nightmare."

"It's not that bad."

"Maybe not for you. You're cool again. I'm seventeen. Seventeen! And I'm back in high school! While you've been reliving the glory days with your hot young wife, I've been living at home with Officer Creeper and his weird lady friend. This is terrible, Garren. I need to get back to our time."

Garren fell silent again.

"Oh, I get it. You like it here. You don't want to go back. What was I thinking?" She put her head down on the desk.

"What *were* you thinking, Sofia?"

"I was thinking how nice it would be to have a friend. You know, someone to talk to, commiserate with…someone who would understand. Do you know what it's like to be a seventeen year old girl? And don't even get me started on the boys."

"I'm sorry it's been so hard for you."

"You have no idea. Yesterday, when I saw you and realized who you were, I couldn't believe it. I mean, what are the odds that you would be my teacher. That's why I asked you about the election. I was trying to see if you were you…I mean you from 2019."

"Yeah, I was pretty shocked to see you."

"Well, here we are. What do you say we get out of here and go get a drink?"

Garren laughed nervously. "You're kidding, right?"

"No."

"We can't do that."

"You were pretty okay with it the other night."

"Last Friday night won't happen for twenty years."

"Maybe for you, but for me it was four days ago…in the past."

Friday night flashed through Garren's memory. The moon. The beautiful woman. The drinks. The blur. He had questions about what happened that night, but he was afraid to ask. "What do you want me to do about this?"

"Gee, let's think about this for a minute. Here's an idea: Fix it!"

"Wha…how can I fix this?"

"You're a smart guy."

"I'm a history teacher."

"Maybe you know someone, like a scientist."

"I doubt anyone would know how to fix this."

Garren went back to his desk. Neither of them knew what to say. So they just sat there. Finally, Sofia got up.

"Well, I guess that's it then. Have a nice evening. I'll see you tomorrow in class, Mr. Rosen."

"Sofia, wait."

"What?"

"I know this is harder for you than it is for me. And you're right, we can't pretend this whatever-it-is isn't happening to both of us. It might be a little awkward, me being your teacher and all, but I am your friend."

"Thanks." Sofia shrugged. "I don't want to have to go through the next twenty years again. My life wasn't that great." She was on the verge of tears.

Garren walked over to the door and checked the hallway to see it if was clear. "Come here." He held out his arms and hugged her for real this time. "You're not alone. I'm with you. We'll figure this out together."

11

Garren dreaded going home. It felt all too familiar, too much like his old life – the morning altercation, the day-long mental replay of what he did or didn't say or do, the inevitable evening rehash of the morning's debacle. Then again, it was apparently their first real argument. While he was a seasoned veteran, hardened by the decade-long war, Kate was a rookie. She had not yet acquired the tactics or amassed the arsenal she would one day use to launch devastating attacks from which he would never recover. Perhaps he could use this to his advantage, not to score an early victory, but solidify an alliance that would prevent the first-time-around hostility. Perhaps it was not too late to get back on track with his second-time-around initiative, the salvation of his marriage. That was his objective. That's what he needed to keep in the forefront of his mind when he saw her again.

Then there was Sofia, his unexpected partner in time. Sure, it was great to have someone to talk to about the most amazing thing to happen to anyone, but it was complicated and dangerous. He (age 30) was her (age 17) teacher. This new reality put a whole new twist on the evening they spent together, an evening that happened four days in the past and might happen again twenty years in the future; an evening still shrouded in the fog of inebriation. What really happened (or will happen) that evening? There was an attraction, he had to admit that. But as far as he could remember, he'd kept his vows to Kate. He was honest about being married and Sofia assured him nothing would happen between them. But that was before the third or fourth drink. What did she call it? *Eden's Curse.* How did she describe it? *At first you think it's no big deal, but then you wake up naked in the woods.* She was mostly right. At first, it didn't seem like a big deal. But then he woke up semi-naked in the forest of the past. There was a lot he just couldn't remember between Tommy's couch in 2019 and his own bed in 2000. He was fairly certain Sofia would be able to fill in the gap. He was less certain that he wanted her to.

Compartmentalization, that's what Garren decided as he drove the speed limit all the way home. He could deal with only one situation at a time. Sofia would have to wait until tomorrow. Kate would be home in an hour or two, he hoped. He also decided he needed some assistance. If fifty year old Garren got him into this mess, maybe thirty year old Garren could get him out.

"What would I have done?" he asked himself. "What *did* I do after our first argument?"

He pulled into the parking lot of the neighborhood grocery. Ten minutes later, he was back in his car with a bouquet of flowers, a box of chocolates and a teddy bear. Yes, he knew it was a cliché, but that's what he did the first time and it seemed to work then. Now for the apology. By his calculation, he had about an hour to work on it before Kate got home.

Rounding the corner onto their street, all his careful planning went out the window. Kate's car was parked on the street in front of their apartment and Kate was sitting on the hood. As soon as she saw him, she hopped down. Garren took the only available spot, three cars behind hers on the opposite side of their one way street. He started to reach for the flowers, but changed his mind as she came walking toward him. Even from a distance he could tell she'd been crying. He got out of his car and met her halfway. She threw her arms around him and held him so tightly he thought she would never let go.

"Don't say anything," she said. "Just listen. I don't know what came over me this morning. Everything was fine and then all of a sudden I heard my parents arguing. Garren, I can't stand the thought of us becoming like them. I don't want to make you feel like you're walking on egg shells around me. I don't want you to feel like you have to apologize every time we disagree. I'm not always right, you know."

Garren was stunned. This was not the Kate he was used to sparring with. He didn't know how to react.

"I love you so much," she said.

"I love you, too."

"Just hold me for a minute."

Garren was happy to oblige.

"Thank you," she said after a long embrace.

"For…what?"

"For not doing anything stupid, like buying me flowers."

"Flowers?" Garren chuckled nervously. "Pff."

"If you want to buy me flowers, do it for no reason. Make-up flowers are insulting."

"Yeah they are."

"How about this? Let's never have to make-up. Let's never argue like that again."

The analytical side of Garren told him that what she was proposing was statistically improbable, if not impossible. Thirty year old Garren would have attempted to correct her naïve assumption. Fifty year old Garren, however, had lived through the despair of pure rationalism. His wounded heart was desperate enough to try something different. Hope.

"Okay," he said. "I like that better. Let's give it a try."

"Do or do not," Kate said in a poor imitation of Yoda. "There is no try."

Garren couldn't help but laugh. He'd forgotten about Kate's fondness for all things *Star Wars*. Her playfulness, which, in the early days, was her way of signaling she was ready for a truce, was the first casualty of the old war. It was something he now hoped to preserve.

"Let's go inside," said Garren. "It's cold out here."

"I'll get your briefcase." Kate started toward his car.

"No!" Garren said when he remembered the stupid make-up gifts on the front seat. "I'll get it later." Not knowing what else to do, he scooped her up in his arms and made for their apartment. "I must get you inside before Darth Vader finds us." He felt silly, but figured that's what thirty year old Garren would have done.

Kate laughed and played along with what she took as a romantic gesture. "Put me down, you scoundrel. I'd rather kiss a wookie."

Garren wanted to come back with the appropriate line, but he was never as much of a fan as she was. He hadn't seen any of the good episodes in more than a decade and he couldn't remember how far into the saga they were in 2000. So he said the first thing that popped into his head. "I'm one with the Force. The Force is with me."

"What?" Kate laughed. "What was that?"

"Uh, nothing. I just made it up."

"Hey, we should watch one tonight. Too bad *The Phantom Menace* isn't out on video yet."

"Yeah, too bad." Garren tried to sound sympathetic.

"We could watch one of the other ones. You pick."

Two and a half hours later, as the ending credits rolled, Garren's eyes snapped open. He glanced in Kate's direction to find her riveted to the screen, her lips curled in utter happiness. "Wow," he said, "that never gets old."

"I know," she replied. "Wanna watch *The Empire Strikes Back*?"

"Gosh, I don't think I can stay up that late. School tomorrow."

"Don't be such an old man. It's only eight o'clock." Kate start gathering the empty dinner plates and silverware.

"Hey," Garren replied, "are you still mad at me?"

"No." She took the dishes into the kitchen. "It's just not that late. And it's not like you have to drive back to your place after. This is one of the advantages of being married and kidless. We get to stay up as late as we want. And if we fall asleep together on the couch, no big deal." She plopped back onto the couch and curled up close to him.

She was right and this was the perfect time for him to start thinking like a newlywed. "I didn't mean I was ready to call it a night. I thought we could just be together."

"I like that." She finger-walked her hand up his arm and behind his neck to play with his hair. "What do you have in mind?"

"We could talk."

"Or we could not talk." Kate crawled into his lap and began kissing his neck.

Garren tried to think of another excuse, but there weren't any. She had him, and there was nothing he could do to stop her. After one final hesitation, he forced the thought of their age difference from his mind and gave in to his desire for her.

12

By the year 2000, Garren had traveled by air only four times in his life. The first two were to California and back when he was fifteen. His parents took him to Lake Tahoe and Yosemite National Park for a family vacation. The last two times were more recent. He and Kate flew to Hawaii for their honeymoon; another gift from his parents. All four times, Garren suffered the effects of jetlag. That was nothing compared to what he now referred to as *time lag*. He figured that's what must have been making him feel so out of sorts the last four days. His senses needed to adjust to their new time-environment. By the morning of Day Five, his mind had fully accepted the fact that he was now a resident of the year 2000. When his alarm clock sounded at 6:00 AM, he immediately accepted the fact that it was Wednesday and he would be spending most of it at Hempstead High School where he would be Mr. Rosen to the hundred or so students who would sit through his classes. The sounds from the kitchen were the expected sounds of Kate getting ready to head out to the gym before her own day of studies. The thought of last night proved that he was no longer hampered by the perception of an age difference between himself and Kate. He got out of bed and fell naturally into the routine of his younger self.

"Good morning, Babe," Kate said when she saw him.

Garren did a double-take. "Good morning, Sweetheart."

She made a face. "I think I'm okay with *Babe*, but let's not get crazy with the cutesy names."

"It's a start."

"Come here to me." She held out her arms until Garren was in her embrace. "I love you." She tip-toed up and kissed him warmly on the lips.

Garren almost commented on last night, which was undoubtedly a bigger deal to him than it was to her, but decided to let it go unspoken. "Mm, I'm awake now, Mrs. Coffee."

"I am so glad you decided to join me on the dark side." She let him go and turned back to finish her snack preparation. "I'll let you borrow my travel mug today, but as soon as you get paid again, you're going to have to get your own. It's on the counter. I got it ready for you."

"That's very sweet of you. Thanks."

"You're welcome." She grabbed her backpack and slung it over her shoulder.

"So, I'll see you tonight," Garren said. "Any thoughts about supper?"

"No, but I have an idea about dessert." She raised her eyebrows at him. "Oh, hey, better give yourself a little more time to get to school. I hear the cops are on the lookout for cool guys in muscle cars."

"You saw my ticket."

"Eighty-five in a forty-five. Yikes! I know I am partly responsible for that one. I'm sorry." She kissed him again, and though it was less passionate than before, something about it conveyed a sense that they were together…really together. "Seriously. Please be careful. I need you to come home to me."

"I will," he replied. "I promise."

Garren drove the speed limit all the way to school. On the way, he saw a police car parked in the grass near the intersection of NW Arterial and Pennsylvania Avenue. He waved as he drove by and Officer Daniels pointed at him. As he pulled onto the campus, he felt a sense of belonging, like he was supposed to be there. He even got a little excited when he recognized some of his students. One of the boys put his hands behind his back and leaned forward, pretending to be handcuffed. The other boys laughed and waved at him. Garren laughed, too, and waved back. Even walking into the school felt more natural and he was glad to be there. What it lacked in collegiate prestige, it more than made up for in high school spirit. Posters predicting a Hempstead Mustang victory over the Bettendorf Bulldogs at the basketball game on Friday adorned the halls. The idea occurred to him that maybe he and Kate might even attend. He acknowledged several of his colleagues with a head-nod as he stopped by the office to check his mailbox. The receptionist greeted him warmly. He couldn't remember her name, but she obviously knew him. Principal Jenson chatted him up as if they were now close friends. Even the attendance secretary, whose face seemed permanently frozen in an expression of suspicion, smiled at him like he had just made her day. Everything seemed to be exactly as it should be, as if the year 2000 had accepted Garren as one of its own.

When he arrived in his class, he found a note on his desk addressed to him by his first name. The handwriting was that of a teenage girl. It read:

> *Garren, I really need to see you.*
> *Meet me in the library at 11:03.*
> *I hate this place.*
> *Sofia.*

Garren sank into his chair. The note was like a calling card from the future. 2000 may have accepted him, but 2020 wasn't ready to let him go. He tucked the note into his jacket pocket and unpacked his lesson book. His first class would be arriving any minute. He needed to be ready.

The school day was divided into six forty-seven minute blocks (Periods 1-4 and 6-7) and a ninety-eight minute Period 5. This longer period was divided into three unequal blocks: A twenty minute study hall, a forty-eight minute class and a twenty-five minute lunch. The students were divided into four groups (A-D) with alternating schedules such that only a quarter of the student body were in the lunch commons at any given time. Obviously a mathematician had designed the schedule. The fact that the three divisions of Period 5 didn't add up to ninety-eight minutes went unnoticed by everyone except a novelist and a few readers who cared to add them up. The math gods had smiled upon Garren at the beginning of the year, assigning him two study periods back to back: Period 4 (10:11-10:58) and the longer Period 5 (10:58-12:36). That gave him an enviable 155 minutes between Current Events and Driver's Ed. Sofia wanted to meet him during Group D lunch at 11:03. That gave them twenty minutes before her fifth period class at 11:23.

The morning passed by with little to no drama. Garren was hitting his stride with his classes and actually enjoying them. He decided to take his study period in the library so he would be there when Sofia arrived. The librarian smiled and nodded at him and watched him until he sat down at one of the study tables. She lost interest when he pulled out his notebook. May as well make good use of the time while he waited.

At 10:59, the noise level in the library went from dead quiet to a muffled rumble as the hallway outside filled with students moving on to their next class. At 11:02, Sofia entered behind three other students. She found Garren and gave him a nod to follow her to the back of the library behind the last book shelf. When they were out of sight of, Sofia dropped her backpack and put her face into her hands. When she looked at him, her cheeks were moist with tears.

"I can't take this," she said, trying to keep her voice down. "Let's get out of here."

"We can't just leave," Garren replied. "We both have classes."

"No *we* don't. This isn't right. You and I, we don't belong here."

"I think we do."

"Garren, please. I need to talk to you and I'd rather not do it here. You have to take me somewhere."

"Where?"

"I don't care. Anywhere, but here."

Garren sighed and scratched his head, trying to figure out how to dissuade her. "Can't we talk after school?"

"He will be waiting to take me home."

"Did something happen?"

She looked away, nibbling her bottom lip. "I got in trouble last night. Now I can't even ride the bus."

Garren had to bite his tongue in order to keep a straight face. "What did you do?"

Sofia rolled her eyes exactly like a teenage girl. "I didn't come home right after school. I have a curfew! I'm a thirty-seven year old woman. I lived in Manhattan on my own for twenty years. Now I'm grounded because I stayed out until six o'clock on a school night. And to make matters worse, I keep crying. These emotions are driving me crazy!" She folded her arms across her chest. "I hate my life."

Garren bit his tongue harder. "Sofia, I am so sorry. I wish I could help, but I—"

"Oh, no you don't." Her face hardened. "You are not going to blow me off. Whether you want to admit it or not, we are in this together. Think about it. Somehow, you and I came here together. And somehow, you and I are going to figure out how to get back...or at least deal with it. I'm not going through this alone this time."

Just then, a girl appeared at the opposite end of their row. She glanced at them, started scanning the books and looked back at them. Realizing they were a teacher and student, a perplexed look came over her. She quickly averted her eyes back to the shelf and made a weak attempt at hunting for her book. After a few seconds, she gave up and backed out of the row.

"We can't talk here," said Garren. "Someone will hear us."

"Well, duh! That's why you need to take me somewhere else, so we *can* talk."

"What do suggest? We can't just walk out of here together. I'm pretty sure I could get arrested for that. And don't forget your foster dad, the cop, already has it in for me. If he caught us, I think he really would shoot me."

"When's your next class?"

"Sixth period. Why?"

"Perfect. Let's go get some lunch and we'll both be back by sixth period. No one will even know we've gone."

"How will you not be missed?"

"I used to cut fifth period all the time. Mrs. Armstrong always liked me and she wasn't very bright. I already told her I had assembly practice."

"Are you a cheerleader?"

"No," she said sarcastically. "I'm going to forget you said that."

"So, uh, when you did this before, how did you get out of the school?"

"Easy. It's all about confidence. Look bored. Walk with purpose, but not too quickly. If you look like you are supposed to be doing it, no one suspects you aren't. Think *Ferris Bueller's Day Off*. Besides, it's the year 2000. People weren't quite so paranoid as they are now…or will be. Err, you know what I mean. I'll meet you at your car in ten minutes."

"I don't know about this," Garren said.

Sofia's emotions must have swung to the side furthest from weepy teenage girl. She locked eyes with Garren, reached into his pants pocket and pulled out his keys. "If you want these back, you know where I'll be."

Garren didn't try to stop her. She had intrigued him in 2019 and that same bold determination intrigued him now. Besides, part of him wanted to talk, too. He waited a few minutes to let Sofia's exit look like a solo act. Then he casually made his way to the door. He tried to look bored while he walked with purpose, but not too quickly. It was harder than she made it sound. He felt everyone knew exactly what he was doing.

On his way out, he stopped by the office and told the secretary he had to run home to get some notes he forgot. She didn't look like she cared. As he left the school, Sofia's observation about the year 2000's lack of paranoia stuck in his mind. He noticed that he didn't have to pass through a metal detector. There were no cameras, no armed resource officer, no signs reminding him to be vigilant. She was right. The first year of the new century was much more trusting than the ones to follow.

Garren arrived at his car first. Without his keys, he couldn't open the door, so he pretended to be looking for something in his briefcase. When Sofia appeared from around the back corner of the school, he almost didn't recognize her. She was sporting a form fitting blazer. Her skirt had somehow become three inches shorter than the school dress code allowed. Her long hair was pulled up and twisted into a loose knot at the back of her head. And she walked with a New York strut that no teenager from Dubuque could possibly have pulled off. She tossed Garren's keys to him and walked around to the other side of the car. Garren made a quick scan of the parking lot. Finding it devoid of human activity, he quickly got into his car and reached across to unlock the passenger side.

Sofia casually slipped in and closed the door. "Stop staring."

Garren fumbled the keys into the ignition and fired up the engine. He wished he had his nondescript Corolla. "Where to?"

"Get on 20 and head west."

Garren was all nerves until they were away from the school. Entering Highway 20, he started to relax. "You look older."

"Like I said, confidence. By this time next year, I'll be tending bar in New York. Yes, I lied about my age. Some places don't check."

"What about the foster dad?"

"He's the reason I left." Sofia stared out the side window and started talking. "Before I killed him."

"It's that bad?"

"I don't want to talk about him anymore. In six months, I'll leave Dubuque and not come back until 2019. I have a sister. She's five years older than me. I haven't seen her since she aged out of the system. She finds me in 2002. We'll keep in touch for a few years, but when her kids start getting old enough to do things, she'll stop calling. She divorces her husband in 2017, tracks me down and stays with me in the city for about a month. She can't take it there, moves back to

Minneapolis, meets husband number two. She called me last summer and told me she was moving to Florida. I waited until she was gone. Then I came back here. I don't know why. I just did. Maybe I had to put some closure on the darkest part of my life. That's my sad story and unless I can figure out how to get back, I'm about to live it all over again."

"Can't you change it?"

Sofia laughed, but it wasn't a joyful laugh. "I've spent the last three days asking myself that same question." She paused for a full minute before continuing. "He's abusive. Not sexually…at least not yet. But he watches me. He controls every aspect of my life. It's like he's waiting for something. All I could do the first time was keep my head down and wait until I graduated. But I'm different now. I know how to defend myself. If he touches me, I'll put him down."

"Wow, Sofia, I had no idea."

"It's not something you lead with when you meet a nice guy. But given the circumstances, I thought you should know."

"If it's any consolation, you turn out pretty good. I mean, the other night at Tommy's party, you seemed like you had it all together."

"I'm a good actor. New York's full of them, though most won't admit it. I guess I was around it so much, it rubbed off on me. That's one of the reasons I left. I was tired of pretending. I wanted something real in my life. Look at me now. I'm pretending to be a seventeen year old girl with her whole life ahead of her."

"I don't know what to tell you except that you don't have to make the same choices the second time around. I'm looking at this as an opportunity to be the husband I should have been the first time."

"Sounds like you've accepted it. You think this is permanent?"

"I don't know what it is. But I figure as long as I'm here, I may as well try to make my life better. This could be a gift."

"It feels more like a cruel joke."

"But it doesn't have to be. Maybe I'm supposed to help you see it differently."

"What, like *It's a Wonderful Life*? Are you my guardian angel?"

"No, not that. More like a fellow traveler with a different perspective."

"Now we're fellow travelers. I was beginning to think you didn't want me along for this ride."

"It's not that. I'm just as confused as you are. I'll admit our current roles here make it more challenging than if we had woken up in 2010. But we can work around that."

"Are you saying you'll work with me? You know, try to figure it out?"

"I can't make any promises that we'll know anything more than we do now, but I give you my word that I won't abandon you. I'll help you in whatever way I can." Garren drove for several seconds thinking about what he had just promised. "We'll have to be discreet. If Officer Daniels finds out about us, he'll kill me."

"What about your wife?"

"What about her?"

"I want to meet her."

"Why would you want to do that?"

"Check out the competition."

Garren flashed her a look. "Seriously."

"I'm dead serious, Garren." In that moment, Sofia seemed all of thirty-seven. Then twenty years vanished as she started to giggle. "Lighten up, will ya? I'm just curious."

"About what?"

"I don't know." She shrugged. "I'd like to meet her. Besides, it only seems fair that if you are going to help me, I should return the favor."

"What can you do for me?"

"Obviously, you screwed it up the first time. I can give you some insider information. Don't let this school girl façade fool you. Inside is an experienced woman. I'm actually older than your wife is now. Think about that. And although we've only just met, I'm pretty sure I know you."

"Do you now?"

"Remember, I'm a bartender. I'm something of an expert when it comes to people. And we did have a pretty good night together."

Garren winced. "Yeah, about that. I'm having some difficulty remembering everything that happened that night. I think whenever we leaped back to this time, it must have done something to my memory."

Sofia laughed. "Or maybe it was all those drinks."

Garren cringed. "Well? Aren't you going to tell me what happened?"

"What's the last thing you remember?"

"I remember sitting on the couch with you. Tommy came over to talk with us. After that…yeah, that's about it."

Sofia made a funny little sound.

"What? What's that mean?"

"I means this is finally getting interesting."

"Aren't you going to tell me?"

"No, I think it will be more fun to keep you guessing."

"At least tell me if…" He couldn't say it.

"Tell you what?" She looked at him as if she were the teacher. "Oh, I get it. You want to know if you and I…" She laughed in earnest.

"Well?"

"Naw, you're going to have to earn that one."

"How am I supposed to do that?"

"You can start by figuring out how to get us back to our time."

"Are you serious?" Garren laughed. "You really expect me to crack the code on time-travel?"

"I can't do it," she replied. "I'm just a dumb kid from Dubuque."

"You *are* serious."

Sofia nodded and she wasn't smiling.

"I don't even know where to begin."

"I guess you better start asking around."

"Who am I going to ask who won't think I'm crazy?"

Sofia starting assessing her fingernails.

"What if I don't?"

She slowly turned to look at him. She had the hardened look of a thirty-seven year old bartender from New York. "I'll incentivize you."

Part Two

The Complication

13

Time was slowing down. At least that's what it seemed like to Garren Rosen. Every time he glanced at the clock on the classroom wall or the watch on his wrist, he was surprised to find that the minute hand had only moved slightly since the last time he looked. As an educated man, a man of reason, he knew that time was one of the most constant aspects of the human experience. It couldn't really be slowing down. But as a man who had actually traveled backward in time, he also knew that time was not as perfect as he once thought. Whatever that imperfection was, it somehow affected two humans by allowing them to slip from one time to another. The year 2020 had lost two of its own and the year 2001 had found them. So for Garren Rosen, the slowing of time was at least a possibility. Then again, it could have been a combination of two somewhat more mundane factors: 1) He was bluffing his way through a lecture on American government. Not that he didn't understand the material, but his dislike of it prevented him from giving it as much attention as he should have. And 2) Sofia Rae had moved to the front row and kept making faces at him that were more than a little distracting. Garren tried to direct his attention elsewhere in the class, but every few minutes she would cough or clear her throat. He would look her way only to find her winking and pursing her lips or anything to get a reaction from him. More than once, Garren had to put his hand over his mouth to conceal his amusement.

At 2:13, just seven minutes before the end of class, Garren started to wind down his lecture. "So we can see from these ten cases how the decisions made by just nine Supreme Court justices can affect the lives of three hundred thirty-four million U.S. citizens."

"Mr. Rosen," said a girl in the second row.

Sofia crossed her eyes and stuck out her tongue. Garren flashed her a *cut-that-out* look.

"Excuse me, Mr. Rosen?"

"Uh, yes, Miss...Frazelle."

"I thought you told us the population of the United States was two hundred and eighty million."

"That's right, Mr. Rosen," said Sofia. "I remember you saying that, too."

Out of the corner of his eye, Garren could see Sofia's smirk. "That is correct. Thank you for catching that mistake. Two hundred eighty million is the population of the United States today. However, by the time you all are my age, it will be over three hundred million, which only supports my argument. As the population increases, the influence of the few over the many increases as well."

"Mr. Rosen," Sofia said.

"Yes, Miss Rae."

"Will you tell us more about what life will be like when we're your age?"

Garren chuckled. He had to expect that from now on everything Sofia said would be packed with double meaning. To the uninformed observer, she would be just another curious adolescent. But to Garren, their shared predicament somehow gave her permission to mess with him. He would have to stay on his toes. "We can only make predictions based on trends we observe in history."

"Okay. What do you think my life will be like when I'm your age?"

"It doesn't really matter what I think. Your future is up to you. You make the choices that determine your path."

"Don't you believe in fate?"

Several students took notice of the taunt in Sofia's voice and sat up to listen. Finally, something more interesting than Supreme Court cases of the past. There was whispering in the back of the class and a few snickers.

"That's getting a bit off topic, Miss Rae. Let's get back to the Supreme Court. Based on the cases we have examined so far, has the Supreme Court ever been wrong? Mr. Quinn."

"Yes. Dred Scott versus Sandford, 1857."

The class settled back into their seats to wait out the last six minutes of class.

"Why do you think the court got it wrong?" Garren asked.

"Because you can't deny someone citizenship because of their race. That's wrong."

"It seems obvious to us now, in the year 2000, but America was quite different in 1857. Slavery was legal in over half of the states. The line between states' rights and federal law was hotly debated. The Civil War was just four years away. Our country was deeply divided. And the Supreme Court, being a product of that time, made a decision that our modern sensitivities find reprehensible. This is why we must study history. It reminds us that we humans are fallible. Even with our best intentions, we sometimes get it wrong. History also teaches us that we have the ability to recognize those wrongs and the responsibility to make the necessary corrections. Just eight years after the Dred Scott decision, Congress passed the thirteenth amendment to the Constitution abolishing slavery in the United States."

Several students yawned. A few near the back of the class began to close their notebooks and ready themselves for a quick dismissal at the sound of the bell. Those near the front, in full view of the teacher, had to wait.

"Yes," said Quinn, "but the Civil Rights movement didn't happen for another hundred years. A lot of people suffered while they waited for those corrections to take effect. Many never saw them."

"Change isn't easy," Garren replied to Mr. Quinn's comment, but he was looking at Sofia. "But it is possible. Even when the course seems fixed, we can alter it. We just have to determine what we want and keep going after it, even when it seems impossible."

"History is written by the victors," Sofia said. "It's easy to be hopeful when you aren't the one who's suffering."

"And yet hope is needed most by those who are suffering."

Most of the class tuned in to the tension between them and sat up again to listen.

"And they can have it if they want it bad enough. Is that what you're saying, Mr. Rosen?"

"Wanting it is part of it, yes."

"And keep on believing. Never say never, right?"

"Persistence is also important."

"Thank you, Justin Bieber. I feel so much better now that you've explained it."

Not everyone was aware that something was going on between Mr. Rosen and Sofia.

"I'm just glad we've gotten over all that mess," said the girl sitting directly behind Sofia. "My dad says that this is the best time to be alive. He predicts the twenty-first century is going to awesome."

Sofia turned in her seat. "I've got a prediction for you. It's not awesome. In fact, it's awful."

"Miss Rae," Garren said, trying to steer the conversation back to safer waters. "This is a history class. Let's try to keep our comments relevant to our subject."

"You're right, Mr. Rosen. This is history and my comments are quite relevant. George W. Bush will be our next president."

"Sofia," Garren cut in. "I'm going to have to ask you to not interrupt our class."

"Go ahead. Ask away. Do you all want to know what else is coming?"

"Sofia, please."

"There's going to be a terrorist attack next year."

"This is not the time or the place."

"Oh, I think it is."

Now the entire class was clued in, though they had no idea what was really happening. When Sofia got out of her desk, Garren made the mistake of reaching for her arm.

"Don't touch me," Sofia snapped and made a show of jerking her arm away from him.

"Sofia," he said, trying to remain calm and evasive. "Think about what you're doing."

"I have thought about this. This is me exercising my ability to recognize the wrongs and accepting my responsibility to make corrections." She turned to address the class. "On September—"

Garren's penchant for historical trivia told him that the phrase *saved by the bell* originated from the old English practice of attaching bells to coffins as a precautionary measure to prevent comatose patients from being buried alive. But in that moment, he took it to mean something else. The dismissal bell prevented Sofia from revealing more about the future and literally saved Garren from having to physically stop her. The class, more eager to end the school day than to figure out what in the world was going on between their teacher and Sofia, noisily collected their personals and made the dash for the exit. Sofia folded her arms across her chest and Garren busied himself with his briefcase while they waited for the room to clear. When the last student exited, Garren shut the door.

"What was that about?" he demanded.

Sofia casually collected her things. "Incentive, my dear Garren. Unless you want more of that, I suggest you get out your rolodex and start making some phone calls."

"Do you realize how dangerous that was? What if these kids actually heard what you were saying?"

"Like they would actually listen to me. But I am glad you see it my way."

"What do you mean?"

"You and I, we're both dangerous here. Either one of us could say or do something that could irrevocably alter the past."

"At least I'm not being reckless."

"Oh yeah?" Sofia laughed. "Let's check the score board. Who decided to play speed racer in a school zone?"

"I wasn't in a school zone," Garren countered.

"You know what I mean. Now shut up and let me continue. Who's chaperoning the Valentine's Day dance? Yeah, I overheard that and I know for a fact you didn't do it the first time because I was there with Eddie Craven, who I will not be going with this time because he's a creep and aptly named. What else? Oh, yeah. Who told their Current Events class about Facebook and downloadable music? I know it wasn't Mark Zuckerberg because he's just a kid right now. And who hasn't done their homework for this class? You again, Mr. Three Hundred and Thirty-Four Million people in the U.S. Oh, and what could possibly go wrong with this one? Who's trying to be the husband he wasn't the first time around? Please, I beg you, please keep the intimate details to yourself. I really don't want to hear it."

Garren stood motionless, unable to respond.

Sofia continued. "What have I been doing during this little fieldtrip to the past? I'm perpetually grounded for being rebellious and disrespectful to my elders. I'm what you would call a troubled child. As for my little performance here…well, that's to be expected from the weird kid." She grabbed her backpack. "Now, if you'll excuse me, I have to meet the foster dad…the cop…in his police car…in front of the school…in front of everybody." She headed for the door.

"Wait."

She stopped, but kept her back to him. "Make it fast. He's not a patient man."

"What do you mean by *weird kid*?"

She didn't answer.

"Sofia?" He noticed she was trembling. "Hey, talk to me."

She shook her head.

"What's going on here?"

"Nothing. I have to go." She started for the door.

Garren caught her arm and turned her around. Her face was moist with tears. "Help me understand."

She took a deep shuttering breath. "Do you really want to know?"

"Yes."

"Okay." She took another breath to steady herself. "Do you remember the kid in school that never quite fit in? The one everybody knows about, but nobody really knows?"

"Yes."

"That's me. I'm that kid."

"Are you kidding me? Look at you. You're smart. You're funny. And I know I'm not supposed to notice this because I'm your teacher, but you are absolutely beautiful. I assumed you were popular."

"Not even close."

"How could you not be?"

"Let's just say nobody wants to hang out with the crazy girl."

"I don't understand."

"I'm kind of an alien."

Garren gave her a sideways look.

"Not *that kind* of alien, but I feel like it. I mean, this isn't my life. I'm not supposed to be here. I'm not even from Dubuque. I didn't tell you because I wanted you to like me."

"Tell me what? I won't think you're weird. I promise."

"Okay, but don't say I didn't warn you. My life started out normal. I was born in Colorado. When I was five, my family…my *real* family…moved to Montana. I was a normal, happy kid. It was a great life. Two years ago, my parents were killed in a car accident. My sister, who was twenty at the time, disappeared. She left me and ran off with some guy. Like I said I won't see her again until two years from now. Anyway, I was put into a foster home. A year later, I was sent here to live with Officer Daniels and that woman. Maybe she's his wife, that's what he calls her, but there's something off about their relationship."

"That's terrible, but it doesn't make you a weird kid."

"No, but this does. I'm not allowed to have any friends. I'm not allowed to use the phone. I can't go anywhere, except for school functions, which I am required to attend. No one can come to my house. My bedroom door has a lock on the outside. I am randomly drug tested once or twice a month. There's more if you want to hear it."

"No, but I still don't get how that makes you an outcast."

"The cop knows everyone in this town. He's a respected servant of the community. They trust him. When he explains how his foster daughter continues to suffer the effects of the trauma she experienced from her biological family, which he saved her from, they believe him. Apparently, I'm on several medications. I'm a chronic liar. And I have deviant sexual tendencies. They're doing their best to save me, but I have a lot of issues to work through. So, I'm not exactly best friend material."

"Why do you stay?"

"I have nowhere to go. And freedom is in sight. My real dad taught me to take the long view. He used to say that suffering can be endured if you can see the end. I'm trying to honor him. In six months, I'll be a legal adult with a high school diploma. And I guess I'll be heading to New York then. At least I know where to go when I get there."

"Wow, Sofia. I don't know what to say, except I'm so sorry you got thrown back into this. Now I understand why you want out so badly. I wish there was something I could do to help."

"You can try to get us out of here."

"You do realize how impossible that is."

Sofia chuckled. "Yeah, about as impossible as us being here, yet here we are."

"You have a point."

"If we can figure out how this happened, maybe we can reverse it."

"If we can't?"

Sofia re-shouldered her backpack. "At least I know he doesn't kill me. I gotta go."

O n his way out of the school parking lot, Garren saw Officer
Daniels yelling at Sofia inside his patrol car. After hearing her
story, he couldn't bring himself to think of the man as her father. He
could barely think of him as an officer of the law. So he decided to call
him Cruller from here on out. For one thing, the guy probably ate a
lot of doughnuts. But more importantly, the nickname sounded like
Cruella Deville, the evil woman from Disney's *101 Dalmatians*. He
knew it was corny, so he decided to keep it as his own private joke.

With Cruller and Sofia in his rearview mirror, Garren started for
home. He intended to go there, study for a while and then enjoy a
quiet evening with Kate, but he couldn't get Sofia out of his mind.
How could he, in good conscience, go back to his peaceful abode
knowing what she was having to deal with? Her words kept playing
over and over in his mind until he couldn't stand it anymore. Instead
of making the right turn that would take him to the apartment, he
turned left toward the university. He had an idea. It was an impossible
longshot, but then again they were in an impossible situation.

Pulling onto the campus of the University of Dubuque, he had a
strange feeling. In less than two years, he will be a member of the
faculty and part of the campus life of UD. But in 2000, he was a
visitor. None of the men and women who will become his colleagues
knew him. If they saw him now, they would assume he was just one of
the 1,500 students. He drove slowly through the campus, not because
he didn't know where he was going, but in order to build up his nerve

for what he was about to do. Given the time of day, it was easy to find a parking spot in front of the University Science Department. He hoped the man he came to see would be in his office.

"Come in." The voice behind the door was that of an older gentleman, refined and shaped by an English accent that had been worn down by decades on this side of the pond. At the sound of it, a lump began to form in Garren's throat. In 2003, the two men will begin a deep friendship that will last until Dr. Finney's untimely death in 2010.

"Dr. Finney." It was all he could do to keep from embracing the man and telling him how much his own life had been enriched by him. "My name is Garren Rosen. I'm a teacher at Hempstead High School."

Dr. Finney was exactly what you would expect of a science professor – a bifocalled man in his sixties, wild hair, large nose and severe eyebrows. He got up from his desk, depositing his glasses into the clutter that was his desktop, and came around with his hand extended. "What can I do for you, Mr. Rosen?"

Garren shook the man's hand, marveling at his presence. "If you've got a minute, I have an odd request."

"In my experience, odd requests are the best kind. I have…" Finney glanced at his watch. "…twenty-two minutes before I have to head across campus. Have a seat." He sat down in one of the two armchairs, crossed his legs and folded his hands beneath his chin. It was a position Garren knew well, as he had spent many hours in this very office discussing the many intersections of their two disciplines. "Topic?"

"Time," Garren said. "Actually, time-travel."

"Theoretical or practical?"

"I'm not sure."

"Perhaps I can help you narrow your focus. What is the thesis of your paper?"

"I'm not writing a paper. As I said, I'm a history teacher at Hempstead—"

"Oh, yes, yes, you did say that. Forgive me. I'm a bit scattered today. History, you say. Ah, so you would be interested in traveling back in time." He chuckled. "That would be a useful tool in your field, yes?"

"Yes, it would. Let me get to the point. I'm considering an assignment I would like to give to one of my classes. I'm going to ask them to imagine traveling back in time to an historical event of their choice and write about it as if they were living it. You know, like a news reporter."

"Excellent idea. Put them into the thick of it. Give them a real feel for history. I like that."

"Although the focus is not on the science of time travel, per se, I want them to be as realistic as possible about the entire experience. So I thought if I could help them understand a little about how they arrive at their destination in history, it might give them some better insight." Dr. Finney peered at Garren over his tented fingers, but didn't say anything. The silence caused him to wonder if the professor had already written him off, so he added, "I asked around and was told that you might be able to help me."

Dr. Finney shifted in his chair. "I have given this subject a fair amount of thought…as much as anyone here I suppose. But mind you, I am no Einstein."

Relieved, Garren leaned forward and pressed the subject. "If time-travel were possible, how would one go about doing it?"

"Well, I suppose one would have to construct a time machine." Dr. Finney chuckled again. It was his nature to add levity to matters of severity. "That's the short answer, mind you. The real answer, of course, is a fair bit more complicated. One would first have to understand time itself. Does it flow like a river? Is it playing out like a film? Is it scripted like the pages of a book? Each of these analogies offers its own requirement as to how one would be able to move back and forth through time. For example, if time is like a river and we are floating along in its current, one would have to figure out a way to move against that current. You could either step out of the river and travel upon the shore to your desired point or you could devise a way to travel upstream; like a motorboat is able to maneuver contrary to the current. If time is like a film, you as the observer would not necessarily have to leave the theater, but you would call up to the projection booth and request that it be run backward or cut to another scene. If time is like a book, then we might conclude that all of history is already written, and the we, the readers, would have to develop the ability to turn the pages against their natural turning."

"I see," said Garren. Actually, he couldn't see, for he was lost somewhere in the river. "Suppose there is no time machine. What if someone just…oh, I don't know…woke up in the past? Can you imagine any way in which that might happen?"

"Ah, a natural, or rather an *un*natural phenomenon."

"Yes, that's more of what I had in mind. Suppose a man went to sleep in one time and woke up in the past. Are you aware of any forces in nature that could cause that?"

"Yes. We wonder what lies within a black hole. We know that the gravitational forces in the vicinity of a black hole are of the magnitude such that it bends light. It is theorized that time itself could be affected. Of course, you would not be able to survive such an experience to know where or when you came out. Wormholes are another possibility. This is posited as an explanation to the equations in Einstein's theory of general relativity. But again, I am afraid one would be hard pressed to find a wormhole, and then again the effects are unknowable. And then there is the theory of—"

"Dr. Finney," Garren cut in, "I'm sorry to interrupt, but that's not quite what I'm looking for. Let me put it to you another way. Suppose a man went to sleep on December 31, 2019 and woke up on January 1, 2000. And now this man is living out the natural flow of history in the year 2000, but he can remember the next twenty years as if he has already lived them. Suppose such a man came to you for help. What would you say to him?" It was a lot more than Garren planned to reveal, but theories weren't helping. He hoped Dr. Finney wouldn't thank him for wasting his time.

"I would say he is in quite a predicament," Dr. Finney chuckled again, but then he stared hard at Garren, his mind working the problem. "But seriously, I would begin by determining whether the man was sane or delusional or simply having a bit of fun at my expense."

"Suppose you found him to be quite sane and serious."

"We seem to have gone far afield from the assignment you are considering for your students."

Garren felt his time with the professor was about to come to an end. Then another idea came to him. "Yes, we have. Dr. Finney, I haven't been completely honest with you. I am a teacher, but this is not for an assignment. I didn't think you'd take me seriously if I told you the truth. I, uh, I'm writing a novel."

"Oh, thank heavens. For a moment, I thought you were going to tell me this happened to you. I'm quite relieved. A novel, you say. Why didn't you tell me that in the first place? I've dabbled in that arena myself." He looked at his watch. "I'm afraid we're running out of time…unlike the character in your story who seems to have been given quite a bit of time. Perhaps you will come back again and we can talk further about your story."

"I understand, and I don't mean to hold you up, but is there anything you can tell me right now that would at least put me on the right track? My character is a little desperate to understand what's happened to him."

Dr. Finney got up and talked as he gathered his notes. "Just thinking off the top of my head, I would want to know something about the conditions of 2019. What was the man doing? What was happening around him? Was he exposed to anything? Are there villains in the mix? What is the last thing he remembers? Did he see or hear or smell or taste anything strange? Of course, I should like to give this some more consideration. Fiction must still be believable. Come back again and we'll talk some more. I'm sure we'll be able to get your character back to where he belongs. Or at least we'll have fun trying, yes?"

"Thank you for listening, Dr. Finney. I will come back. And thank you for the insight. You've given me some things to think about."

"Good day, Mr. Rosen."

As Garren left Dr. Finney's office, he heard the old man muttering to himself about time-travel. Perhaps he'd made more progress than expected. The professor was at least pondering the problem. Maybe their next conversation would yield some real answers. He hurried back to his car where he intended to write down some of the things Dr. Finney wanted to know about the conditions of 2019. No sooner did he get outside than he heard his name. He stopped and turned around.

"Kate. I didn't expect to run into you."

"What are you doing here?"

"Just something for school."

Kate looked up at the building. "In the science department?"

"Yeah, just a thing I'm working on. How's your day going?"

"Better now." She looked at the building again and then put it out of her mind. "I was going to the library to study, but since you're here, do you want to get a cup of coffee?"

"Sure."

Coffee with Kate was a welcome distraction from Sofia's sad story and the problem of time-travel. It also confirmed Sofia's accusation. Garren did prefer this time. Even if it were possible to get back to 2020, he didn't think he would take it. In fact, if he could stop time and just be with Kate in that very moment, he would be tempted to do it. The expression on her face and the sound of her voice as she recounted her morning lecture made him fall in love with her all over again. This was the real Kate, the Kate with whom he should have been sharing that boat on the river of time, the Kate who should have been with him on New Year's Eve 2019. Whether he altered history or not, he determined right then and there to prevent the other Kate from ever taking her place. He would help Sofia if he could, but he was not about to jeopardize his chance at a better second time around.

"Garren, did you hear what I said?"

"Huh?"

"You zoned out on me again. What are you thinking about?"

"Time…" It slipped out before he knew it, and then the desire to tell her the truth came roaring back to him. Why couldn't he tell her? Dr. Finney didn't think him crazy. Of course, the truth was hidden in a fictitious story, but at least it gave him a way to talk about it. Maybe he could do the same with Kate. She would never believe he was actually writing a novel, but she might believe he was reading one. "… travel. I was thinking about time-travel. It's this book I'm reading."

"Oh, yeah? What's it called?"

"What's it called?" Garren scolded himself for not coming up with a title first, and the only time-travel movie he could think of was *Terminator.* "Uh, it's called, uh…" Glancing around for anything that sounded like it might be the title of a book, he spotted a blue receptacle next to the trash can. "*Recycle.* Yeah, I think that's it. *Recycle.*"

She bought it. "What I would give to be able to read a novel again. As soon as I finish my degree, I'm going to read all the Harry Potter books. So, tell me about it?"

"What? My book?"

"Yeah, what's it about?"

Garren could hardly believe it. He could finally tell her what was happening to him without actually telling her. "It's about this guy who goes to sleep in one time and wakes up twenty years earlier. And he gets to relive those years and fix everything he did wrong the first time around."

"When he wakes up, he knows everything that will happen to him," Kate guessed.

"Not exactly. He remembers the big stuff, but he can't remember everything. I mean, can you remember everything you did twenty years ago?"

"I was only five."

"Okay, ten years ago or even five."

"Oh, yeah. That would be pretty frustrating."

"Believe me, it is. I mean that's part of the story. He knows what his life could become if he does nothing, so he tries to change it."

"Does he?"

"I don't know. I'm only about a third of the way into it. But he's trying."

"What happened to his younger self?"

"What do you mean?"

"If the older version of himself went back in time, his younger version had to go somewhere."

"I haven't thought about that."

"Maybe he switched places and now his younger self is living in the future."

Garren really hadn't considered this possibility. What if thirty year old Garren woke up in his fifty year old life? He shuddered to think of what he might be doing. "That could be bad."

"You know what else would be bad?"

"What?"

"If he woke up back in his original time before he had a chance to fix anything."

"Gee, I haven't thought about that either."

"If that happened to me, I would write myself some notes."

"Notes. Why? About what?"

"About everything. Think about it. If the guy might switch back at any moment, he could at least leave messages for his younger self so he knows what's coming – investments, decisions, ideas, accidents, tragedies. He could be his own teacher."

"How did you think of all that?"

Kate shrugged. "Same reason we have cases of water and toilet paper in our apartment. I just think of what could happen. Anyway, I hope I didn't ruin your book."

"No, not at all. I really have no idea how the story will end." Garren felt the urge to hug her, just in case he was suddenly sucked back to the future, but also because she had provided some ideas he should have already considered. He made a mental note to stop by the bookstore and buy a new notebook.

15

G arren arrived at school early on Thursday morning hoping to
catch Sofia before the first bell. He wanted to tell her about
his meeting with Dr. Finney and give her a gift. Inspired by Kate's
comments about time-travel, he stopped by the bookstore and
purchased two matching blank books. He'd already designated them
time journals in which he and Sofia would record as much as they
could remember about the next twenty years. They would agree to
put each other's contact information on the first page, along with
a note explaining their connection. That way, if a correction did
occur and they were suddenly returned to 2020, their younger selves
might benefit from their knowledge of the future. The thought of
his younger self troubled him ever since Kate mentioned it. Where
was he now? *When* was he? Could they have really switched places?
Was thirty year old Garren wandering around in the year 2020 as
his older self? What must that be like? For all the good he was trying
to do in the past, he might also be making things worse for himself
in the future. Thinking about it made his head hurt. Best to focus
on the task at hand. He and Sofia were living in a past that was far
better for him than it was for her. He couldn't abandon her to her
circumstances. He had to help. The time journal wasn't the way back
to 2020 she wanted, but it was something. At the very least, it was a
distraction. At best, it might help her see some good in a situation
that so far was all bad.

At 7:25, the ten-minute warning bell rang. Still no sign of Sofia. Garren abandoned his post in the commons and made his way to his first class. Maybe he'd missed her, or maybe she was just running late.

The morning hours passed sluggishly like they do at the Department of Motor Vehicles. Garren sympathized with his students. Most of them sat in their desks like mannequins; physically there, but mentally somewhere else. Unlike them, he didn't have the luxury of staring blankly at nothing or doodling mindlessly in the margins of his notes. He was the teacher and it took all of his mental strength to stick to his lesson. With each bell, both he and his students breathed a sigh of relief that another period of the high school experience was safely archived in the vault of the past, never to be endured again. That is, unless another glitch in time sent one of them back to repeat it. That was now a possibility, but Garren could deal with only two time-travelers at a time. At the end of each class, he stood at the door and scanned the moving masses for Sofia. They were connected now. Even if he couldn't get her back to the future, he felt obligated to be there for her in the past…or was it the present?

Eleven o'clock found Garren in the library. It was the most public place where he could camp out without looking too much out of place. Perhaps Sofia would come looking for him there like she had the day before. At 11:03, the fifth period bell rang and the halls became deserted again. A handful of students were in the library. A few of them cast suspicious glances his way, wondering why a teacher had invaded the student domain.

In an effort to look like he belonged there, Garren took out his time journal and opened it to the first page. Its blankness dared him to make the first mark. It was as if time itself were waiting to see whether he would actually go through with it. Then a series of question marks formed over his great idea. Was it even permissible for him to record things yet to come? Was it morally right? Wasn't the future supposed to be undetermined, blank like the pages before him? Wouldn't committing it to the ink of his pen be a violation of its freedom? Who was he to commit the timeline of history to a fixed course of events? Or was it fixed? Was history bound to play out exactly as he remembered it? The fact that he was even able to consider such a thing suggested it was not; that it could be changed. After all, was he not attempting to alter his own history? That felt right for his own life, but what about the other lives he was affecting by his efforts? And what if his time journal were to fall into the hands of someone else? What right did he have to deprive a native of this time the wonder of experience, the discovery of each day as it happened? Garren closed the book and backed away as if it were something dangerous. Then it occurred to him that the threat resided within himself. He was the anomaly here. It was his knowledge of the future that would turn a harmless journal into a potential weapon. More questions came. What if the outcome of the next five presidential elections were to become known to the losers? What if people knew what Disney was going to do to *Star Wars*? What if he prevented the 2005 resurgence of disco? Those were minor *what ifs* compared to things he didn't want to think about. If he abandoned the idea now, the journal could become what it was intended to be, a record of the past or a wish for dreams that may or may not come true. Still, there were the advantages he and Sofia could give to themselves – investment tips, a warning about a bad decision, a head start on a great idea. If they were careful, agreed to some guidelines, they could avoid screwing up the timeline of history and still provide their younger selves an advantage. Small consolation for the cruel hand time had dealt them. Yes, *them.* Sofia's troubles had become his troubles. While he would make good on his second time around with Kate, he would also bear as much of Sofia's suffering as he could for her. They were in this together, bound by their immigrant status. He opened and closed the book three more times before he cautiously began jotting down some initial thoughts.

By the time the sixth period bell rang, Garren had filled ten pages of the journal. He'd composed his letter to himself, explaining as much of the situation as he could, including Sofia. He would get her contact information next time he saw her. He'd also written a list of guidelines along with a stern warning to keep the journal a secret. Then he had the beginnings of a rudimentary outline of the next twenty years. The big events were easy. The small ones would take more thought. Proud of his initial efforts, he placed the journal into his briefcase and hurried to his next class.

The Driver's Ed. lot was located behind the school. It wasn't elaborate, just a cordoned off section of the junior parking lot with orange cones and a few wooden cutouts of pedestrians that had suffered mercilessly at the hands of juvenile pranksters. Three matching Geo Metros were parked in a line, each emblazoned with decals that read: WARNING: STUDENT DRIVER. Two of the cars bore the marks of their service. The third, referred to simply as *the good car*, was reserved for those students who had proven themselves in the lot and were deemed ready for the public streets.

Garren was surprised to find Principal Jenson and Coach Carmichael talking with his students.

"Mr. Rosen," said Principal Jenson. "Come with me."

Garren heard some snickering from the students and someone said, "Busted."

When they were a good ways from the group, the principal stopped. "It has come to our attention that you were involved in an incident with a police officer early Tuesday morning."

"Yes, Ma'am."

"Did you receive a speeding ticket?"

"Yes, Ma'am."

"Mr. Rosen, I am sure I do not need to remind you that teaching is more than simply relaying information. It is about setting an example. We are role models for our students. Therefore, our behavior both on and off campus matters. We do not have the luxury of leaving our jobs at the end of the day. When we encounter a student beyond these walls, we are still responsible to set a positive example."

"I understand," Garren said.

"Then I do not need to tell you that this is a very serious matter."

"No, Ma'am." Garren understood the mixed emotions all students must feel when they are reprimanded for bad behavior: Shame, embarrassment and the urge to retaliate with sarcasm. He didn't say it, but he thought, *But I'll bet you're going to tell me anyway.*

"What if our students begin to think that because their teacher can drive like a…like a…like a speed demon, they can do the same? What if one of our students follows your poor example and hurts themselves or someone else? What if one of these precious children dies because of your recklessness? Do you realize how serious this is?"

"Yes, Ma'am." Garren thought she was a little over the top, but he kept himself in check.

"I like you, Mr. Rosen, and our students like you. So I take no pleasure in informing you of the consequences of your actions."

"Are you firing me?"

"No, but I have no choice but to remove you from the Driver's Education program. Coach Carmichael will take the remainder of your classes."

Garren was actually relieved. He didn't particularly like Driver's Ed. to begin with. Besides, he wouldn't mind another study period.

"And you will take Coach Carmichael's Freshman P.E. class."

"Oh?"

"Is that a problem?"

"No, Ma'am. Just unexpected, that's all."

"Good. Then I suggest you go to the gym. Your students are waiting for you."

As Garren made his way to the gymnasium, he felt more than a little slighted. Gym class was bad enough. Freshman gym class was the worst. But he did bring it upon himself. Had he just kept his cool that morning, he wouldn't have been speeding and he wouldn't have been pulled over and he wouldn't have....Then it hit him. His carelessness had started a chain of events with untold consequences.

Freshman P.E. turned out to be everything Garren feared. There was no written curriculum. Whatever plan the coach followed was likely committed to memory from years of repetition. The boys were immature, obnoxious and dangerously out of control. The girls were timid, self-conscious and mortified to be seen in the mandatory uniforms. Once he identified the class leaders, he pretty much let them run whatever game they were playing. By the end of the period, no one had been hurt and everyone seemed to have their proper clothes on. All-in-all, not a complete disaster. He would have to put some thought around the days ahead, but that would have to wait. He was eager to get to his last class and Sofia.

As students began trickling in, Garren tried not to look too eager. He couldn't risk tipping any of them off to his special relationship with Sofia. He occupied himself by writing the day's topic and a few bullet points on the board; sneaking an occasional glance over his shoulder at her empty desk. When the bell rang, he went to the door and looked both ways down the hall.

"Has anyone seen Sofia Rae today?" he asked.

No one responded. One of the boys in the back of the class leaned over and whispered something that caused the girl next to him to snicker.

The punk annoyed Garren, but he couldn't show it. "Has anyone talked with her since yesterday?"

"She's probably on West 6th," said someone. This caused the class to laugh.

Garren picked up a book and slammed it on the desk, silencing them. "Hey! Let's show some respect."

West 6th Avenue was the location of the Dubuque Juvenile Detention Center. Apparently, Sofia's assessment of her reputation was accurate. Her classmates believed the lies planted by Officer Daniels and no doubt concocted a few of their own. The cruelty of youth surprised him as much as his blindness to it. All of this had gone on the first time around. Sofia had endured it right under his nose, but he was too fixated on his own life to notice the hurting girl in the front row. Not this time. Now that he knew her and the hard road she'd already traveled once, he couldn't remain silent.

"Do any of you even know Sofia? Where she came from? The kind of life she's had? The kind of person she is? Well, do you?"

"I heard she got in trouble at her last school," said one of the boys. "And she's already on probation here."

"Yeah, I heard they had to take her away from her family because they couldn't handle her," said another.

"I heard she spent time in a mental hospital."

"I was warned to stay away from her."

"I heard she's a witch or something."

"Okay, okay," said Garren. "That's enough. You've heard some things, but you don't *know* anything. You don't know that she's smart and funny. You don't know how brave she is. You don't know that she has this ability to read you in a minute, but she'd never use it against you. You don't know that she's not afraid to be honest and that makes you want to be honest, too. You don't know how great she is because you'll never give her the chance to show you."

"How do you know all that, Mr. Rosen?" The question came with a hint of suspicion.

"Yeah, how do you know Sofia so well?"

In truth, it had been less than a week since Garren and Sofia met, and although they'd only really spoken a few times, he knew her in a way he knew no one else. They shared a secret that connected them in a way no other human being could even begin to understand. Looking at the inquisitive faces of his students, he realized he may have said too much. So he decided to say a little more.

"I'm going to tell you something you probably won't hear from anyone else. In a few months, you're going graduate and get on with your lives. You'll go to college, have careers, get married, raise families. It will be great for a while. But you'll blink and twenty years will pass. You'll hate your job. The excitement will have gone from your marriage. Your kids…let me tell you about your kids. They'll be about as old as you are now, and they're going to see you exactly the same way you see your parents. Any coolness you think you have now will be long gone. No one will care that you used to be popular or that you played football or were voted cutest couple. They won't even care what your grades were. And then one day you're going to see her, the girl everyone used to whisper about. It might be in a bar in New York or at a New Year's Eve party, but when you see how cool and beautiful she is…well, you're going to wish you'd gotten to know her when you had the chance. I've seen the future…" Garren paused when he saw the expression on their faces. "What I'm trying to say is there's more to life than high school. And you are so much more than your high school reputation. Don't believe everything you hear. Let people show you who they are. You just might be surprised by what you find. Now, let's talk about next week's exam."

16

Sofia's absence haunted Garren, causing his mind to play a game of worst-case-scenario. The last time he saw her, she was slunk down in the passenger seat of a police car with Cruller going off on her. What if things got out of hand? What if Cruller tried to hit her again? What if Sofia made good on her promise to put him down? Although the size differential put her at a disadvantage, he would not expect her to fight back. And whatever skills she might have acquired over the next twenty years could tip the scales in her favor. What if she'd done it and was now on the run?

Garren knew he couldn't just wait to see if she would show up at school the next day. He had to see her. On his way to the office, he hoped to find it unoccupied or so busy with everyone trying to get home that no one would notice him. Either way, he had to find Sofia's home address. Rounding the corner, he saw the office aide talking on the phone and an idling computer next to her. Then he remembered Sofia's advice. He slowed his pace, tried to look bored and sat down next to the aide. He'd never tried to access the student directory before, but figured it wouldn't be too difficult. The directory was easy enough to find, but when he clicked on it, a password window appeared. He must have done something to draw the attention of the aide because within seconds a slip of paper with a single word written on it slid into view. He looked up to find her smiling at him, but still talking on the phone. He mouthed the words *thank you* and opened the directory. A quick search produced what he was looking for and he was on his way.

He half-hoped to find Sofia waiting for him at his car. A vision of her tossing his keys to him flitted through his mind. What if they had been seen leaving the school together? Gossip travels fast in a small town. What if Cruller got wind of it and that's why he was so upset? Another vision flashed through his mind: Officer Daniels lying on the floor with a kitchen knife in his chest, the wife screaming, Sofia fleeing in a stolen car. Would she take the police car or the family sedan?

Garren got into his car and fired up the engine. He was tempted to let the muscle car perform as it was intended, but he kept his cool and eased his way through the lot and entered the long line of cars waiting to exit the campus. The wait was agonizing. Every student he saw, whether walking or in a car, was happy in the freedom of another day's end. These were the same students who either ignored Sofia or perpetuated the lies about her. None of them knew her. None of them cared. It occurred to Garren that he was probably the only person on the planet who cared what happened to this lost and lonely girl. Even if they weren't bound together by time, knowing the truth about her, he would have gone after her all the same.

Finally, he was next to enter the flow of traffic. The urge to muscle his way in was strong, but he resisted at the sight of a police car approaching from the left. He waited and feigned boredom. As the cruiser closed in, its lights flashed and the siren chirped. Officer Daniels peered at him over the top of his mirrored sun glasses and made a two-fingered gesture to indicate he was watching. Garren had seen the trope a hundred times in movies and television shows. By 2019, it had become a cheesy cliché, but perhaps in the year 2000 some still found it intimidating. Garren was too relieved to see Cruller was still alive to do anything but stare. Hopefully, that meant Sofia wasn't in as much trouble as he feared. Rather than taking the chance of catching up to the police car, Garren flipped on his left turn signal and took advantage of the next opening.

Without his smart phone or GPS, Garren had to find Sofia's house the old fashioned way. He stopped three times to ask directions, but no one had ever heard of the obscure residential street. After two more stops, he found a printed street map. Then he had to figure out how to use it. Fortunately his young eyes were able to decipher the microscopic print. What should have taken ten minutes turned into a thirty minute hunt, but he was there – 111 Woodmoor Drive, first house on the right. It was a nice house on a large, well-tended lot. It seemed to Garren too extravagant for a police officer's salary. Then again, his impression of the man rendered other streams of income entirely within the realm of possibility.

Garren rolled past the house, taking in as much of the scene as he could without looking like a stalker. He didn't want to catch the attention of the neighbors. A man like Cruller likely had a finger on the pulse of his own neighborhood. The lurking of a suspicious vehicle, especially one as distinctive as Garren's, would get back to him. The house looked vacant – empty driveway, garage closed, curtains open except for one of the rooms upstairs. Could that be Sofia's bedroom? He zeroed in on it, hoping to see some movement. Supposing she was up there waiting for him to come and rescue her was too much to expect; a product of his modified worst-case-scenario. Cruller was still alive, but that didn't mean Sofia was out of the woods. He continued on Woodmoor Drive all the way to the end and turned around. He could make one more slow pass. More than that would be too risky. Slowing down just a little, house now on his left, he casually glanced toward it, focusing his attention on the suspected window. Still no movement. He stopped at the entrance to the neighborhood, waiting for a truck to pass. He made one more glance at the house in his rearview mirror and determined to come back later. Perhaps in the dark with lights on in the house, he might catch a glimpse of her.

Garren didn't quite know what to do. He had a few hours before Kate would be home. He could drive around to some of the area shopping spots on the slim chance that he might find Sofia walking around. Would she do that? Not if she were grounded. She might, however, if she were left unattended and was gutsy enough to think Cruller wouldn't find her as he patrolled his beat. Glancing at the map, it looked like a mile or two to the nearest commercial area. Not out of the question, but the temperature was only about thirty degrees and the wind was starting to pick up. It would be a tough hike. With nothing to lose, he headed that way.

His instincts were right. No sooner did he pull into the lot than he spotted a group of what appeared to be teenagers going into a coffee shop. Bundled up as they were, it was impossible to tell for sure if they were any of his kids. Of course, Sofia would not be part of their group, but the fact that they were there confirmed that young people did that sort of thing in 2000. Maybe Sofia was nearby. Cruising through the parking lot, it became apparent to him that he was not going to find her. In order to keep hope alive, he told himself that it was more likely that she would see him. He drove to the end of the lot and turned around to make another pass. Again, he felt conspicuous. He considered parking near the coffee shop and going in, but then he would have to buy something. He had already spent his last few dollars on the street map and Kate would ask him about the expenditure when the bank statement came in. He decided to just sit in his car for a minute and think.

He was already mentally spent from a full day of teaching, and his concern for Sofia had depleted his emotional energy. Try as he might, he couldn't think of anything else to do. It was looking more and more like he would just have to wait until the next day and hope Sofia would show up with a mundane reason for her absence, like a cold or something. He was just about to give up and head home when he saw something he hadn't seen in years. A payphone. Snatching the piece of paper with Sofia's address, he was pleased with himself that he had the foresight to write down her phone number. Now all he needed was a quarter. Fishing in his pocket for the change he received from the purchase of the map, he found a dime and three pennies. A quick search through the ashtray and under the seats yielded a gum wrapper, a French fry, a pair of concert ticket stubs, a hair clip with three blonde hairs that did not belong to Kate and a quarter. He jumped out of his car and quick-stepped it toward the phone, tossing the artifacts of his past into a trash can along the way. He deposited the quarter and punched in the seven digits. If anyone other than Sofia answered, he would hang up. In the unlikely event Cruller had caller ID on his home phone, it wouldn't matter anyway.

The phone rang five times before there was a click and a female voice told him that no one was there to take his call, but if he left his name and number, someone would get back to him. The voice sounded young and flirty. Not that he needed proof that Sofia was telling him the truth, but it did support her assessment of the wife. A picture of Sofia's 2000 experience was becoming clearer and it wasn't good. Dejected, Garren hung up the phone without leaving a message and returned to his car.

Feeling as if he had failed her, he drove home in silence. Radio off, speed a few miles below the posted speed limit, he would not allow himself even the simple pleasure of driving as long as Sofia's whereabouts remained unknown. He wasn't even sure how he would be able to enjoy Kate's company when she got home. He considered telling her about Sofia. At least that would explain his mood. But what could he tell her? How could he account for his concern for the girl without revealing the whole crazy story?

When Garren arrived home, he was surprised to find the door unlocked. "Kate?"

"We're in here," a man replied.

"Tommy? What are you doing here?" Rounding the corning into the living room, he was caught up in a strong embrace. "Sofia! You're here." He tried to hold her back, but she persisted.

"Just let me be like this for a minute."

"Okay." Garren looked to Tommy for an explanation, but only got a shrug and a blank stare.

After a minute, he gently pulled her arms from around him and held her so he could get a look at her. He sucked in at what he saw. "What happened?"

Sophia's lip was swollen and cut, and her left eye was blackened. She winced as she tried to smile. "You know."

"Do you want to tell me about it?" Garren asked.

"Not now."

"Dude," said Tommy, "Over here."

Garren led Sofia to the couch. "You okay for a minute?"

"Yes."

Garren joined Tommy in the kitchen. "What happened? Where did you find her?"

"Here," Tommy explained. "I came by to get something to eat and found her huddled at your door. She said she was a friend of yours. I couldn't leave her out in the cold, so I let her in. I hope that was okay."

"Yes, of course. What time was that?"

"Around noon. Yeah, I didn't want to leave her alone, so I stayed. She's a little freaked out. I think she was in an accident or something." Tommy leaned in. "I think she must have hit her head."

"Why do you say that?"

Tommy looked like he was trying to find the right way to put it. "She mentioned that she's from the future."

Garren put his hands to his face and massaged his temples. "She said that."

"And get this," Tommy continued. "She said she knows both of us...from the future. That's weird, right? Because that struck me as weird."

"Okay." Garren returned to the living room. "Not quite what I had in mind, but let's see where this goes. Let's all have a seat."

Tommy took the chair and Garren sat down on the couch.

"First," Garren said to Sofia. "I've been worried sick about you. I went to your house. I called. I'm so relieved you're not…I'm glad you're okay. How did you find my apartment? Never mind. That doesn't matter. Do you want to tell me what happened?"

"No." Sofia cut her eyes toward Tommy. "Later."

"Okay…so how do we do this?"

"I told him. He knows, Garren."

"I heard. And you thought that was a good idea?"

"We need allies. People who know the truth and can help us."

"Why him?"

"First of all, he's your best friend. I figured we could trust him. And secondly, he's Tommy. I figured of all people he might actually believe us."

"He thinks it's weird."

"So do I," Sofia said. "This whole thing is crazy, but it's happening to us, Garren. And we need some help."

"What?" said Tommy. "You're from the future, too? Whoa."

The threesome sat in silence for a full minute. Sofia leaned into Garren's side and closed her eyes. Tommy looked like he was trying to solve a brainteaser. Garren just sat there, relieved to know Sofia was safe.

"How did this happen?" Tommy asked, his voice low and thoughtful.

"We don't know," Garren replied. "We just woke up in this time."

"When?"

"Five days ago. New Year's Day."

"What time are you from?"

"2020. Actually, the last thing I remember is New Year's Eve 2019, but I guess it's 2020 now. We were at a party at your apartment."

"We're still friends in 2020." Tommy chuckled. "That's good to know. But I still live in an apartment. That's kind of sad."

"It's a very nice apartment. One of those singles only places."

"Still single," Tommy said. "Figures."

Another minute passed as Tommy tried to wrap his head around it. "You don't look fifty."

"Huh?"

"In 2020, you'll be fifty years old. You still look like you. What's that about?"

"I guess my older self is still there."

"So, technically, you didn't really travel through time."

Garren was taken aback. "What do you mean?"

"There was no actual transference of matter. Nothing tangible from 2020 appeared in 2000. So, technically, you're still you."

"Well, yes, but in my head, I'm fifty. I have all the memories of the next twenty years."

"But technically, you're only thirty."

"Will you stop saying *technically*? The fact is, last week was 2019 for us and now it's 2000."

"How do you know you're not crazy?" Tommy offered.

"I've thought of that," Garren conceded. "But the same thing happened to Sofia. We can't both be suffering from the same delusion."

"It's not out of the realm of possibility," Tommy said.

"I'm not crazy," Sofia said without sitting up. "But I'm getting there."

"What does she mean by that?" Tommy asked.

"It's a long story. Let's just say this has been a lot easier for me than it has been for her."

"I can see that. Maybe we should put some ice on your face."

"I'm fine," she growled. "Keep talking. Believe it or not, this is helping."

Tommy leaned forward in his chair. "Do you mind if I ask you a few questions about the future?"

"Go for it," said Garren.

"Are there flying cars yet?"

"No, but self-driving cars are starting to show up in some cities."

"Have we put a man on Mars?"

"Nope," Garren replied. "But the Chinese are close to going back to the moon."

"What about money. Do we still use cash?"

"Not much. Everything is electronic."

Sofia sat up. Tommy's line of questioning suggested he was moving toward belief. She wanted to see when it happened.

"Teleportation?"

"No."

"Alien contact?"

"No."

"Robots?"

"Yes, but not what you're thinking. Artificial intelligence is the thing and it's practically everywhere."

"Who's the president of the United States?"

"Donald Trump."

Tommy laughed. "That figures."

"Who won the Super Bowl in 2019?

"No idea. Didn't watch it. Didn't care."

"Are the Stones still together?"

"Farewell Tour in 2018. Their second or third. I lost count."

"Do we still have hair?"

"Yes, but it's gray."

"What about Sofia? Is she my girlfriend?"

"You wish," Sofia replied. "But no. Nice try though."

"Okay," said Tommy. "That's cool. I don't need to hear anymore."

"So…you believe us?"

"I believe you believe it."

"Oh no you don't," said Garren, clearly put off. "That's what people say when they don't want to say what they really think."

"Dude, you didn't travel through time."

"Yes, we did."

"You can't prove it."

"Ask us some more questions. Anything."

"Okay. Does Kate know about her?" Tommy nodded toward Sofia.

"What's that supposed to mean?"

"You tell me. By the looks of it, you've got some kind of teacher/ student thing going on here and somebody found out about it. My guess is whoever did that to her is probably looking to do a lot more to you."

Sofia was too shocked to say anything. She scooted to the far end of the couch and glared at him.

"That's not it," said Garren.

"That makes a lot more sense than you went to sleep in the future and woke up in the past."

"I don't like where this is going. I think you should leave, Tommy."

"Dude, you're my best friend. You know I've got your back. But it looks like this fantasy you two cooked up is about to blow up."

"I told you, Tommy. That's not what this is."

"What about the other day? Kate was pretty mad about something. Did Kate find out?"

Garren stood up. "I asked you to leave."

"Okay, Man." Tommy got up. "I'm going. Most guys date two girls at a time before they get married."

Garren grabbed Tommy by the collar and dragged him toward the door.

As Tommy exited the apartment, he called out, "I'm still your best friend. Call me if you need a place to stay…that goes for you, too, Sofia."

Garren slammed the door. "Can you believe that guy?" He stomped back into the living room and dropped into the chair.

Sofia was clearly rattled by the unexpected turn of events. "I'm sorry, Garren. It's all my fault. I thought he would believe us."

"It's not your fault. That idiot knows me better than that. He knows I would never do something like that. Some best friend."

"He's right. This is what it looks like. This is what people will think."

"No they won't."

"They already do."

"What?"

"Someone saw us leave school yesterday."

Garren was silent as he let the revelation sink in.

"And they told the cop."

"He did this to you." Garren's was voice edged with anger. "I'm gonna get him."

"No, you're not. He's dangerous."

"He can't get away with this."

"He already has. And he's already spreading a story about what happened. Apparently, I snuck out last night. I got beat up. He found me in a bar near the river. Once again, the problem child gets rescued by super-dad."

"That's ridiculous. No one will believe that."

"They'll believe it before they believe one of Dubuque's finest enjoys beating up his foster kid."

"You can't go back there. I won't let you." Garren got up and paced around the room. "We'll figure something out. I'm not going to let him hurt you again. We'll think of something."

"I'm sorry I got you into this mess. I'm not that kind of person. I was feeling sorry for myself and—"

"What's done is done." Garren sat back down in the chair. "We just need to come up with a plan."

"I have one. I'm leaving town."

"You can't do that."

"Why not? I leave in six months anyway. I already know where to go. I know where I'm going to live. I know who's going to hire me. I'll just start sooner this time."

"You know I can't let you do that."

"Why not?"

"I don't want you to go. We're partners, remember? We've got to figure this thing out."

"Garren, I think it's time we faced reality. We're never going to figure this out. Whatever *it* is, whatever reason *it* happened, this is our reality now. I'm happy for you. You've got Kate. Make it work this time. I don't want to mess that up for you. Who knows? Maybe I'll parlay my knowledge of the next twenty years and become a millionaire. But for now, I think I owe it to you to leave you alone. I've caused enough trouble for you."

"Sofia, let's think about this."

"I've been thinking about it all day. I'm not going back to that house. I can't stay here. If you could give me a ride to the bus station and a little money, I'll be out of your life."

Garren thought for a moment, then said, "You're right. We need to get you out of town, but not that way. I don't know how yet, but I'm going to help you get someplace safe. And we're going to keep working on this together. I talked to a friend of mine yesterday at the university. He might be able to help us. But for now…oh boy…I'm going to grant your request."

"What request?"

"You're about to meet my wife."

17

Kate was in a good mood when she got home. Her Monday through Thursday class schedule meant it was the weekend. Of course, there was plenty to read and study, but for the next three days her schedule was her own. She smiled at the sight of Garren's Camaro parked in its usual spot across the street. She noticed the occupied police car parked four cars behind it, but put it out of her mind as she walked up the stairs to their apartment.

"Hey, *Babe*, I'm home. I have to admit, that's starting to grow on me. Whoa! What the—." Startled, Kate started backing up toward the door.

"Hi, Kate?" Sofia got up from the kitchen table. "Of course, you're Kate. I'm Sofia. Wow, now I understand why Gar...I mean, Mr. Rosen—"

"What are you doing in my kitchen?"

"Uh...that's a long story."

Kate eyed the stranger. Her face softened at the sight of Sofia's blackened eye and swollen lip. "Garren?"

From the bedroom, the sound of a toilet flushing and running water preceded Garren's appearing. "Kate, I'm so glad you're home." He went to her and kissed her on the forehead. "I see you've met Sofia. She's one of my students."

Kate looked at the girl again, assessing the intruder. "Why is she here?"

"She's in a bit of trouble and came here for help."

Sofia did her best to look like a frightened seventeen year old. She sank back down into the chair and hugged one knee to her chest. She fidgeted with her hair in a futile attempt to hide her injuries. She was a good actor. In reality, she was an angry thirty-seven year old bartender from New York trying to get a read on this other woman.

"Shouldn't she be at home with her parents?" Kate asked.

"That's part of the problem," Garren replied. "She can't go home."

"Is she pregnant?"

Sofia shot her a look, but recovered her school girl pretense.

"No," said Garren. "It's not that. She's…maybe we should sit down." He pulled a chair out for Kate and took the one next to it.

Kate lowered her backpack to the floor and sat down. She glanced at the open journal on the table and noticed the page was half-filled with girl-script. Sofia closed the book and folded her hands upon it.

"What happened?" Kate directed her question to Sofia. "Who did this to you?"

Sofia sat up and ran her hand through her hair, trying to look like she was trying to regain her composure. "My foster dad." She even managed to make her voice sound weak and quivery.

Kate immediately responded. "You poor girl. Why?"

"He, uh…" Sofia sniffed and wiped at a tear that wasn't there. "He gets angry when I disappoint him. I disappoint him a lot."

Kate reached across the table and placed her hand upon Sofia's. "That's terrible. Isn't there someplace else you can live?"

Sofia shook her head and glanced down at Kate's hand and the time journal beneath it. "My real parents died two years ago. I have an older sister, but I don't know where she is."

"What about relatives?"

Sofia shrugged. "It was just the four of us. Now it's just me."

"You must have friends."

Sofia looked to Garren and chuckled in the way people do when the words are too difficult to say.

Garren spoke for her. "You know how kids are. Sofia is new to the school this year. They haven't gotten to know her."

"Mr. Rosen is more than just a great teacher," Sofia said in response to what she guessed Kate was thinking. "He really cares about his students. I've been talking to him about my situation. He's been encouraging me a lot. My plan is…or was…to hold on until graduation. Then I can get a job and place of my own. But now, I don't think I can wait. I'm really scared."

"There must be something that can be done. Have you gone to the police?"

Sofia and Garren exchanged looks. Garren said, "That's why this is so bad. The foster dad is a cop."

Kate's eyebrows came together as the situation developed in her mind. "Do you think he's looking for you?"

"He will when he gets home and discovers I'm not there," Sofia said.

"What time does he get home?" Kate looked at the wall clock. It was a quarter past five.

"Soon. Why?"

"It's probably nothing, but I noticed a police car parked on the street when I came home."

"Oh, crap. It's him." Sofia grabbed the journal and jumped up from the table, scrambling to find her jacket.

Garren got up as well, went to the door and looked through the peephole.

"What's wrong?' Kate asked. "Why would he look for her here?"

As soon as the words were out of her mouth, there was a loud knock on the door. Garren spun around and held his finger to his lips. Sofia scanned the apartment for a back door, but there wasn't one. She went to the window and looked down. It was about fifteen feet to the concrete sidewalk below. Not completely out of the question, but a drop from that height would hurt. Kate grabbed her arm as she tried to open the window and shook her head. Then she led her into the bedroom.

"Stay in here," Kate said. "We won't let him find you."

When Kate returned to the living room she found it empty, but she heard voices from the other side of the door. Looking through the peephole, she could see the encounter. The police officer was clearly angry as he jabbed his finger into Garren's chest. She put her ear to the door to listen.

"This is a small town, Rosen. People see things and they talk about them. And people are talking about you and my daughter."

"People see what they want to see and they talk before they know the whole story."

"Then how about you tell me the whole story."

"I'm Sofia's history teacher. That's all. But I'm sure there's a story behind those bruises on her face. I know what you did. If you ever touch that girl again, I'll—"

"Threatening a police officer? For a teacher, you're not that smart."

"You beat that girl and you don't even deny it?"

Officer Daniels was quiet for a moment as he thought about how to reply. "If anyone comes after me, they better come with a lot more than a few self-defense techniques. I teach those classes. As you know, the teacher always knows more than the student."

"The truth is going to get out. It always does."

"I could say the same about you."

"Are we done here?"

"Just a word of caution. Actually, consider this a threat. If I hear about you talking to my daughter about anything that doesn't have to do with history, you and I are going to have an encounter. Do you understand me?"

"Yeah, I hear you."

Kate jumped back as Garren burst through the door, slamming it shut behind him.

"Garren?" she said. "What was that about?"

"Nothing. Just a little misunderstanding."

"What are people saying about you and that girl?"

"Nothing."

"Young girls' fathers don't get that angry about nothing. What aren't you telling me?"

"*Foster* father." Sofia appeared from the bedroom. "And not a good one. I assure you, it's nothing. I needed someone to talk to and Garren, I mean, Mr. Rosen listened. He's helping me deal with my situation."

Kate's women's intuition was on high alert. "Maybe you should be talking with kids your own age."

"Kids my age." Sofia bit her bottom lip to keep from laughing. "I don't relate well to *kids* my age."

Garren sensed the tension between them. "Sofia's not like the students at school. She's an old soul."

"That's true," Sofia said.

"Well…" Kate walked the three steps into the kitchen and leaned against the counter, arms folded. "Old soul or not, she's still a minor, and—"

"Barely," Sofia countered. "I'll be eighteen in a few weeks."

Kate narrowed her eyes and trained them upon Garren. "And *you* are the adult. A man came to our home and accused you of messing around with his daughter."

"*Foster* daughter," Garren said.

"Really? You're correcting me? Garren, this is serious. She came here looking for you. Do you not see what this looks like?"

"Yeah, I do, but it's not like that."

"Then what is it exactly?"

"I told you."

"No. You didn't. Not everything." Kate's posture and the tone of her voice was beginning to look and sound a lot like the Kate of the future. "I'm not dumb. I have attractive professors, too, you know."

"What's that supposed to mean?"

"It's obvious she has a crush on you. You're the good looking, cool teacher. It happens. I get it."

"What are you talking about?"

Kate shook her head and laughed. "You just proved my point. How can some men be so intelligent and so clueless at the same time?"

"I know," Sofia chimed in. "They can turn a perfectly innocent comment into an invitation to hop in the sack with them. But tell them straight up how you feel and it's like you're speaking a different language."

"Exactly," said Kate. "And then when you point it out to them, they get all defensive like it's our fault."

Garren was taken aback by the sudden alliance.

"Tell me about it," said Sofia. "They're boys in men's bodies. Last guy I dated…third date, he takes me to meet his parents and introduces me as his girlfriend. Then he tells them I could be the one. When I asked him about it later, he said he was only kidding. I didn't know whether to be relieved or offended. I told him I didn't want to see him again. Next day, his mother calls me and asks me to give him another chance."

Kate cocked her head. Garren caught Sofia's attention and gave her a look that brought her back to the current reality.

"Of course, I told her I was way too young. Like I've totally got my whole life in front of me, right?"

After an awkward silence, Kate said, "Back to the problem at hand. What are you going to do about this, Garren?"

"Who, me?"

Kate looked around the room. "There's only three of us. I'm new to this party. She's the victim. That leaves you, Rosen. What's your plan?"

"I was hoping we could help Sofia together."

Kate glanced at the clock. "It's five-thirty. If we hurry, we might be able to get her home before the foster dad."

"I told you I'm not going back there," Sofia protested.

"You can't stay here."

"We can't just turn her away," Garren said. "She has no place to go."

"Garren," Kate said firmly, "she is not staying here."

"I hate to impose," said Sofia, "but if you could loan me some money and take me to the bus station, I'll be fine."

Kate saw the determination in Sofia's eyes. "Where would you go?"

"I've got friends in New York. If you can just help me get there, I won't bother you anymore. And I'll send you the money in a few weeks. I know it's a lot to ask, but I'm out of options."

"You don't have to do this," said Garren. "Your future is not set in stone."

Sofia chuckled and drummed her fingers on the journal that was still on the table. "From where I stand, it sure looks like it. One way or another, I'm going to New York. If you can't help me, I guess I'm on my own. Mrs. Rosen, I'm really sorry about all this. Please, don't be angry at him. He's only been trying to help me. I promise that's all." She grabbed her jacket from the couch and put it on, and slipped the time journal into the pocket.

Garren was paralyzed by all the things he couldn't do. He couldn't return Sofia to her abusive foster parents and he couldn't let her just slip away to New York. He also couldn't feed the apparent suspicions of an inappropriate teacher/student relationship. And he couldn't tell Kate the entire truth. His brain was frantic to find something he could do, but every thought trail ended with another *couldn't*. He slumped onto the back of the couch, defeated.

"I'm sorry, Sofia," he said at last. "I don't know what to do. I don't think we have enough money for a cab to the bus station, let alone a ticket to New York."

"I understand." Sofia pulled her jacket closed and zipped it all the way up to her chin. "Thanks for trying."

"Hold on a minute," said Kate as Sofia reached the door. "We're not going to let you become another runaway statistic."

Sofia turned around, her face a mixture of hope and caution. "You mean I can stay here tonight?"

Garren glanced from Sofia to Kate, trying to guess what she would say.

"No. When you turn up missing, your foster dad might come back here. I have a better idea." Kate walked over to the wall phone and placed a call. After a few seconds... "Denise, hey, it's me. We need a favor. Can we come over?"

18

"Your sister," Sofia said from the backseat of Kate's car. Garren was driving. "What's she like?"

Kate turned in the passenger seat to answer. "She's nice, in a big-sisterly kind of way."

"I have a big sister. She split on me after our parents died."

"I'm sorry to hear that. Denise would never do that. In fact, she's kind of a mother hen."

"Great. Just what I need, another foster mom."

"What you need is a place to stay." Garren didn't know if he was talking to Sofia, the troubled teenager, or Sofia, the disgruntled time-traveler. Either way, he was a little surprised by her attitude. A little appreciation would have been nice.

"Are you sure she'll go along with this?" Sofia asked. "I mean, she'll be okay harboring a fugitive, yeah?"

"She has a heart for the oppressed," Kate replied. "One look at your bruises and she'll let you stay as long as you like. She's sort of between relationships at the moment, so she'll probably welcome the company."

"Does she ask a lot of questions?"

"I'd say she's more of a talker than an asker," Garren said. "Wouldn't you say that, Kate?"

She gave him a hard look. "I'd say my sister is a wonderful person who, at times, might try a little too hard."

"Perfect." Sofia caught sight of Garren looking at her in the rearview mirror and read his expression. "She sounds nice. I really do appreciate this. Hopefully, I'll be gone before I wear out my welcome."

It was dark as they rolled up in front of Denise's house, a modest single-story in one of Dubuque's older neighborhoods. A root from one of the giant trees in the front yard had buckled the asphalt, forming a speed-bump size hump at the end of the driveway. The car rose and fell as Garren navigated it, careful to hit it in just the right spot so it wouldn't scrape the underside of the car. It had been years, but he remembered how to do it.

"This is it," Garren said as he switched off the engine, the nostalgia of the old place washing over him. Simpler times.

Sofia took in her surroundings, what she could see of them. Streetlights never made it to this part of town and most of the houses had their curtains drawn. The only visible lights were single-bulb porch lights. Actually, not a bad place to lay low for a while. "Looks nice."

The short walk from the driveway to the house put things in perspective for Sofia. It had gotten even colder since the sun set and the sky was crystal clear. The night would prove bitterly cold. While she wasn't all that keen on bunking with a stranger, it was better than sleeping outside. She would have to make the best of it.

The door opened as they stepped up onto the porch. For some reason, Sofia expected a much older woman, probably a little frumpy, bad hairdo, maybe a cat in her arms and one of those voices that makes you wish for a good stiff drink or three; anything to numb the senses. But Denise was quite the opposite. She was young, maybe only a year of two older than Kate, and attractive. Long dark brown hair fell softly around a pretty face. When she welcomed them in, her voice was low and relaxed; bordering on soothing. At her feet was a puppy of mixed breeding; the lovechild of the neighbor's golden lab and a vagabond pit bull, with a little beagle somewhere in either parent's lineage. His little mouth was half open, giving it the impression of a smile, and his tail wagged with such wild abandon that his backend wobbled causing his hind feet to slip on the hardwood.

"Hi guys. What a nice surprise." Denise stepped back and the puppy stayed right with her.

"Thanks for seeing us on such short notice," said Kate. "I'd like you meet one of Garren's students. Her name is Sofia. Sofia, my sister, Denise."

The flash of confusion on Denise's face was quickly replaced with a compassionate smile. Kate was right about the effect of Sofia's bruises. "Hello, Sofia. It's nice to meet you."

"Hi."

"Come in," said Denise. "It's too cold outside."

Sofia watched the sisters hug as Kate entered the house. She could tell they were close; one more reason to envy Garren's wife.

They gathered in the living room, a cozy space with a fireplace, extra-large pillows on the floor and soft blankets draped over the backs of the couch and chair. A thick novel and a pair of reading glasses occupied the table near the couch. No ashtray or wine glass in sight. No sad music on the radio and no pictures of ex-boyfriends. Denise was handling her singleness pretty well. Sofia wondered how long it had been since the last guy. Garren would probably know when the next one was due.

The sisters dropped onto the couch in a way that suggested that was their usual spot. Sofia sat in a mismatched wingback chair. Garren grabbed a chair from the dining room and set it in the open space, closer to Kate's side of the couch than Sofia. The mood was uncomfortable at first. Kate still wasn't sure what to make of Sofia. Sofia was clearly guarded. Denise was eager to understand why her sister had insisted on meeting that evening with no mention of the young girl. Garren wanted to get it over with.

"I guess I'll start," he said. "As Kate said, Sofia is one of my students. She's a great kid in a tough situation."

Sofia cringed at the introduction, but didn't break character.

"She lives in a foster home," he continued, "and it's not good. The, uh, father is abusive."

Denise gasped. "He hit you?"

Sofia nodded and looked down at her hands. The puppy waddled over to her and laid down with his chin on her foot.

"You can hold him if you want," Denise said. "His name is Bon Jovi, but you can call him Bon or Jovi. He responds to either one. Actually, he'll come to you no matter what you call him if he thinks you'll pet him. Mostly he just likes to have his tummy rubbed. He's my little buddy."

Sofia picked up Bon Jovi and set him in her lap. The puppy immediately snuggled in and laid his head in the crook of her arm.

"He likes you," Denise said.

"Getting to the point," Garren continued, "she can't go back to her foster home, and it would be awkward for her to stay with us."

Kate delivered the request. "We thought maybe she could stay here for a few days…until she can find a more permanent solution."

"Of course," Denise said without hesitation. "I've got plenty of room. Jovi has already given his approval. She can stay as long as she likes. What about school? I might be able to give her a ride in the morning, but I don't get off work until four-thirty at the earliest."

"I'm not going back to school," Sofia said. "I can't go back there."

"But graduation is only a few months away," Kate noted. "You can't quit now."

"My birthday is only a few weeks away," Sofia countered. "I'll get my GED later."

"Is it really that bad?" Denise asked.

Sofia flipped her hair to reveal her black eye. She even managed to conjure up a tear. "I can't let them see me like this. And I can't let *him* find me. Next time will be worse."

Denise practically melted. Kate sensed Sofia was laying it on a bit thick, but the marks on her face were impossible to ignore.

"One problem at a time," Garren cut in. "Denise, thank you. Let's give it the weekend and see how things develop. Sofia, are you going to be comfortable here?"

She looked down at Bon Jovi, who was asleep in her lap, then at Denise, who was smiling sympathetically. "Yes, this is perfect. Thank you, Denise. I promise, as soon as I can figure out my next move, I'll be out of here. Would it be okay if I spoke with Mr. Rosen in private?"

"Sure," said Denise. "I need to start making supper anyway. Kate, you wanna give me a hand?"

Kate took one more analytical look at Sofia and her husband before following Denise into the kitchen.

"That went better than I thought," Garren said. "Nice acting, by the way. For a minute there, I almost forgot your real age."

"I wasn't acting. Obviously, I'm not as tough as I thought. He really did hurt me."

"If it's any consolation, you look tough."

"Gee, thanks. I hope this heals before I get to New York. Street brawler isn't quite the look I'm going for. And poor little abused orphan girl doesn't fit my profile either. I had to work hard to convince my first boss to hire me. And friendship didn't come any easier. I had to rely upon my assets."

Garren's eyes widened. "Which ones?"

"Positive thinking, Mr. Rosen, a winning smile and a can-do attitude." She made her voice sound overly cheery.

Garren gave her a sideways look.

"What do you think I had to do? Nightclubs aren't bastions of higher learning. They don't check grades. But they do have certain aesthetic standards and you have to be able to make people believe you like them. Potential friends are no different. Let's just say I presented myself in the way that met their criteria."

Garren nodded as he absorbed this part of Sofia's story.

"No, I didn't sleep with anyone."

"I didn't say you did."

"You were thinking it. Don't tell me you weren't. Remember, I can read people. And you're easier than most. And for the record, I'm not that kind of girl."

"Okay, okay," said Garren. "So I'm not good at reading people. I'm still trying to figure you out."

"Believe it or not, you know me better than anyone else. And not just because we're from the same temporal neighborhood. I've never been this open with anyone."

"Are you just saying that to make me believe you like me?"

Sofia snorted and shook her head. "Never mind. New subject, please."

"Okay." Garren glanced toward the kitchen to gauge his time. "I'm going to see Dr. Finney again tomorrow and press him a little bit on suggestions for the plot of my novel, which I must say, was a pretty genius idea. I forgot to tell you, he said my character should try to reconstruct the particulars of the moment just before he leaped back in time. We should do that. Let's write down everything we can remember from that night. Maybe something will give us an idea how this happened, and Dr. Finney can help us think of how we might be able to...what? Why are you looking at me like that?"

"I spent all day thinking about this. Let's be honest. We're never going to figure it out. And even if we did, there's no way to re-create whatever brought us here. We're stuck. I can only think of two good things about this whole mess."

"Oh, yeah? What?"

"Your time journal idea is pretty good. We should take full advantage of our knowledge of the next twenty years. We should write down everything we can remember, but not for our younger selves who may or may not ever come back here. We need to write it down for us. Maybe Tommy is right. Maybe we aren't time-travelers after all. Maybe we're just us and somehow the memories of the next twenty years got downloaded into our brains. Who knows? Maybe

I've never even been to New York, but I just know what's going to happen when I get there. We'd have to be morons not to take advantage of that knowledge."

"Actually, that was Kate's idea. She thought of the time journals."

"Smart woman. You better not screw it up with her."

"I'm trying. Believe me, I'm trying."

Sofia looked like she wanted to say something, but couldn't decide if she should.

"You said there were two good things. What's the other one?"

Sofia looked down at Bon Jovi, still asleep in her lap. When she looked up, she had a distant look about her like someone reliving the past (or future). "You. Whatever this is, I'm glad I'm going through it with you. You're a good guy, Garren."

"You're not so bad yourself, Sofia."

"You know what I mean. I like you."

"I like you, too."

Dear clueless Garren. Sofia sighed. "You know I am going to New York. I have to. But I'll try to stay until my birthday. If we're going to take full advantage of these time journals, we should make sure we remember the next twenty years as accurately as possible. We'll have to compare notes."

"I agree."

"And we should probably get cellphones so we can stay in contact when I'm gone."

"Absolutely."

"And…" she hesitated in order to choose her words. "…if things don't go according to plan, we can be there for each other."

"Hey, it's all going to work out. Things will be even better than they were."

Sofia faked a smile.

"But you're right," Garren added. "If something happens, anything at all, we've got each other's back."

"Yeah…that's what I was thinking. Hey, you should probably get back to Kate. Don't want to give her the wrong impression about us."

"You're right. I better go."

"When will I see you again…to compare notes?"

"Maybe Sunday. I'll think of a reason to come back over here."

"You know, your Dr. Finney might be on to something. Maybe we should try to recreate the conditions of the night we left. If nothing else, at least it will be fun." She winked at him.

"I probably shouldn't ask this," Garren said sheepishly. "How fun?"

Sofia giggled. "I'll let you read about it in my journal."

Garren's face flushed.

"Garren, we should probably get going," Kate announced as she returned from the kitchen. "Sofia, I won't pretend to understand what you're going through, but I do care about you. Will you at least take the weekend to think about your options? I'm concerned about you going all the way to New York by yourself."

Sofia nodded. "I promise I won't do anything unless I'm sure how it will turn out."

"I appreciate your optimism, but no one can be sure of the future."

"I'm pretty sure...ninety-five percent."

Kate turned toward Denise. "Thank you, Sis. Call me if you need anything."

"We'll be fine," Denise said.

As Garren got up from his chair, he whispered to Sofia. "Watch out for Bon Jovi. He's gonna bite me one day. I'll need stitches."

The ride home was a bit chilly at first. Garren drove and Kate stared out the side window. After several minutes...

"You do realize that girl has a crush on you," Kate said without shifting her gaze. "You need to be careful."

"She's just scared and she doesn't have any friends."

"You really are naïve." Kate shifted in her seat to look at him and put her arm across his shoulders. "A woman's attraction begins with her emotions. You taking an interest in her and trying to help tapped into that. Given her home situation, she sees you as her rescuer. Add to that your good looks and above average cool factor, you're like a superhero to her."

"Pff, I think you might be reading too much into this. But you're obviously paying attention in your psych class. So that's good."

"Seriously, Garren. There's definitely a connection between you two. I saw it. Denise saw it, too."

He started to protest.

"Hear me out," she persisted. "I'm not accusing you of anything. I just don't want my husband to let his naiveté get him into trouble. Whether you know it or not, there is a connection. I trust it's completely innocent on your part. You're a good guy trying to help one of his students. I'm glad you're like that. It's one of the many things I love about you. But she is an impressionable, very attractive young woman. All I'm saying is you need to be careful that you're not leading her on."

"I wouldn't do that."

"Not intentionally, but it happens."

There was so much he wanted to say in order to explain the connection and assure her, or maybe himself, that there was absolutely nothing going on between himself and Sofia. But older Garren knew from experience that the more he tried to explain himself, the deeper whatever hole he had dug became. His older wisdom prevailed. "I see your point. I agree. I need to be careful."

Kate let a full minute pass. "I do trust you."

"Thank you."

Another minute passed.

"Because I know you would never hide anything from me."

Garren felt himself slip deeper into the hole he'd been digging ever since he arrived in 2000. Perhaps this was the moment he should lay all his cards on the table. He played it out in his mind: *Actually, there is something I've been meaning to tell you. You know how ever since my birthday you've been saying there's something different about me? Well, there's a really interesting explanation. You see, I'm from the future. I'm actually the fifty year old version of myself. Or at least I think I might be. I suppose I could be this younger version with all the memories of the older version. But I don't know how to prove it either way. Oh, and the same thing is happening to Sofia. That would explain the connection between us.*

"You wouldn't hide anything from me, would you?"

"Who me? No, of course not." He gathered up his cards and held them tightly to his vest. He needed to change the subject quickly before he dropped one. "Say, are you getting hungry?"

Everybody's working for the weekend
Everybody wants a little romance
Everybody's going off the deep end
Everybody needs a second chance, oh
From the Canadian rock band Loverboy (October 1981)

Friday. The end of the first week back at school after the long winter break. Teachers and students alike were ready for the weekend. Neither wanted to be confined to a classroom until a bell told them to go to the next where another bell would tell them to go to the next until the final bell granted them release until Monday when it would start all over again. In and around the official procedures of the day, conversations were had and plans were made for the fifty-five hour and fifteen minute reprieve. There would be parties and dates and phone calls and encounters, all of which held the promise of romance and adventure and misadventure. There would be staying up and sleeping in. There would be intentionality and life on the whim. Real life would retake center stage again and the students, faculty and staff of Hempstead High School would become real people again.

Garren felt the pull, same as everyone else, though for him the gravity of it was more intense. He'd already lived this weekend once. To be sure, he must have enjoyed it. He and Kate must have spent those hours wrapped in the warm glow of newly wedded bliss. But he could no more remember the particulars of that weekend than he could remember the details of any other weekend of his past. It must have been enjoyable, though it most likely came and went with little or no fanfare. This second time around, however, he was more keenly aware of a weight of significance. Though every moment of a person's life carries that weight, there is something about living them again that makes a person more attuned, more sensitive to the significance of being. Surely life is a gift, each moment an integral part of the whole. Each moment is affected by those that came before and affects those that follow. Delete one and the whole thing falls apart. Change one and the whole thing becomes something different; an altered version of the original. Garren and Sofia had changed hundreds of moments and were therefore living an altered version of their own lives. All that, plus the urgency of Sofia's situation and his own marriage shifting and adjusting to the knowledge he possessed and his efforts to be a better husband the second time around, made everything more weighty.

He managed to get through his classes, playing the role of an ordinary school teacher without giving away his true identity. Although he knew she wouldn't be there, he was surprised by the effect of her absence. His final class of the day was incomplete, off-balance; Sofia's empty desk a silent reminder of the reality that only she and he knew. He paused at her name as he called the roll. A snicker followed whispers from the back of the classroom. Garren knew it had something to do with her. He wanted to call it out in her defense, but he didn't want to call any more attention to his already noticeable favoritism. He let it go. The next forty minutes crept by at an agonizing pace. Garren heard himself drone on and on about something neither he nor his students thought important. He watched three of his students doze off, their heads bobbing as muscles relaxed and suddenly tensed. He was aware of a conversation in the form of note-passing happening off to his right. He saw several students either writing or doodling in their notebooks. The rest were mere crash test dummies with blank faces, entranced by the cadence of his voice ticking off the points of his lecture. Twice, he threw in a comment so absurd that anyone paying even a modicum of attention would have reacted with at least a variance of facial expression. The test proved his suspicion. He was alone. Everyone else was gone.

The bell rang with enough force to wake the dead. Consciousness flooded the classroom like a tsunami, reanimating their host bodies with a singular purpose. Chairs scraped atop linoleum squares and clanged against metal desks. Backpacks rustled as notebooks were thrust inside and hoisted upon shoulders. A cacophony of many voices rising to be heard swelled to a decibel level such that Garren's reminder to read chapter 23 in Tomlinson and answer the questions at the end went unheard.

Alone for real, Garren drank in the silence. He'd made it through his first week in the past. Aside from a few mishaps, he'd done okay. In spite of a few minor alterations, he hadn't destroyed the fabric of time and space. He checked himself by recalling a few details of December 31, 2019. Apparently, he hadn't done anything to prevent himself from making it to that moment and then leaping back in time. So he hadn't created the time paradox he'd always thought of as a good reason for the impossibility of time-travel into the past. *Not bad for a rookie time-traveler*, he thought, and then laughed to himself at the absurd reality of it. He really was a time-traveler. Granted, it wasn't quite the same as in the movies. He didn't have a machine. He didn't pass through a portal. He was completely unaware of any*thing* that caused the phenomenon. Finney's words played out in his mind: *Replay the circumstances*. Obviously, something had caused Sofia and him to leap twenty years into the past. Then Tommy's words rang loudly: *You are not a time-traveler. You have no proof.* Maybe he was right. Maybe he only thought he had memories of the next twenty years. Maybe he was delusional. Maybe he was losing his mind. No, that couldn't be it. Sofia's shared experience proved it was real…or was it? What he needed was a test. He needed to identify something that he knew would happen and then watch it play out. Unfortunately, the only event he could remember from 2000 was the presidential election still ten months away. What did that say about him as an historian? He made a mental note to run this by Sofia. Perhaps she could offer a test event nearer on the horizon.

There were two ways off of the Hempstead High School campus. The main exit allowed for two lines of cars turning either left or right onto Pennsylvania Avenue. There was a traffic light there timed in such a way to accommodate the high volume of cars leaving the school at the end of the day. The other was Keymont Drive that cut east through a quiet middleclass neighborhood. Residents complained about the daily flood of traffic for years, but the city refused to block the exit citing safety concerns. Of the two, the main exit was the best bet. More traffic, but better flow. Garren hedged his bets and headed that way. After ten minutes, which seemed like twenty, he was turning right onto Pennsylvania road.

Garren immediately noticed the police car parked in the drop-off zone in front of the school's main doors; not unusual for that time of day. Reflexively, he checked his speedometer and saw that he was driving two miles under the posted speed limit. With no reason to be concerned, he let his mind drift to more important things. The weekend was upon him and the thought of spending it with Kate made him smile. Twenty yards passed the driveway, he glanced into his rearview mirror. The flashing blue lights didn't register at first. Probably one of the kids behind him got a little too eager for the weekend or cut someone off. But when the police car whipped in behind him and he saw that it was Cruller, Garren's smile faded. Having already passed Rosemont Street, he continued another hundred yards to the Dubuque Assembly of God and pulled in. He thought about going all the way to the back of the parking lot, but decided to park in the shade of the only tree on the premises. Without its leaves, it didn't completely hide him from Pennsylvania Avenue, but it provided enough cover so that his second traffic stop of the week wasn't on full display for the Hempstead student body or Principle Jenson.

"Good afternoon, Officer Daniels," Garren said after he rolled the window halfway down. He decided not to get out of the car this time and he kept his hands on the steering wheel. He wasn't about to give Cruller a reason to play tough cop again. If that was his game, he'd have to earn it.

"Mr. Rosen," said Officer Daniels in a professional tone. "Would you mind stepping out of the car?"

A request, not a command. "May I ask why, Officer? I wasn't speeding."

Cruller looked down at him over the top of his aviator sunglasses. "Get out."

Garren wondered what his rights were in such a situation. Did a police officer have the authority to demand an exit from a vehicle without stating the reason? He hated to give up the safety of his closed door, but if he didn't comply it might be enough to flip the crazy switch in Cruller's head. Then it would be handcuffs and his face on the hood all over again; and this time would undoubtedly be rougher than before. He might even get to ride in the back of Cruller's car down to the station. Then his weekend would be shot, Kate would have another reason to suspect him of some shenanigans and he might be forced to give up Sofia's location. He slowly opened the door and got out.

"You know what this is about," said Cruller. "I want to know where my daughter is."

Garren wanted to correct him – *foster* daughter – but decided to play dumb. "Is she not at home? I was concerned when she didn't show up for class today."

Cruller stared hard at him. "Cut the crap, Rosen. I know there's something going on between you two and she doesn't have anywhere else to go. So why don't you make this easier on yourself and tell me where she is? If you don't, I can make your life very uncomfortable."

"I honestly don't know what you're talking about." Garren had lied more in the last week than in his entire life. He hoped he was getting good at it.

"Don't lie to me."

So maybe he wasn't as good as he thought, but he wasn't about to betray Sofia. "I don't know what to tell you."

"Maybe after a day or two in lock-up you'll think of something."

"You can't arrest me. I haven't done anything wrong."

"Civilians," Cruller chuckled. "Possession of stolen property. Carrying a concealed weapon. Possession of a firearm on school property. Possession of an illegal substance. Intent to distribute an illegal substance."

"I don't have any of that stuff."

"You do if I say you do. I can add to that: Resisting arrest and assaulting a police officer."

Garren tried to read the man to see how far he would carry such a bluff. He was never good at poker either.

"Or you can just tell me what I want to know and you can get on home to that pretty little wife of yours," Cruller snorted. "Or maybe you prefer young girls. Is that it? Is that why you became a teacher, so you could be around all these pretty little girls?"

It was all Garren could do to keep from lashing out at the man.

Cruller pushed some more. "Sofia is rather attractive, don't you think? And she's almost eighteen. Almost legal."

Garren flinched and balled up his fists.

"That's it, Rosen. Come at me." He dropped his hands down to his sides and stuck out his chin. "Take a shot."

Garren forced himself to relax. "I don't know where your... daughter is, Officer Daniels."

"All right, Rosen, if that's the way you want to do it..." Cruller reached for his handcuffs.

Garren took a step back. "If you arrest me, I'll tell them what you did to her. I'll expose you as a child abuser."

"It would be your word against mine." Cruller was almost laughing. "In the real world, police officer trumps high school teacher."

"What about Sofia's word? And she's got the marks to prove it."

"Prove what?" Now Cruller did laugh. "I've got witnesses that say they saw her down on Bells Street getting mouthy with some tough girls. I've got a complaint from a club owner about her trying to talk her way in. I've got a 911 transcript from the woman who found her trying to break into her car. Let's see what you've got – an impressionable young girl who's fallen under the influence of her teacher. Sorry, Rosen, but I don't think your case is going to hold up. So, why don't you save yourself a world of trouble and tell me where she is?"

It did seem as if Officer Daniels held all the cards, and either way he played it, Garren was going to lose. Someone's future was about to be changed. He could almost hear the deck of time being shuffled from which a new hand would be dealt. The question was which of them would be living that new hand? Save Sofia and he would be saddled with a criminal record and a termination on his résumé. That wouldn't bode well for his career at the university. Plus, he might lose Kate even sooner than the first time around. Give up Sofia and that could mean an even worse life for her. No telling what the psycho would do to her. Actually, he had a pretty good idea and that made him sick. Whatever force had sent him back into this predicament was not playing fair.

"Funny thing is…" Cruller dangled the handcuffs in front of Garren. "If you'd have just waited a few more months, we'd be having a completely different conversation. So what's it gonna be?"

Garren heard what Cruller said, but had no idea what he meant. At the last possible moment, as the words that would change his life forever were on his tongue, the force that seemed intent on wrecking his life came to his rescue. The radio in the police car came to life.

"Calling all units. Robbery in progress at Dubuque Bank and Trust on John F. Kennedy Road. Shots fired. One officer down. All units respond."

The bank was less than a mile away. Cruller was likely the closest police officer. The opportunity to catch or shoot a real bad guy was too much to resist. He shook his finger at Garren and jumped into his patrol car. With lights flashing, siren screaming and tires screeching, he left Garren with more time to consider his options.

He wanted to go home. He wanted to be with Kate. He wanted to just be the man who had been allowed to go back for a do-over. But the way back had become complicated. He wasn't the only one with a second chance. Another life was on the line and it was apparent now that he had a part to play in making sure that life didn't get sucked into a worse situation than before. He wasn't convinced New York was Sofia's best long-term plan, but it was plain to him that she couldn't stay in Dubuque. At least not Dubuque in the year 2000. Garren jumped into his car and turned left onto Pennsylvania Avenue, away from his home and toward the university.

"Yes, I have been giving the problem in your book some thought." Dr. Finney coaxed the fire in the bowl of his pipe back to life.

"You have?" Garren had no doubt that his old friend would devote part of his great brain to any problem posed by him, if for no other reason than friendship. That he would do so for a complete stranger affirmed the character of the man he remembered and thought so highly of the first time around. The thought of repeating that friendship was a great consolation to the trouble of the last few days.

"Mind you, I must give priority to my classes and my own scientific enquiry. I have a few projects of my own in the works."

"Of course. I wouldn't want to impose."

"However, there is a place for recreational thinking. All work and no play makes Jack a dull boy."

The two once and future friends laughed together as Dr. Finney's first name actually was Jack.

"Now on to the problem at hand," Dr. Finney said. "You've written your man into quite a quandary. He has awakened in his own past with no knowledge of how he arrived there and no proof that he has actually come from the future. He must wonder if he might be having an hallucination or if he might be going insane."

"Those thoughts have crossed his mind."

"But you say there is another character who is experiencing the same phenomenon."

"Yes, a woman he met the night he traveled back in time."

"There's always a woman." Dr. Finney winked and waved his pipe in the air. "That cancels out insanity…unless this woman is not real. Could he be imagining her?"

"No, she's very real."

"Just a thought, but it is your story. Could this woman be the catalyst, the cause of the phenomenon? Is she some sort of enchantress?"

"I don't think so."

"What do you mean, you don't think so? You're the author. How will you write her? She either is or she isn't."

"She isn't. In this time, she's just a scared girl. In fact, she wants to get back to her own time more than my main character. No, she's not the cause." Garren let his emotions show more than he intended and Dr. Finney picked up on it.

"It's not unusual for an author to become attached to his characters, even to imagine them as real. I suppose this is natural and even necessary to write a convincing story. What's her name?"

"Uh, Sofia."

"Tell Sofia I did not mean to accuse her. I'm just looking for an angle."

"No offense taken," Garren chuckled. "Yeah, I guess I have become a little attached."

"Well, Mr. Rosen, I'm afraid you have not given us, or your characters, much to work with. You say there is no time travel device, no observable anomaly, no event that would cause such a thing to occur."

"An event." Suddenly, part of his last evening in 2019 came back to him. "Actually, there was an event. Two hours before they traveled back in time, the moon was struck by an asteroid."

"They observed this?"

"Yes, a lot of people saw it."

Finney thought for a moment. "I cannot make a real scientific case, practical or theoretical, to suggest such an event would open a portal or cause a temporal displacement, but this is a novel. Ah, the luxury of fiction. Your task is not to prove an actual event, but simply invite your readers to momentarily suspend the rules they know to be true and consider new ones. Why couldn't a lunar event be your cause? Most people know that the moon affects the ocean's tides. Research is being done on the influence of the moon on seismic activity and plate tectonics here on the earth. The moon also affects humans. Hospital emergency rooms report an increase of cases when the moon is full. Police officers report an increase in crime. The word *lunatic* describes a person who experiences periodic insanity believed to be associate with the phases of the moon. In a fictional world, it is quite plausible that the moon could also have some influence on time. Vis-à-vis, a significant disruption in the moon's stasis would have some kind of adverse effect upon time itself. You do, however, owe it to your readers to be convincing. You must at least seem to know what you are talking about. This is where I can help you. I can give you the scientific jargon and theories. Give me some time and I might even be able to draw some causal connections between a lunar event and temporal anomalies."

"Wow," said Garren. "That's a lot to think about."

"Indeed, it is. One question: How many more people are affected by this lunar impact?"

"How many?"

"You said the impact was witnessed by many people. If it is the cause, then it stands to reason there would be more affected than just two."

"Gosh, I haven't thought of that."

"A thoughtful reader would. I'm not a literary critic, but it seems to me that a good novelist should anticipate the questions his readers will ask. Of course, you shouldn't be expected to answer all of them, but the big ones – yes."

"I'll keep that in mind." Garren wished he were writing a novel. Dr. Finney's insights were keen, but not very helpful. Even if he could demonstrate how the asteroid impact had in fact caused the temporal anomaly, it would be impossible to reverse it. "Dr. Finney, can I run another possibility by you?"

"Sure. I've got a few more minutes."

"I am consulting with another friend who suggested my characters didn't actually travel through time. She thinks it might be mental."

"Back to my question about hallucinations or insanity."

"Not quite. My friend wonders if my characters might have received the memories of events that will occur and experiences they will have."

Dr. Finney took a long drag from his pipe as he considered this new angle. "Extreme precognition. I'm afraid that's outside of my field of expertise. I suggest you speak with Dr. Marcus."

"The philosophy professor?"

Dr. Finney leaned forward as if to share a bit of inside information. "He respects the university's reputation as a conventional institution, but his real passion is metaphysics and the paranormal. I find him to be open-minded, but not irrational. Tell him I recommended you speak with him."

"Thank you, Dr. Finney. I will."

20

G arren walked through the door and into the warm embrace of his lovely bride. She hugged him tightly and kissed him with all the passion of the end of a long separation.

"I missed you." She planted another one on him.

"I missed you, too." Garren enjoyed another extended osculation, but couldn't help wondering what had sparked it. The morning didn't yield so much as a cold peck on the cheek.

Kate pulled away and led him by the hand to the couch.

"I like where this is going," he said.

Kate flashed a coy smile. "Maybe later, but right now I need to say something."

"Okay."

"I want to apologize."

"For what?"

"For not trusting you with that girl."

"Oh, well, I know how it must have looked to you."

"No, let me finish. I admit I jumped to conclusions. I've just never seen you act that way around another woman…and she is more woman than girl. It just caught me off guard, that's all. But I thought about it and I understand. She's in trouble and you want to help. I love that about you. Now for a confession. I probably wouldn't have reacted like I did if she weren't so attractive and if she didn't so obviously have feelings for you. Of course, I can hardly blame her. But I still think you need to be very careful. Protecting her is admirable, but giving her even the slightest notion that there's something more can be just as harmful. You could end up hurting her just as badly."

"Sofia doesn't have feelings for me."

Kate gave him a look. "Do I have to spell it out for you again? Trust me, she does. I can see it in her face every time she looks at you."

"But—"

"Don't try to explain it. Don't even try to understand it. Just trust me on this. Sofia has a major crush on you, and if you aren't careful, you're going to break her heart."

Garren shrugged because he had nothing to say. Deep down inside, he knew she was right. Sofia had so much as said it that night at Tommy's. What could he say? Some guys just have that effect on women. Of course, the effect works both ways. If he were honest, he had to admit he was attracted to her...that night at Tommy's when Kate was so distant and he was so lonely. But here, in the second time around, with Kate so physically and emotionally with him, his feelings for Sofia were strictly platonic.

Kate continued. "I'm not keen on the idea of a young woman like that stepping out on her own in New York, of all places, but maybe it is the best option. I called Denise today. She and Sofia talked most of the night. Apparently, she does have friends in New York who can take her in and watch out for her. She said they can even get her a job. Denise has agreed to let her stay until her birthday. That way she'll be a legal adult. Then we can all chip in and get her a bus ticket and a little getting started money. What do you think about that?"

"I'm not at all comfortable with New York either, but you're right. It probably is the best option at this point. I know she'll be okay, but I know where that road is going to take her. I just wish for something better for her."

"None of us knows the future. Hopefully, she will get her GED. Maybe she'll go to college. She'll probably meet a really nice guy, get married, have a family and a really great life. We have to be hopeful."

Garren loved his wife's optimism, but his knowledge of Sofia's future wouldn't let him share it. He faked a smile and nodded. "Yeah, you're probably right."

"So, do you forgive me for overreacting?"

"Not that you need to be forgiven, but yes. I'm sorry for springing this on you like I did. And I'm sorry for giving you the wrong impression. I want you to know that I'm hearing you about me needing to be careful around Sofia. I do understand. Thank you for pointing that out. I also need to thank Denise for taking her in."

Kate put her arms around him and leaned hard against him, forcing them both to lie down on the couch. "You can thank her tomorrow. We're going over there for dinner. But for tonight, can we not talk about this anymore?"

"Sure. Do you have something else in mind?"

"I do. Let's go out."

"I'd love to, but unless you hit the lottery, we won't have any extra money until next week."

"It's not the lottery, but…" A sly grin played on her lips. "…I did do the laundry today. Look what I found in one of the dryers?" She pulled two twenty dollar bills out of her pocket. "No one else was there, so finders keepers, yeah?"

"In that case, you're buying."

The weekend was off to a great start. Garren was back on track, being the husband he should have been the first time around. Kate was responsive, still enamored by what was, for her, the novelty of marriage. They held hands, gazed into each other's eyes, enjoyed the meandering conversation that drifted so effortlessly between tender words of affection and the humor of the many little inside jokes they shared. For the moment, the things that could ruin this perfect evening had been pushed aside. Kate was not thinking of the young woman named Sofia. Garren had stopped telling himself that he had already lived this evening once before and he had ceased looking for details that could jog his memory. Together, they were able to enjoy it for what it was, a simple night out.

And then Tommy showed up.

"Hey, you guys." He dropped clumsily into the empty chair next to Kate, sloshing his drink as he landed it roughly on the table. "Whoa, the Eagle has landed." He tried unsuccessfully to wipe the spill with his shirt sleeve. "Sorry about that. What are you guys doing here?"

"Having dinner," Garren replied, stating the obvious.

Kate liked Tommy, partly because he reminded her of an Owen Wilson character – the lovable under-achiever whose heart kept him so solidly in the moment that his head could not think far enough ahead to see the consequences of his actions. As a result, Tommy skipped merrily through life, leaving a trail of one-night stands and missed opportunities in his wake. The only constant was his friendship with Garren – they'd known each other since high school – and now Kate. She was fully aware that when she married Garren,

Tommy was part of the deal. "Hi, Tommy," she said. "Are you here alone?" She knew the answer, but hoped the reminder would send Tommy back to the evening's love of his life.

Tommy thought for a moment. "No, no. I'm here with some friends." He scanned the restaurant and pointed to a table occupied by two very attractive, smartly dressed women. "That's Melissa and…" He scrunched up his face, looked up and did this thing with his hands like he was ticking off items from a list. "No, it's Marissa and…don't tell me…Tawny. Yep, that's it, Marissa and Tawny. Do you want to meet them?"

"No, that's all right," said Garren.

"They seem nice though," offered Kate.

"Oh, yeah, they're great. They're from South Carolina, here for some kind of conference. A couple of real southern belles."

"Where did you meet them?" Kate asked.

"The gym."

"Are you still going to the Hilton?" Garren knew Tommy couldn't afford a real gym membership. He also knew his friend could be creative when properly motivated. Meeting women was always a proper motivation.

"I prefer the Hotel Julien these days."

"Hilton kicked you out, eh?"

"It was mutual. We agreed that I would be better served elsewhere. Turns out they were right. The Julien has hotter women."

"Well, thanks for coming over, Tommy," said Kate. "It's always great to see you."

"Speaking of hot women," said Tommy, "you wouldn't happen to have the number for that Sofia girl, would you?"

"No," Garren replied, irritated that he would ask.

"How do you know Sofia?" Kate asked.

"I met her yesterday at your place. Oops, maybe I shouldn't have said that. Sorry, Bro."

"It's okay," said Garren. "Kate knows all about her."

"And you're not mad?" Tommy gave Kate an approving nod. "Extra cool points for Kate."

"There's nothing to be mad about," said Kate. "But you ought to be ashamed of yourself. She's only seventeen years old."

"Almost eighteen," said Tommy. "Besides, Garren was in his twenties when you were seventeen."

"I didn't know Garren when I was seventeen."

"Doesn't matter," Tommy said with a shrug. "You're together now."

"Yes, but I was twenty-three when we met."

"And now you're what? Twenty-five? Barely out of your teens. While Garren here is in his thirties. That's practically middle-aged. I, on the other hand, am still in my twenties."

"You're twenty-nine," Garren pointed out.

"Doesn't matter. The way I figure it, Sofia and I are actually closer in age than you and the old man here."

Kate liked Tommy, but she wasn't about to let his charm alter the facts. "Or you could use real math. I am only five years younger than Garren. You are eleven years older than Sofia. And she's still a minor!"

"Not for long," Tommy countered.

"You're disgusting!" Kate's irritation was beginning to show. "How can you think of another woman…*girl*…when you've got two real women waiting for you? How you meet so many women is a mystery to me. I think you should take your drink and get back to your dates."

"Speaking of mysteries," said Tommy, unfazed by Kate's logic, "what do you think of Garren claiming to be a time-traveler from the year 2020? Which, by the way, would make him fifty years old. Talk about robbing the cradle."

"Tommy," said Garren, "Kate's right. You should go now."

"And not just Garren," Tommy continued. "Sofia is from the future, too. She's actually thirty-seven. And for the record, I'm not opposed to dating older women. So what about that?"

"Tommy," said Garren. "That's enough."

"What is he talking about, Garren?" asked Kate.

Tommy explained. "Yesterday, when I found Sofia waiting outside your apartment, she told me she was from the future. I thought she was putting me on. Then Garren got home and the two of them tried to get me to believe it. Now I'm not saying time-travel is impossible. In fact, I think it would be pretty awesome. But if you tell me you're from the future and expect me to believe it, you better be able to back it up with some hard evidence. Sorry, buddy, I just don't believe your story." Tommy took a sip of his drink. "But it is a great story, Bro. What do you think, Katie?"

"Garren?" said Kate. "Is that true? Did you and Sofia tell him you were from the future? Why would you do that?"

"Like Tommy said, we were just putting him on. It was a joke."

"It didn't seem like a joke when you threw me out," said Tommy. "You seemed pretty mad that I didn't believe you."

"It was all part of the gag," Garren said. "Sofia wanted to see how far we could take it."

"But it's not funny," said Kate. "It's not even clever. It's just weird."

Garren scratched the back of his head. "Well, yeah, now that we're talking about it. But in the moment, it was interesting."

"So, what?" said Kate. "You and your student just thought it would be interesting to tell someone you are from the future? Why?"

Garren thought fast. "It was a challenge. In class we've been talking about the reliability of the historical record and how some things are fiercely defended even in the face of new evidence. Conversely, I pointed out how some people are willing to believe unconventional ideas that challenge the accepted narrative. For example: The moon landing. There are some who believe it was a hoax. In order to demonstrate, I challenged the class to conduct some experiments to see how difficult or easy it is to get someone to believe something unbelievable." Even as the words were coming out of his mouth he could see Kate mentally challenging the veracity of his story.

"You're teaching your students to lie. That's a terrible idea."

Tommy, however, bought it. "Dude, that's awesome. Do you want me come in and speak to your class? I could tell how I totally saw through it. I could be your example of how they need to think about life and stuff. I knew you weren't really from the future. Well, now that that's settled, I really should be getting back to Melissa and Tanya."

"Marissa and Tawny," said Kate.

Tommy winked at her and clicked his tongue. "Right."

Kate stared at Garren for several long seconds. "What's up with you and time-travel? This isn't the first time you've mentioned it."

"I don't know. I find it fascinating."

"It's one thing to be interested in something fantastic like that, but when you start trying to make people believe something that isn't real, that's not normal. And to involve your students like that…that's not right. Is there something else going on, Garren, that you need to tell me?"

Garren still wanted to tell Kate the truth, but this was definitely not the right time. He was already out on a limb as it was. Any more talk of time-travel would likely send him crashing to the ground. "No. It was just a silly idea that got out of hand. I shouldn't have done it."

Kate looked down at her plate. "If my kid were in your class, I'd tell her to take an F on that assignment."

Tommy, Garren thought. He looked over and saw the three of them laughing. Tommy, in his usual animated manner, was dishing out some elaborate story about himself and the two beauties were totally into it. How did Tommy get away with lying to impress women and he couldn't even tell his own wife the truth?

"Garren, did you hear what I said?"

"I'm sorry, what?"

"I said there's no point in letting this ruin our evening. Let's stop by the video store on the way home and get a movie. Maybe they'll have *Back to the Future.*"

—⁓—

"I can't believe you've never seen this," Garren said as the credits rolled. The video store didn't have *Back to the Future*, but they did have *Ground Hog Day*.

Kate replied, "I was eighteen when this movie came out. I'm sure my parents saw it."

"Hey, what's that supposed to mean? Didn't you like it?"

"No, it was fine. It's just not the kind of movie I would have watched then. I never really got Bill Murray."

"Are you serious? Bill Murray is the best."

"I'm sure my dad would agree with you."

"Are you saying I'm old?"

"Sometimes you act a little older than you are…especially since you turned thirty."

"Gee, thanks." Garren got up from the couch. "I think I'll shuffle off into the shower, have some warm milk and turn in."

"Hey, if you're not too tired…" She winked at him.

"I'll make it fast."

Kate grabbed her backpack from beside the couch and pulled out a book she was reading for one of her classes. Garren usually took long showers; enough time to finish one of the assigned chapters. Halfway down the first page, she came upon a quote that would fit perfectly into a paper she was writing. She reached for the pen on the table to make a note, but found it out of ink. She tossed it back onto the table and looked for another one. You'd think an apartment shared by two academically inclined people would have plenty of pens lying about, but there weren't any in sight. Spotting Garren's briefcase, she opened it and started rummaging around. In between the notebooks containing Garren's lesson plans, she spotted a leather bound book; the kind one would use for a journal. It wasn't like Garren to keep a journal and she wasn't prone to snooping. However, given the way Garren had been acting lately, the temptation was strong. She glanced toward the bathroom. The shower was still running. He would never know if she just took a peek. No, that would be a breach of the trust upon which their entire relationship was built. She wouldn't violate that. Finding a pen, she turned her attention back to her assignment, however the mysterious journal would not leave her mind. She read two paragraphs of her book only to become aware that she had no idea what she had just read. All she could think about was that journal. Trying to force it out of her mind only made it worse. In order to deal with it, she began to rationalize: *It's probably not a real journal. It's probably just another notebook filled with job related information. Or it's a calendar. Or maybe it's a grade book. Garren always complained about how the standard grade books lacked style. It's not a real journal.* Rationalization complete, Kate set her book aside and retrieved the leather book.

Her first impression was that it was new. The pages were still smooth with a uniform edge, as if they had not yet been opened. Fanning through them, she found a blur of unmarked whiteness; a recent purchase. Her second impression was that it was not inexpensive. The cover was not fine leather, but still it was leather… or perhaps imitation leather. Either way, it wasn't like the cheap $4.99 journals she'd seen in the university book store. The price tag on the back cover read $19.99. Why would Garren spend money they didn't have on an expensive blank book? Perhaps it was a gift for her. Garren knew she liked to journal. But her birthday wasn't for several months and their anniversary was further than that. The next occasion would be…Valentine's Day. Was this his Valentine gift to her and he just hadn't wrapped it yet? Ah, how sweet. She almost dropped it back into the briefcase, but something made her open to the first page. There she found Garren's unique script. But instead of being addressed to her, this was written on the first page:

Thursday, January 6, 2000

> *Garren, if you're reading this, you made it back and so did I. I guess whatever happened to us corrected itself and we are back to where…or when we belong. It feels strange referring to myself in the plural. After all, we are the same person. But acknowledging the situation, it seems appropriate to make the distinction.*
>
> *I am tempted to describe my experience thus far, to talk about how great Kate is, but I have not yet decided the impact my activities may or may not have upon your*

*return. Suffice it to say, I have accepted this experience
as a gift, a chance to right some wrongs and be the
man I should have been...the man I hope you will be. I
suspect you understand what I am trying to say, having
experienced this phenomenon from the other side. What
must you have thought of how our life turned out?
Hopefully, your time there served as a wake-up call, and
now that you are back, you will continue upon the path
that I have tried to put us on. I wish us the best and hope
that upon my return, I will find that our efforts will have
succeeded.*

*But now, I turn to the purpose of this journal. Consider
it a gift. Use it wisely. Learn from it. Make wise decisions.
What follows is my recollection of the next twenty years
(2000-2019). Forgive me for not remembering more
accurately. I will make note of dates about which I am
certain. The rest should be taken as close approximations.*

*Before I begin, I need to tell you that you are not alone.
A woman by the name of Sofia Rae has experienced the
same phenomenon. Perhaps you met her. She was (or will
be) an acquaintance of Tommy's. We met on December 31,
2019 – the night we switched places. Anyway, she was a
student of ours at Hempstead High School, class of 2000,
but in all likelihood she is now living in New York. Her
phone number is: _____. Please contact
her. She could probably use a friend who understands.*

*Well, that's about it by way of introduction. It would
have been amazing to cross paths, but this whatever-it-is is
weird enough as it is. Be assured, I've done my best to take
care of your life. After all, it was mine, too.*

Good Luck, Garren

It is uncertain how much of the page Kate was able to read
before the water cut off and Garren called out for her to bring him
a towel. She snapped the book shut and jammed it back into his
briefcase. She was as curious about the strange message as she was
guilty for having read what was obviously not meant for her eyes.
Whatever it was, it was personal. Strange, to be sure, bizarre even,
but personal. And whatever the explanation was, she would have
to trust Garren. Whether she would ever try to read it again was

unknown to her. It would be better if Garren shared it with her on his own under the right circumstances. Perhaps she could create the right circumstances.

21

Next morning, Kate woke to find Garren already up and in the living room. She could smell the coffee and hear the television set at low volume. She slipped out of bed and tip-toed to the door. Peeking around the corner, she saw him sitting on the couch with his back to her. He was watching one of the cable news stations.

"What are you doing?" she asked as she made her entrance.

Garren jumped at the unexpected greeting and slid something down into the couch cushion. "Oh, hey, just catching up on the news. Did I wake you?"

"No." She came around, kissed him on the head and sat next to him. "Why are you up so early on a Saturday? It's not even seven o'clock."

"Couldn't sleep."

"So you decided to watch this? Poor man's cure for insomnia."

"Something like that. See that guy?" Garren pointed at the television. Two commentators were discussing the man in a still photo between them.

"He looks familiar. Who is he?"

"Osama bin Laden. He's on the FBI's Ten Most Wanted."

"What'd he do?"

"He's responsible for bombing the U.S. embassies in Kenya and Tanzania a couple years ago. Killed two hundred and twenty four people."

"Oh."

"He's going to kill a lot more."

Kate listened to the broadcast for a minute, trying to catch up with what they were saying. "Why do they say that?"

"He's calling for a holy war against Jews and Crusaders. He says Muslims should kill Americans anywhere in the world."

"You don't think that could happen here, do you?"

"It happened in '93. A truck bomb in the parking garage underneath the World Trade Center. They were trying to bring it down."

"I forgot about that. I'm sure they've got ways of guarding against that sort of thing now."

They watched some more. Kate quickly became bored, but Garren was mesmerized by the pre-9/11 confidence the commentators shared with his wife. In that moment, the weight of his foreknowledge pressed upon him, and with it an overwhelming sense of responsibility to do something, tell someone, if not prevent it, at least warn people. But how? What could he say that anyone would believe? Without realizing it, he mumbled his thoughts: "Not against airplanes."

"What did you say?"

Against his better judgment, he decided to test the waters. "Airplanes. They could hijack a couple commercial airliners and fly them into the towers. That'll bring them down."

"The World Trade Center." A crease formed between Kate's eyebrows as her analytic mind went to work. "Both buildings?"

"It could happen."

"That's some theory. Is that what they're saying?" She nodded toward the television.

"No." Garren was tired of lying, but he couldn't just open the front door to the whole truth. But perhaps a window. "I've imagined such an attack on the U.S. It's possible."

Kate pondered the scenario. "I imagine it's not easy to hijack a commercial airliner. Gaining control of two at the same time would be quite a feat. Getting both hijackers to follow through on a suicide mission puts it in the realm of the highly improbable, if not impossible. But assuming an airplane strike could topple a building that size, which I doubt it could, getting the same results in both buildings would be like two people drawing the same poker hand out of two separate decks. The odds are astronomical."

"When you say it like that, it is hard to believe, yet…" Garren let the thought hang in the air while his memory of that terrible day filled in the rest of the details: Not two, but four hijacked planes, three downed towers in New York, three gaping holes – the side of the pentagon, a field in Pennsylvania, the heart of America.

Kate waited for him to finish. When he didn't, her own mind began to draw seemingly unrelated ideas together: Garren's journal, one mysterious line in particular – *What follows is my recollection of the next twenty years (2000-2019)* – and now his ominous prediction – *He's going to kill a lot more* – followed by specific details – *commercial airliners into the World Trade Center.* This from the man with an admitted disdain for speculation. He chose his profession because he preferred discovery of the facts of history over guess work about the future. Garren Rosen, PhD. could spend hours discussing an event that happened thousands of years ago or reminiscing about last summer's cruise up the river – the man could tell a story – but he became antsy after five minutes of talk about things that may or may not happen next year. The chronology of their relationship was testimony to this characteristic. Though immediately attracted to each other, it was Garren who set the pace – slow. They spent time together, became friends creating their own history. Then after a year of casual, non-committal interaction, which had given Kate the idea he may never come around, Garren asked her out on a real date. Between dinner and dessert, he expressed his true feelings. She reciprocated. Three months later, he proposed. Three months after that, they were married. History without much speculation. All this to say, Garren's sudden preoccupation with the future was out of character.

"Okay," Kate said, "you've given me the *who*, the *what* and the *how*. How about the *when*?" She was more interested in how he would reply than what he might actually say.

Garren sensed something was up. It wasn't like her to keep pressing a matter, especially one without any observable evidence. It was Kate's own no-nonsense approach to life that made her amendable to such a brief courtship. Once she made up her mind about something, she saw no point in waiting. He eyed her suspiciously. "Next year."

Safe answer. More than enough time to forget all about wild speculations. Now she wondered if he might be messing with her. She could play, too. "Care to narrow that down a bit?"

"Oh, I don't know." Garren shrugged. "Late summer, early fall… maybe September."

"Okay, I see what's going on here." Kate got up and went into the kitchen. "You're testing your believability theory on me. If we're going to play *guess the future*, let's talk about something less tragic. What else you got, Future Man?"

"I wasn't trying to get you to believe anything," he replied. "Just making an observation. But since we're on the topic, if I really did want you to believe I am from the future, what would it take to convince you?"

Kate returned to the couch, cradling a steaming cup of coffee. "None of that next year stuff. You'd have to tell me something that's going to happen soon. And nothing vague or obvious. It would have to be something specific and unexpected. What outfit do I wear to Denise's tonight?"

Garren chuckled. "I'm a time-traveler, not a mind-reader." Saying it out loud felt good, even if Kate took it as part of the game.

"Okay, who wins the Super Bowl? I'll make it even easier. Who plays in the Super Bowl?"

Garren sighed. "Do you even know me? It has to be something I actually care to remember. Like how you look right now."

Kate smiled behind her coffee cup. "What else?"

"I remember the way you play with your hair when you're studying and how you stick out your tongue when you're in deep concentration."

"I do that, don't I? Keep going."

"I remember how excited you were when we finally moved into a house and bought our first washer and dryer."

"Now that's a good memory. When was that again?"

"June 2002."

"This is fun. Tell me more."

Garren propped his feet up on the coffee table and let his mind go back to the early days of their marriage. "I remember how much fun we had, how you made everything an adventure. I remember going out and pretending we didn't know each other just so we could flirt with each other in public. I remember making out in elevators. I remember faking accents so people would think we were from somewhere exciting. I remember our spy weekend when we checked into a hotel using aliases and pretended we were on a mission. That one nearly got us arrested."

"Wait a minute," Kate interrupted. "That does *not* sound like us."

"Not yet, but once you graduate we get a little crazy for a couple years."

"Time out." Kate made a T sign with her hands.

"What?" Garren snapped out of his nostalgia.

"I get your point. You can sound pretty convincing. If I didn't know you were just making stuff up, I'd be tempted to believe you."

"See? I'm pretty good at this, yeah?"

"A little too good. Promise me you'll never try that on me for real."

Garren chuckled and tried to make it sound genuine. "I doubt I'd get away with it. You're too smart."

Silence settled upon them, except for the news anchor who had gone on to another topic. Kate sipped her coffee while Garren replayed the last few minutes of honest conversation, wondering how he might actually get her to believe him. Finally, Kate spoke up.

"Some of those things you made up sound fun. Want to go downtown and ride a few elevators?"

"As you wish, m'lady," Garren replied in his best British accent.

—✦—

They were still laughing when they pulled onto Denise's street. The day had turned out to be even more fun than Kate expected and Garren remembered. They'd put on their nicest clothes and hung out at Dubuque's fanciest hotels pretending to be European entrepreneurs investigating business ventures in America's heartland. At the Hilton, they were Fredrick and Greta Vaterhausen, industrialists from Germany. The Hotel Julian received the honor of welcoming Italy's hottest new fashion designers, Anton and Monique Vitano. They thought they were busted when they ran into Marissa and Tawny in the lobby. Monique was brilliant, letting it slip that they were scouting models for a new American line of eveningwear. The girls from South Carolina insisted on buying them coffee after which phone numbers were exchanged for autographs. And yes, the elevators were fun, too.

"That was fun, but it didn't prove anything," said Kate.

"What do you mean?" Garren asked.

"It didn't prove you are from the future. You didn't remember this day. You cleverly planted a suggestion."

Garren shrugged. "Maybe."

"And we shouldn't make it a habit."

"Why not?"

"We just spent the afternoon lying through our teeth."

"Pretending."

"Call it what you like, we deceived people. It kind of bothers me how easy it was. I mean, it was hard at first, but after a few minutes, I totally got into it. Now I feel kind of dirty."

"It was just a little fun. It's not like we hurt anyone or stole anything."

"So begins a million stories that end with 'and they spent the remainder of their days in prison.' I don't think Anton and Monique should come back to Dubuque."

"You're probably right, but you have to admit it was fun."

"Okay, I admit it. But from now on, let's make reality even more fun."

"Hey, guys, come on in," said Denise. "Sofia and I will have dinner ready in a few minutes."

Kate and Garren peeled out of their coats and hung them on hooks behind the door.

"She's in a good mood," noted Garren.

"I know," Kate agreed. "Wonder what's up with that."

They walked into the kitchen and found Sofia and Denise laughing.

"You two seem to be enjoying yourselves," said Kate.

"Oh, yeah," said Denise. "Sofia and I have had the best day."

"What did you guys do?" Garren asked.

"You know, girl stuff." Denise looked at Sofia and the two of them busted out laughing again.

"Okay then," said Garren. "I guess I'll be in the living room."

"I'll set the table," said Sofia.

"Wow," said Denise as if just noticing Kate's appearance, "you look amazing. What's up with the fancy clothes? And is my sister wearing makeup? What's up?"

"Nothing. Just something Garren and I did today. I'll tell you about it later. So, this is working out…having Sofia here?"

"She's great," Denise replied. "It's not like babysitting at all. She's smart and funny and wise beyond her years. If I didn't know better, I'd never have guessed she's still in high school. She has an old soul."

"Really."

"Oh, yeah. She's like this really cool, confident, outgoing woman in this young schoolgirl body. It's kinda weird."

"What do you mean?"

Denise lowered her voice. "We stayed up really late last night talking. I thought I'd be the one trying to help her, but it turned out the other way around. We started talking about guys. I told her all about my ex. She listened. She offered some really good advice. It was like talking with someone who has, you know, been around and really gets people. I literally had to keep reminding myself she's a teenager. She's not at all what I expected."

"Huh." Kate plugged this new information into the narrative of the last couple days. "That's great. I'm glad she's not an inconvenience to you."

"Not at all. In fact, I told her she could stay here as long as she likes."

Kate's attention was drawn to the little catch-all table in the corner.

Denise tended to something on the stove and continued, "I'm trying to talk her into staying at least until graduation, but she insists on going to New York."

On the table, Kate noticed a leather-bound journal exactly like the one she found in Garren's briefcase. "That's great. You think she's open to it?" As Denise talked, Kate opened the book to the first page and began reading the following:

> *These are my tragic memories. Hopefully, in case of a merciful reversal, they will prove to be helpful instructions. I can't believe this is happening to me. As if my life didn't already suck, now I have to relive it. Ugh, I just want to crawl into a hole and sleep the next twenty years. My only consolation is G. Whatever caused this misfortune (I won't give it credence by naming it) didn't affect me alone. G is here with me, but he's just as helpless to do anything about it as I am. The difference is he's happy about it, which makes it that much harder on me. That's another thing I refuse to give power to by putting it into words. At least I know I won't have to see him much longer. Irony: My solace is also my pain.*
>
> *2000 – Leaving Dubuque is easy. The old man's safe is in his closet. I forgot the combination, but the idiot has it written on the wall behind his shirts. There's a couple grand in there, but leave the gun. I didn't need it and it was a hassle to hide. The bus ride to New York was long, but uneventful. I sat in the back and pretended to sleep the whole way. New York was hard at first. Don't waste your money on a hotel. Go to the C3 Church on W 46th St. and find Dave and Laurie. They are good people. They let me stay there for a few weeks. You need to find Nikki Starr as soon as you can. I met her on the subway in late June or July. She came to my rescue when I was being harassed by some guy, which tells you something about her. We hit it off and I moved in*

with her when her roommate bailed in August (I think – it's hard to remember specific details). Anyway, that's a touchy subject, so don't ask about it. You can also find her at The Pyramid Club on Avenue A between E. 6th and E. 7th Street. She DJs and tends bar on weekends. She's a total 80s chick – twenty-three, pretty, petite; looks like Pat Benatar. I don't want to give too much away because she might think you're up to something, but here are some things that can get a conversation started: She has a cat named Mars, favorite movie is Pretty in Pink (I know, just go with it), favorite book is Lord of the Rings (reads it over and over), her mom kissed Eddie Van Halen back in the early 80s – she kissed his son a few years ago (loves to talk about that), and she's never driven a car (embarrassed by that). She puts up a tough front, but she's a sweetheart. Saved my life more than once. If you can, try to warn her off of a guy named Pierre. He hurts her bad. Watch out for her brother, Stan. He's good looking, but he's bad news. DO NOT go out with him. I regret that. What else? Oh, Nikki will get you a job at The Pyramid, but let her bring it up. She will also introduce you to her friends. The thing to remember is you've got to play it cool with these people. They can be cynical, they don't trust easily and they don't do needy. You'll be fine. After all, I made it without this tutorial.

As with Garren's journal, it is unclear how much Kate read before Sofia came back into the kitchen to get the silverware. She flipped the cover closed before she was discovered, but she'd read enough to put two and two together. Her husband and Sofia were up to something.

Dinner was delicious, but Kate was too distracted to enjoy it. She let Garren and Denise do most of the talking, which was unusual, and she could tell they noticed it. Garren regaled Denise and Sofia with the afternoon's exploits at the hotels. Denise responded appropriately with big-sisterly shakes of the head to hide her longing to have someone with whom she could have such adventures. Sofia was appropriately amused, though Kate thought her attention to Garren was a little much. Every look and smile seemed to carry an expression of affection. When Sofia touched Garren's hand as he passed the salt, Kate believed they lingered. Fueled by the mysterious journals, Kate's imagination concocted a scandalous narrative that made posing as Italian fashion designers and scoring free drinks seem like child's play. Dessert was served with an extra dollop of chill from Kate's side of the table, followed by another lie that she wasn't feeling well and thought it best to call it an early night. She hugged Denise and coolly nodded at Sofia, then grabbed her coat and walked out into the cold.

"It's probably something she ate at the hotel," Garren offered to Denise's and Sofia's questioning looks. "I'm sure she'll be fine. Dinner was great. Thanks, both of you."

Denise hugged him. Sofia's intuition caused her to hang back and conclude the evening with a, "Goodnight, Mr. Rosen. I hope your wife feels better."

The ride home wasn't any better. Kate stared out the passenger side window so Garren couldn't see her face. Every time he tried to engage her, she shut him down with one-word replies. Arriving at their apartment, she didn't wait for him to open her door, but got out and walked quickly up the stairs and used her own key to open the door. By the time Garren caught up with her, he found her rifling through his briefcase.

"Where is it?" she demanded.

"Where's what?"

"Your journal. I want to read it."

"Kate—"

"Don't pretend you don't know what I'm talking about. I saw it and I saw Sofia's, too." Her voice was starting to quiver. "Could you two be any more obvious?" And then the tears came. Kate was mad – at Garren for being a man, at Sofia for being so irresistibly gorgeous, and herself for not being strong enough to contain her emotions. Why couldn't she just be mad at Garren? It was all his fault.

"Katie, I can explain." He shouldn't have called her Katie.

The tears stopped as her eyes narrowed and the muscles in her jaw tensed so much that she could barely be heard. "The journal...now."

Garren paused, tapped his chin with his index finger and shook his head. "Okay." He walked over to the couch and pulled the journal from beneath the cushion. "There's more to this than you think."

Kate snatched the journal from his hand, stormed into the bedroom and slammed the door. Garren dropped onto the couch. After several minutes, he shed his coat, kicked off his shoes and stretched himself out. Obviously, he was going to be there for the night.

22

"I'm ready to talk now."

Garren cracked open his eyes. A quick glance toward the window told him it was still dark outside. The only light was coming from the kitchen behind him. Kate was sitting cross-legged in the chair facing him, his journal in her lap. It didn't look like she had slept at all. He probably shouldn't have either. Pushing himself into a sitting position, he winced at the stabbing pains in his neck and back. Strange, since it had always been such a great napping couch. Perhaps the furniture was in cahoots with Kate and he deserved it.

"Why is Pluto not a planet?" she asked.

It wasn't the question he expected and this wasn't the way he'd hoped Kate would learn the truth, but it was happening. Finally, no more hints. No more lies and half-truths. No more testing the waters. It was time for the truth as strange and unbelievable as it was. Then it would be up to Kate whether to believe it or not. He shrugged. "I don't know. It might be a planet again, but I can't remember for sure. That might have been a rumor."

She made a face and looked down at the journal. "They made *Harry Potter* into a movie."

"Eight movies."

"Are they good?"

"We like them."

Kate nodded and looked back down. "Why should we buy stock in Amazon? You starred it and underlined it twice."

"It's huge. Everybody shops Amazon...for everything."

"Google?"

"Also huge."

"Apple?"

"Even bigger."

"What's an iPhone?"

"It's a cell phone, but it's more than a cell phone. It's actually a little computer, but it does more than that one we have on the desk over there. Everybody has one or something similar to it. It literally changes the way we live."

"Hmm." Kate turned the page and her eyebrows went up. "You're wrong about my dad's job. You wrote that he works for John Deere."

"He does work for John Deere."

"Garren, you know my father. You've been to his store – Morley Farm and Supply. It's been in our family for three generations. He would never work for a big corporation like that."

"I can't remember when, but he does...he will."

"Don't you remember Thanksgiving? He offered you a *real job* whenever you get tired of talking to people about the past? You got kind of offended."

"Oh, yeah," Garren said with a chuckle. "I forgot about that."

Kate shook her head with a smirk. She got him on that one. Then she became serious. "You don't mention our kids." She said it as a statement, but Garren could hear the question in her voice.

"We, uh, we can't have kids."

Kate's face registered the pain of the revelation. "Is that why we..." She took a shuddering breath. "Is that why *I* become..." She read the section out loud. "2009 – Kate is obsessed with her career. She blames it on the economy and fear of losing her job, but I know it's something else. We are more like roommates than lovers. I think I'm losing her."

"That's part of it, but it was me, too. I wasn't there for you like I should have been, but I am now. Kate, I think this is why I came back. I'm being given a second—"

She cut him off, not wanting to hear that. "You wrote: September 11, 2001. Everything changes. Explain."

Garren would rather have stayed on the topic of them, to get her to understand that he'd spent the last week trying to salvage their marriage, but she was calling the shots.

"Talk about September 11," she pressed.

He thought he had given a thorough explanation of the impact of 9/11 upon America and the world, but again, she was calling the shots. He repeated some of what he had written, elaborated on some of the points. He could tell she wasn't really listening.

She interrupted him again. "Sofia is mentioned in your introduction, but that's all. You don't mention her again. Why not?"

"There isn't anything to say. She's not a part of my life."

"This doesn't make any sense." Kate closed the journal and placed it on the coffee table. "Is this some kind of fantasy?"

Garren shook his head. "I know what it sounds like, but it's not."

"What is it then? Are you looking for a way out of our marriage?"

"No."

Kate crossed her arms and stared hard at him. "What exactly is your relationship with Sofia? Do you love her?"

"No!"

"Then what is it?"

Garren rubbed his forehead between his eyes. "I know this sounds crazy, but it's what I've been trying to tell you since…" He took a breath and blew it out. "Since I got here."

"Got here? From where?"

"Not where…*when*."

Kate covered her mouth. "I don't know whether to laugh or cry. Garren, you're scaring me."

"I know. I'm sorry. I just don't know what else to say."

"How about the truth?"

"I'm trying."

"Try again. From the beginning."

"Okay." Garren shifted on the couch and took a moment to collect himself. "Last week…New Year's Eve…for me it was the year 2019. I went to a party at Tommy's apartment. I had too much to drink. When I woke up on New Year's Day, it was the year 2000. I can't explain how it happened, but it did. I have no proof other than my memories of the next twenty years, which I am trying to write down in case whatever happened to me switches back. I promise you, Kate, that is the truth."

"Where am I in 2019?"

"You're at Denise's house. She lives in Des Moines. You've been there since before Christmas."

"Are we separated?"

"I guess you could call it that."

"What about Sofia? Where does she fit into all this?"

"The same thing happened to her."

"Do you know her in 2019?"

Garren hesitated, not liking where this was going. "Not really. I met her at Tommy's party."

Kate nodded. "Did you sleep with her?"

Garren wanted more than anything to tell her he didn't, but he was done lying. "I honestly don't know."

Kate raised her eyebrows.

"Like I said, I drank a lot that night. I don't remember much about it."

Kate stared at him for several seconds, trying to decide how far to take this. "Tell me what you do remember. I want to know everything that happened that night."

He shifted again. "I wasn't gonna go to Tommy's because I thought you would be home. I tried to call you, but your phone went straight to voicemail. I tried to locate your car, but you'd turned off the locater. I was upset and angry. Tommy called me again. I didn't want to spend New Year's Eve alone, so I went. I arrived at Tommy's. We watched the asteroid hit the moon. And then we went inside."

"Hold on," Kate cut in. "An asteroid hit the moon?"

"Asteroid. Meteor. I don't know what it was, but yes."

"Go on."

"We went inside. We were watching the news about the moon and this woman and I started talking about it."

"Sofia?"

"Yes. She said she'd just moved back here from New York. She'd met Tommy at the gym, he invited her to his party, she came. Let's see…we talked, I told her I was married, she guessed we were having some problems, we talked some more, we had a few drinks…and then the next thing I know, I'm in our apartment with you on January 1, 2000."

Two full minutes passed as Kate replayed the events of the last week. "Why didn't you tell me sooner?"

"I tried. I have tried so many times. I didn't think you would believe me."

Another minute.

"In 2019, did you know Sofia was a former student?"

"No. I had no recollection of her."

"Did she know it was you?"

"I don't think so. We didn't talk about high school."

Kate paused again as she did the math. "The night you met her, you would have been a day shy of fifty and she would have been thirty-seven?"

"Yeah."

"I imagine she's a very beautiful woman."

"I'm not going to lie to you anymore. She's attractive. Yes, beautiful."

"I guess I can't blame you. Lonely man. Beautiful younger woman. I see how that must have made you feel. So, um, when you came back to this time and you saw her, what was that like? Did you recognize her?"

"Not at first. She figured it out before I did."

Kate started and stopped a few times before landing on what she wanted to say next. "Quite a story. Two people attracted to each other, travel into the past together to do what? Make things right? Be with the one they should have been with?"

"Yes. No! Kate, no. I mean, yes, make things right. No, not to be with each other. I'm with you, Kate. It's always been you."

Kate let another minute pass. "I think I understand now."

"You do? That's great." Garren breathed a sigh of relief. It was touch and go there for a while, but she was taking it much better than he thought.

"I have a plan. Do you want to hear it?"

Finally, they were working together. "Yes, I do." He leaned forward, ready to move forward as a team.

"I'm gonna go out for a while. You're gonna pack whatever you need. And when I get back, you'll be gone. I don't care where you go, I just want you gone."

Garren was too stunned to reply.

Kate continued. "I need some time to process. Since we don't have iPhones yet, I will leave a message with Tommy as to when you can come back to get the rest of your stuff. I won't be here. Don't try to find me." She got up from the chair, calmly picked up the journal and threw it as hard as she could. Garren felt the breeze as it passed by his head and he heard something break in the kitchen behind him. "Since this is where we end up anyway, let me save you the trouble of the next twenty years." Then, as calmly as any other day, she put on her coat and lifted the keys from the hook by the door. She went back into the kitchen and retrieved the time journal. "I'm not done with this." Then she was gone.

Emotional paralysis, if there is such a thing, prevented Garren from going after her, which was probably for the best. He'd said all there was to be said. Any more would only make things worse. With nothing else to do, he waited for his legs to start working again. Then, like a robot, he put what he needed into a backpack and stepped out into the cold night.

Garren spent the night driving, his mind too wrecked to think about anything. Like the driverless cars of his own time, he was following a program downloaded into his brain from a lifetime in the same town. He went to his parent's house and pulled into the driveway. The house was dark and he didn't want to have to explain, so he left there and drove to Tommy's apartment. The light was on and he could hear music, but he was in no mood for a party. Next thing he knew, he was driving slowly past Denise's house. The house was dark except for a light in the room he assumed Sofia was in. She might be awake. The insane thought came to him that he would go to her window and he would tell her about what happened with Kate. But then his sanity returned and he left before he did anything stupid. He drove to the school, pulled into the lot, parked in his usual spot and switched off the engine. He thought about staying there, but after a few minutes he could feel the cold creeping in. He couldn't sleep anyway, so he decided to keep driving.

Chance or fate or just a random impulse sent him south on Highway 61. An hour and a half later, he rolled into Davenport in need of gas and a restroom. He found both at a 7-11. After using the facilities, he grabbed a Coke and a bag of doughnuts. Realizing he didn't have any cash, he pulled out his *emergency only* credit card. He almost put the doughnuts back, but then decided they qualified. At the checkout counter, he noticed a digital clock on the wall. It read two o'clock, but that didn't matter. He was a man out of time. He snorted at the thought.

Back on the road, he continued south on I-74, which would become I-155 outside of Peoria, and then turn into I-55 all the way into St. Louis. Somewhere around Galesburg, he switched on the radio. It was a little before three. The first clear station he found was airing a late night talk show called *Coast To Coast AM*. He'd never heard of the program and didn't care what it was. He just needed another voice besides the one in his head telling him how badly he'd messed up. Jumping in mid-topic, it took him a few minutes to catch on to what the host and his guest were discussing. He actually laughed out loud when he heard the guest say the words *time-travel*. Yes, they were actually talking time-travel, not the science behind it, but the evidence for it: Old photographs of people and objects that looked like they were from a different time period; modern technology discovered among ancient ruins; hieroglyphs on an Egyptian tomb depicting a modern airplane, helicopter and boat; Leonardo da Vinci's drawings of machines that would not exist until four hundred years after his death. Had Garren heard this two weeks earlier, he would have dismissed it as a hoax, over-active imagination, wishful thinking, pure entertainment. But now he gave it his serious attention and with that came clarity.

He'd experienced flashes of insight before, moments when the answer to a problem (usually of an historical nature) suddenly came to him. This was like that, only more intense. His view of history had just been injected with a proposition he'd never considered. The historical perspective he had developed over the years had been turned, and he was now able to see it from an entirely different angle. This new paradigm flashed before him like a bold headline: Time-travel as an active agent in the history of humanity? Then the questions came: Was Leonardo da Vinci a time-traveler? What about the guy who carved the hieroglyphs on that pharaoh's tomb? How many of the historical figures he studied and taught had been affected by the same phenomenon that plucked Sofia and himself out of 2019 and dropped them into 2000? Had the members of the historical hall of fame done amazing things and affected the course of history because they, like himself, possessed experiential knowledge of the future? If so, what did that say about history? Was it fixed or could it actually be changed? And what did that say about reality? Were there multiple versions? And what did that say about Garren Rosen and Sofia Rae? Were they chosen for something special? Were they part of the select few sent back in time (or to another version of reality) to do something or correct something? Is that how history worked? He would have to rethink the entire historical narrative.

The revelation may not have saved his marriage, but it may have saved him. Somewhere around Peoria, Garren turned around and headed back to Dubuque. He needed to talk to Sofia.

Part Three

The Solution

23

Not much happened on January 9, 2000. A quick Google search will tell you that Harrison Ford and Julia Roberts won People's Choice awards for their work in motion pictures and Drew Carey and Calista Flockhart won for television. Dan Marino won his last career NFL game. Google won't tell you that the author of this novel turned thirty-five that day. Nor will it tell you what happened in Dubuque, Iowa, to a man named Garren Rosen who arrived in this particular timeline eight days earlier with his memory of the next twenty years still intact.

Still amped up by his revelation about time-travel and its possible influence on history, Garren arrived back in Dubuque just as the sun was making its appearance. He'd slept only two of the last twenty-four hours, but his mind was reeling, pondering the possibility that any number of historical figures may have actually been time-traveling agents from the future. Pivotal events, coincidences and other unexplainable circumstances he could never quite wrap his mind around suddenly made sense. It explained Copernicus's concept of a heliocentric solar system a century before Galileo's improvements and use of the telescope proved him correct. It explained Columbus's insistence that he could reach the East Indies by sailing west. It accounted for the unlikely victory of the American colonists over the superior British army and for the collective brilliance of the Founding Fathers. It even explained the uncanny similarities between Morgan Robertson's 1898 novel, *The Wreck of the Titan: or Futility*, and the

1912 sinking of the RMS Titanic. It explained the rapid changes of the last hundred years – from candle light, horse-drawn buggies and full-body swimming apparel to artificial intelligence, off-world habitats and thong-bikinis in a single lifespan. It always seemed to Garren as if they were following a script. Now he knew why. Maybe all this wasn't the natural progression of human achievement and societal change. Perhaps history bore the fingerprints of people like Sofia and himself who were selectively transported backward in time to spark certain events and affect certain changes.

Were it not for the shambles he had made of his marriage, Garren's new appreciation for his situation would have made him the happiest man on earth. To be sure, he would gladly exchange his role as an agent of Time for another shot with Kate, but it would take another miracle for that to happen. Unless he could go back in time and relive the last week, he would just have to allow nature to take its course…let time heal…hope that some other cliché would somehow bring them back together. Perhaps if he could discover his mission and get that right, Time would reward him with a second chance at his second chance. But for now, he needed to compartmentalize. Convincing himself that tracking Kate down would be the worst thing he could do, he set his mind on the only other person who carried as much risk.

Pulling up to Denise's house, he was relieved to find the driveway empty. Seven o'clock on a Sunday morning, Denise's car should have been there. Chances are Kate had called her and the sisters were together. If she, or they, returned to find him there, he would be a dead man. Hopefully, Sofia was still there. Of course, she was on Kate's *persona non grata* list, same as he. She was either there or Denise had taken her someplace else on her way to meet Kate. Garren shook his head to clear out all the pointless speculation and rang the doorbell. Seconds later, the door opened. Sofia was dressed, backpack slung over her shoulder like she was about to vacate the premises.

"Boy, you got guts." Sofia looked past him as if to make sure no one else was there. "C'mon." She pushed past him and made her way to his car.

"Dare I ask what happened?"

"First, get us out of here."

In the safety of Garren's car, with Denise's house in the rearview mirror, Sofia hugged her backpack to her chest and closed her eyes.

"You okay?" Garren asked.

"Mm-hmm."

"What happened?"

"Your wife..." Sofia took a breath. "...*really* mad."

"Was she there? Did you see her?"

"No. Called thirty minutes ago. Denise filled me in. Long story short, doesn't want to see either of us...ever. Had you not shown up, I'd be hoofin' it. Got to get us some cellphones. Tried calling. Where were you?"

"Illinois." Garren shook his head as the Kate compartment in his brain begged for his attention. "Did she say anything else?"

"Wrecked her car."

Garren snapped a glance at her. "What! Is she hurt?"

"She's fine. Minor. Probably didn't help, though. Don't know what happened. Called from a gas station. Denise went to her. Be back soon."

"Are you sure you're okay?" Garren asked.

"Yeah, why?"

"You're talking in rapid fragments."

"I do that when I'm stressed. Sorry."

"It's okay. Take a minute." Garren drove in silence, resisting the urge to launch into his revelation. They headed north, for no other reason than he'd already gone south.

When they were out of town, Sofia spoke. "Am I correct in assuming you told her what happened to us?"

Garren glanced at her and smiled. "Welcome back. I was about to call our English department to help me translate."

"Cute. Seriously, you told her?"

"I had to. She found my journal. Actually, I'm relieved. I'm not happy that it went sideways, but I'm glad I told her the truth. I'm not a good liar."

"That explains why she thinks you're crazy. I heard that word, among others, through the phone. She's as scared as she is mad. She also thinks you and I are having an affair."

"Yep. I told her everything about New Year's Eve."

"I can see how she might come to that conclusion. I guess I owe you an apology."

"For what?"

"For not giving you the whole story about that night. It might have helped." Sofia looked out the side window so she wouldn't have to see his face. "Not exactly my finest moment."

"Sofia, you don't have to—"

"Yes, I do. I owe it to you." She took a deep breath and blew it out. "The woman you met that night is not really who I am...or not who I want to be. I've had a hard life. I survived by creating this persona of a confident woman. But I'm really not. I'm scared and self-conscious like everyone else. I really can read people, that part is true, and that's what I see. We're all pretty much the same. Some of us are just better at hiding it than others. I went to Tommy's that night expecting the usual, people pretending to be something they're not in hopes of finding something they can't even explain. I'm not judging because I'm the same way. I play the game just like everyone else. If there is a difference, and I'm not sure there is, I have strict rules and I never break them. Anyway, when I saw you, I figured you were just another player looking to score." She paused.

"Why did you talk to me?"

"You were good looking and you had this lost boy vibe about you. I figured I'd enjoy the scenery, have a few laughs, let you think something was going to happen and then leave you with a fake phone number and a story to tell your buddies."

"That's a pretty cynical way of looking at people."

"I agree. I'm not proud of it, but it's kept me from getting hurt... well, hurt again."

"I see."

"Do you want to know when I broke my own rules?"

Garren glanced at her, but didn't reply. He wanted to hear, but he didn't want Sofia to say anything she didn't want to say herself.

"When you told me you were married. I've met a lot of married men and none of them ever told me, at least not in the first few minutes. I thought you were either stupid, arrogant or totally in love. It didn't take long to figure out which one. So, I figured I'd stick close to you because you were safe."

"How does that violate your rules?"

"You disarmed me. I let my guard down. *Rule #1: Flirt, but never admit attraction.* I let that slip. Don't you remember?"

"I also remember you said we were the only two people there who weren't looking to hook up."

"That was me trying to recover...throw you off."

"You didn't have to."

"I know. Instinct, I guess."

"That's not so bad, you know. Like you said, everyone tries to keep their real self hidden from the world. We're lucky if we find just one person who can see behind the mask and accept us for who we really are."

"Yeah. I came really close to taking off my mask. Of course, the alcohol might have helped a bit. That's when I broke *Rule #2: Two drink maximum. No exceptions.*"

"I'm sorry I was such a bad influence."

"No you weren't, but that's when I almost broke *Rule #3*."

"I'm afraid to ask."

She turned back to the side window. "You should know that nothing happened between us. It could have. I even…I even suggested we…" She laughed nervously. "I'm really embarrassed right now."

"That's okay. Enough said."

Sofia wiped her face with the back of your hand and turned to face him. "You were so kind to me. Even as you were rejecting me, you did it in a way that didn't make me feel like a tramp. You even thanked me for the compliment."

"Sofia."

"I'm not finished. I want you to know nothing happened; not even a New Year's kiss. I left you alone in Tommy's room, fully clothed, your fidelity intact."

"Thank you for telling me. That's a relief, yeah? If we had…you know…this would be awkward."

"This *is* awkward."

Garren looked at her and for the first time saw her as a seventeen year old girl. "Okay, so we had a close encounter. But that's in the past. There's nothing we can do about it now."

Sofia tilted her head. "Actually, it's in the future, and correct me if I'm wrong, but isn't that exactly what you've been trying to do for the last week…do something to change the future? If you can salvage your marriage and if I can salvage my life, neither one of us will be at Tommy's party in 2019. It will be as if we never met. Or will it? Huh, I wonder what will happen when we get to that night again. Do you think we'll ever see 2020? Or will we end up back here again?"

"I don't know. If we could just figure out how this happened, I suppose we could prevent it from happening again. What else do you remember about that night? What did you do after you left me?"

"I went outside to clear my head. I was walking through Tommy's apartment complex. It must have just hit midnight because I heard people cheering and I saw fireworks. Then I felt really warm and everything got blurry. I thought I was going to pass out so I started running back toward Tommy's. And then I woke up here in 2000."

"There has to be something else. Something affected us. Do you remember seeing or hearing or smelling anything unusual?"

Sofia closed her eyes to concentrate. "Wait a minute. It wasn't midnight. I remember the countdown clock Tommy had programmed onto his television. It was only 11:30. I remember him asking me where I was going. He wanted to come with me. I told him I would be back before midnight. I went outside. I was walking. I saw...oh, no."

"What is it?"

"That wasn't cheering I heard. It wasn't fireworks. It was...oh my gosh! Garren, stop the car now!"

He glanced at her to find her face had gone white. As soon as he pulled over to the side of the road, Sofia was out and staggering toward the rear of the car. Garren got out and found her bent double, hands on her knees, throwing up what little was left in her stomach. He caught her by the arm as she teetered forward and helped her into a kneeling position. He pulled her hair back and held her steady as she continued heaving. When she was done, she collapsed into his arms. He held her, feeling her arms wrapped tightly around him and her body trembling against his own. After a minute or two, he felt her grip relax and her breathing settle into a rhythm as she regained control. She pulled away from him and sat cross-legged on the asphalt, elbows on her knees, fingers laced behind her head.

"Are you okay?" Garren asked after another minute.

"I-I think so." Sofia leaned back against the rear quarter-panel of Garren's car.

"What happened? What do you remember?"

"I'm not sure. I think I might have seen the end of the world."

"What?"

"Okay, maybe not the end of the world, but something very, very bad. The sky...it was...on fire. And it was falling all around. Everything was burning. People were running and screaming. And the moon...I saw it come apart. Whatever hit it, there must have been a lot more."

"Whoa," said Garren. He leaned back next to her and felt her hand find his.

"I remember it all now. I saw Tommy's apartment get hit. There's no way anyone at that party survived. Garren, I saw you die." She leaned over and put her head on his shoulder. "I'm sure I died, too."

"But we didn't. We're here."

"How can we be sure? Maybe we're both dead."

"Or maybe we were saved. Maybe something reached in at the last second and pulled us out and sent us back here. Maybe that's why this is happening to us. Maybe that's our mission."

"What do you mean, mission?"

"Maybe we're supposed to tell someone…warn them. I don't know, maybe we can prevent it."

"How?"

"I don't know, but I'd say we've got twenty years to figure it out."

24

Why us? Why here? Why now?

These questions and others like them were bandied about all the way to McGregor, about an hour and a half north of Dubuque. Answers proved elusive and Garren was getting irritable from hunger and lack of sleep. He needed a break. If he and Sofia had been sent back to prevent the extinction of the human race, or just the residents of Dubuque, it could wait until after breakfast. Now comfortably settled in a booth at Maggie's Diner, their stomachs happily satisfied, Sofia resumed the investigation.

"Assuming you are right and the universe has sent us back to save the world, what can we do?"

"I don't know," said Garren, "but I have to believe that whatever or whoever did this has a plan. We must have been chosen for a reason."

"Now we're the chosen ones. You're pretty convinced this is intentional and not some fluke or glitch in time."

"It makes sense. It puts purpose behind it."

Sofia stirred her coffee. "Okay, I'll ask again. Why us?"

"I guess that's what we need to figure out. Maybe in this version of history, you don't become a bartender. Maybe you take a different path and become a scientist."

"Ha! You should see my grades. I'm not dumb, but I'm no scholar. The world of academia and I never clicked. Nah, it's not me. You, on the other hand..."

Garren chuckled. "There's a reason I'm a history professor. The rearview mirror has always been more appealing to me than the road ahead."

"Maybe I should drive," Sofia quipped. "Seriously though, is that true?"

"I'm afraid so."

"You'd rather live in the past than venture into the future?"

"Yep."

"No wonder you're liking this so much."

"What can I say? I love history."

"Have you ever considered what that says about your love life? It's a wonder Kate married you. From what little I know about her, she strikes me as a forward-thinking girl. How did you two get together?"

"Opposites attract. Unfortunately, that's not true for the long haul. Without something to hold them together, opposites will eventually repel each other."

"Now that you see it, you can do something about it. That's my philosophy. Everything in life is a teacher to help us do better the next time. A punch in the face is good incentive to learn how to duck. So you screwed up with Kate today. Win her back tomorrow."

"That's rich coming from someone who's resigned herself to repeating her own past."

Sofia squinted at him. "You got me. Wanna hear a secret about bartenders?"

"Sure."

"We're notorious for giving advice, but we suck at taking it. Or at least I do. I guess I just have a very low bar of expectation for myself."

"I don't get that. You seem like someone who could do anything she puts her mind to."

"I've learned how to present well, but in truth I'm a box of broken pieces."

"Maybe this time you can avoid some of the damage."

She shook her head. "You can't avoid what's already happened. Even with this do-over, I can't forget what I know."

"I guess we both have some things to work on. And we can help each other. But we should probably put our heads together on the bigger mission. Your revelation about our time changes everything. Even if we could go back, what would we be going back to?"

"I see your point. But if we're supposed to do something about it, where do we start? Again, why us?"

Garren thought for a moment. "Maybe we can't fix it, but we know someone who can."

"Who do we know?"

"Unfortunately, most of my colleagues are pretty much like me."

Sofia faked a yawn. "That explains why you looked so desperate at Tommy's party. I could tell that wasn't your scene."

"Hey, my friends know how to have a good time," Garren shot back in mock offense.

"I'll bet." Sofia rolled her eyes like a seventeen year old. "Dr. Rosen, look what I found in this old box. It's a letter from somebody no one's ever heard of. Let's get the guys together Saturday night and read it."

"Is that really what you think of me? I'm boring?"

"Not boring." Sofia nibbled her bottom lip as she assessed him. "Studiously alluring."

Garren raised his coffee mug. "Here's to geek appeal." He knew she was flirting with him, but he let it go; too tired to be the teacher. He was, however, happy for the ease of their banter. That's what he remembered most about the first time they met. She was funny, smart and so easy to talk to. In truth, he was attracted to her that night. But now with Kate back in the picture and Sofia looking all of seventeen, whatever attraction he felt had changed to a fatherly—make that big brotherly—affection. "What about your crew? Who do you know?"

"I met Kevin Bacon at a party. He's a nice guy."

"And he knows everyone. As soon as we get to a phone, you can call him."

"I think I will."

"All right then, problem solved."

"Ready to leap?"

Garren cocked his head.

"You know...*Quantum Leap*."

"Oh, yeah. You watched that?"

"My sister and I used to pretend we were leapsters."

"You're a geek, too?"

"At least I grow out of it."

"Ouch." Garren stuck out his bottom lip.

"You better put that away before I bite it."

For a second, he thought she just might. "You're pretty feisty in the morning."

"Twenty years in New York, Babe." She winked at him.

Now it was his turn to assess her. The seventeen year old version sitting before him was a fair preview of the woman he met at

Tommy's – quick-witted in an easy-going sort of way. He could almost picture her tending bar, handling customers in various degrees of intoxication. She possessed an allure that drew you in and a force that warned you she was no push-over. He wondered how many men had made a play for her. The number had to be large. He also wondered how many she turned down and how she did it. He could see her tactfully dismissing the nervous ones who knew before they even asked that they didn't have a chance. The aggressive ones were probably shot down before they knew what hit them. Then he wondered about the men who got through that lovely barricade. Surely, there had to be a few. If circumstances were different, he wondered if he…no, he couldn't let his mind go there. Back to the task at hand. "You know we can't stay here. We need a plan."

"I know," she replied. "It's just nice to not be looking over my shoulder…or getting tossed out of someone's house. For the first time since we got here, I'm starting to relax."

"I know what you mean. It's nice to be honest with someone who doesn't think I'm lying or crazy."

"Someone who understands what I'm going through."

"Exactly."

"Someone from the same time."

Garren nodded his agreement.

"So, what do we do? I can't go back to Dubuque."

"I agree. And as much as I hate to admit it, New York is probably your best bet. At least you have friends there."

"*Will have* friends," she amended. "I'll be arriving a few months earlier this time. The circumstances of our meeting will be different."

Garren detected a hint of reservation, but wanted to stay positive. "We'll have to figure out a way to stay in touch. We'll get cell phones. In a few years, we can connect on Facebook."

"Facebook friends." Sofia chuckled, but there was something serious in her eyes. "Or you could come with me. We'd be good together."

Garren was caught off-guard. He was used to her flirtation. He didn't expect a full on proposition.

"You said it yourself," she continued, "opposites attract. And we have something to hold us together: *Our* time, *our* reality, the one you and I belong to." Then she played the ace. "The one where Kate left you and we found each other."

"We had one evening together. That's not much to go on. Besides, this is our time now and we've both got a second chance to get it right."

"What if this is *our* second chance? What if getting it right means you and me together?"

"I'm just as married now as I was when we met."

"And Kate is just as gone."

Stalemate. Sofia had played all her cards. Garren was out of chips. They sat there, each staring at their empty plate. Finally, Sofia got up and pulled a twenty from the pocket of her blue jeans. "I got this." She dropped it on the table and headed in the direction of the restrooms.

Garren waited at the table for her to return. After ten minutes, he got up and wondered around the diner's waiting area. He read the bulletin board and learned that Johnny Jack had a tractor for sale, Mary Lukenstraus was offering a free introductory piano lesson, and a cat named Muffin had been missing since New Year's Day. Glancing at his watch, he noted fifteen minutes had passed since Sofia went to the ladies' room. When she appeared, her eyes were red and her face bore no expression. She walked past him without acknowledging him.

He followed her out into the cold morning air. "You okay?"

She stood with her arms crossed, waiting for him to open her door. She got in without answering, closed the door and buckled her seatbelt.

Her silent treatment felt a lot like the last several years with Kate. He'd learned to deal with it by busying himself with projects around the house and the reading of many books. The difference – this was Sofia and the close proximity of the front seat of his car amplified the tension. After several minutes on the road, Garren couldn't stand it any longer. He pulled over at the next place to stop and switched off the engine.

"This isn't working," he said. "We can't just keep driving without direction. And being upset with each other isn't helping."

"I not upset at you," she said, her voice void of emotion.

"You seem upset."

She pressed her lips together and shook her head once.

"Do you want to talk?"

"Obviously not."

Garren drummed his fingers on the steering wheel. "Would you like to make a suggestion as to where we go?"

"I don't care."

"Well, there's the river. Wisconsin is on the other side. We could turn around and head north into Minnesota. Or we could go back to Dubuque. Do you prefer one over the other?"

"Any place where I can catch a bus to New York. Unless you want to take me there."

"I can't. I've got school tomorrow."

"Then I guess it really doesn't matter. Just drop me anywhere."

Garren looked at his watch. It was 9:15. He reached over and pulled a map from the glove compartment, studied it for a minute and then tucked it in between their seats. He started the engine and pulled back onto the highway. As they crossed the Mississippi River, Sofia glanced at him and then back out the side window.

"Where are you taking me?" she asked.

"Milwaukee. It's about three hours."

When they crossed the Wisconsin River a few minutes later, she asked, "What's there?"

"Airport. I'm not going to let you ride a bus that far. It's not safe."

"I don't have that much money."

"Don't worry. I've got an emergency credit card. I'll see if I can get you some cash when we get there."

"You look tired. Want me to drive? I do have my license."

Garren glanced at her and saw a hint of an expression on her face. He was caffeinated enough to keep driving, but he sensed Sofia wanted to contribute. Besides, maybe an offering of trust would smooth things over. "Sure. I appreciate that."

He pulled over at what looked like a gravel quarry and got out. Sofia slid over behind the wheel and adjusted the seat and mirrors. Garren got in and pushed his seat all the way back.

"I don't think I've ever ridden on this side," he said.

"You're not one of those guys, are you? 'Cause if you're going to criticize my driving, we can switch back right now."

"No, I'm not that way at all. I should warn you, it's got a pretty big engine."

Sofia fired it up and revved it a few times. She dropped it into gear and punched it. Garren was thrown back into his seat. He started to say something, but held his tongue when he realized she could handle it and was obviously trying to get a rise out of him. She cut her eyes toward him, snorted and eased off the accelerator, letting the car find its cruising speed at just above the posted speed limit.

"So, three hours, huh?" she said.

"Yep. You still mad at me?"

"Never was."

"Want to talk about it?"

"Not really."

"So, we're good?"

"I don't think any of this qualifies as good."

"Sofia, I'm sorry. I just—"

"Shh," she cut him off. "There's no point in dragging it out. I told you how I feel about you. That's not what you want. There's nothing more to say about it."

"I just want to make sure you're okay."

"I'll be fine."

"Are you sure?"

"Would you stop?! Geez!"

"Okay, okay. It's just that you seemed so upset back at the diner and then you just turned it off. I'm not used to that."

"Rule #5: Know when to quit."

Garren did a mental calculation. "What about Rule #4?"

She gave him the squint-eye. "You don't get to know that one."

25

"I am so mad right now." Kate rested her elbows on the table and cradled her head in her hands. The couple at the next table couldn't help overhearing, but Kate was too angry to notice or care. "I just want to throw something."

Denise smiled sympathetically at the eavesdropping couple and moved Kate's coffee mug out of her reach.

"How did I not see this coming?" Kate continued, speaking as much to herself as to Denise. "There are things we both need to work on, but that's normal, right? It takes time for two people to learn how to live together. Marriage doesn't mean you've arrived, but it does mean you're both committed to getting there together. Am I right about that?" Denise started to respond, but Kate wasn't done processing. "It's just so unbelievable. Why would he...? How could he...? Ugh! I can't even say it. No, I have to. Why would my husband get involved with another woman? Not even a woman...a girl...his own student. It doesn't make sense."

The couple at the next table had heard enough. They quickly finished their coffee and left. Now alone at the back of the café, Denise felt a little more free to speak.

"Maybe it's not what it looks like," she offered.

Kate lifted her head and rested her chin on her folded hands. "Seriously? You saw how she looked at him."

"Okay, so Sofia has a little crush on her teacher. What girl hasn't entertained the idea of forbidden love? I do it all the time. It doesn't mean Garren feels the same way about her. Kate, he loves you."

"Then how do you explain this?" Kate retrieved a time journal from her purse and slid it across the table.

"Why do you have Sofia's journal?" Denise asked.

"It's Garren's. They have matching journals. Isn't that cute?"

Denise looked at it, trying to make sense of the odd coincidence.

"Look at it," Kate said.

Denise flipped open the cover and read the first page. "What's this?"

"Some kind of fantasy."

"I don't understand."

"I saw Sofia's journal, too. Hers is a message to herself about going to New York; instructions on where to go and who to meet. She refers to him as G. Whatever this is, they are in it together."

"Okay, it's weird, but it doesn't sound like they are *together* together. Maybe it's some kind of creative writing project."

"I might believe that if Garren taught English. No, not even then."

"Did you talk to him about it?"

"Oh, yeah."

"What did he say?"

"He said…" Kate resumed the head-in-hands posture. "He said it's real."

"What's real?"

Kate chuckled at the absurdity of what she was about to say. "He claims that he and Sofia are from the future."

Denise laughed out loud.

"See? This is what I'm dealing with. Now you know why I kicked him out."

"You're serious."

"*He's* serious. Denise, he really believes he's from the future. He's got this whole elaborate story all worked out."

"What is it?"

Kate sat back, crossed her legs and folded her hands upon the table. "Apparently, he's from the year 2019. He and I are separated. Probably my fault. He went to a New Year's Eve party at Tommy's. Sofia was there. They had some drinks. He passed out. Then he woke up here in this time. Oh, and the moon gets hit by an asteroid or something."

Denise's mouth hung open and her eyebrows had crawled up onto her forehead. "He said that with a straight face?"

"Yes. He really believes it." Kate shrugged and shook her head. "I wanted to believe it."

Denise traced her finger around the top of her coffee mug as she considered what Kate had just said. "What about now? Do you believe him now?"

"No. Of course not."

Denise analyzed her sister's face. "But you want to."

"No. Yes." Kate looked down for a second and then looked up. "Maybe. I don't know. I want to believe my husband is telling me the truth. But time-travel? Really?"

"Can you think of any other explanation?" Denise asked.

"He's delusional?"

"Maybe."

"And that helps me how?"

"It gives us three options. You want to try something?"

"Sure."

"Okay. Let's think it through. Option One: Garren and Sofia concocted a story to hide their affair. Option Two: They are both mentally unstable and need some serious psychiatric help. Option Three: Something unexplainable happened, and they really are time-travelers from the future."

"If you're trying to make me feel better, it's not working."

"I'm trying to help you make sense of this. You know Garren. Which of these three options is most plausible?"

Kate nibbled her bottom lip. "None of them."

"Until there's another, you have to believe one of them is the truth. Now let's think about it. Take the first option. Assume for a minute that Garren and Sofia are having an affair. What's the evidence?"

"She's obviously attracted to him and she's young and beautiful."

"She's *too* young and not as beautiful as you," Denise countered, "but she is attracted to him. Is he attracted to her?"

"He's protective of her."

"Why?"

"Her parents died and left her alone. Her foster dad is a creep. She's got nowhere to go."

"Does that mean he's attracted to her?"

"I don't know. Not necessarily. But still, he might be."

"Has he been spending time away from home? Do you guys spend time apart?"

"Except for work and school, we're always together."

"How has he been with you? Has he been distant? Distracted? Unattentive?"

"No. In fact, this past week has been amazing. Until this happened, I'd have said we've never been closer."

"So based on the evidence, do you believe Garren is having an affair with Sofia?"

Kate weighed the evidence. "No. The evidence doesn't support it. But how do you explain their journals?"

"Yeah, that part is suspicious, but why make up a story no one would believe? What could they possibly gain from it? How does it help them?"

Kate thought for a minute. "It doesn't help them at all. It only makes them seem guilty."

"Option Two," Denise said. "Garren and Sofia are both delusional. They've both entered into the same fantasy. Again, what's the evidence?"

"The journals speak for themselves."

"That's one mark in the crazy column. Is there anything else that would make you believe Garren is experiencing a mental break from reality?"

Again, Kate gave the idea her full consideration. "He has been different since his birthday…more attentive…more interested in what I'm studying…what I think about. He's been going out of his way to show me he loves me."

"Does that suggest crazy?"

"No." Kate almost smiled. "He's been really sweet."

"If this whole business with Sofia wasn't happening, and the journals didn't exist, is there any reason to believe Garren is having any kind of mental breakdown?"

"No, not at all."

"Can we take Option Two off the table?"

"Yeah, I think so."

"You know what that leaves us."

Kate nodded, then shook her head. "But that's not possible."

"But what if it is?"

"C'mon, Denise. Are you saying you believe him?"

"I'm not saying I believe it. I'm not saying I don't. We're just working through the options. Let's say for a minute that time-travel is possible. Would that be a reasonable explanation for the evidence? You said Garren's been different since his birthday. That was New Year's Day. If time-travel were possible and the Garren you've been with this past week is really the Garren from twenty years in the future, could that explain the way he's been acting?"

"I guess so."

"If time-travel were possible and Sofia came back with him, could that explain why he is so protective of her?"

"I suppose."

"If time-travel were possible, could it explain what they've written in their journals?"

"Yes, but—"

"Hold on a minute. If time-travel were possible, could it explain the events of the last few days?"

"Yes. *If* it were possible, but it's not."

"Again, I'm not saying I believe it, but it is an option and we cannot disprove it."

Kate frowned.

"May I make a suggestion?" Denise asked.

"Would it matter if I said no?"

"I am your big sister."

"Go ahead then."

"Let it play out."

"What? You want me to act like everything is normal?"

"No. I want you to keep paying attention until the evidence either disproves two of the options or makes one of them undeniable."

"You think that will happen?"

"It has to. Something is going on. There is a real explanation. Now that we identified the options, you have a system by which to evaluate what happens next."

"Are you saying I need to let Garren come back home?"

"You could keep him at a distance and drive yourself nuts trying to put it together with only some of the pieces, or you could let him back in and get to the truth."

"What if I don't like the truth?" Kate asked honestly.

"Of those three options, which one would be the worst?"

"That's easy. The affair."

"If that's the truth, at least you'll know he did it to himself. You'll know he blew the best thing that ever happened to him. What if it goes the other way?"

"And my husband is a time-traveler?" Kate actually giggled. "Oh my gosh, I can't believe I just said that. If that's the truth..." She became serious. "If that's the truth, then he needs me now more than ever."

"If I were you," Denise offered, "I'd return this journal and tell him to keep writing. He'll prove himself one way or the other."

"If I ask you something, will you be totally honest with me?"

"Totally."

"What do you believe?"

Now it was Denise's turn to weigh her options. "I honestly don't know."

"Will you help me find the truth?"

"Yes."

"Will you help me deal with whatever truth we discover?"

"I'll either ruin him myself, buckle his straight jacket or become your publicity agent. I'm in."

———

One hundred seventy two miles to the east, another conversation was taking place at a coffee shop across from Gate 23 at the General Mitchell International Airport in Milwaukee.

"I guess this is it," said Garren. "Are you sure you're going to be okay?"

Sofia shrugged. "I did okay the first time."

"Yeah, but you're arriving on scene a few months early."

"I know where to go. I'll be fine."

"You've got my number. You'll stay in touch, right? If you need anything, I can help."

"I know how to survive. Besides, this time I have the advantage."

"If you knew then…"

"What's that?"

"Tommy's party. We talked about that question we heard on the radio: If you knew then what you know now, what would you do differently? I guess we'll find out. But seriously, you'll call me?"

"I've been thinking about that. I think it might be best if I didn't."

"What about our mission? You and I are supposed to save the world."

Sofia smiled. "That's a nice thought, but let's be honest. Time screwed up. It sent the wrong heroes back. Honestly, what can a history professor and a bartender do to alter the forces of nature? I certainly can't."

"But we have to keep in touch. We're from the same time zone. Let's say every New Year's Eve we talk just to see how each other is doing."

"I don't think that's a good idea."

"Why not?"

"Because." She took a sip of coffee to stall. "I was hoping to leave without having to say this, but here goes. Kate's only partly right about me crushing on you. Seventeen year old Sofia does have a crush on her history teacher."

"I'm flattered, but I'm not that—"

"Shut up and let me finish. I'm not her anymore. I've moved past school girl crushes. Garren, I fell for you. At Tommy's party, all the while I was trying to be cool and casual, I was falling hard. I lied to you about my coming back to Dubuque. I didn't come back to stay. I was just passing through on my way to California. It was a stupid poetic gesture – last night of the year in the place that nearly destroyed me. For twenty years, I used my past as an excuse for what I had become. I didn't want to do that anymore. I wanted to face my past and know that I was done being affected by it. I even drove by the old house to prove to myself I could do it. I was about to leave town when I ran into Tommy. And he was Tommy. I took his invitation as one last challenge that I could go where I want and leave when I wanted to. I was on my way out when I met you. I don't know what it was, but I was drawn to you. As the night wore on, I let down my guard and it happened. I broke my rules and let myself fall."

"You fell for a drunk idiot?"

"Yeah, I lied about that, too. The first three drinks hit you pretty fast, but you stopped after that. After about an hour and something to eat, you were as sober as you are now. We spent the rest of the night talking until I made a fool of myself and suggested we…you know."

"Why can't I remember any of that?"

"Probably the same reason I couldn't remember what happened after that. In *Quantum Leap*, Sam suffered gaps in his memory, too."

"Makes sense, I guess."

"There's more. When I woke up back here, I was freaked out. I spent the entire weekend locked in my room. I only went to school to get out of the house. When I walked into class and saw you, I couldn't believe it. I just stared at you the entire class trying to figure out if it was you or the other you. I've never been a big believer in fate, but when I realized the same thing had happened to you, I began to believe that maybe I was being given a second chance, and it was with you. My fall was complete…until I heard you talk about Kate. So, there it is. I've completely dropped my guard. I'm all out of secrets. I love you, Garren, and that's why I don't think we should try to stay in touch. It's just too painful."

"Sofia," Garren began, but was mercifully interrupted.

"Final call for United Flight 1953 to New York LaGuardia. All passengers for United Flight 1953 report to Gate 23 for immediate boarding. This is the final call."

Sofia got up and shouldered her backpack. "Thanks for the ticket. I'm sorry I can't pay you back."

"Wait." Garren got up and reached for her arm.

"Don't," she said, pulling away from him. "Don't say anything you'll regret."

"I'll regret it if you get on that plane without me saying something."

"Write it in your journal." She started for the gate just a few steps away. She was the last passenger to board and the attendant was starting to close the jet way door. "I'm coming," she called out, waving her ticket. "Hold the door."

"Sofia." Garren tried to follow her but was cut off by the gate attendant.

"I'm sorry, Sir, but this flight is ready for departure."

"Sofia!" Garren strained to get one last look at her as the door closed. He ran over to the window in hopes of getting her attention as she boarded the plane. Not that he could actually communicate anything to her, but he wanted her to know he was there and that he wouldn't leave until the airplane's departure prevented her from altering her plans. He watched United Flight 1953 back away from the terminal and begin its slow roll to the runway. When it disappeared from view, he turned and walked slowly toward the airport exit. Outside, he made his way to the parking lot. A jet had just taken off and was making its climb. He couldn't tell if it was Sofia's flight, but he waved anyway, just in case she might be looking for him.

26

Garren was in no hurry to get back. Not allowed to go home and not wanting to hang out at Tommy's, he turned the two and a half hour trip into an all-day affair. Without a GPS, he used the Rand McNally map to navigate his way along the smaller state roads between Milwaukee and Dubuque. He got lost a few times, stopped to experience two of the dozen small towns he passed through and added an extra hundred miles to his trip. He ate lunch in a diner that looked exactly like it did in the 1950s and browsed a few shops stocked with trinkets and other locally made items he had no intention of buying. He needed time to think and process all that had happened in the last week—the mess he'd made of his marriage and how he'd failed Sofia. If time had chosen him, Sofia was right, it had made a huge mistake. Everything he'd tried to do had gone wrong. If the fate of anyone rested in his hands, they were in real trouble. At one particularly low point, he considered not going back at all. He even pulled over on the side of the road and traced a path to New York. But then he returned to his senses and made a beeline back to Dubuque. He'd veered off track too many times as it was. If he had any hope of getting anything right, it would be there. Anywhere else would simply be another detour with the potential of messing up someone else's destiny.

The sun was setting by the time he rolled into the town. Keeping below the speed limit in order to avoid another encounter with Cruller, he drove passed his apartment and saw Kate's car parked in its usual spot. The light in the living room was on. He ached to be with her, but he knew any attempt to engage her would only make things worse. With nowhere else to go, he made his way to Tommy's place.

"Dude," said Tommy when he opened the door. "What's up?"

"Nothing," Garren replied. "Can I crash here tonight?"

"Mi casa su casa."

Tommy's apartment was everything you might expect it to be. Garren wrinkled his nose as he was assaulted by the myriad smells – burnt popcorn, stale beer, dirty clothes and man-funk. He'd considered going to his parents' house, but figured Tommy wouldn't grill him. Besides, Kate indicated that any correspondence from her would be routed through Tommy. He could endure a night or two of bachelor pad – hopefully no more – if it meant a peaceful misery and the chance to talk to Kate.

Garren sat down on the couch and sank several inches further than he should have. The springs had long been broken as was the leg on one corner. He was familiar with "Old Marge," having been her former owner and having spent many a night on her. No one could remember the origin of the moniker, but the old girl was legendary. "Sleeping with Marge" was a euphemism for crashing at whatever residence that housed her. She'd been with Tommy ever since Garren set up house with Kate back in November.

"Want some pizza?" Tommy asked. "It's yesterday fresh."

"Sure."

Tommy retrieved a pizza box and two beers from the refrigerator. He handed the box and one bottle to Garren and opened the other as he plopped down in the recliner. True to his character, Tommy didn't ask Garren any questions. He either didn't know anything or he was giving him space.

"What are you watching?" Garren asked, more to break the silence than anything.

"Documentary about ancient weaponry. These guys are trying to build a trebuchet using thirteenth century tools and materials."

"Trebuchet," said Garren, appreciating the elegant sound of such a deadly weapon.

"Catapult," Tommy offered.

"I know what a trebuchet is."

For the next twenty minutes, Garren ate cold pizza and watched five middle aged men in medieval garb construct a contraption that looked like something from the set of *The Lord of the Rings*. For a few minutes, he felt like himself, his younger self. The nostalgia of the days when he and Tommy used to just hang out doing exactly what they were doing now was a much needed relief from the fiasco that his life had become. He almost didn't bring it up, but it was during times like this that the two friends used to discuss life, women, music, cars and women.

Before he knew it, Garren heard himself say, "Kate and I are in a situation."

"Yeah, I know. She called about an hour ago."

Garren did a double-take. "What'd she say?"

"She wanted to know if I'd seen you. She sounded upset. You know, normally I can't stand it when girls get all emotional, but there's something about Kate that makes it sound kind of sexy. Then again, everything about Kate—"

"Tommy! You're talking about my wife."

"I know. You have a sexy wife. Am I not supposed to notice?"

Garren waved him off. "Did she say anything else?"

"She said if I saw you, I should tell you she wants you to come home."

Garren jumped up from Marge. "Why didn't you tell me that sooner?"

Tommy shrugged. "You seemed interested in the show."

"I gotta go." Garren made for the door.

"Dude, you comin' back? There's a show about ancient Egypt on next." Tommy grabbed the last slice of pizza and settled back in his chair. "Okay, then. I'll see you later."

Fortunately for Garren, Tommy lived just a few miles away from his and Kate's apartment. His chances of running into Officer Daniels or any other officer of the law were slim, which was good because in his eagerness to get back to Kate he exhibited a flagrant disregard for the posted speed limit. He pulled in behind Kate's car, sprinted to his building and took the stairs two at a time. He paused to regain his composure before entering.

"Kate?" he called out. "I saw Tommy. He told me you wanted to talk."

"I'm in the bedroom."

He found her sitting cross-legged on the bed, his journal open in front of her. "How are you doing?" He already knew the answer to that question from her rigid posture and the serious look on her face, but he had to ask anyway. But she didn't have to answer.

"Were you with Sofia today?" There was a note of accusation in her tone.

"This morning." There was no point in lying.

Kate nodded as if she expected it. "Where is she now?"

Garren glanced at his watch. "Probably somewhere in New York."

"How did she get there?"

"I drove her to Milwaukee and bought her a plane ticket."

She nodded again. "How do you feel about her being gone?"

Garren started to sit down on the bed but changed his mind when he saw from Kate's expression that she wasn't ready for that, so he leaned against the wall. "I'm concerned about her. New York is a big city for a girl her age."

"Thirty-seven isn't that young," Kate said. "Besides, she knows where to go and who to meet."

"Well, yeah, but…" Garren eyed her, trying to determine whether she was being serious or facetious. "…she's a few months ahead of schedule."

"Right." Kate nodded again. "What's it like knowing things before they happen?"

Garren chuckled. "It's not as easy as you might think. It's not an exact replay."

"Explain."

"Circumstances start out the same, but I'm able to affect the outcome. I'm not reliving each moment as I did the first time. I'm twenty years older. My perspective has changed. So I'm acting differently and making different choices. Besides, I can't remember much that happened this far back. This is all twenty years in the past to me."

Kate raised her eyebrows. "You don't remember our first year of marriage. I must not have made much of an impression."

"No, it's not like that. I remember the broader picture – the mood, the feel of it – but it's the details that elude me. I don't remember specific conversations, so I don't know what people are going to say. I don't remember the day-to-day events, so I don't know when the phone is going to ring or whether I break a glass. But I do remember what it felt like to be married to you. And sometimes I recall a moment, like a little snapshot. It's like déjà vu, only more intense."

"This moment right now…this didn't happen the first time?"

"No. This is new."

"So you have no idea how it's going to turn out?"

"No."

"It could be very different for you."

"It could be, yes."

"Twenty years from now, you'll have two different sets of memories for the same time."

"I guess I will."

"And they will both be just as real to you."

"They probably will."

"But for me, there will only be one set."

Garren nodded.

"What happens to the other version of me?"

Garren blinked. "I-I don't know."

Kate flipped to a page in Garren's journal and read aloud. "By 2010, Kate and I are more like roommates than a couple. Work becomes our identity. In 2012, Kate takes a new position at work that requires her to travel a lot. We hardly see each other. In 2014, Kate and I take separate vacations. She goes to the Bahamas with Denise. I go to Chicago." She closed the book. "Is this my future?"

"It's what I remember."

"But I haven't done any of these things."

"Not yet."

"Am I destined to become this person?"

Garren rubbed the back of his neck. "I don't know."

Kate flipped the book open to a random page. "If you change something, what happens to the original?"

"I'm not sure what you mean."

She ran her finger down the page and read. "January 1, 2015 – Terrorist Attack in Times Square one minute after midnight. Thousands die. If you could prevent it, what would happen to all those people?"

"I guess they'd go on living."

"In a different reality than the one you know?"

"I-I don't know. What are you getting at?"

"I'm trying to understand what you're telling me. If you change something are you really altering history, or are you creating another reality? Does the original version still exist?"

"I have no idea. I'm still pretty new at this."

Kate looked intently at him like she was trying to see beyond what was there. "Are you the man I married three months ago, or do you belong to this other Kate?"

"I don't know."

"Because I'm not that woman. I make my own choices. You don't get to write my life."

Now he understood what she was getting at. "Kate, that wasn't my intention."

"But that's what you did. You've written the story of our marriage and you've cast me as the villain." Kate's emotions were beginning to show. "I don't know which is worse. If this is real, then this is what I become. If this is some kind of joke, then this is what you think of me."

"I never meant for you to read it."

"What difference does it make? You wrote it. This is how you think of me. I just don't understand why? What purpose does it serve? Who did you write this for? Did you write it for her?"

"No."

"Tell me the truth. Did you have an affair with her?"

"No. I love you, Kate. Only you."

"Then who did you right this for? Who was supposed to read this?"

"I wrote it…" Garren felt himself backed into a corner. "I wrote it for myself."

Kate tilted her head. "Why? So you could justify your feelings for Sofia?"

"No. I told you, I do not have feelings for Sofia."

"Then what possessed you to write these things?"

Garren didn't want to say it, but he had no other answer. "You did."

"I did?" Kate got up from the bed, her body rigid and her face tense with anger. "You're actually going to pin this on me? Maybe you are from another reality because I don't know you."

"Kate, please let me explain."

"Get out."

"Kate, listen. That day at the university when I told you about that book I was reading…the one about the guy who went back in time."

Her eyes narrowed and the muscles in her jaw hardened.

"There was no book. I was trying to tell you about myself."

She snatched the journal from the bed and advanced on him. She looked as if she intended to bludgeon him with it.

"You said that if that happened to you, you would write everything you could remember in a book so that if you switched back, your younger self would know what's going to happen."

She closed the distance, backing him up against the wall.

"I wrote this so that if I switched back with my younger self, he…I mean *I* wouldn't make the same mistakes again."

Kate's face contorted as if she were in pain. "You really believe this, don't you?"

"It's true."

She blinked and new tears began to trickle down her cheeks. "If you were having an affair, at least I could hate you. But I don't know what to do with this."

"Believe me."

"I can't. I can't accept this. It's just not possible. Garren, I'm scared for you. You need to get some help."

He threw up his hands. "I don't know what else to say. I promise you this is the truth. I don't know how or why it happened, but I promise you it's real. This is really happening to me. And I'm scared, too. Mostly, I'm scared of losing you."

Kate's breath caught in her throat. She tried to speak, but couldn't. All she could do was shake her head. Now with tears streaming down her face, she calmly handed him the journal and walked out of the bedroom. Garren stood there for a minute, too stunned to move. Somehow he'd succeeded in making the worst case scenario even worse. When he finally found the will to move, he went into the living room where he found her sitting on the couch, hugging a pillow to her chest. Everything in him wanted to make one more appeal, but the verdict was in. He convinced her he was not having an affair only to make her believe he was crazy.

"I'll be at Tommy's." He placed the journal on the kitchen table and left the apartment. This time, he believed, for good.

He drove around town for nearly an hour before getting to Tommy's. By then he'd shed all the tears he had and he was exhausted.

"Hey, Tommy," he said as he let himself in.

"Oh, hey. You missed the first one on ancient Egypt, but I think there's another one."

Garren dropped back onto the couched and sank into the cushion. "I'm just gonna sleep if that's okay with you."

"Sure, Man."

Garren kicked off his shoes and stretched out his legs. A minute later, he was sleeping with Marge.

27

Monday started out like a low grade fever. Not bad enough to be canceled and confined to the sweet solitude of bed rest, hot soup and motherly care, but just enough to be annoying. The faculty and students of Hempstead High School filed in like automatons running on last year's programming. The somber mood of the masses was enough to cool even the most school spirited down a few degrees. Instead of a rousing "We're the Mighty Mustangs!" it was more like "the old gray mare ain't what she used to be." But for Garren, it was even worse. After a restless night with Marge, his back was killing him and he couldn't turn his head to the left without feeling like something important was about to snap.

"Good morning, Mr. Rosen," said the attendance secretary whose name he couldn't remember. "Officer Daniels is here to see you. He's waiting in your classroom."

Oh, great.

"He's with your new student. You need to sign this."

"What is it?" Garren received the form from her and noted the header: *Department of Social Service.*

"She's another one of Officer Daniels's foster children. The custody papers are still being processed. Should be complete by this afternoon. Until then, we are assuming legal guardianship, which means you get to be a foster dad during first period. Sign at the bottom please."

"I've never heard of this. Is this standard practice?"

"Apparently, it is. They arrived with a social worker first thing this morning. Said they wanted to get Lana plugged in right away. I hardly think all this is necessary, what with him being a police officer and all, but he said it had to be done by the book. He's such a good man."

"Thanks." Garren slipped the form into his briefcase and turned to leave.

"Um, Mr. Rosen," said the secretary. "You're supposed to sign it before you go to class. He was quite insistent about that."

"I'll sign it later," Garren replied.

"I'm sorry, Mr. Rosen. He said I was supposed to watch you."

Garren retrieved the form and laid it on the counter. Reaching for his pen, he scanned the font six print. There was a lot of it. He was just about to sign when something caught his eye. He made a show of checking his watch. "I just remembered I'm late for a meeting. I promise I'll sign this as soon as I'm done." He jammed the form back into his briefcase and made his exit.

"Mr. Rosen, wait!" the secretary called out, but he was already halfway down the hall.

Garren ducked into a vacant classroom and pulled out the form. Buried in all the legalese, he found his name attached to a statement of confession to the following charges: Contributing to the delinquency of a minor, child endangerment, obstruction of justice, possession of alcohol in the company of a minor, conspiracy to commit indecent acts with a minor, assault and battery, kidnapping.

"What the…" Garren read the charges again. "Could this get any worse?"

"Hey, Garren. You lost or just hiding?"

Garren looked up to find another teacher whose name he probably used to know standing in the doorway. "Oh, hey. Yeah, I was just getting myself prepared."

"I hear that. You can stay as long as you like, but the hellions will be here any minute."

"Thanks, but I better be getting on to my class."

Garren was tempted to leave the school entirely, but then he figured an unexpected absence would only make him look guilty. May as well face the music. He took a breath and headed for his classroom.

Officer Daniels was in uniform, half-sitting on the edge of Garren's desk with one foot tapping the floor. Next to him was a shifty looking man in a dark suit who looked like he wasn't used to wearing suits. A sleepy-eyed girl of about fifteen was sitting in the front row.

"I was beginning to think you wouldn't show."

"Officer Daniels. What a pleasant surprise."

"Did you get my message?"

Garren cocked his head. "Oh, you mean my confession." He patted his briefcase.

"I take it you didn't sign it."

"Nope."

Cruller shrugged. "It was worth a shot."

Garren nodded toward the dark suit man. "I take it he's not really DSS."

Cruller got up and moved next to the girl. "Lana, Sweetheart, I want you to go with Mr. Diggs out into the hall while I have a chat with your teacher."

The girl got up and followed Dark Suit out of the classroom.

"I hate to see a pretty little girl like that look so sad," said Cruller when they were alone. "Poor thing lost her parents in a car accident. I'm just trying to give her a good home so she can heal."

"That sounds oddly familiar. Sofia's parents were also killed in an accident."

"You're right. That *is* an odd coincidence. Speaking of Sofia, where is she?"

Garren shrugged. "I don't know what her first period class is, but I'm sure the office can help you."

"I doubt she's here today. In fact, I haven't seen her all weekend. That makes her a runaway or an abductee."

"You don't look very concerned, Foster Dad."

"We'll find her. The entire police force is on the lookout. Actually, I'm running down a lead right now." Cruller glared at him.

Garren conjured up a look of concern. "Gosh, I hope you find her soon."

Cruller studied Garren's face, then chuckled. "Think you're smart, huh? You took her somewhere." He clicked his tongue. "No matter. She'd of probably run off soon anyway."

"What do you want, Officer Daniels?"

"You know something, Rosen? I thought you were just some dumb shlub who accidently stuck his nose in the wrong pond, but now you're struttin' around like the big dog. I warned you to stay out of my lane, but you didn't listen. You crossed a line, Son. Now I'm going to up the ante. You stole one of my chickens. Now I'm putting the bounty on yours."

"Wow, that's a lot of metaphors. What are you trying to say?"

"My associate thinks you've got a hero complex. I think that little minx sweet talked you into takin' her away from me. Either way, doesn't matter. I was getting tired of her anyway. Too old, too clever, too aware of her surroundings. You saved me the trouble of having to remove her from the equation, but in the process you put yourself smack dab in the middle of it."

"The middle of what?" Garren asked.

Cruller looked like he was enjoying himself. "I think I've given you enough to chew on. Now let's see how smart you really are. Here's the rules: If you keep your nose out of my business, Sofia becomes just another runaway who never gets found and I don't follow through on those charges. You play the hero again and you'll need one yourself."

"Why give me a choice at all?"

"We live in Dubuque. Not exactly a hotbed of activity, if you know what I mean. Not like Chicago. I thought you and I could spice things up. So, you wanna play?"

Garren thought he had the man figured out, but now he wasn't sure about anything. He stared dumbfounded as Cruller walked over to the door to let Dark Suit and the girl back into the room.

"Lana," he said, "you listen to your teacher and learn a lot, okay? When this class is over, Mr. Rosen will help you find the next one." He knelt down so that he was eye level with her. "And when school is over, I'll be here to pick you up. You're gonna come and live with me for a while. We're gonna be good friends."

The girl nodded sheepishly. "Okay."

Cruller caught Garren by the arm and pulled him toward the door. "One more thing for you to keep in mind. I noticed that pretty little wife of yours works out early in the morning. There are a lot of bad people in this world. Be a shame if she crossed paths with one of them. Yep, pretty wife." Cruller smiled and winked, then looked back over his shoulder. "Lana, Sweetie, you be a good girl now. Make lots of friends."

No sooner had the two men left than students began filing into the classroom. Garren went to the white board so he wouldn't have to face anyone just yet. He was shaking and he could feel his heart pounding. What had he gotten himself into? What kind of man was Officer Daniels, really? The noise in the room increased several decibels with the clatter of chairs, the shuffling of papers and the din of last minute conversations. When the bell called the class to order, Garren pulled himself together and took attendance. Twenty eight names were called. Twenty six answered that they were present.

"Okay," said Garren. "Before we get started, I'd like to introduce our new student. This is Lana. I want you all to give her a warm Mustang welcome. Now, who can tell me where we left off last week?"

Forty-five minutes later, the bell ended Garren's lecture on the development of the feudal system in 9th century Europe. It wasn't his best. Cut off from Kate, and now with Crazy Cruller playing some insane game that he still didn't understand, he was more than a little distracted. "Tomorrow, we'll talk about the Knights Templar. Read chapter six in your Hancock text."

Everyone exited the class except for Lana.

"Oh, yeah," said Garren. "I'm supposed to help you find your next class. Do you have your schedule?"

Lana handed him a yellow slip of paper. Garren read the name at the top. "Okay, Lana Karr, where do you go next?"

"That's not my name."

"It's not?"

The girl shook her head. "My real name is Svetlana Karabelnikoff."

Now he detected the slightest hint of an accent and he could see her heritage in her eyes. But that's not all. The unusual name sounded an alarm in Garren's mind. Where had he heard that name before? "Tell me your name again." He knew what she said, but he wanted to hear it again.

"Svetlana Karabelnikoff."

"Why does this say Lana Karr?"

"Mr. Diggs said I should use this name."

"Where are you from, Svetlana?"

"I live in Eureka, South Dakota...*lived* in Eureka."

The significance of her name was right on the edge of his recollection. The name Diggs sounded familiar, too. A little more information might bring it all the way in. "What happened to your parents?"

"They told me they were killed in a car accident."

"How did you end up in foster care? Don't you have relatives?"

"It's complicated."

That's what people always say when in fact the situation is not complicated at all; just something they don't want to talk about. What did it matter to Garren anyway? He wasn't about to let himself get sucked into Cruller's game. "I'm sorry this is happening to you. C'mon, let's get you to your next class."

"Mr. Rosen?"

"Yes?"

"I need to tell someone. They never showed me."

"Showed you what?"

"The accident. They should have shown me pictures of the car or something for me to identify. I don't think there was an accident. I don't think Mr. Diggs works for the foster care people. I don't think that police officer is a good man. You probably won't believe me, but I think I've been kidnapped."

Okay, so maybe it was complicated. Garren tried to hide the fact that he was thinking the same thing. "Why do you think that?"

"It was the day before Christmas break. Mr. Diggs and another man came to my school and said my parents had been in a car accident. When I went with them, they told me my parents had died and I was being placed in foster care. They took me to a house out of town. There was a man and woman there and two other girls. They were nice, but strange. They didn't have a TV. The telephone didn't work. They locked my bedroom door at night. They never let us be alone together, and when I tried to talk about what happened, they would either play another game with us or send us to our rooms for some quiet time. A couple weeks later, they moved us to a farm. Mr. Diggs was there and the other man – Mr. Diggs called him Gene – and there were four other girls."

Garren gasped as the pieces fell into place – the news story on the radio his last day in 2019, this girl with the unusual name. This was her. "This farm, is it near a town called Oskaloosa?"

"I don't know."

"When you were there, did you see a cellar or some kind of underground shelter?"

"Yes, that's where we slept. How do you know?"

Garren felt sick. The faceless victim of a twenty year old murder, long dead and likely forgotten, now stood before him in the flesh and very much alive. Her face, vivid with all the details of a real person, shifted through expressions of fear and confusion and hope. Eyes blinked trustingly as quivering lips told a story – macabre in another time, to be determined in this one. Garren regained his composure as students began arriving. "Svetlana, we need to get you to your next class."

"You don't believe me." Her countenance fell under the weight of despair.

"I do." Garren put his hand on her shoulder. "I believe every word. I also believe your parents might still be alive. I just don't know what to do next. Let me think for a minute." He couldn't believe he'd stumbled onto a murder before it happened. Yes he could – he was a time-traveler from the future. He could believe anything. Still, his knowledge of this piece of the future stunned him. But the really shocking part was that Officer Daniels was a serial killer, or at least he was involved with one. And the really *really* shocking part was that he, Garren Rosen, could do something to stop it. This had to be the reason time had selected him to go back to this particular moment. Sofia's mission to save the planet was still twenty years in the future, but his was standing right in front of him. Saving Svetlana was his mission. "Come with me."

He led her out into the crowded hallway where hundreds of students were pressed together like cattle. She grabbed his hand and huddled close to his side.

"It's okay," Garren said. "Just stay close."

When they arrived at their destination, Garren was relieved to find the class was small in number and the teacher was one whose name he remembered. "Miss Reeves, this is Svetlana. It's her first day."

"Hello, Svetlana," said Miss Reeves.

"Good morning."

Garren's mind was still reeling. For the second time that morning, he thought about ditching school, this time with Svetlana, but again he was afraid of the suspicions it would raise. He looked at her class schedule and committed it to memory. He was about to hand it to Miss Reeves, but didn't. "I'll walk her through her schedule. She's a bit nervous and we seem to be hitting it off."

"Suit yourself." Miss Reeves returned to the white board to finish whatever she was writing.

"Are you going to be okay?" Garren asked.

Svetlana nodded.

"Okay, then. I'll see you at the next break."

"Mr. Rosen."

"Yes?"

"Don't forget me."

"I won't. I promise."

And he didn't. After each class, Garren rushed to where he had left her. And each time, as he led her to her next class, he tried to reassure her that he wasn't going to abandon her. But then came the end of the day. He knew Cruller was outside waiting for her. If she didn't show, the game would kick into high gear and Garren wasn't ready for that. Believing that Cruller wanted to play things out a bit, and counting on the fact that Sofia had survived all those months at his house, Garren put on his best face. They talked as he walked her to the school's main entrance.

"Svetlana, I know you don't want to do this, but you need to go with Officer Daniels. He won't hurt you."

"I'd rather go with you."

"Me, too, but we just have to be a little patient. Go home with Officer Daniels and promise me that you won't tell him anything we talked about, okay?"

She nodded.

"If he asks you anything about me, tell him you didn't see me the rest of the day. Can you do that?"

She nodded again.

"Do you trust me?"

"Yes."

"Then give me tonight to figure something out. Tomorrow I'll have a plan."

"Okay."

Garren could tell she was nervous, but trying to be brave. As soon as she exited the school, he ran into the admissions office and peeked through the window. Cruller was right where he knew he would be – leaning against his cruiser, right hand resting on his gun, mirrored aviators covering his guilty eyes, stupid grin on his face. Garren held vigil until they disappeared from his sight. He exhaled the breath he'd been holding. "Garren, you better come up with a plan."

28

"Dude, you need to lighten up." Tommy slurped down the last of his Raman noodles and set the empty bowl on the floor beside his chair. "I get it that you'd rather be home with Kate, but maybe that's your problem. You're…I don't know…too available…too there. You're not a challenge anymore."

Tommy was only partly right. Kate weighed heavily upon his mind, but so did Svetlana. "You know something, Tommy? That's one of the great things about marriage. You don't have to play games anymore. You don't have to wonder."

"What if wonder is the very thing that makes life worth living? Why do you think the lioness does all the hunting? Because her mate is just hangin' around all the time. She misses the excitement of their courtship. She wants to be out there chasing something. She needs the thrill of that hunt. Kate's a lioness. If you don't let her hunt you, she'll be huntin' something else."

Garren gave him a sideways glance. "That's your philosophy on women."

"It's instinct. They can't help it."

"Let me guess – Discovery Channel?"

"Dude, television is only the textbook. Experience is my teacher and I'm a straight A student, if you know what I mean."

"You think it's a problem that I would rather be in my own bed with my wife than spend another night on this couch?"

"Show some respect. Marge has been there for all of us. Remember that time in our old apartment when that weird chick fell asleep and then moved into my room and wouldn't leave and I had to sleep on Marge for a whole month?"

"She wouldn't leave because you told her she could stay."

"Oh, yeah. She was really cute. Do you remember her name? I think she had a guy's name, like Johnnie or Billie. She could totally pull it off though because she was hot. Hey, remember that night…" And on he went for a good five minutes.

Garren ran his hand over his face and let his head fall back against Marge's motherly shoulder. He was in no mood for Tommy's meandering journey down Memory Lane. When it was apparent that he wasn't going to ride along, Tommy unmuted the television.

"Next on the History Channel, Cold War Espionage."

"I could be a spy," Tommy said. "I mean, how hard could it be? The trick is to not look like a spy. That's why Roger Moore was the greatest James Bond ever. He totally looked like an insurance salesman." And Tommy was off on another pointless ramble.

Garren tuned him out until something he said caught his attention. "What was that?"

"What was what?"

"What did you just say?"

"I said a slushy brain freeze would be a much more effective form of interrogation than a tub of water. It just makes sense. You know they want you to talk, so just hold your breath until they let you back up. Brain freeze, on the other hand—"

"Before that. You said something about embassies."

Tommy backtracked to that part of his ramble. "Oh, yeah. A country's embassy, no matter where it is in the world, is still considered part of that country, which means it's outside the jurisdiction of the host country. That's why if you ever get in trouble in another country, all you have to do is get to the U.S. embassy and they can't touch you. Now that's good information."

"It sure is." Garren couldn't get Svetlana out of his mind. Although she didn't say it, she was obviously Russian. Was she born in Russia? Was she still a Russian citizen? "The Russian embassy wouldn't care about a local police department, would they?"

"Nope."

"Where's your phone book?"

Kate was unaware that her natural instinct was to get out there and hunt. She missed Garren and wished this whole mess would just go away so she could have her husband back. But she wasn't a weak little lamb either. She couldn't pretend nothing had happened. Garren was either lying to her or he was losing touch with reality. And somehow – she couldn't quite put it together - that girl Sofia had something to do with it.

She got up, went into the kitchen to refill her wine glass and returned to the couch. The coffee table was strewn with books she hadn't touched since everything went down with Garren. Amongst them was Garren's time journal. She snatched it up and skimmed through what she'd already read. She chuckled, not because she thought it funny, but because the length to which Garren had gone to play out this fantasy of his was so ridiculous. Of all things, time-travel?

The phone rang. Kate tossed the journal back onto the table and got to the phone by the fourth ring.

"Hello."

"Hey, Sweetie, it's mom. Sorry to call so late. I hope I'm not interrupting."

"No, I'm just reading. Is everything all right?"

"We haven't spoken in a few days. How are you guys doing?"

"We're fine."

"Good. That's good."

Pause.

"So, uh, is something wrong?" Kate asked.

"No, no. Actually, it's good news. I just don't know how you'll react."

"What is it?"

"Your father and I have decided to sell the store."

"What? Why?"

"We've been thinking about it for a while and we feel the time is right. We'll both turn fifty next year. If we're going to do something big, we figured we should do it now while we're able."

"But the store has been in the family for generations."

"That's part of the reason. It's got a great reputation, but no heir. We have two beautiful daughters who are living their own lives. We realized a long time ago that hardware and farm equipment didn't appeal to either of you. We held on to the store this long because we thought maybe one of our sons-in-law might want it. Garren has no interest in it. And Denise...well, it might be awhile before we get another son-in-law."

"That's what Garren and dad were talking about at Thanksgiving."

"Don't feel bad. We don't. It was a nice idea, but you and Garren have your own interests."

"Do you have a buyer?"

"We've had one since last year. Every time we turned them down, they'd come back with a better offer. When we realized you and Garren didn't want it, we decided to accept. We're getting four times what we would have asked."

"Wow, that's great, I guess. How do you feel about it?"

"Honestly, I'm relieved. The store made us a decent living, but not enough to really save for our retirement. We're getting enough to make up for all those years we should have been saving. Katie, this is good for us."

"What are you going to do now?"

"That's the part you're not going to like. We're moving to Moline. Your dad has accepted a job with John Deere as one of their Midwestern regional reps. It's a great salary plus benefits. I'm going to take some time off and explore my options."

"Wow, dad working for a big corporation. Do they realize what kind of man they're getting?"

"That's why they recruited him. They want someone who understands the small farmer. They need someone those farmers will trust."

"They hired the right guy. When will you move?"

"Dad starts his new job on February 14."

"Valentine's Day."

"We don't need a designated day to celebrate our love. Anyway, I'm going to stay on at the store for another month to get the new owners up to speed. They're a young couple from Montana. Reminds me a lot of us when we were that age."

"I'm happy for you, but I'm going to miss being able to come over any time I want. We've never lived apart."

"It's not like we're moving to the other side of the country. Moline is only an hour and fifteen minutes away. We can meet for lunch every week if we want to."

"I'd like that. Let me know when you start packing. I want to help… Mom?"

"Yes, Sweetheart."

"I love you and dad so much. I want you to know that if this is what you both want, then I want it for you, too."

"I'm so glad to hear you say that. Denise wasn't quite so understanding at first, but she came around. So, that's our big news. We're John Deere people now."

"I never thought I'd hear either of you say that."

"Like your dad always says: People in suits are the same as people in overalls. They're all the same kind of naked inside."

"He's a wise man, in a weird sort of way."

"That's one of the many reasons I love him. I'm sure you feel the same way about Garren."

"Yeah. Hey, Mom, do you know if dad ever mentioned anything about working for John Deere to Garren?"

"No. We haven't seen you guys since before the new year and Dad didn't accept the job until today. I tell ya, everything happened so fast, we haven't talked to anyone until tonight."

"So there's no way Garren could have known about the store or you guys moving to Moline."

"No. Why do you ask?"

"Oh, nothing. I just like to know what my husband knows before I share big news like this. I'm sure he'll be just as excited about it as I am. Thanks for calling."

"We love you, Katie. Goodnight."

"Goodnight." Kate hung up the phone and snatched up Garren's time journal.

———

"It's not listed." Garren tossed the phonebook onto the couch. "Why did I expect the Dubuque phonebook would have the number for the Russian embassy?"

"Is my best friend a spy?" asked Tommy "Because you've got the perfect cover. No one would ever suspect someone like you…teacher and all."

"No, Tommy, I'm not a spy."

"A spy would have to say that." Tommy looked around as if to make sure no one else was there. "But you can give me a signal if you are, right? Blink your eyes if you're a spy." He stared at Garren.

After thirty seconds, the dryness in the air forced Garren to blink.

Tommy snickered. "I knew it. Does Kate know? Is that why she threw you out? She's tired of all the lies, yeah?"

"Tommy, I'm not a spy."

"You blinked."

"You have to blink. Everyone blinks."

"Then why all this talk about embassies…the *Soviet* embassy?"

"You do know the Soviet Union collapsed in '91."

"That's what they want you to think. In case you missed it, Yeltsin resigned week before last. His replacement is a guy named Vladimir Putin. I think he'll be Russia's new president."

"You're right, he will be. But what about him?"

"He's KGB."

"*Former* KGB."

"Uh, no. Once you're KGB, you're always KGB. Putin's plan is to revive the Soviet empire and be a world superpower again…maybe *the* world superpower."

"I didn't know you were so up on this stuff." Garren was impressed that Tommy paid attention to anything beyond Tommy.

"I've been meeting a lot of smart women lately. A guy's gotta stay relevant." There was the real Tommy. "So, what's with all the interest in the Russian embassy? If you're not a spy are you thinking about defecting? 'Cause usually it's the other way around – you know, a Russian ballerina or scientist wanting to defect to the U.S."

That's it, Garren thought as a critical piece fell into place. The 2019 news said there was no record of Svetlana's disappearance. Did her family defect to the U.S.? Were they in some kind of secret protective custody? Was that why her parents didn't report her missing? Garren picked up the phonebook and flipped to the government pages. He ran his finger down the listing until he found the number to the FBI tip line. "I need to use your phone."

Kate scanned the pages of the time journal. When she found the entry she was looking for, she read it out loud: "*2015 – Mr. Morley retires from John Deere. Kate's parents move back to Dubuque from Moline, Illinois.* How could he have known this?" She read some more. "*2017 – Kate's parents take Alaskan cruise. 2018 – Kate's parents take European vacation. 2019 – Kate's parents join Faith Community Church. Mission trip to Nicaragua.* Huh, my parents become religious." She turned the page and read about her sister's failed relationships. "Sad, but I can see that happening." She continued reading. Somewhere between the housing market collapse of 2008 and Obama's second term, she found herself on the threshold of belief. She flipped back to the first page and re-read the introduction.

"Oh, Garren."

Garren was still on hold with the FBI when there was a knock on the door. He stretched the curly cord to its limit in an attempt to gain some privacy while Tommy answered it.

"Hey, Kate," Tommy said. "Come on in."

A second later, there was a click in the receiver and a voice: "You've reached the Federal Bureau of Investigation 24-hour tip line. State your name and the nature of your call."

Garren stepped back into sight of the front door and saw Kate's beautiful face. "I'm sorry. I'll have to call back later." He terminated the call and placed the phone back on the wall. "Kate, you're here."

Kate pushed past Tommy and stopped just short of Garren's reach. She looked at him intently. "How did you know?"

Garren wasn't quite sure what she meant.

She pulled the time journal from her purse and held it up. "How do you know these things?" She needed to hear him say it one more time.

"It's what I remember. Kate, are you saying you believe me?"

She nibbled her bottom lip. "My mom called tonight and told me they sold the store and are moving to Moline. My dad took a job with John Deere. She said no one knew that until today, but it's here. You wrote it in your journal. How did you know?"

"I remember it."

"So all these things are going to happen?"

"I guess so, unless I do something to change them."

"Sofia. You don't see her again until December 31, 2019?"

"I suppose I could try to find her, or she could decide not to come back in 2019. I really don't understand how it works, but apparently we can change some things."

"Like our marriage."

"Yes. Definitely our marriage."

"I want to ask you something and I want you to answer truthfully. How old do you think you are?"

Tommy wandered into the kitchen and leaned against the counter. He wanted to hear it, too.

Garren chuckled and then became serious. "To me, I'm fifty years old. Kate, do you believe me?"

She held up a finger. "I have another question. If I asked you to forget all this time-travel stuff, would you do it for me?"

Garren's shoulders slumped in defeat. "I wish I could. I really do.

But if I can't be honest with you about who I really am, then how would you be able to trust me about anything else?"

Kate drummed her fingers on the journal. "I guess that's it then. You've made your choice and I've made mine." She leaned against the counter next to Tommy.

Garren felt his throat tighten. "I'm so sorry, Katie."

"You know what this means, Tommy?"

"Uh-uh."

"It means my husband is old enough to be my father."

Garren and Tommy both looked at her.

"You believe him?" said Tommy.

"You believe me? said Garren.

Kate handed the journal to Tommy. "I don't understand it, but the evidence is what it is. Come here."

"So, you believe me."

"Yes." Kate launched herself into his arms and wrapped herself around him. "I'm sorry it took me so long."

"It's okay." Garren held her tightly and breathed in the scent of her. "I don't blame you for doubting all this. I know it's crazy."

Tommy opened the journal and flipped through it while Garren and Kate kissed. After a minute, which is a long time to stand next to two people who are kissing, he interrupted them. "Hey, Garren."

"Yeah, Buddy."

"What's a YouTube?"

For the next hour, Kate and Tommy grilled Garren on what was going to happen over the course of the next twenty years. At first, they wanted to know details about their future selves, but quickly discovered that such information created, as Tommy put it, *a creepy vibe.* They all agreed that it would be better to stick with general history and popular culture, at least until they got more used to the idea. Kate enjoyed knowing that people still did things like take walks in parks, meet friends at coffee shops and curl up with a good book. At the same time, she was fascinated by the influence of technology: The connectedness brought about by smart devices and the Internet and social media; the rise and reliance upon artificial intelligence; the efficiency of automation which would quickly lead to the relinquishing of such tasks as vacuuming, bill paying, remembering phone numbers and birthdates; and the near instant gratification of Amazon. She intuitively estimated that the future would be both easier and more complicated. Tommy was just happy to know that the mighty Van Halen was still rocking with Diamond

Dave at the helm. Although he was totally bummed about Michael Anthony's departure and thoroughly confused by Wolfgang and Chickenfoot. When asked what he liked most about the future, Garren confessed there wasn't much.

When they'd heard enough for one evening, Tommy asked, "How does this time-travel thing work?"

"I honestly don't know," Garren replied. "Like I said, I went to sleep in 2019 and woke up here."

"Have you tried to get back?"

"I wouldn't even know where to begin. If I'm honest, I don't think I'd go back even if I could."

"So, you're just going to relive twenty years of your life. Not sure how I'd feel about that."

Garren put his hand on Kate's knee. "I'm feeling pretty good about now."

"That must be some trip to get old and then get to be young again."

Garren chuckled. "It has its advantages."

"It's like the ultimate do-over."

"Yeah, it is."

"Have you considered *why* this happened?" Kate asked. "I mean, why you? Why Sofia? Why not Tommy and me?"

"Maybe it did happen to us, but we landed somewhere else," Tommy offered. "You and I could be talking to another Garren in another time, trying to convince him *we're* the time-travelers. Or maybe it happened to everybody and all of history is littered with people from 2019. Maybe 2020 is the end of the story and that's just what happens to everybody who's still alive; they get rebooted. Man, this is awesome. I can't wait to see where I end up."

"Wow, Tommy," said Garren. "I don't remember you thinking about stuff like this."

"Maybe I'm not the same guy you used to know. Maybe I'm smarter and more interesting. I might even be better looking. What do you think about that?"

"I guess anything is possible."

"Seriously, you guys," said Kate. "Why do you think this happened to you, Garren? Do you think it's just a fluke or is there some purpose behind it? If there is some kind of intelligence behind it, maybe you were sent here to do something…to correct something."

"Actually, I've been giving that a lot of thought. At first, I thought I was being given a second chance at being a better husband. I still think that, by the way." Kate smiled and placed her hand on his. "But I do think there's something else I'm supposed to do. Cruller, I mean Officer Daniels brought a new foster kid to school today. Her name is Svetlana and I think she's in trouble."

"Dude, what's with you and these young girls? Is she good looking?"

"Tommy, I'm serious. On my last day in 2019, I heard on the news that they'd found the remains of seven young women at a farm in Oskaloosa. One of them was identified as Svetlana Karabelnikoff. This morning, she shows up in my class."

"How do you know it's her?" Tommy asked.

"How many Svetlana Karabelnikoffs can there be in Iowa? Besides, what she told me matches up with what I heard on the news. She said that she and six other girls slept in an underground bunker on a farm. I also heard the name of the guy who locked them in that bunker – Something Diggs. He was with Daniels this morning. I met him."

"Do you remember Svetlana as your student the first time?" Kate asked.

Garren shook his head. "No. Today was twenty years ago for me. I don't even remember Sofia."

"I would remember Sofia," Tommy said. "You say I meet her in 2019? I bet she's hot."

"Tommy!" Garren and Kate said simultaneously.

"Let me get this straight," said Kate. "You heard on the news that Svetlana Karabelnikoff is found dead in 2019."

"Yes, but she probably died twenty years ago, which is now."

"But she's still alive."

"Yes. I met her this morning."

"You realize how crazy this sounds."

"Yeah, I've been living this crazy for the last nine days."

"Okay, crazy aside, let's think it through. Assuming she wasn't in your class the first time, because you might remember a student with the name Karabelnikoff, why is she now?"

"I don't know. Maybe something changed. Actually, something did change. The first time, Sofia stayed here in Dubuque with Daniels until after graduation. Then she moved to New York. This time, she left early. Which means Daniels doesn't have her, which means—"

Kate finished his thought. "Which means he got another girl. What's this guy's deal?"

"I know he's a jerk," said Garren. "And he's got it in for me."

"Explain that," Kate said, now in investigation mode.

"He and I had a little chat this morning. He's pissed because he thinks I took Sofia away from him. Now he's dangling Svetlana in front of me to see if I'll get involved again. If I do, he said he'd…"

"What?" Kate pressed. "What will he do?"

"He implied that he could make something bad happen to you."

"Oh." Kate's face registered this unexpected twist. "He sounds twisted."

"He sounds like a perv," said Tommy. "I admit I think Sofia is a total babe, but apparently we meet when she's like thirty-something, so it's totally cool. This guy's obviously got a thing for young girls and he's using the foster care program to get them. Who knows? Maybe Sofia's leaving actually saved this girl's life. Daniels probably is a scumbag, but he might not be a murderer."

"But Diggs is a murderer," Garren said, "and Daniels is involved with him somehow."

"What did the news say about Diggs?" Kate asked.

"He's serving a life sentence for killing a man and woman sometime this year. He's dying of cancer in 2019. Oh, and he confesses to kidnapping and human trafficking."

"That explains a lot," said Tommy. "Maybe murder isn't his main gig. If he intended to sell those girls, he probably didn't kill them. Maybe they just got left in that bunker when he got arrested and couldn't get out. That doesn't excuse what he did, but it could mean those girls aren't in immediate danger."

"That's awful," Kate said as she imagined how those girls must have died a slow, terrifying death. "We have to do something. Garren, I think you're right. I think you were sent here to save those girls. We need to call the police."

"Or not," Tommy said. "This Daniels guy is a cop. Even if he's not a killer or a human trafficker, he's somehow involved with the guys who are. He's either a customer or he's covering for them. Maybe Svetlana was part of a deal. He either bought her or they gave her to him as a bribe. Either way, we can't go to the police."

"Tommy's right," said Garren. "It would be our word against his. And who do you think they'll believe?"

"Good point," said Kate. "But there's got to be someone. Another police department?"

"How about the FBI?" Garren offered. "I was calling their tip line when you got here. I'll call them back."

"What are you going to tell them?" Tommy asked. "What are you going to say when they ask how you got this information? If you tell them you heard about it on the news last week when you were in 2019, they'll charge you with pranking the FBI. You don't prank the FBI."

"I don't have to tell them about the news. I have Svetlana. She's been to the farm. She's seen the other girls. She knows where the bunker is."

"I still don't get how she fits into all this," Kate said. "Is she an orphan? Is she a runaway?"

"They kidnapped her," Garren explained. "Diggs and some other guy came to her school claiming to be social workers. They said her parents had been killed in an accident and that she had to go with them. She trusted them because she didn't have reason not to. But since then she's figured out it was a scam."

"Why doesn't she try to escape?" Tommy asked.

"She is," Garren replied. "I'm her way out."

Kate's mind was still trying to complete the picture. "Why would Officer Daniels let her go to school? I mean, he got her from Diggs and this other guy. He knows they kidnapped her. I hate to think this way, but it's kind of obvious why a man acquires a young girl from kidnappers. Why risk losing her?"

Garren replied, "Sofia told me he never touched her sexually."

"But he did hit her," Kate said. "I saw the bruises. That still doesn't answer the question. Why let her go to school?"

"It's all part of the scam," Tommy offered. "I've heard about this. These human traffickers use kids to get other kids. It's a total mind game. They brainwash them so they don't even know they're being used. Then they get them to befriend other kids and the whole thing starts over."

"It's a mind game all right," said Garren. "He's using her to test me. This is some kind of game to him and Svetlana is the game piece."

"That still seems so unnecessarily risky," said Kate. "He's got to know that he could be implicated."

Garren shrugged. "I don't get the impression he's all that smart."

"Then we take him down," Tommy said with confident resolve.

"I agree," said Garren. "But he's still dangerous."

"And those other guys are serious criminals capable of murder," Kate added. "I wonder if they've done it yet, killed that man and woman. Maybe we could save them, too."

Garren looked at his wife and best friend, relieved beyond words that they believed him and grateful to have their help. "So we all agree that something has to be done. Now all we need is a plan."

Kate looked at Tommy. "Do you have any coffee?"

"I think so."

"Good. We're going to need it. We're not leaving here until we have a plan to save those girls. And I'm calling Denise. Oh, by the way, she's half way there to believing you, Garren."

"Really?"

"Yeah, you think you can convince one more person tonight?"

"I'll give it a shot."

"Denise," said Tommy. "Your sister, Denise?"

"Yeah, why?"

"No reason. Just curious." Tommy disappeared into his bedroom and reappeared a few minutes later with his hair combed and wearing a nicer shirt. "Okay. Let's get this party started."

29

Next day, Garren arrived at school early, parked in a spot near the entrance of the building and waited. As soon as Officer Daniels pulled into the drop-off circle, he got out of his car and paced himself to be at the front door in time to meet them.

"Officer Daniels," he said politely. "Good morning, Lana."

Cruller looked like a man holding all the cards. "Lana, Sweetheart, why don't you go on in where it's warm while I have a word with your teacher?"

Svetlana looked questioningly at Garren.

"You can find your way to class, yes?" Garren winked at her such that Cruller couldn't see.

As soon as she was in the school, Cruller's demeanor shifted from the friendly father-type to a man who had spent most of his life dealing with the worst of humanity. "Didn't expect you to seek me out like this."

"I thought a lot about what you said yesterday. I want to apologize for my actions. I was completely out of line. I'm sorry if anything I said or did caused Sofia to run away like she did. If she comes back, I assure you I will be nothing more than her teacher. The same goes for Lana. I've learned an important lesson never to interfere in the personal lives of our students. I won't make the same mistake again. You have my word."

"Nicely done," said Cruller in mock acceptance. "It's refreshing to hear a teacher admit he still has some things to learn. But I'm not buyin' it. I've been around enough liars to spot one."

"Why would I lie to you? Do you think I want to play this game?" Garren wasn't sure how much longer he'd be able to fake his compliance, but he had to stick with the plan. "If it were just me, maybe, but I can't leave home every morning wondering if I'll ever see my wife again. I received your warning loud and clear. I've got too much to lose. All I want to do is go about my business and leave you to yours."

Cruller eyed him suspiciously. "I'm disappointed in you, Rosen. I thought you had more backbone than that. Then again, maybe it was more about Sofia than you all along. She did have a way about her. All the same, I'm keepin' my eye on you. If I get even a hint that you're warming up to my daughter, it's game on. You read me?"

"Yes, Sir."

"See you around, Teach." Cruller climbed back into his cruiser and left Garren to consider his next move.

He went straight into the school and found an empty office, closed the door and dialed home. Kate picked up on the first ring.

"Garren?" she said expectantly.

"Yeah, it's me. I don't think he believed me, so we need to go with Plan B. If you don't hear from me by ten fifteen, it's still a go. We'll see you guys around noon."

"You saw Svetlana…she's okay?"

"Yeah, she looks fine."

"Tell me again we're doing the right thing."

"We are. I know it."

"Be careful."

"I will."

"I love you, Garren."

"I love you, too." There was silence on the line, but he could tell she was still there. "You okay?"

"Yeah, I'll just be glad when this is over."

"It will be soon."

"Noon then." Kate sighed heavily. "I'm going to be a nervous wreck until I see you."

"We'll be there. I promise. I gotta go now."

"Okay. Bye."

Garren heard the click, then said to himself, "We have got to get some cell phones."

———

As soon as the line cleared, Kate called Denise. "Hey, Sis, I just spoke with Garren. So far, so good. Svetlana is at the school."

"Did he see him?"

"Yes, but he doesn't know if he believed him. So we're going with Plan B. Meet me behind the university library at nine o'clock."

"I'll be there."

"Don't forget to get Tommy on the way. I'll call him and let him know to look for you."

"Uh…that's okay. You don't need to do that."

"I want to make sure he's awake."

"He's awake."

"How do you know that? Oh…never mind. I don't want to know. I'll see you at nine."

Kate hung up the phone and paused at the thought of her sister and Tommy. It was such an unlikely pairing that she'd never even considered introducing them. They did meet once at the wedding, but Denise was still with what's his name and Tommy was occupied with the girl he brought. But now that she thought of them together… no, they were from completely different universes. She thought of Garren's journal. No indication there that their paths ever crossed again, let alone converged. Then she started thinking like a time-traveler's wife. Things were different now. Sofia's early departure created a brand new chain of events and in effect spawned an entirely different history; one in which Denise and Tommy meet a second time and…Kate pushed the possibilities aside. She didn't have time to think of them now. She didn't know if she wanted to think of them at all. She pulled on her coat, slung her backpack over her shoulder, grabbed her keys and headed out.

The sight of the police car parked on the other side of the road stopped her in her tracks. Not that she didn't believe Garren when he said Officer Daniels would probably have one of his buddies keep tabs on her, but it was the first tangible evidence that all this intrigue was actually happening. She steeled herself and got into her car, trying to act like everything was normal. She pulled out of her spot and drove to the corner, turned left and glanced in her rearview mirror. Sure enough, the cop was following her.

—⁂—

Garren found Svetlana sitting in the front row in the desk closest to the wall. The rest of the students were filing in and chatting the last few minutes before the bell. After the way Sofia was treated, he was keen to the fact that no one seemed to even know Svetlana was there. But given the circumstances, he was glad. He went to his own desk and casually called her to him.

"How are you?" he asked, keeping his voice low and trying to act like a teacher.

"Okay. I don't like staying with that man. I don't like how he looks at me."

Garren lowered his voice even more. "You won't have to go there ever again. I'm taking you away from here today."

Svetlana's eyes widened. "How?"

"I told you I'd have a plan. I need you to meet me in the library after third period. Can you do that?"

She nodded.

Garren looked at the clock and saw that he had exactly one minute before the bell. "We're taking you home. You'll be with your parents tonight. Okay?"

Svetlana's lip began to quiver and her eyes began to tear up. She mouthed the words, "Thank you."

The bell rang at exactly 7:35. Garren called roll and launched into his lesson. Svetlana kept her eyes glued to him the entire class. At first, he found her distracting, knowing what she'd been through and what she must be thinking. But then he found assurance in her stare; confirmation that he was fulfilling his purpose in time. The class ended at 8:22. On her way out, Svetlana caught his eye and thanked him again with a slight nod of her head.

At 10:06, Garren packed his briefcase and left the tranquility of his classroom. The halls were overly crowded as usual, a stark contrast to the wide open spaces he was used to at the university. There, he could actually stroll at a leisurely pace and converse with students who happened to be going his way. High school was the antithesis of that. At the sound of the bell, the deserted ghost town halls morphed into the streets of Pamplona. Garren held his briefcase in front of him like a shield against the stampeding masses. He was relieved to reach the library and find Svetlana waiting for him. He gave her a nod to follow him to the table furthest from the door.

Sitting opposite her, he pulled a notebook out of his briefcase and laid it open. At least he would try to look like they were discussing something school related. "We're leaving in just a few minutes. You ready?"

"I think so," she replied.

"This will be the hardest thing you have to do today, but it will be easy. A good friend of mine taught me this. You know where the cafeteria is?"

She nodded.

"There's a short hallway to the right of the food service line that leads to an exit at the back of the school. Wait here for ten minutes, then go there. Go out the exit and stand outside the door. I will come to you in my car. Now the key to doing this right is to look like you're supposed to be doing it. Don't run, but walk like you need to be somewhere. Try to look like you've done this a hundred times. If you can look bored, all the better. Do you think you can do that?"

"Yes."

"I'll get as close as I can. As soon as you see me, get in the back seat and lay down on the floor. There's a pillow and blanket. Try to make yourself small and cover yourself."

"What if somebody stops me?"

Garren fished a small pad of hall passes from his briefcase and filled in the necessary information. "Show them this."

She took the pass and put it in her shirt pocket. "Can you get in trouble for this?"

"Probably."

"Why are you doing it?"

"I might be able to explain it to you one day, but for now it's just the right thing to do." He repacked his briefcase and got up. "Ten minutes. Cafeteria. Exit. See you soon."

The plan was a good one. It was pretty much identical to when Garren and Sofia ditched a few days ago. It worked flawlessly then. There was no reason to believe it wouldn't work flawlessly now. Garren strolled toward the office to inform the secretary he needed to leave and to ask her to call in a substitute for his last two classes. Then this happened.

"Mr. Rosen. Just the man I need to see. Come into my office, please."

"Principal Jenson," Garren replied. "Can this wait? I'm in a bit of a hurry."

"Are you on your way to class?"

"No, but—"

"Then you can spare me a few minutes. My office." She didn't wait for his reply.

Garren checked his watch.

"Mr. Rosen," Jenson said from the doorway to her office.

Garren followed her in. She closed the door behind him. He smiled and tried to look interested. Perhaps he could hurry things along with charm and attentiveness.

"What can I do for you?" he asked.

"The Valentine's dance. Have you given much thought to it?"

"No, I haven't. I thought I was just chaperoning."

"I've decided to introduce something new this year: Valentine Sweetheart Dances. And I want you to be the Match Maker for the evening."

"Excuse me? I'm not familiar with that."

"Haven't you ever been to a Sweetheart Dance?"

Garren shook his head.

"Throughout the evening, the students will submit the names of their friends they want to see dancing together. Before each slow dance, the Match Maker – that's you – reads out the names and they have to dance together."

"That sounds horrible."

"It's sweet. Now I want you to make it interesting. Spice it up. Pretend you're Cupid. Make it romantic. Create a mood."

"Are you sure we should be creating a mood for these kids?"

"Oh, yes. We did this when I was in school. It's lots of fun." She leaned in like she was letting him in on a secret. "The clever students will actually submit their own names along with someone they're sweet on. Who knows? We might even see the budding of young romance."

It was all Garren could do to keep from throwing the time-out flag and pointing out the obvious differences between Principal Jenson's 1950s high school experience and the sexually charged 2000s. He didn't have time to get into all that with his boss, so he capitulated. "That actually does sound nice. I'd be happy to play Match Maker. Now, if you'll excuse me, I really need to be going."

"I've made a list of ideas for romantic banter for you. Would you like to see it?"

"Yes, but not until I can sit down and give it my full attention. E-mail it to me."

"Okay, but some of it might need some explanation. And I thought maybe you and I could come up with a little routine for the students, or a skit. I just want to make it fun for them."

Garren was already backing out of her office. "All great ideas. Let's get together soon and plan it out."

Principal Jenson followed him out. "Would you consider wearing a pair of wings and holding a little bow and arrow?"

"We'll talk about that, too. Goodbye, Principal Jenson."

That little detour cost him five minutes and he still hadn't asked the secretary to arrange for an afternoon substitute. And wouldn't you know it, she was on the phone. After another minute, Garren glanced at the clock on the office wall. Svetlana would be leaving the library soon and he wasn't even at his car yet. He looked at the secretary, trying to politely communicate that he needed to speak with her.

"Uh-huh," she was saying. "Uh-huh…I know, right? The same thing happened to me last week. The nerve of some people."

Garren cleared his throat.

"Hey, let me call you back. One of the teachers needs me; the one I told you about…No, I'm not gonna say that…Shush, you're awful… Goodbye, Mom." She ended the call. "Sorry about that, Mr. Rosen. What can I do for you?"

—*wv*—

Svetlana made it to the cafeteria without a hitch. Fourth period was well underway and everyone was where they were supposed to be. The only persons to see Svetlana make her way past the long rows of tables were the cafeteria workers preparing for the first lunch rush in less than an hour. Had they noticed her at all, they would have assumed she too was exactly where she was supposed to be. Besides, their responsibility to ensure the students weren't up to any mischief didn't start until 10:58. So Svetlana had free passage all the way to the short hall that led to the exit. But when she got there, the sign on the door stopped her in her tracks: EMERGENCY EXIT ONLY. ALARM WILL SOUND IF DOOR IS OPENED. She looked around for another way out, but there wasn't one. She started to go back to the main entrance, but stopped as it would put her on the opposite side of the school and increase her chances of being intercepted. So she turned back to the emergency exit as her only way out. Examining the door, she couldn't find anything to suggest an alarm except for the sign – no visible wires or magnets or electronic sensors, no special hardware, no emergency light or siren. She examined the cinderblock wall in which the door was located and saw no enhancements. Of course, the security measures could have been hidden within the walls, but she remembered seeing a plaque indicating the school was built in 1969. The front of the building had recently been remodeled and there were many upgrades throughout, but the building itself was thirty years old, long before a town like Dubuque would even think about security systems in their public schools. That suggested to her that any security measures added to this particular door would be visible. Bracing herself for an error in her reasoning, she leaned into the door, heard a click and felt the door open. Stepping quietly through the door, she glanced up at the door frame to confirm her evaluation. She was correct. The sign was bogus. She was free.

But Garren wasn't there and she wasn't alone. Further down the backside of the building, just outside the back doors to the band room, two kids were leaning against the wall. They straightened up when they heard the door open, ready to make a run for it, but relaxed when they saw that it was just another kid. Svetlana saw smoke rise from between them and detected a faint sweetness wafting in the breeze from their direction.

"Hey," one of the kids called out to her.

Svetlana offered a timid wave.

That was the extent of their interaction, a simple acknowledgment of each other's presence. But there was meaning in it. In that exchange, there was a camaraderie based solely on their shared desire for freedom at the risk of getting caught. And along with it, an agreement that whatever the other was up to stayed between them. However, alliances among criminals are fragile.

The two boys stiffened as something caught their attention from around the corner that Svetlana could not see. Then they broke out in a sprint in her direction. Passing her, they dropped two baggies and a lit joint at her feet. Seconds later, they were gone around the next corner. A second or two after that, an overweight resource officer came chugging around the corner where the boys had been moments earlier. Seeing her, he made a beeline in her direction. He was only thirty feet way and running as fast as he could, barely enough time for Svetlana to react. Her first few steps put her in the direction of her cohorts, but movement in the parking lot drew her attention away from the building. Gambling on it being her real ally, she ran toward the only moving car in the lot.

Garren saw what was going down, so he altered his plan. Slowing, but not intending to stop, he leaned over and opened the passenger door. "Get in!" he yelled as he rolled up next to her.

Without hesitation, she dove in, closing the door behind her. Garren was surprised by her ready commitment to the stunt and the fluidity of her movement; as if it were not the first time she'd done something like that. Still operating according to plan, she slid down until she was mostly sitting on the floor in front of the passenger seat. Garren glanced in the rearview mirror in time to see the resource officer fumbling with his notepad. The description of his car and license plate would soon be radioed to his supervisor, who in turn would most likely call it in to the local police department. It was only a matter of minutes, if that long, before Cruller would be notified. Then it would be game on and he would probably lose his job. At least he wouldn't have to create a mood for a bunch of hormone-driven teenagers at that stupid dance.

Throwing caution to the wind, Garren peeled out of the school parking lot and accelerated east down Pennsylvania Avenue. He tried to keep his speed down, but they needed to get out of Dubuque before being spotted. Weaving through traffic, he reached the end of Pennsylvania and took the forty-five degree left turn onto University Avenue and followed it around until it put him onto N. Grandview Avenue. A few blocks more and he would see the signs for Highway 20.

Blue lights appeared in his mirror a block from the onramp. Knowing the highway would mean certain apprehension, he altered his plan again, blowing past the onramp and continuing straight down N. Grandview. Taking advantage of his car's superior engine, he put some distance between himself and his pursuer. A right bend in the road gave him a few seconds of cover. That was all he needed. In a maneuver that surprised even himself, he took a hard right onto a side street, another immediate right and then a left into a neighborhood. He slowed down and started picking his way back toward the highway. Unfamiliar with this part of town, he hoped he wouldn't inadvertently end up at a dead end.

"Not bad," Svetlana said as she pushed herself up into the seat. "Have you done this before?"

"You mean running from the cops? No. First time. How about you?"

She didn't reply; just smiled and fastened her seat belt.

"No, I mean it," Garren said. "The way you jumped in back there and the fact that you seem to be enjoying this suggests you're not the timid school girl you let on to be."

"My parents taught me to utilize my assets. I'm small, so people naturally think that about me. That makes it easy to conceal what I can do."

Garren gave her a look. "What *can* you do?"

"I know how to survive."

Garren thought about the news report. Everyone has limitations. Still, he was impressed and more than curious. "Did your parents teach you how to jump into a moving car?"

Svetlana looked out the window, but he could tell she was smiling.

"Don't want to talk about it, eh? That's okay, I understand. We don't really know each other that well. But we do have a long road trip ahead of us. If you want me to stay awake, you're gonna have to keep me company." Garren found his way back onto S. Grandview not far from the onramp.

"You missed the highway," Svetlana said when Garren passed it.

"You caught that, huh? Well, I know a few things, too. By now, every cop in Dubuque is looking for this car. We need to ditch it." He turned left onto Bennett Street. "Our new car is right up here."

Svetlana read the sign on the huge building to her right. "University of Dubuque Heritage Center."

30

"I like your car better." It was the first thing Svetlana said since leaving Dubuque thirty minutes earlier.

"So do I," Garren replied from behind the wheel of Kate's 1982 Chevy Citation. He was beginning to wonder if she would talk at all. "But no one's looking for this car."

"I'm not complaining. You said I had to help you stay awake."

"I'm okay for now."

Svetlana let another minute pass, then noted, "We're heading east. South Dakota is northwest."

"You're very observant. Did your parents teach you that, too?"

She turned her gaze back out the side window. "Where are you taking me?"

"Still don't want to talk about your folks. I don't mean to pry, but your avoidance is only making me more curious."

"So is yours. Why are we going east?"

"How about a trade? I answer your question and you answer mine. I'll go first. We're going to Madison, Wisconsin to meet up with my wife, her sister and a friend of ours. We'll exchange vehicles and get on the Interstate to South Dakota."

"You planned all this out?"

"That's two questions, but yes."

Svetlana nodded as she digested the information. "Switch cars. Leave town heading east. Switch cars again. That's pretty good. Did your parents teach you how to cover your tracks?"

"I'll add sarcasm to your list of hidden talents. And that's your third question. No, my parents don't think like this."

"But you do. Observation, not a question."

Now it was Garren's turn to clam up.

Svetlana turned in her seat to look at him. "I think we both have secrets."

When she didn't continue, Garren said, "Maybe we should both put our cards on the table. We've got a long trip ahead of us and it's going to get a lot more crowded. If there's anything you want to tell just me, now would be the time to do it."

Several minutes passed. Garren sensed she was trying to decide whether and how much to disclose. He wanted to press, but his own secret gave him a greater appreciation for her reluctance to reveal the secret she was carrying. Granted, she probably wasn't a time-traveler or extraterrestrial or anything cool like that, but whatever it was, it was still important to her. He was about to change the subject when she opened up.

"I'm sorry I'm being so evasive. My family…trust doesn't come easy for us. My parents taught me a lot of things, but trust isn't one of them. I've never really let anyone in, if you know what I mean."

"I can respect that. I won't ask you to tell me anything you don't want to, but if there's anything that will help me get you back home, I hope you'll tell me."

Svetlana pulled a small book from the inside pocket of her coat. From the book, she removed a photograph and handed it to him.

"Nice looking family."

"My mother wears her hair short now and my father shaves his face every day."

"People change when they get older." He handed the photograph back to her.

"Sometimes people change because they have to. If you meet my parents, they will introduce themselves as Peter and Mary Karr and they will call me Lana. They will say they are both only children, born in Kansas in a town no one has ever heard of, and that their parents are deceased. They will tell you they met in a small college in Missouri that no longer exists. They will say I was born in Chicago while they were visiting friends who no longer live there. They will say we traveled around the United States in an RV until I was old enough to begin school. Then we moved to Eureka where we have lived for the last ten years. My father will tell you he works for a construction company and my mother is a stay-at-home mom. We are quiet people who keep to ourselves. We have no pets. We never entertain guests. We often take weekend trips to obscure places no one visits. Most of the people on our street have never met us."

"But it's not true, is it?"

"This is what my parents taught me to say about our family."

"I would never ask you to disobey them."

"But if you ask me which parts I like, I will tell you."

"Okay, which parts of your family story do you like?"

"I like that my parents are good people and they love each other and they love me. I like that we traveled around the United States before landing in Eureka. I like that my father works for a construction company. I like that when we are in Eureka, we are very quiet people and we don't have any pets." She leaned over and whispered. "That last part is true, but I don't like it." She sat up straight, then leaned over and whispered again. "Also, I've never been in an RV and the only ruler my dad knows how to use is a slide ruler."

"Is that photograph real?"

"Yes. I must have been three when it was taken. My mother gave it to me years ago and said I must never let anyone see it. I keep it in my book of things that are true."

"Why did you show it to me?"

"I'm tired of lying. I want someone to know who I really am. There's something different about you. You seem safe to me."

"I get that a lot."

"I feel like I can trust you. I've never had that before, except with my parents."

"I'm honored."

"Of course, you can't tell anyone, not even your wife. In fact, if you meet my parents, you can't tell them I told you anything."

"Your secret is safe with me."

"You think you know my secret?"

"I have a pretty good idea."

"Then I may as well tell you their real names. My mother's name is Nadia and my father is Petros. My mother told me that picture was taken the day before we left Russia."

"How old are you?"

"Fifteen."

"If you were three years old in that picture, that was twelve years ago. 1988. Three years before the collapse of the Soviet Union." Garren's pretty good idea solidified into certainty. "That explains a lot."

"What does it explain?"

What Garren was thinking was how the news story got her name right. The photograph and the *book of things that are true* must have been found with her remains. It also explained why she was the only one publically identified. There would have been no record of a missing girl named Svetlana Karabelnikoff and no way to notify next of kin. He wondered if Petros and Nadia were still alive in 2019 and if things had changed enough for them to come forward and claim the remains of their daughter.

"Mr. Rosen? What does it explain?"

"Your name. It explains why those men think your name is Lana Karr."

"Mr. Diggs knows my real name."

"Did you tell him?"

"No. They called me Svetlana when they picked me up from school. I thought my parents sent them and used my real name to tell me it was safe to go with them. When they told me they were both dead, that's when I realized something was wrong."

"If they know your real name, they must know the truth about your parents. Getting you home may not be the end of it. Svetlana, I think your parents' cover has been blown."

They drove for a while in silence, both considering the implications. Working with the extra information that he knew, Garren tried out a few scenarios. 1) Diggs and his accomplice were Russian agents sent to round up Cold War defectors. No, they would have gotten the entire family. 2) Diggs and company were middlemen working on a tip and Svetlana was a bargaining chip to get her parents to do something. No, they wouldn't have passed her on to Cruller. 3) Diggs was just a two bit hustler who stumbled into something and saw an opportunity to nab a girl who probably wouldn't get reported missing. That didn't explain how Diggs discovered Svetlana's identity, but it was the most likely given what Garren knew. All Svetlana could think about was her parents and whether they were even alive. If what Garren said was true, that their truth had been discovered, they were all in danger, even Garren and his friends.

"Can we talk about something else?" Svetlana said after a long sigh.

"Sure. Would you like to listen to some music?"

"No. What's your first name?"

"Garren."

"May I call you that?"

"Looks like we've moved beyond the whole teacher/student thing."

"Yes, we have, Garren. It feels weird to call you that, but it's better than Mr. Rosen."

"Are you saying I have an unusual name, Svetlana Karabelnikoff?" They both laughed.

"Garren," she said. "I told you my secret. Now tell me yours."

"Then you'll really think I'm weird." Garren let out a leftover chuckle. "Believe it or not, my secret is even more complicated than yours. I doubt you'd believe it."

"Try me."

"You might question my sanity."

"Have you told anyone else?"

"Yes."

"Did they believe you?"

"Not at first."

"But you convinced them."

"Yes. I guess I did."

"Then convince me."

"It wasn't easy. It took some time."

Svetlana kicked off her shoes and put her feet up on the dash. "We've got nothing else to do. Tell me your story. I promise to hear you out. However, I must warn you, if it's embarrassing I'll probably laugh."

Garren glanced at her and saw something in her eyes that made him want to tell her. So for the next thirty minutes, he told her everything. He told her about New Year's Eve 2019 and Sofia and the moon and passing out. He told her about waking up on his birthday in the year 2000. He told her about Kate and how he'd spent the last week and a half trying to save his marriage. He told her about his run-in with Officer Daniels, who he nicknamed Cruller, and how he helped Sofia leave Dubuque five months earlier than the first time. He told her about Dr. Finney and some of his theories about what happened and how he and Sofia were writing time journals just in case they switch places again with their younger selves. He told her everything he could think of except what he knew about her future. If things worked out in this time line, Svetlana Karabelnikoff would live a long and happy life, never knowing what happened in the other time line.

"Well, that's it," he said when he had run out of things to say. "At least you aren't laughing."

"I don't believe it," she replied.

"See? I told you."

"No, that's not what I mean. I didn't tell you what my father really does. He's a theoretical scientist."

"And?"

"And this is his thing. This is what he does. He's been theorizing about time-travel since before I was born. Garren, you are the outcome of my father's life work."

"So, do you or do you not believe it?"

"Yes, I believe it. Oh my gosh, he is gonna flip out when he meets you. Wow!"

"What about your mom?"

"She's a scientist, too, but she's more into the applied sciences. Guess what I'll be when I grow up?"

"Farmer?"

"No, silly. I'm destined for science. Both of my parents come from scientific families. My mom was actually an apprentice for my dad's father. He introduced them. Funny story. My grandfather had to trick them into going on their first date because neither of them thought they had room in their lives for romance. His experiment must have worked because six months later they were married."

"What's your mom's specialty?"

"Lately, she's been working on my grandfather's research. It's kind of out there."

"Time-traveler here."

"My grandfather invented something called a pulse burst transmitter back in the 1960s. It was supposed to make interplanetary communication sound like a local phone call. He lost his funding when the U.S. landed a man on the moon. The entire space program was punished for losing the Space Race. The government confiscated his only working prototype, but they didn't get his notes. Those ended up as a wedding present to my mother. They've become something of a hobby for her."

"That's not so hard to believe."

"Not the science, but the application. She wants to use it to communicate with aliens."

"Really?"

"What? Don't you believe in extraterrestrial intelligent beings, Future Boy?"

"Since you put it that way. Hmm, so who do your parents work for now?"

"The United States government."

"Do you know what they're working on?"

"They never talk to me about their real work. Just their hobbies."

Garren drummed his fingers on the steering wheel as he continued working on their situation. "If your parents are helping the United States government, then the United States government should want to help them, right?"

"It seems like they would, but governments can't always be trusted. My family knows this all too well."

"I might have a few bargaining chips of my own."

Svetlana cocked her head.

"Let's just say my knowledge of the next twenty years might prove valuable. But that's enough intrigue for now. Let's talk about something really important. What do you do when you're not diving into moving vehicles and being all scientific? Who is the real Svetlana Karabelnikoff?"

—◊◊◊—

They passed the Madison City Limits sign at noon on the dot. Ten minutes later, they found the intersection of W. Broadway and Monono. Working with only a printed map the night before, they guessed it would be a good place to meet up and park Kate's car. They guessed right. There was a large shopping center, two hotels and an office building. Rolling up to the intersection, Garren spotted Kate waving from the parking lot on the right. After a brief introduction, they parked Kate's car at one of the hotels and piled into Denise's 1998 Honda Accord. They stopped at a Taco Bell to take care of two basic life needs and were back on the road in less than thirty minutes.

It was decided that Denise would drive and Tommy would navigate the first leg, allowing Svetlana to ride in the back with Garren and Kate. It was crowded and a little awkward sitting so close together, and Garren felt obligated to fill the void with conversation. But since Denise was still a little freaked out by the fact that Garren was a time-traveler and Garren was the only one who knew Svetlana's family secret, he couldn't think of much to say. Mercifully, Denise switched on the radio to an easy listening station. Tommy was out in five minutes and Denise was singing along to a medley of Barry Manilow tunes.

"How old are you, Svetlana?" Kate asked when she couldn't take the silence any longer.

"Fifteen."

"What do you like to do?"

"I like to read. There's not much else to do where I live."

"Do you have any brothers or sisters?"

"No."

"Pets?"

"No."

Kate gave Garren a look inviting him to help make some conversation. He returned a look that indicated he was tapped out.

"We've still got a long way to go yet. Garren, do you know how far it is to Eureka?"

"About ten hours."

"Ten hours," Kate repeated. "Yup, we're going to be in this car for ten hours. Svetlana, that's such a pretty name."

"Thank you."

"And your last name – Karabelnikoff – is that Russian?"

"Yes."

"Have you ever been to Russia?"

Svetlana looked to Garren for help. All he could offer was a shrug. She reached into her jacket pocket and pulled out her *book of things that are true*. She withdrew the photograph and handed it to Kate. "That's me with my parents. It was taken the day we escaped from the Soviet Union. Now we live in South Dakota in a government safe house with false identities. My parents are scientists. They work for your government. I don't know what they do, but my mother is interested in aliens and my father has theories about traveling through time. He'll be very excited to meet Garren for reasons I assume you all are aware of. Does everyone here know Garren's secret?"

"Pretty much, yes." Garren and Denise made eye contact via the rearview mirror.

"That's ours. How about you guys? Does anyone else have a secret?"

"I wasn't really asleep," said Tommy. "I just don't like this music. Garren, remember your lucky date shirt you never let me borrow? Not that I needed it, but I borrowed it and then lost it. I also let Dave borrow your Led Zeppelin records. He still has them. What else? Oh yeah, sometimes I lie about myself to get women to go out with me."

Denise shot him a look. "Is that all?"

"I want to get a tattoo, but I'm afraid it will hurt too bad to finish and then I'll have only a partial tattoo that will look stupid. Yep, that's about it for me."

"Wow, Tommy," said Kate. "That's a lot of information, but I don't think that's what Svetlana had in mind."

"Actually, that's perfect," she replied. "This is what people do on road trips. They get to know each other. What kind of tattoo do you want to get?"

Tommy turned in his seat. "I'm thinking an eagle holding an American flag all across my back."

"I'd like to get Stalin on this arm," Svetlana said with a straight face. "And the hammer and sickle on my neck." This was met with uneasy silence. "Sheesh, I'm only kidding...Go U.S.A...Baseball, yeah."

Tommy laughed and then everyone else joined in on the joke.

"I already have a tattoo," said Denise.

"You do?" exclaimed Kate. "Does dad know?"

"No. And you're not going to tell him."

"What is it?" Tommy asked.

"I'm not sure how I feel about you yet," Denise replied. "I will say this, if I ever catch you lying to me, you'll never see it."

"Ooo," said Garren and Kate at the same time.

"You better not pull anything on my sister," said Kate.

Tommy had to get the last word in. "For clarification, she did say *catch*."

From there on out, the mood was light. With the elephant in the car exposed, it somehow made it seem less serious. Talk of tattoos and a slew of other things was a welcome distraction from what they all were thinking might be waiting for them in Eureka. Even Garren's time-travel situation seemed less mysterious and more like an enhanced game of reverse trivial pursuit. When the conversation drifted in that direction, everyone had questions about the future they wanted Garren to answer. And the more they got to know Svetlana, the more she seemed like one of the gang. She proved to be quick witted with a good sense of humor. Even Tommy, who was usually the most entertaining one in the room, relinquished the spot light to Svetlana's sometimes humorous tales of life as a Russian ex-pat in her tiny South Dakota town – wheat capital of the world and birthplace of Allen H. Neuharth, founder of *USA Today*, thank you very much. All in all, it was a good way to pass the miles.

31

The nightlife in Eureka, South Dakota consists of two bars – Prime Time and Wolff Den – both of which close at 1:00 AM. But most of the town's 1,101 residents, mostly of German and Russian heritage, are in by nine and asleep by ten. Eurekans are mostly hard-workin', God-fearin' folk who don't look favorably on horsin' around or layin' about when there's work to be done…and there's always work to be done. So when the city-slickers from Dubuque came rollin' into town with their fancy import car just after last call, no one noticed.

"We're here," said Garren from the driver's seat. No one had said a word in the last hour and he didn't know if anyone else was awake.

"See that gas station on the right?" Svetlana said from the back seat. "You can turn right onto any of the next four streets."

Garren detected something in her voice. It could have been from sleepiness or the emotion she must have been feeling at the moment. As they turned onto 9th Street, Denise sat up. She was snuggled up against Tommy in the back seat. In the front passenger seat, Kate also stirred awake.

"Wake up, Tommy," said Denise. "We're here."

Tommy opened one eye and squinted at the lone street light on the corner.

"There's my school on the left," said Svetlana. "Our church is behind it." Four blocks later, she said, "Turn left at the stop sign. Follow this street and take the fourth left."

"North Lake Drive?" Garren asked as he approached the turn.

"That's my street. We're the second house on the right."

Garren stopped in front of a house lit only by a single bulb porch lamp.

"I don't see any cars," said Kate. "Do you think they're home?"

"The garage is around back."

Garren cut off the engine. No one moved, not even Svetlana.

"I'm nervous," she said.

"Would you like us to come with you?" Kate asked.

"Just Garren, if that's okay."

Kate nodded and Garren got out of the car. He opened Svetlana's door and offered his hand. She took it and held tightly to his arm as they approached the house. It was very cold, but he knew that wasn't the cause of her trembling. She was starting to lose it.

"It's okay," Garren said, trying to comfort her. "You're home."

They climbed the three brick steps and Garren rang the bell. They waited long enough for Garren to think no one was home. He was about to ring the bell again when a light blinked on in the window furthest to the right. He heard a sound he identified from countless movies as that of a pump shotgun being racked.

"Who is it?" It was a man's voice. He sounded irritated and understandably so. Nothing good ever happens after midnight.

"Papa, it's me, Svetlana."

The door flew open and there was a shirtless Petros Karabelnikoff, his face a mixture of bewilderment and guarded hope. "Doch-ka?" Then the shotgun came around and landed straight at Garren's chest. "Who are you?"

Garren's hands went up and he stepped backward off the steps.

"No, Papa!" shouted Svetlana. "He's my friend. They brought me home to you."

Petros looked past Garren to the car in front of his house. "How many?"

"Uh-Five, Sir," Garren stammered. "Sir, we only want to help."

"Papa, we can trust them."

Petros, overcome by his desire to hold his daughter, lowered the shotgun and leaned it against the wall. As Svetlana stepped into his embrace, Nadia appeared next to him and immediately began to weep. Garren took another step back to give the family time to reunite.

In the television show *Quantum Leap*, whenever Sam completed a mission, whoever or whatever was calling the shots would send him to another time and set up the premise for the next episode.

Garren braced himself to be shot back to 2019. But that's not what happened. There was no leaping, no fading out, no whooshing into another time. He was still there in the cold early morning hours of January 12, 2000, standing outside a little house on the prairie. He was about to return to the car when he heard a friendlier Petros call out to him.

"Drive your car around back. And don't use your headlights."

Before Garren could reply, the door was shut and locked and the only light in the house blinked off. He walked back to the car and found three sets of eyes eager for a report.

"What happened?" Kate asked.

"He told me to move the car."

Garren backed the car up and then drove down the driveway, around the house and into an open garage. As soon as he was in, Petros lowered the door.

"Follow me." The man led them through the darkened house to stairs that led to the basement. They entered what could only be described as a reading room because that's all there was to it. Svetlana and her mother sat huddled together on one end of a large dark brown sectional that looked like it came straight out of the 70s. A quick survey of the room revealed two walls solid with full bookcases and the other two tastefully decorated with pictures of prairie landscapes and barns. Nothing about the room, except maybe the titles of the books, suggested anything but Midwest Americana. Garren tried to survey the library, but was prevented by his host.

"Please sit down." Somewhere between *who are you?* and *follow me*, Petros had found a shirt. Though it wasn't obvious, Garren was fairly certain the man was never too far from a weapon. But he did seem a lot friendlier. "I am Peter and this is my wife Mary."

"Papa," Svetlana said, "They know who we are. I told them everything."

Petros looked more frightened than upset. "Please understand, we are so grateful to have our daughter back, but your knowledge of us puts us all in danger."

"We won't tell anyone," said Garren. "You have our word. We are no threat to you, but I'm afraid someone else might be. Do you know a man by the last name of Diggs?"

"No."

For the next thirty minutes, Garren and Svetlana explained the whole thing, from Svetlana's abduction by Diggs all the way to their flight from Dubuque. Again, Garren left out the part about the news from 2019 and Svetlana left out the part about Garren being a time-traveler. Garren, however, did emphasize the fact that Diggs somehow knew Svetlana's real name.

Then Petros recounted what he and Nadia had been through for the last six weeks. "When Svetlana did not come home that day, we went to the school. They said two men came with a note from us saying they were to bring Svetlana immediately to the health center. They said there had been an accident."

"The school just let them take her?" Denise asked.

"This is a small town. People trust one another. By the time we knew anything, she had been gone four hours. We knew she had been abducted, so we stayed home waiting for a ransom phone call. We waited and waited, but no one called."

"What about the police?" asked Tommy.

"The closest police department is thirty miles away in Leola. We have one sheriff and one deputy for the entire county. They are no help to us. Given our circumstances, we do not deal with the local authorities. We have a contact in Washington. He said they would look into the matter, but of course, they found nothing. So we have been waiting and praying for a miracle. Tonight, God has answered our prayers. He sent you to bring our daughter back to us. Thank you."

"I'm glad we found her," Garren replied, "but as I said, this isn't over. Someone knows who you are. What will you do now?"

"We will have to relocate. I will contact our man in Washington and tell him to start the process."

"You're taking this better than I expected."

"We live knowing this can happen at any moment. We are prepared. We will leave immediately."

"Right now?" Tommy said. He was hoping to get some sleep in a real bed.

"Yes. It is too dangerous to stay here. The men who took Svetlana could be here any moment."

"Where will you go?"

"We have a plan. Now, if you will excuse us." Petros and Nadia got up.

"Hold on a minute," said Garren. "There's something else. The people who took Svetlana have six other girls. We need to save them, too."

"Then our prayers go with you."

"No. You don't understand. I can't do it by myself and we can't go to the police there because at least one of them is in on it. I want to call the FBI and I want Svetlana to talk to them."

"No FBI." Petros was quite adamant.

"Svetlana knows exactly where those girls are being kept. She can lead them straight to them."

"We do not have dealings with the FBI. I am sorry. It's too risky. Go home and then call whoever you like." They started to leave.

"Those girls will die unless we get to them soon," Kate said.

"You do not know that."

"Actually, I'm certain of it," said Garren.

The way he said it stopped Petros. "How do you know?"

"Give me ten minutes to explain."

"Please, Papa," Svetlana said. "You will want to hear this."

When everyone sat back down, Garren began. "The reason I know those girls will die if we don't rescue them is because…" He paused, wishing he didn't have to reveal this part. "I heard on the news how the police had found their bodies."

"Then it is too late," said Nadia. "They are already gone."

"Not yet," Garren said. "The bodies aren't found until the year 2019."

"You are a psychic?" Nadia asked.

"No. I'm from the year 2019."

Petros got up. "Nadia. Svetlana. Get your bags. We're going."

"Please, Sir." Garren got up and stepped in front of the stairs. "I know you believe this is possible. Svetlana told us. Now you need to believe me."

Petros considered the man blocking his way. "Svetlana told you of my work and you use it to manipulate me?"

"No, Papa," Svetlana said. "I didn't tell him until after he told me his secret."

"My husband is telling you the truth," Kate said. "I know it sounds crazy. It took me a while to come around, but I believe him."

"I believe him, too," said Denise. "And I'm usually pretty skeptical about that kind of stuff."

Then Tommy chimed in. "Sir, I've known this man for years. Believe me, he could never make up a story like this."

"It's true, Papa. Just listen to him."

Petros leveled his gaze upon Garren. "How did you do it?"

"*I* didn't do anything," Garren explained. "I'm just the traveler. Actually, there are two of us. A woman came back at the same time."

"How?"

"We don't know."

"Then who sent you?"

"We don't know that either."

"Tell me about the device."

"There was no device. It just happened."

"A natural phenomenon?"

"I wouldn't say there's anything *natural* about this. All I know is I went to a New Year's eve party at Tommy's apartment." He nodded toward Tommy. "I met a woman there. We had a few drinks, I fell asleep, and the next thing I know is I'm in my own apartment on January 1, 2000."

Petros pointed at Tommy. "This man is from 2019, too?"

"No. He's still there. I mean his older self is still there. This is the younger Tommy."

Petros returned to the couch, thinking. "How old are you?"

"I would have turned fifty on January 1, 2020, but I'm thirty here."

"So, when you traveled backward in time, you assumed the physical appearance of the man you were in this time. Fascinating."

Garren took this as a good sign. He sat down on the couch across from Petros.

"Do you have any physical proof that you are from the future?"

"No, just memories."

"Then this could be a delusion. Do you have a history of mental illness?"

Garren chuckled. "No, but I admit I've thought of that."

"But you have no way of proving what you say is true."

"I can prove it," Kate said. "My parents just sold a business that has been in our family for generations. They are moving to another town so my father can go to work for a large corporation. No one could have predicted they would do that, but Garren knew it before it happened."

"How did you know this?" Petros asked.

"I remember it."

"Do you have other memories of this time?"

"Yes, but this time was twenty years ago to me. I remember big things like George W. Bush beats Al Gore in a contested election. I remember where I lived and worked and that Kate and I have been married for only a couple months. I remember Tommy here is my best friend. But I don't remember details or conversations any more than you could remember those things from twenty years ago."

"I suggest you document as much as you can remember," Petros said. "As time progresses, you will have your proof."

"I've already started."

"Good. Now, have you changed anything?"

Garren and Kate glanced at each other. "I may have changed a few things."

"Tell me," Petros pressed.

Garren thought for a moment. "I didn't go to a movie because I remembered getting into a fight."

"Is that why you changed your mind?" Kate asked.

"Insignificant," Petros declared. "Have you done anything that could alter the future?"

"The woman I mentioned, the one who came back with me, she moved to New York about six months earlier than the first time."

"Is that all?"

"We've having this conversation. That didn't happen before."

"Listen to me. This is very important. You must understand how precise the time continuum is. You may get away with minor changes, but you do not know the impact your actions could have on a future that, if what you are saying is true, has already been determined. The fact that you know who becomes the next president of the United States places the fate of the entire world in jeopardy. Suppose you did something that resulted in the death of Mr. Bush. You will, in effect, have created an alternate timeline. You may already have done so without even knowing it. If what you say is true and you relive these next twenty years, you may discover a very different 2019 than the one you left. Have you told anyone else about this?"

"No one outside this room."

"You must commit yourself to two things: First, you must live your life exactly as you lived it before. You must resist the urge to change anything. And second, you must tell no one. If certain parties learn about you, they would either use you to their advantage or confine you to prevent you from being used by someone else. You cannot allow that to happen, for that also would alter your timeline. Do you understand what I'm telling you?"

"Yes."

"Good, good." Petros got up and started to pace.

"What is it?" Nadia asked. "What are you thinking?"

Petros stopped pacing and looked hard at Garren. "You cannot save those girls."

"Why not?"

"If what you know about the future is true, they have no part in it. Saving them now would alter the future in ways we cannot imagine. By saving one life, you could destroy others. I know this sounds heartless, but it is reality...or it is one of several possible realities. No man should have the right to decide what that reality is for the rest of humanity." Petros ran his fingers through his hair. "This is why we should not tinker with time."

"But this is your life's work, Papa," Svetlana said. "I thought you would be happy to know it is real."

"My little doch-ka. I proved my theories long ago. My work now is to prevent this very thing from happening. We simply cannot risk the alteration of history."

"What if we've already changed history?" Kate asked.

"Have you?"

"I think we better all sit back down," Garren said. "I was hoping I'd never have to say this, but if we're going to save those girls, I have to."

Petros shook his head. "I'm sorry. I cannot allow you to save them."

"We've already saved one."

Petros followed Garren's gaze toward Svetlana. "Doch-ka?"

Garren nodded. "They found seven bodies in 2019. Your daughter was one of them."

Nadia instinctively pulled Svetlana to her. Petros covered his mouth with his hand. The rest of them just sat there considering the implications. History had changed and a couple who would have mourned the loss of their precious doch-ka now had her back. Or an alternate reality had been created in which one couple's worst nightmare had a happy ending. Either way, there were six other families standing at a crossroads, waiting to learn the fate of their daughters. And the people in that room had the ability to determine that fate.

"Petros," Garren said. "Maybe time isn't as inflexible as you thought. It permitted one change for you. Will you help us change it for those other girls and their families?"

Petros looked at his wife and daughter, the two most precious things in his world. One had been taken and then returned; an answer to his prayers. If God had made such an allowance for him, perhaps He intended to make the same allowance for those other families. If God used Garren to bring his little girl home, then maybe He intended to use Svetlana to help those other girls get back home as well. He walked over to Garren and put out his hand. "We will help you save those girls."

"Thank you, Petros," Garren said as he shook the man's hand.

"But first we must leave this place…and no FBI."

32

Friday, January 14, 2000

G arren woke to the press of a silky smooth leg against his. "I don't want to get up."

"Neither do I, but those notes won't study themselves." Kate climbed over him, kissed him on the forehead and hopped out of bed. From the bathroom she called out, "And those applications won't fill themselves out either."

He groaned and pulled the blanket over his head. "I hate looking for a job. Can't I wait until Monday?"

"If you would have brought a sports almanac back from the future with you, you wouldn't need to find a job."

"Very funny. I still can't believe the school fired me."

"You kidnapped a student."

"Gee, you're all kinds of encouragement this morning."

"That's the way they see it. They had to do something."

"Yeah, but that's not what happened."

"People believe what they want to believe and they love to talk about it. I got pity looks all day yesterday."

"You try to do the right thing and end up getting punished. That's not right."

"You altered the timeline. Maybe time is getting back at you."

"But we saved one girl's life, and hopefully others. I wish they'd call. I hate being shut out like this."

"We did our part. Now it's up to the authorities." Kate came back into the room, sat down on the edge of the bed and started rubbing his back. "Hey, I'm with you. You know that, don't you?"

"Yes."

"Everything will work out. Those girls are going to be fine and so will we. If I need to take a break from school for a while to get a job, I can do that."

"None of this was supposed to happen."

"But it is." Kate chuckled. "Looks like no one can predict the future after all, not even you."

Just then, the phone rang. Kate answered it. "Hello…Oh, hey, Tommy…No, we're just getting up…Why?…Okay, thanks." She hung up the phone. "Tommy said we need to turn on the news. C'mon."

Garren grabbed his sweat pants and put them on as he followed Kate into the living room. She clicked on the television.

> *The Dubuque City Police Department is reeling this morning following the arrest of one of its own. Officer Rowdy Daniels was taken into custody late last night on charges of kidnapping and child endangerment. Details are sketchy, but we have learned that two other officers have turned themselves in, claiming they had knowledge of Daniels's activities, but were threatened by him to remain silent. Sources close to the investigation tell us evidence has been found linking Daniels with two other men, Delmar Diggs and Eugene Ponder, who were arrested Wednesday during a raid on a farm near Oskaloosa where six young women were being held against their will. All six women were taken to a nearby hospital and later released to their families. We will continue following this story and update you as details are made available.*

"You did it!" said Kate as the newscast switched to the weather. "You saved those girls' lives!"

"Yeah, I guess *we* did."

"Don't be so ho-hum about it. Think about it. You gave seven children back to their families. That's seven families who won't have to go through life with a giant hole in their heart. You did that."

"I know. I'm just thinking about the way we did it. It's not like we prevented something tragic from happening. We undid something that did happen and in doing that we set in motion a countless chain of events that didn't happen the first time."

"Yeah, like seven lives full of hopes and dreams and love."

"Petros was right. By changing the past, we create an uncertain future."

"News Flash: The future is supposed to be uncertain. That's life. No one gets to know the whole story. You live it one moment at a time. We do the best we can today and deal with tomorrow when it gets here. That's reality for all of us, even you."

"What about me? I actually do know the future, or at least the next twenty years of it."

"Yes, you have an advantage over the rest of us. But is it so different from the advantage of money or beauty or talent? What you have is a gift and you used that gift to save the lives of seven girls. You have to decide what you're going to do with the rest of these twenty years. You can't change some of the things you want to and then cry foul because you don't like some of the consequences of those changes. Cause and effect is something we all have to deal with, even time-travelers." She paused to get his reaction. "I'm not fussing at you. I've never been more proud of you and I've never been more in love with you than I am right now. But if we're going to make the best use of this wonderful gift, we need to understand it better. And yes, there will be unintended consequences. We'll just have to live with those."

"You're right. I guess I wanted it both ways. I wanted to change the bad things and keep the good. But you're absolutely right. I need to do the right things regardless of the consequences."

"I tell you what. Why don't you forget about those job applications for today? Take a hero's day off and start fresh on Monday. I've got to get ready for school. We can talk more about this when I get home. Okay?"

"You're pretty great, you know that? I'm so glad we've got each other."

"That's right. So don't screw it up. This may be the only second time around you get."

Kate went into the bathroom to finish getting ready for school. Garren turned his attention back to the television. There was a campaign ad for George W. Bush.

"I wonder what George would do if he got a do-over."

Garren spent the rest of the morning writing in his time journal. Encouraged by the success of his first real mission and inspired by Kate's pep talk, he turned a more serious eye to his situation. He thought long and hard about the next twenty years, writing down everything he could remember, trying to paint a coherent picture of the way things were, or would be. He tried to employ his unique perspective so that he could see things he not only could change, but should change. Try as he might to avoid it, one date in particular kept coming back to him. September 11, 2001 was still a year and a half away, but he knew that somewhere in the world, men were already scheming. He spent an entire hour staring at the date he had written at the top of an empty page. Was it possible? Was it right? Was he responsible to do something? His thoughts were interrupted by the telephone.

"Hello."

"Hi, Garren. It's me.

"Sve—"

"Please, do not use my name. Did you hear what happened?"

"Yes. Kate and I saw it on the news this morning. That's great. We couldn't have done it without you. Please thank your parents again for me."

"We made a pretty good team, didn't we?"

"Yes, we did. It's too bad those girls won't ever know it was you who led the way to that bunker. They never would have found it without you."

"That's okay. We know."

"Yep."

"My father wishes to speak with you, but don't hang up. I've got something else to tell you."

"Hello, Garren. How are you?"

"I'm okay. Say, I just want to thank you again for letting your daughter stay involved. You should be very proud of her."

"We are very proud. Let me get to the point. We are being relocated."

"Where?"

"I cannot tell you, but I wish to see you again. If you are in agreement, perhaps we could meet. There is much I would like to discuss concerning your experience."

"Sure. I'd love to. Name the place and time and I'll be there."

"I will be in touch. You have given me much to consider. Perhaps we are meant to work together."

"I've got a lot of free time now. I lost my job. The school thinks I kidnapped your daughter."

"We heard about your misfortune, but I have good news for you. My contact is meeting with the school administration today to give them a more favorable account of the last few days. Of course, you understand my daughter cannot be named, but they will know what you did to save those girls. I suspect they will be more than happy to have a hero teaching their students. You should expect a call soon."

"Thank you. The truth is all I want."

"Unfortunately, the entire truth cannot be revealed. As I said to you when we last spoke, it would not be in your best interest to advertise your situation. Please take this advice from someone who knows about such things. If you are interested, I can introduce you to some trusted associates who may be able to help you make the best use of your...insights."

"Yes, I am very interested."

"Good. We will speak soon. Now my daughter has something else to tell you."

"It's me again. I want to thank you again and everyone else for helping me get home. I will always be grateful to you."

"I'm glad I could help."

"My father says I might be able to see you again at your meeting."

"That would be great."

"Then I can show you my new puppy."

"Hey, you got a pet. That's wonderful."

"Yes, we rescued her from the shelter. It seemed appropriate. We both have secrets."

"What's her name?"

"I call her Deja. It's French for *remember*. I can tell her anything and we can help each other remember who we are."

"That's a great name. I look forward to meeting her and seeing you again. Soon, I hope."

"Me, too. My dad says I have to hang up now. Tell the others I said hello."

"I will."

"Goodbye."

"Goodbye."

As soon as he ended the call, Garren was struck by the name of Svetlana's dog. Coincidence? Or was there a connection?

33

New Year's Eve 2019

There's a farm a few miles outside of Oskaloosa, Iowa where young women can go to find sanctuary once they've been delivered from the sex slave industry. They come from all over the country to rest and heal and rediscover their identity as human beings rather than commodities bought and sold. They can stay as long as they need to at no cost thanks to an anonymous benefactor. All that is required is that they respect themselves and each other and abide by a few simple house rules. *Lana's Safe House* is one of twenty such residences scattered throughout the Midwest providing shelter and support to as many as fifty women at each site. This one is managed by two couples, the wives of which met at this very location twenty years earlier under very difference circumstances. They were fortunate enough to have been rescued at the front end of their ordeal, before any lasting damage had been done. Their shared experience opened their hearts to girls and young women who were not as fortunate; those who bear the deep wounds and ugly scars inflicted upon them by the worst of humanity.

The quiet morning was interrupted by the buzz of a cellphone.

"Lana's House, this is Janet…Good morning, Sir…Very well. Yourself?…That's wonderful…mm-hmm…mm-hmm…Yes, I have them right here. We are currently at thirty five full-time and fourteen sleep-overs…Thank you, Sir. I'll tell them. And you have a happy New Year, too…Okay, goodbye."

One hundred eighty miles away, Garren Rosen laid his cellphone on the desk in his office at home.

"Everything all right, Babe?" Kate asked as she entered with a steaming cup of coffee. She set it on the desk and maneuvered herself onto his lap.

"Just checking in on our girls. Everyone seems to have had a nice holiday."

"That's great. A package came for you today. It's from your parents. An early birthday present."

"Let me guess. It's one of those automatic coffee makers...the Baristabot. They should be calling any minute."

"Okay, Smarty-pants. I'll give you a pass since it's your last *second-time-around* day. But tomorrow you start living like the rest of us."

"I can't wait. It's been great and all, but I'm tired of being a time-traveler."

Kate leaned her head on his shoulder. "None of this would be possible if you weren't. Just think about all the lives you've touched. Think about us. Where were we twenty years ago today?"

"Twenty years ago today, you and I weren't even on the same timeline. You were still a newlywed and I was wondering if we even had a marriage."

"Okay, twenty years ago starting tomorrow. Think about everything we've done since you came back to me."

"It feels like I crammed two lifetimes into one."

She gave him one of her *enough with the time-travel thinking* looks. "This hasn't exactly been easy on me, either. I feel like I've spent the last twenty years playing catch-up to what you've already experienced. I can't wait for tomorrow, either. It will finally be a brand new day for both of us."

"You do realize I'll be seventy years old tomorrow."

"Shut up and kiss me."

He did. Then they did some more.

"Yeah, this twenty has been way better than the first twenty."

Garren's cellphone buzzed.

"That's my mom and dad."

Kate slipped off of his lap and let him take his pre-birthday call in private.

"Ah, Kate. There you are," said a female voice as soon as she stepped out of Garren's office. "It is currently nineteen degrees Fahrenheit.

Today's high will be thirty eight degrees at 1:13 PM with an overnight low of eleven degrees. The skies will be clear so you will be able to see the lunar asteroid strike. The moon is waxing crescent with a twenty six percent visibility. Asteroid Mea-Ta-11761 will strike the surface of the moon in the southern hemisphere at 10:06 PM local time. Scientists at NASA believe the impact will eject a plume of lunar soil that will be visible from Earth. NASA spokesman, Earl Frost, said earlier this week: 'We want to assure everyone that the event poses no threat to our planet, but should prove to be a spectacular show for the end of the year.'"

"Thank you, Deja. Oh, Deja, would you do me a favor?"

"Yes, Kate. I am happy to fulfill any request as long as it does not exceed the parameters of my programming."

"Would you please take the day off?"

"I'm not sure I know what you mean, Kate."

"Just don't be so attentive today. Let Garren do things for himself."

"I can do that. Kate?"

"Yes, Deja."

"Why does Garren not like me?"

"He likes you."

"Then why does he not allow me into his office? I can be of great assistance to him in his work and study. I can keep track of appointments, answer enquiries, take dictation, provide background music or soothing nature sounds. For a full list of my services, consult the Deja app on any smart device."

"He's kind of old school. He likes to do that sort of stuff for himself."

"I do not understand, but I will comply."

"Thank you, Deja."

"You're welcome. Talk to you later."

Kate finished getting ready and met Garren in the living room. "So, how would you like to spend your last do-over day?"

"I just want to be with you every moment."

"You're worried about tonight, aren't you?"

"I'm nervous. What if it happens again?"

"It won't, but so what if it does? You'd get to be young again. I'd be young again."

Garren let out a loud sigh. "I don't know if I could do it again."

Kate shrugged. "I guess we'll just have to wait and see. This time I won't leave your side. If it does happen, maybe I'll get to go with you. That wouldn't be so bad, would it?"

"It would be better."

"Try to put it out of your mind. You do still want to go to Tommy's and Denise's party tonight, yes?"

Garren chuckled. "I think Tommy is more excited about it than we are. If we cancel on him, I think he'll come over here and get us. I still can't believe he rented that apartment just for tonight. He's nostalgic for something he hasn't even done yet."

"He's doing it for you. Besides, it won't be exactly like last time. Their kids will be there."

"Tommy's changed a lot, hasn't he?"

"Yeah, but in a good way. He and Denise have been great together. They really get each other. If nothing else, you saved Tommy from himself."

"And the single female population of Dubuque as well."

"Do you think Sofia will come?" Kate asked.

"I doubt it. She never liked Dubuque."

"I wonder what became of her. Do you think she made any changes?"

"Do you remember that doomsday asteroid Space X diverted from a collision course with Earth a couple years ago?"

"Yeah, they were talking about that on the radio this morning. It was supposed to hit us tonight, right around midnight. Some people say Elon Musk may have saved the planet. Others are saying it was just another one of his publicity stunts."

"It was real all right, but it wasn't all him. If anyone should get credit for saving the planet, it's Sofia."

"Why do you say that?"

"The first time, no one knew it was coming. Right before Sofia leapt back to 2000, she saw it, or pieces of it, hit. She thought she saw the end of the world. She told me she believed that was her mission."

"Why didn't you ever tell me about it?"

"I didn't want you to worry. I told Petros about it years ago. He did some checking around and told me it was already being taken care of. I knew Sofia was involved somehow. Then when it was announced that Space X had successfully diverted a doomsday asteroid, I took that as a message that she was okay."

"Other than that, you've never heard from her?"

"I would have told you."

"Have you tried to contact her?"

"A few times. She's never been on any social media. She's not listed in any data base I know of. I guess she doesn't want to be found."

"Or maybe she got married and dropped her maiden name."

"I hope so. I hope she's had a happy life."

Kate grabbed his hand and got up. "C'mon, let's do something. We've got a few hours before the big event. I heard there's a Moon Pool down at Jake's. You can bet on whether anything will happen when the moon gets hit by that asteroid. Want to make one more sure bet?"

"Like we need any more money."

"Okay, want to go downtown and pretend we're Italian celebrities?"

Garren smiled. "I'm kind of tired. Do you mind if we just stay home?"

Kate sat back down beside him. "Want to watch some *Twilight Zone*?"

"Really? You'd do that?"

"If that's what you want to do. I'm not leaving your side until after midnight. Not even if you beg me."

Garren leaned back and let Kate get comfortable in his arms. "I definitely have the coolest wife ever."

———

Night fell for the last time in 2019. Garren and Kate put on their party clothes and got ready to go.

"Wow, you look amazing," said Garren when he saw her.

Kate twirled around to let him see her whole outfit – a black party dress that fit just right in all the right places.

"I think you're prettier now than ever."

"You're not so bad yourself, but is that what you're wearing?"

"It's what I wore the first time."

"Take your shirt off." She went into the guest room and returned with a large box. "I got you something. A little pre-birthday present."

Garren opened the box and whistled as he pulled out a new leather jacket.

"Keep looking. There's more."

He pulled out a shirt and slacks that looked great with the jacket. "You shouldn't have."

"Tonight is not like it was twenty years ago. It's going to be different. Now let's go and have some fun."

Five minutes later, Garren appeared in his new outfit.

"That's more like it," Kate said. "I should probably warn you. There might be a few more surprises before the night is over."

"That sounds ominous."

"All good, I promise."

It was a little after nine o'clock when they arrived at the apartment Tommy lived in in another time. Garren parked his '79 Camaro – yes, he did prevent Tommy from totaling it this time – and went around to open the door for Kate.

"We're early," he said. "Last time, people were already standing out here looking at the moon by the time I got here."

They both looked up and paid their respects to the unsuspecting crescent floating in a cloudless sky. In a little over an hour, an uninvited intruder would alter its appearance forever.

Inside the apartment, the mood was a lot different than Garren remembered. The only person he recognized from last time was Tommy. All of his swinging single friends, mostly hot women, had been replaced by middle-age couples and families. The music was more subdued and the beverage offering was a lot more kid friendly.

"Garren. Kate." Tommy hugged them both. "I was getting ready to call out the search dogs. Glad you guys made it."

"Hey, Sis." Denise, ever by Tommy's side, hugged Kate. "Hey, Bro." She hugged Garren and kissed him on the cheek. "You both look great."

"So do you," Garren said, and he really meant it. Although he didn't talk about, except with Kate, he liked this version of Denise much better than the other one.

"Are you ready for your next surprise?" Kate said.

Garren made a face. "Yes?"

"Where is she, Tommy?" He nodded toward the living room. "C'mon." She took his hand and led him over to a couple sitting on the couch.

"Svetlana!" Garren said. "I thought you were in Germany."

She got up from the couch and hugged him. "I am, but I heard there was this big party. So, here we are. This is my husband, Felix. Felix, I'd like you to meet Garren and Kate."

Felix unexpectedly hugged Garren like he was an old friend. "Finally, I meet the man who saved my Svetlana's life. I owe you a great debt of gratitude."

When the hug was complete, Garren stepped back. "It was a team effort."

Felix proceeded to hug Tommy and Denise – again – and then Kate. And then he thanked everyone again and again.

"So, tell me," said Garren when he was able to get a word in, "what are you doing now? What are you working on?"

Svetlana leaned in. "It's confidential, but since you're partly responsible..." She beckoned him closer.

Garren leaned in until his ear was next to her lips.

"Deja."

Garren pulled back. "Huh?"

"I'm part of the team that developed her."

"My wife is being modest," said Felix. "She recruited, financed and led the team that developed the system. Now they maintain her."

"How am I partly responsible?" Garren asked.

"If you hadn't saved me, Deja wouldn't exist."

"Wait a minute. You invented Deja?"

"Shh," Svetlana held up her hand. "Yes, and I named her after my dog."

Garren's mind began to swirl with the problem of time-travel. If Svetlana invented Deja in this timeline, who invented her in the timeline in which she died?

"I hate to interrupt," said Kate, "but your next surprise just got here."

Garren looked behind her. "Petros! Nadia! Now all of my favorite people are here. How have you been?"

"Fine. Fine. But it has been too long, Brother. How are you feeling?"

"Good. Why do you ask?"

"Tonight. You know..."

"Oh, that." Garren took a breath and blew it out. "I guess we'll see."

"I have something important to tell you. Can we talk?"

"Sure."

"Okay, everybody," Tommy announced. "Thirty minutes to impact. At ten o'clock we'll all go outside. But first, I've got a game to help us get to know each other. Come on, everybody take a card."

"Look at him," Kate said. "He's like a little kid."

"I'm sorry, Petros," said Garren. "Can we talk later?"

"Of course." Petros smiled in concession. "But we must talk before midnight."

For the next thirty minutes, Tommy's game had everybody laughing and becoming friends. Then, at exactly 10:00, everyone began migrating out into the parking lot. The air was frigid. Couples huddled together and stared up at the sky. But Garren couldn't take his eyes off of Kate. She was looking up at the moon, smiling like a kid on the Fourth of July.

"You look amazing."

She shifted her gaze to him. "It's exciting. Don't you want to see it."

"Been there. Done that. But you…I'll never get tired of looking at you."

Someone called out "Thirty seconds." A few people started to count down. At five, everyone joined in.

"Five….Four….Three….Two….One!"

1.3 seconds later, everyone jumped and gasped as an explosion erupted from the lunar surface. There was a brilliant flash followed immediately by a giant plume of lunar soil ejected from the surface.

"Whoa!" said one of the kids, followed by several other expressions of amazement and then the chatter of twenty people telling each other what everyone saw.

Kate giggled. "I'm actually seeing what you've been telling me all these years."

"Now do you finally believe me?" Garren teased.

"I guess so. What happens next?"

"We go inside."

Most of the crowd was ready to get back in the warmth, though a few of the tougher kids lingered outside to see if anything else would happen. Inside, someone had turned on the television to watch the news coverage of the event. The up-close images showed very little as the entire moon had been blotted out by a tremendous cloud of dust and debris.

"Want something to drink?" Kate asked.

"Sure. I'm feeling wild tonight. I'll have a Coke."

"Be right back."

Even though he'd seen it before, Garren felt himself drawn into the news coverage. It was still an amazing event and he was interested to test the accuracy of his memory.

"What a way to ring in the new year."

The voice came from behind him, but he knew right away. Although he half expected it, when he turned around, he could barely say her name. "Sofia?"

"What's wrong? Never see a time-traveler before?"

"I didn't think you'd come."

"I wasn't going to, but an old friend convinced me."

Garren followed her gaze toward the kitchen and saw Kate talking with Tommy and Denise and the Karabelnikoffs. She smiled and waved, then went back to her conversation.

"Gosh, where to begin? There's so much I want to tell you and so much I want to know about you. Nice work saving the planet. I'd love to hear how you pulled that one together."

"Meh," she shrugged. "My part was easy. Elon and I go back a ways."

"I figured you must have met him."

"Met him? We dated off and on for a couple years. We parted on good terms."

"What else have you been doing? Did you make any other changes? Do you still live in New York?"

"Slow down. We've got 'til midnight."

Garren looked at his watch. "You're wondering what's going to happen, too."

"Let's not talk about that. Can I get you a drink?"

"Oh, no you don't. I'm not doing that again. In fact, I quit drinking right after we went back."

"Yeah, I haven't mixed a drink since 2001."

"That's great, yes? So, what happened after you left?"

"At first, I didn't have much choice. I had to survive, so I followed my old tracks. I found my old friends, got my old job, fell into the same routines. As we got closer to September 11, I started dreaming about it. Have you had weird dreams?"

"The worst. It's like being in a movie theater with two different movies playing at the same time."

Sofia laughed. "That's exactly what it's like. Anyway, every morning I'd wake up in a cold sweat. I knew I had to do something. I called everyone I could think of, but no one would believe me. I started warning people to stay away, but everyone thought I was either crazy or pranking them. That morning, I went to the towers at around seven and just started begging people not to go in. They thought I was high. I was actually in the process of getting arrested when the first plane hit. After that, I was just one of the crowd. I hung around until it was only fire fighters running into the building. I tried to warn them, but they were doing their job. I left a few minutes before the first tower fell. I wandered the city for days, trying to help where I could. That's when it clicked. I knew I was supposed to use my knowledge to help others."

Garren nodded. "I had the same revelation. It's frustrating though because some things you can't fix. They happen anyway."

"Yeah, I don't know if I saved anyone that day, probably because I didn't go about it the right way."

"What do you mean?"

"I figured it out. Actually I remembered something I learned the first time around. The key to getting people to do what you want is to let them think it was their idea in the first place. That's how I got Elon to go after that asteroid."

"It probably didn't hurt that you…well, you look great."

"It doesn't work on everyone." She winked at him and touched his arm. "But anyway, I have been able to help a lot of people."

"Saint Sofia."

"I wouldn't go that far. I've also helped myself quite a bit. I've became obscenely wealthy. But enough about me. I see you didn't screw things up with Kate."

"No. I did a lot better this time."

"Still teaching?"

"Yes. It's all I've ever really wanted to do. But I have gotten involved in a few side projects, nothing too noticeable, and I also improved my standard of living."

"Kids?"

"Nope. Some things are unchangeable."

"I'm sorry to hear that."

"It's okay. We dealt with it a lot better than the first time. What about you? Did you ever get married?"

"Like you said, unchangeable. But I'm okay with how my life turned out."

"Just okay?"

"I would have liked to change one thing." She reached for his hand. When he didn't reciprocate, she let it go. "Well, it was really nice to see you again, Garren."

"Yeah, I'm glad you came. Maybe we could, you know, keep in touch."

Several seconds passed without either one saying anything. Then Sofia abruptly said, "Goodbye, Garren."

"You're leaving so soon?"

"Yeah, I have to do this thing."

"Now? It's not midnight yet."

She pushed her way through the crowd toward the guest room to get her coat. Garren went after her, but was intercepted by Petros.

"Garren, is this a good time to talk?"

"Not right now."

Sofia reappeared with her coat on, brushed past him and went outside. Garren started after her, but was thwarted by a strong hand on his arm.

"It's important," Petros urged.

"It'll have to wait." Garren shook himself free and went outside. "Sofia!" He caught up with her in the parking lot.

"Go back to Kate," she said, refusing to look at him.

"I don't want you to leave like this. Can we talk?" He touched her arm.

"There's nothing else to say. What's done is done." She pulled away from him.

"Sofia, please."

She stopped and turned. "After all this time, you still don't get it."

"Get what?"

"I'm in love with you, Garren. I know that doesn't make any sense to you, but it does to me. So before I embarrass myself any more, I'm gonna go."

She took one step backward, hesitated and then reversed course. The next thing Garren knew, Sofia was in his arms. She reached up with both hands and pulled his face toward hers. They kissed under the wounded moon.

"Come with me," she whispered.

"You know I can't."

She laid her head on his chest and held him tightly. "Faithful to the core. I should have tried harder twenty years ago."

"My response would have been the same. I'm in love with Kate."

Sofia stepped back and composed herself. "Then go to her." Garren made one more attempt to say something that would put things right, but she cut him off. "Goodbye, Garren."

Finally getting it, he started back toward the apartment. The sound of a low tone made him turn around. He thought he saw her walking in the pool of the street lamp, but then she was gone.

Inside the apartment, the party was in a slow simmer. Midnight was approaching and eyelids were getting heavy. Kate was waiting for him.

"Is everything all right?"

"Sofia had to leave. That was nice of you to call her."

"I didn't."

"Huh. She said she got an invitation from an old friend. I figured it was another one of your surprises."

"It wasn't me, but I'm glad she came. She didn't stay very long. Is she doing okay?"

"Seems to be."

"Thirty minutes, people!" Tommy called out. "If we don't get this party crankin', this old guy ain't gonna make it. Who wants to play another game?"

"Can we talk?" Garren said. "I need some fresh air."

Kate followed him through the sliding glass door. "You okay?"

From the balcony, Garren could see the spot where he last saw Sofia. "She kissed me and asked me to go with her."

Kate was more than a little stunned, but kept it in. "What did you say?"

"I told her I'm in love with you. Then she left." He put his arms around her. "It's always been you, Kate. I knew it the moment I saw you."

"What do you think happened to us the first time?"

He shrugged and shook his head. "A lot of things on my part. Pride. Arrogance. Unrealistic expectations. I took you for granted. I loved the idea of marriage, but part of me wanted to stay single. I was so busy thinking you should be the wife I wanted that I wasn't the husband you needed or wanted. I wasn't all the way there for you when you needed me the most. The bottom line is, I failed us."

"You've really thought this through."

"I've had more time than most."

"I'm sure I contributed. I'm not perfect."

"I think that's what tripped me up the first time. I thought you were and I was certain that I was. And then when we weren't, I didn't know what to do with that."

"And the second time around?"

"I know better."

Kate looked at her watch. "Five minutes to midnight. Any final revelations before you pick up where you left off?"

Garren was quiet for a moment. "I have two. I think my failures the first time gave me what I needed to succeed the second time – perspective, wisdom, grace, warning, determination."

Kate nodded. "And the second?"

"For some reason I've been thinking about that story of the tortoise and the hare."

"This ought to be good."

"There's more to the race than just getting to the finish line. My first time around, I was like the hare – running full speed to beat everybody else or asleep in my self-confidence. This time, I paid a lot more attention to the course. I noticed a lot of things I missed the first time."

"Maybe you should write a book: *Things I Learned As a Time-Traveler.*"

"Nobody would ever believe it."

The glass door slid open. It was Tommy. "Hey, you guys. They started the countdown. The ball is about to drop."

Garren and Kate rejoined the party, which was now gathered around the television. On the screen was a replay of what happened at Times Square an hour earlier. At thirty seconds until midnight, the Waterford crystal ball began its slow descent. The digital display where the ball would land counted down the seconds. At ten seconds, everyone joined in.

"Ten…Nine…Eight…"

Garren grabbed Kate's hand.

"Seven…Six…Five…"

He held his breath.

"Four…"

Kate let go of Garren's hand and wrapped her arms around him. "I'm not letting go."

"Three…Two…One!"

The ball reached the bottom of the track, engaging the switch that sent the new year to the Times Square Jumbotron. Garren and Kate gasped as they read it: 2000. A second later, the third digit flickered and morphed into a 2. The host of *Dick Clark's New Year's Rockin' Eve* caught it.

"Whoa! Did you see that? For a moment there we skipped all the way back to 2000, but we're okay now. Welcome to the new year 2020!"

As "Auld Lang Syne" played, couples kissed and teenagers filled their cups from the adult punch bowl. Garren and Kate gazed into each other's eyes.

"We made it," Garren croaked out around the lump in his throat.

"Yes, we did," Kate replied. "Yes, we did."

They kissed and slow danced and kissed some more. And for the first time in twenty years, Garren Rosen had no idea what would happen next.

The End

(But stay to the end of the credits.)

About The Author

Michael E. Gunter

At the age of ten, Michael saw his first episode of The Twilight Zone. At Eighteen, he became a follower of Jesus Christ. In 2001, he discovered his passion for writing. Today, he writes about the mysteries of life from a biblical Christian perspective.

"There's more going on here than we think. I believe there is a Greater Reality than the one we perceive with our physical senses; a Great Mystery that defies conventional thinÅking. Writing is simply our response to that Mystery, our attempts to understand it," says Michael.

Michael explores the Great Mystery from multiple angles. His work in fiction reaches out to other worlds, backward and forward to other times, and inward to the heart of humankind.

When Michael is not writing, he enjoys his family, playing guitar, connecting with his readers and supporting other independent artists.

Find All of Michael E. Gunter's Books on Amazon.com

A Life Not Wasted
Blackwell
Defying Gravity
Departure
Ka-Rel
Klyvian

—⁓—

As soon as the last line of "Auld Lang Syne" faded for another year, Frank Sinatra started belting out "New York, New York." The Sky-cam over Time's Square gave everyone at Tommy's party a view of the city that never sleeps. Dubuque, however, is not that kind of city and Tommy's guests were ready to call it a night.

"Great party, Tommy," someone said.

"Yeah, thanks for having us," said someone else.

"Thank you guys for coming." Tommy stood at the door and bid goodnight as more than half of the guests left the apartment.

Garren and Kate, still enjoying the newness of everything, continued dancing. Tommy, shivering from the cold, grabbed Denise and joined them.

"Happy Birthday, Buddy," he said. "Hey Kate, how's it feel to be dancing with such an old man?"

"It feels perfect," she replied and planted another one on Garren's lips.

Doorbell.

"I'll get it." Tommy walked the few steps to the door and opened it, then stepped back to let the newcomer in.

She was shaking from the cold and something else. "I-I'm sorry to disturb your party. My name is Sofia and I need help. I don't know where I am or how I got here. I found this note in my pocket. It said to come here and ask for someone named Garren Rosen. It says he can help me. Does anybody know a Garren Rosen?"

Petros was the first to respond. "Come in, Child. You are among friends here." He walked her over to the couch. "Garren, I think it's time we had that talk."